THE WINEMAKER

Noah Gordon

BARCELONA
eDITIONS

OPEN ROAD

INTEGRATED MEDIA

This is a work of fiction. Names, characters, places, and incidents either are the product of the author's imagination or are used fictitiously. Any resemblance to actual persons, living or dead, businesses, companies, events, or locales is entirely coincidental.

Originally published in Spanish as *La Bodega* by Roca Editorial de Libros, S.L. in Spain in 2007.

Cover design by Mario Arturo

Image © The Art Archive/Gianni Dagli Orti

Author photo by Jamie Beth Gordon

ISBN: 978-1-4532-7109-4

This 2012 edition published by:
Barcelona Digital Editions, S.L.
Av. Marquès de l'Argentera, 17 pral.
08003 Barcelona
www.barcelonaebooks.com

This 2012 edition distributed by Open Road Integrated Media
180 Varick Street
New York, NY 10014
www.openroadmedia.com

For Lorraine, always

Whether at Naishapur or Babylon,
Whether the Cup with sweet or bitter run,
The Wine of Life keeps oozing, drop by drop,
The Leaves of Life keep falling, one by one.
>—*The Rubaiyat of Omar Khayyam*
>Translated by Edward Fitzgerald

Land is about the only thing
That can't fly away.
>—*The Last Chronicle of Barset*
>Anthony Trollope

Blessed is he who has found his work;
Let him ask no other blessedness.
>—*Past and Present*
>Thomas Carlyle

Where have all the young men gone?
Gone for soldiers every one.
When will they ever learn?
When will they ever learn?
>—*Where Have All the Flowers Gone?*
>Pete Seeger

PART ONE

The Return

Outside the village of Roquebrun
Province of Languedoc, Southern France
February 22, 1874

1

Going Home

*O*n the morning when everything changed, Josep was working in the Mendes vineyard, and by midmorning he had settled into a trance-like routine, moving from vine to vine, removing the dry, tired branches that had borne the fruit harvested in October, when each grape had been juicy as a ripe woman. He pruned with a ruthless hand, leaving economical vines that would produce the next generation of grapes. It was a rare, lovely day in what had been a sour February, and despite the chill the sun seemed to surge in the vast French sky. Sometimes when he came upon a shriveled grape that had been missed by the pickers, he salvaged the Fer Servadou raisin and relished its spicy sweetness. Whenever he reached the end of the row, he made a pile of the prunings and took a flaming vine from the previous burning to ignite a new fire, the bitter stink of the smoke adding to his pleasure in the work.

He had just finished firing a pile when he looked up and saw Leon Mendes making his way across the vineyard, not pausing to speak with any of the other four workers.

"Monsieur," he said respectfully when Mendes reached him.

"Senyor." It was their little joke, the proprietor addressing him as if Josep were the proprietor and not the peon, but Mendes wasn't smiling. He was gentle but as direct as always. "I spoke this morning with Henri Fontaine, who has recently returned from Catalonia. Josep, I have very bad news. Your father is dead."

Josep found himself as if clubbed, unable to speak. *My father? How could my father be dead?* Finally, "What was the cause?" he said stupidly.

Mendes shook his head. "Henri had heard only that he had died late in August. Henri knew nothing more."

". . . I'll go back to Spain, Monsieur."

"Are you certain?" Mendes said. "After all, he is gone."

"No, I must go back."

"And shall it be . . . *safe* for you?" Mendes asked gently.

"I believe so, Monsieur. For a long time I've been thinking about returning. I thank you for your kindnesses to me, Monsieur Mendes. For taking me in. And teaching me."

Mendes shrugged. "It's nothing. One never stops learning about wine. I deeply regret the loss of your father, Josep. I remember you have an older brother, is it not so?"

"Yes. Donat."

"Where you live, does the eldest inherit? Shall Donat get the vineyard from your father?"

"Where we live, the custom is for the eldest son to inherit two-thirds, with any younger sons sharing the remainder and given jobs that provide a living. But it's my family's custom—because we have so little land—that *all* goes to the eldest son. My father always made it clear that my future was with the army or with the Church. Unfortunately, I am fit for neither."

Mendes smiled, but the smile was sad. "I can't disapprove. In France, splitting properties among surviving children has led to some ridiculously small farms."

"Our vineyard is made up of only four hectares as it is. That's barely enough land to support one family when the grapes grown on it are used to make cheap vinegar."

"Your grapes start out fine enough. They have pleasant, promising flavors—too good, in fact, for cheap vinegar! Four hectares run properly can give a crop to make good wine. However, you need to dig cellars, so the wine doesn't turn sour in the heat of summer," Mendes said mildly.

Josep had great respect for Mendes, but what did the French winemaker know of Catalonia or of growing grapes from which to make vinegar? "Monsieur, you've seen our little casas with their dirt floors," he said too impatiently, numbly thinking of Padre. "We don't have great chateaus. There is no money for the construction of grand bodegas with wine cellars."

It was obvious Monsieur Mendes didn't wish to argue. "Since you don't inherit the winery, what shall you do in Spain?"

Josep shrugged. "Find employment." Almost certainly not with Donat, he thought.

"Perhaps not in your village? Spain's Rioja district has a few vineyards that would be fortunate to have you, for you're a born grower of grapes. You sense their needs, and your hands are happy in the earth. Of course, Rioja is not Bordeaux, though they make a few passable reds there," he said loftily. "But if ever you wish to return here to work, you will find quick employment with me."

Josep thanked him again. "I don't believe I'll go to Rioja or come back to Languedoc to work, Monsieur. Catalonia is where I belong."

Mendes nodded his understanding. "The call of home is always loud. Go with God, Josep," he said. He smiled. "And tell your brother to dig a cellar."

Josep smiled too and shook his head. Donat would not dig a hole even for a shithouse, he told himself.

"Leaving? Ah . . . Good fortune, then." Margit Fontaine, Josep's landlady, received the news of his departure with her secret, almost sly, little smile—even, he suspected, with pleasure. A middle-aged widow, she still had a lovely face and a body that made Josep's heart thump when he first saw her, but she was so completely absorbed with herself that after a time she had lost any allure. She had provided him with careless meals and a soft bed she had sometimes shared scornfully, treating him like a dull pupil in her strict sexual academy. *Slowly, purposefully. Gently! Jésus, boy, you are not running a race!* It was true she had meticulously taught him what a man could do. He had been intrigued by the lessons and by her attractiveness but there were never tender feelings between them, and his pleasures were limited because he came to dislike her. He knew that she saw him as a rawboned country youth, an uninteresting Spaniard who spoke Occitan, the regional language, badly and French not at all. So with an unromantic adieu he departed early the next morning the way he had come to France, quietly and unnoticed, disturbing no one. Hung from one shoulder, he carried a cloth bag containing sausages, a baguette, and a bottle of water. From his other shoulder, he carried a rolled blanket and a gift from Monsieur Mendes, a small skin of wine on a rope strap. The sun was gone again, the sky was gray as a dove's neck; the day was cool but dry, and the surface of the dusty road was firm, good conditions for walking. Fortunately, his legs and feet were hardened by work. He had a long way to go and set himself a purposeful but unhurried pace.

His goal for the first day on the road was to reach a chateau in the village of Ste. Claire. When he arrived there late in the afternoon, he stopped at the small Church of St. Nazaire and asked a priest for directions to the winery of a man named Charles Houdon, a friend of Leon Mendes. When he had found the winery and had given Monsieur Houdon the felicitations of Monsieur Mendes, he received Houdon's permission to sleep that night in the barrel room.

As evening fell, he sat on the floor next to the casks and ate bread and sausage. Houdon's barrel room was spotlessly clean. The heavy sweetness of fermenting grapes didn't quite mask the harsh scent of new oak wood and the sulfur that the French burned in their bottles and barrels to keep them pure. In southern France they burned a great deal of sulfur, fearful of all disease but especially phylloxera, a plague that was ruining vineyards to the north, caused by a tiny louse that ate the roots of the vines. This barrel room reminded him of the one in Mendes' winery, though Leon Mendes made red wines, and Houdon made only white wine from the Chardonnay grape. Josep preferred red wine, and now he gave himself the indulgence of a single swallow from his wineskin. The drink was a small burst, sharp and clean—vin ordinaire, common wine even workingmen could afford in France, yet better than any wine Josep had tasted in his village.

He had worked two years for Mendes in the vineyard, another year filling in as a cellarman, and a fourth year in the barrel room, blessed with the opportunity to taste wines whose qualities he had never imagined. "Languenoc is known for decent vin ordinaire. I make honest wine, somewhat better than ordinary. Occasionally, through poor fortune or stupidity, I make rather poor wine," Monsieur Mendes had told him, "but most of the time, thanks to heaven, my wine is good. Of course, I have never made a *great* wine, a wine for the ages, such as the vintages created by the fabled wine-makers like Lafite and Haut-Brion."

But he never stopped trying. In his unrelenting search for the ultimate cru—a perfection he spoke of as "God's wine"—whenever he achieved a vintage that spread joy over gullet and palate, he beamed for a week. "Do you detect the fragrance?" he would demand of Josep. "Do you sense the depth, the dark scent that teases the soul, the floral smell, the taste of plums?"

Mendes had given him knowledge of what wine could be. It would have been merciful to have left Josep in ignorance. The thin, sour stuff created by the vintners of his village was poor wine, he now realized. Horse piss, he told himself morosely; probably it would have been better for him to have stayed in France with Mendes and strive to make better vintages, instead of courting danger by returning to Spain. He comforted himself with the assurance that by now it must be safe for him to go home. Four years had passed without a single indication that he was being sought by the Spanish authorities.

He didn't like the bitter realization that generations of his family had used up their lives making such bad wine. Still, they had been good people. Hard-working people. Which brought him again to his father. He tried to picture Marcel Alvarez but could remember only small, homely details—his father's large hands, his rare smile. There was a gap from a missing lower tooth in front; the two teeth next to the gap were crooked. His father had a crooked toe, too, the small toe of his left foot, from wearing bad shoes. Some of the time Padre had worked without shoes—he liked the feeling of soil beneath his soles and between his gnarled toes. Lying back, Josep indulged in memories, for the first time allowing himself to enter a true state of mourning, as darkness drifted into the room through its two high windows. Finally, distraught, he fell asleep among the barrels.

The next day the air turned sharper. That night Josep wrapped himself in his blanket and burrowed into a haymow in a farm field. The rotting hay was warm and made him feel a kinship with all the burrowing creatures waiting for the sun. He had two dreams that night. First the bad dream, the terrible dream. Then, mercifully, he dreamed of Teresa Gallego, and when he awoke he remembered the dream about her very clearly, in delicious, torturous detail. A waste of a dream, he told himself. After four years, no doubt she was married or working somewhere far from the village. Or both.

Mid-morning, he had a stroke of fortune when a carter gave him a ride on a wagonload of firewood pulled by two oxen with red wooden balls on the sharp tips of their horns. If a billet fell from the load, Josep would leap off and replace it. Otherwise he rode for more than three leagues atop the load in comparative luxury. Alas, that night, his third night on the road, wasn't spent in any sort of comfort. Darkness found him afoot in wooded country, with neither village nor farmhouse in sight.

He believed that he had traveled beyond Languedoc and that the forest in which he found himself was part of the province of Roussillon. He didn't mind the woods in daylight; indeed, during the hunting group's existence he had enjoyed its forays into the woods. But darkness in the woods wasn't to his liking. There were neither stars nor moon in the sky, and it made no sense to walk the forest track without being able to see. At first he sat on the ground with his back against the bole of a large pine, but the great soft hissing of the insistent wind through so many trees soon unmanned him, and he clambered into the lowest branches of the pine tree and climbed until he was well off the ground.

He crammed himself into a crotch and tried to cover as much of himself as possible with the blanket, but it was a sorry attempt, and the cold won out as he perched in the tree in great discomfort. From the blackness around him there was an occasional sound. The hooting of a distant owl. A mournful call of doves. A high-pitched . . . *something* . . . that he imagined was the scream of a rabbit or some other creature being murdered.

Then, from the ground directly below, the rasp of bodies brushing against one another. Grunting, snuffling, a loud snort, the scrape of earth being pawed. He knew it was wild pigs. He couldn't see them. Perhaps there were only a few, though his imagination painted a large pack. If he fell, even one boar could be lethal, with those terrible tusks and sharp hooves. Doubtless the brutes were smelling his sausages and cheese, though he knew they would eat anything. Once his father had told him that in his youth he had seen wild pigs tear into and eat a living horse with a broken leg.

Josep clung tightly to the tree branch. After a time he could hear the pigs moving away. Everything was quiet again and shivering cold. It seemed to him that the dark lasted forever.

When daylight finally arrived, he didn't see or hear animals, and he came down from the tree and breakfasted on sausage as he walked the narrow road. The sleepless night had left him tired, but he went at his usual pace. Around noontime the trees thinned and then there were fields and a good glimpse of the higher mountains ahead. An hour or so later, when he had gained the Pyrenees, it began to rain very hard, and he took refuge through the open door of a barn attached to a handsome masia.

Inside the barn a man and his son stopped mucking out their cows' bedding and stared. "So what is it?" the man said brusquely.

"Passing through, monsieur. If I can wait in here for a few moments, until the worst of the rain is gone?" Josep saw that the man was looking him over carefully, clearly less than pleased with what the rain had brought him.

"All right then," the farmer said, moving slightly so he could continue using his sharp hay fork while watching the stranger.

The rain continued to teem. In a little while, instead of just standing, Josep picked up a shovel that was leaning against the wall and began to help the other two in their work. Soon they were listening with interest as he told them about the wild pigs.

The farmer nodded. "Mean bastards, those damned swine. And they breed like rats. They're everywhere."

Josep worked with them until the whole barn was mucked. By that time, the farmer was mollified and friendly and said he could sleep in the barn if he liked. So he spent that night cozy and dreamless, with three large cows giving off heat on one side of him and a great pile of warm dung on the other side. In the morning, while he was filling his water bottle in the spring behind the house, the farmer told him that he was just west of a heavily used pass through the mountains. "It is where the mountain range is thinnest. It is a low pass and you could walk across the border in three and one-half days. Or, if you go west for two leagues you come to a higher pass. Few people use it, for it is a good deal longer than the other pass. It would take you an extra two days, and you would walk through some snow, but it is not deep . . . Also, on the high pass there are no guards at the border," the farmer added knowingly.

Josep dreaded border guards. Four years before, in order to avoid the border guards, he had stolen into France, trying to follow faint trails through the mountain forest, lost much of the time, expecting at any moment to slip into a chasm, if border guards didn't shoot him first. He had learned then that the people who lived along the border knew the best routes for smuggling, and now he took this man's advice.

"There are four villages along the high pass at which you may seek food and shelter," the man said. "You should stop at each one for the night, even though there may still be a few hours of light that would allow walking, for outside of the villages there is neither food nor protected places to sleep. The only segment of the pass over which you must hurry, to avoid being caught in darkness, is the long walk leading to the fourth village."

The farmer told Josep that the high pass would bring him into Spain far to the east of Aragon. "You should be safe from Carlist militiamen, though fighters in red berets move deep into the Spanish army's territory now and again. Last July they went all the way to Alpens and killed 800 Spanish soldiers," he said. He looked at Josep. "Are you involved in that disagreement, by chance?" he asked carefully.

Josep was tempted to tell him he had almost worn the red beret himself, but he shook his head. "No."

"That's good sense. Jésus, you Spanish couldn't have more terrible enemies than when you fight each other," he said, and Josep was tempted to take offense but, after all, wasn't it true? He contented himself to say that civil war was hard.

"What is all the killing about?" the man asked, and Josep found himself giving this farmer a lesson in Spanish history. How, for a long time, only royal first sons had been allowed to inherit the Spanish monarchy. How, before Josep had been born, King Fernando VII, having watched three of his wives die without a babe, was given two daughters in succession by his fourth wife, and persuaded the Cortes to change the law in order to name his first-born, Isabella, as the future queen. This had made piss-mad his younger brother, the infante Carlos Maria Isidro, who would have inherited the kingdom from Fernando.

How Carlos had rebelled and fled into France, while in Spain his conservative followers had joined together to form an armed militia that had been fighting ever since. What Josep didn't say was that the struggle had caused him to flee from Spain himself and had cost him four years of his life.

"I don't give a damn whose royal cul covers the throne," he said bitterly.

"Oh, aye, what good does it do a sensible common man to fret about such things?" the farmer said, and he sold Josep a small ball of cheese made from cow's milk at a very good price.

When he began to walk through the Pyrenees, the high pass turned out to be little more than a narrow, twisty path that rose and fell, rose and fell. He was a mote in unending vastness. The mountains stretched before him, wild and real, sharp brown peaks with white caps, fading into blue well before the horizon. There were sparse forests of pine, interspersed with naked cliffs, tumbled rocks, contorted earth. Sometimes at an elevated height he stopped and stared, dreamlike, at a stunningly revealed vista. He feared bears and wild pigs but met no animals; once, far-off, he saw two groups of deer.

The first village he came to was no more than a tiny cluster of houses. Josep paid a coin to sleep on the floor of a goatherd's hut, next to the fire. He spent a miserable night because of tiny black vermin, bugs that supped on him at their leisure. The next day, he scratched a dozen itchy spots as he walked.

The second and third mountain villages were larger and better. He slept one night near a kitchen stove, and the next night on a workbench in a cobbler's shop, bugless and with the rich, strong scent of leather in his nostrils.

He started out early and energetically on the fourth morning, conscious of the warning the farmer had given him. In places the trail was difficult to walk but, as the man had said, only a short section, the highest point, was covered by snow. Josep wasn't accustomed to snow and didn't like it. He could imagine breaking a leg and freezing to death or starving in the awful white expanse. Standing in the snow, he made a single chill meal of his hoarded cheese, eating it all as if he were already starving, letting each precious bite melt slowly and deliciously in his mouth. But he neither starved nor broke a leg; the shallow snow slowed him but wasn't a hardship.

It seemed to him that the blue mountains would march before him forever.

He didn't see his enemies, the Carlists in their red hats.

He didn't see his enemies, the government troops.

He saw neither any Frenchman nor any Spaniard, and he had no idea where the border was located.

He was still marching through the Pyrenees like an ant alone in the world, tired and anxious, when the daylight began to fail. But before darkness he came to a village where old men sat on a bench in front of an inn, and two youths threw a stick for a skinny yellow dog that didn't move. "Go after it, you lazy cunt," one of them called. The words were in Josep's kind of Catalan, and he knew he was close to Spain.

2

The Sign

Seven days later, early on a Sunday morning, Josep reached the village of Santa Eulália, where he could have walked safely in the dark, knowing every field, every farmhouse, each tree. It appeared to be unchanged. Crossing the little wooden bridge over the Pedregós River, he noted the thinness of the trickle through the riverbed, the result of half a dozen years of drought. He went down the narrow street and through the tiny plaça bordered by the village well, the communal wine press, the blacksmith's forge, the grocery of his father's friend, Nivaldo, and the church whose patron saint shared its name with the village. He met no one, although some people already were in the Santa Eulália Church; when he passed, he heard the quiet rumble of their voices at the Mass. Beyond the church were a few houses and the veg-etable farm of the Casals family. Then, Freixa's vineyard. After Freixa's, Roca's vineyard. And finally Josep reached the vineyard of his father, nestled between the Fortuny family's white grape vineyard and Quim Torras's plant-ings of black grapes.

A small wooden sign on a low stake had been hammered into the ground.

FOR SALE

"Ah, Donat," he said bitterly. He might have guessed his brother would not want to keep the land. He didn't become angry until he saw the condition of the vineyard, for the vines were in sorry shape. They hadn't been pruned and were overgrown and sprawling, all the neglected spaces between the vines rampant with grass, thistle, and weed. The masia almost surely had not changed in appearance since it had been built by Josep's great-grandfather. It was part of the land, a small building of stones and clay that seemed to grow out of the earth, with the kitchen and a little pantry on the ground floor, and stone stairways leading to two small bedrooms on the second floor and an attic where grains were stored under the eaves. There was an earthen floor in the kitchen, and the upstairs floor was plastered, the plaster stained deep red with pig's blood and waxed regularly through all the years until now it seemed like dark, polished stone. All the ceilings had exposed rafters, logs taken from trees felled by José Alvarez when he had cleared his land to put in vines, and the roof was made of tall hollow reeds that grew on the river banks. Split and woven, they made a strong support for the roof tiles fashioned from gray river clay.

Inside, there was grit everywhere. On the kitchen mantle, the mahogany-cased French clock—his father's wedding gift to Josep's mother when they had married on December 12, 1848—sat silent and unwound. The only other things in the house that Josep valued were his father's bedstead and trunk; both had been decorated with elaborate carvings of grapevines by their creator, his grandfather, Enric Alvarez. Now the carvings were gray with dust. Soiled work clothing lay on the floor and on the roughly made chairs and table, next to dirty dishes that contained mouse speckles and the remnants of old meals. Josep had been walking for days on end and was too weary for thought or act. Upstairs, it didn't occur to him to use his father's room, his father's bed. He kicked off his shoes, dropped onto the thin, lumpy sleeping mat his body hadn't touched for four years, and almost immediately knew nothing.

He slept through that day and the night, awakening late the next morning with a terrible hunger. There was no sign of Donat. Josep had only enough water left in his bottle for a swallow. When he carried an empty basket and a pail toward the plaça, the alcalde's three sons were in Angel Casal's field. The two older ones, Tonio and Jaume, were spreading manure and the third, the youngest one-Josep couldn't remember his name-was plowing with a mule. Working, they didn't take notice as he passed them and went to the grocery. In the gloom within the small shop was Nivaldo Machado, almost but not quite the same as Josep had remembered. He was skinnier if that was possible, and balder; the hair that remained had turned more completely grey. He was pouring beans from a large sack into small bags, and he stopped and stared with his good eye. The bad eye, the left one, was half shut.

"Josep? Praise be to God! Josep, you're *alive!* Damn my soul, is it you, Tigre?" he said, using the nickname he, and only he, had used all of Josep's life.

Josep was warmed by the joy in his voice, moved by tears in Nivaldo's eyes. The leathery lips gave two kisses, the wiry old arms wrapped him in abracada.

"It's me, Nivaldo. How are you?"

"I'm fine as ever. Are you still a soldier? We all thought you were dead, for certain. Were you wounded? Did you kill half the army of Spain?"

"The army of Spain and the Carlists have both been safe from me, Nivaldo. I haven't been a soldier. I've been making wine in France. In Languedoc."

"Truly, in Languedoc? How was it there?"

"Very French. The food was fine. Right now, I'm half starved, Nivaldo."

Nivaldo smiled, visibly happy. The old man threw two sticks on the fire and set the stewpot on the small stove. "Sit."

Josep took one of the two rickety chairs as Nivaldo set two cups on the tiny table and poured from a pitcher. "Salud. Welcome back."

"Thank you. Salud."

Not so bad, Josep told himself as he drank the wine. Well . . . as thin and sour and harsh as he remembered, yet comfortingly familiar.

"It's your father's wine."

"Yes . . . How did he die, Nivaldo?"

"Marcel just . . . seemed to become very tired, his last few months. Then one evening we were sitting right here, playing draughts. He got a pain in his arm. He waited until he won the game and then said he was going home. He must have dropped dead on the way. Donat found him in the road."

Josep nodded soberly, drank his wine. "Donat. Where is Donat?"

"Barcelona."

"What is he doing there?"

"Lives there. Married. He took a woman he met where they both work, in one of the textile mills." Nivaldo looked at him. "Your father always said that when the time came, Donat would accept his responsibilities in the vineyard. Well, the time came, but Donat doesn't want the vineyard, Josep. You know he never liked that kind of work."

The smell of the heating stew made Josep swallow. "So, what's she like? The woman he married?"

"A nice enough female. Her name is Rosa Sert. What can a man tell about another man's woman, just by looking? Quiet, a little homely. She came here with him several times."

"He's really serious about selling?"

"He wants money." Nivaldo shrugged. "A body feels the lack of money when he takes a wife." He took the pot from the stove, lifted off the cover, and spooned a generous portion of stew onto the plate. By the time he served a hunk of bread and added wine to the glasses, Josep was already shoveling food into his mouth, tasting black beans, sausage, lots of garlic. If it were summer, there would have been green beans, eggplant, perhaps kohlrabi. But now there was a taste of ham, bits of stringy rabbit, onions, potato. It was said that Nivaldo rarely washed out the stew pot, because as its contents shrank, new ingredients found their way into the stew.

He emptied his plate and accepted a second helping. "Is anyone interested in buying?"

"Always there are a few people interested in land. Roca would kill for it, but there is no chance he can manage to buy. Same for most of the others—there is no money at all. But Angel Casals wants land for his son Tonio."

"The alcalde? But Tonio is his first-born!"

"He is a slave to brandy, drunk much of the time. Angel can't get along with him and doesn't trust him to take over the farm. The two younger boys are good workers. He will leave everything to them, and he seeks to find land for Tonio."

"Has he made an offer?"

"Not yet. Angel is waiting, letting Donat sweat so he can steal the land at the best price. Angel Casals is the only one I know who can afford to set up a son with bought land. This village goes from poor to poorest. All of the younger sons leave to live elsewhere, same as you did. None of your friends are still here."

"Manel Calderon?" he asked casually.

"No. I have not heard a word about him for four years, either," Nivaldo said, and Josep felt a familiar fear.

"Guillem Parera?" he said, naming the member of the hunting group who had been his closest friend.

"Shit, Josep. Guillem is dead."

Dead? "Ah, *no.*"

I told you. You should have stayed with me, you fucking Guillem.

"Are you all right, Tigre?" Nivaldo said sharply.

"What happened to him?" he asked, afraid to hear the answer.

"After he went with you and the others, evidently he left the army too. We heard he turned up in Valencia and found work repairing the cathedral, moving those big stone blocks. One slipped and crushed him to death."

"Oh . . . A bad way to die."

"Yes. A dying world, my young friend."

Crist, poor Guillem. Nervous and depressed, Josep stood finally. "I need beans, rice. Chorizo—a great big hunk, Nivaldo, if you please. And oil and lard." The old man got the items together for him and threw a small cabbage into the basket as a welcoming gift. He never charged anyone for stew or wine, so Josep added a few coins to the bill when he paid. It was the way things were done with Nivaldo.

He couldn't help himself. "Is Teresa Gallego still here?"

"No. She made a marriage a couple of years ago, to a shoe repairer, Luis . . . Montres, Mondres . . . something like that, a cousin of the Calderons, who came to the village from Salamanca for a long visit. He wore a white suit at the wedding and speaks Spanish like a Portugués. He took her away to Barcelona, where he has a cobbler's shop on Sant Doménech del Call."

His fear realized, Josep nodded, tasting the bitterness of regret. He folded his dream of Teresa and put it away.

"You remember Maria del Mar Orriols?" Nivaldo said.

"Jordi Arnau's girl?"

"Yes. He left her with a big belly when he went off with your lot. She bore a little boy, Francesc, he's called. Later, she married your neighbor, Ferran Valls, who gave the child his name."

"Ferran?" Older, quiet man. Short, wide body, big head. Widower, no children.

"He's dead too, Ferran Valls. Cut his hand and was carried off fast by the fever, less than a year after they married."

"How does she live?"

"Valls' vineyard is Maria del Mar's now. For a time last year Tonio Casals lived with her. Some feared they'd marry, but she soon realized he's mean as a snake when he drinks—and he always drinks. She drove him off. She and her boy keep to themselves. She works hard, tends the land as if she's a man. Raises grapes and sells wine to become vinegar, same as everybody else," Nivaldo said.

Nivaldo looked at him. "I once walked away from soldiering, too. Do you want to talk about what happened to you?"

"No."

"It's all changed, there in Madrid, but not as your father and I had hoped . . . We put you on the horse that didn't win," Nivaldo said heavily.

"Is there anything I can do to welcome you home?"

"I can use another bowl of stew," Josep said, and the old man smiled and got up to get it for him.

Josep went to the churchyard and found the grave where Nivaldo said it was. There had been no room for his father next to where his mother lay. Her grave looked the same.

Maria Rosa Huertas
Wife and Mother
2 January 1835–20 May 1860

His father had been buried off to one side, in the southeast corner just left of the cherry tree. Each year the cherries on that tree were large, purple temptations. The villagers avoided the fruit, fearing it had been nurtured by the corpses in the graves, but his father and Nivaldo always had picked the cherries.

The earth of his father's grave had had time to settle but still was bare of grass. Josep grieved, pulling the few weeds almost absent-mindedly. If he had been at the grave of Guillem he might have spoken to his old friend, but he felt no connection to either of his dead parents in this churchyard. He had been eight years old when his mother died, and he realized that he and his father never had found meaningful words to say to one another.

His father's grave had no marker. He would have to make one.

Eventually he left the churchyard and went back to the plaça. He tied his pail to the rope and dropped it into the well, noting the interval before he heard the splash.

As he had seen from the river, the water level was low. When he had recovered the brimming pail, he drank deeply from it and then filled it again and carried it home with care to store in the two cántirs, the water jugs that would keep it cool.

This time, as he walked past the alcalde's field, his presence was noted. Tonio and Jaume stopped what they were doing and stared. Jaume lifted a hand to him. Josep's hands were occupied with the basket and the pail, but he shouted a cheerful *hola!* in greeting. In a few minutes, when he set down the pail to flex his cramped hand, he looked back and saw that the youngest Casals brother—the boy's name was Jordi, he remembered suddenly—had been sent to follow him to ascertain that he was indeed Josep Alvarez, come home.

When he reached the Alvarez masia, he set the basket and the pail on the ground. The wooden FOR SALE sign came out of the dry ground easily, and he whirled it overhead before letting it fly into a deep clump of brush.

Then he looked down the road and smiled to see young Jordi Casals fleeing like a panicked animal to tell his father and his brothers what he had witnessed.

3

Cleaning the Nest

𝒯he evidence of Donat's slovenly housekeeping disgusted Josep, yet when he began to work, he was drawn not inside the casa but to the vineyard. He cleared weeds and pruned vines, the same tasks that had been his final work at the larger Mendes vineyard. What he had done well and with pride for wages in France, he resumed now with overwhelming pleasure on this small, scruffy piece of land that had belonged to his family for a hundred and eight years. Far back into the early days of Spanish agriculture, his people had been serfs and then day laborers in the crop fields of poverty-stricken Galicia. In the year 1766 things had changed for the Alvarez family when King Charles III had noted that much of the countryside consisted of fallow land without workers, while the villages were crowded with men without land— discontented and therefore politically dangerous. The king had appointed Conde Pedro Pablo de Aranda, a military leader who had distinguished himself as a Captain-General of the armies, to oversee a program of ambitious land reform, parceling and redistributing public lands as well as tracts that had come to the Crown through the purchase of extensive properties from the Catholic Church.

One of the first of these transactions involved 51 hectares of isolated, rolling hills on the Pedregós River in Catalonia. The land was empty of habitation, and Aranda had ordered it divided into 12 sections of four hectares each, with the remaining three hectares surrounding a small stone building, the long-abandoned Priory of Santa Eulália, which he designated as a church. To receive the land the Captain-General chose 12 retiring combat veterans, senior sergeants who had led troops under his command. As young soldiers all of them had fought in petty campaigns and bloody insurrections. Each of the sergeants was owed back pay, not huge amounts but a respectable sum when added together. Except for small allowances given to each new farmer so he could put in a first crop, the claims for back pay were settled by the land grants, a by-product of the program that pleased Aranda in a year of financial difficulty for the Crown.

Only one of the twelve tracts was truly outstanding for agricultural purposes. This good field was located in the southwest corner of the new village, on a former course of the river. For centuries, in the rare years of high water, swollen currents had collected topsoil upstream and deposited it at a crook in the river, building a thick cap of rich alluvial soil. The first grantee to inspect the new village had been Pere-Felip Casals, who had chosen the fertile corner eagerly and without hesitation, assuring the prosperity that had brought his descendents political power and made them, generation after generation, alcaldes of Santa Eulália.

Josep's great-grandfather, José Alvarez, had been the fourth retired soldier to inspect Santa Eulália and accept his land. He had had dreams of becoming a prosperous wheat farmer, but he and the other sergeants, born peasants all, had knowledge of soils and had observed that every remaining tract was composed of slatey soil or dry limestone earth, a chalky, stony medium.

They had talked gravely and at length. Pere-Felip Casals had already started to plant potatoes and rye on his fertile piece. The others knew they would have to be resilient. "It isn't possible for many crops to thrive in such inhospitable shit," José Alvarez had said wearily, and the other sergeants had agreed.

From the very first planting, each of them had grown a crop that thrived in the burning sun of summer and renewed itself in the respite of the mild winter in northern Spain. A crop that could burrow deep into the dry, stony ground until its roots sucked and swallowed whatever meager moisture was held by the earth.

Each of them had planted grapes.

The land reform movement didn't get far. The Crown soon decided to encourage a system that leased large tracts to tenants-in-chief, who in turn rented tiny bits of land to indigent farmers. In less than two years Aranda stopped giving away land, but the farmers of Santa Eulália had been given clear titles and were landowners.

Now, more than a century after the land grant, fewer than half the tracts in Santa Eulália were owned and operated by descendents of the retired soldiers. The other pieces had been sold to landlords and were tended by pagesos, peasant grape growers who leased tiny bits of land. The living conditions of owners and renters were scarcely different, but in addition to farming larger tracts, those who owned their vineyards were secure in the knowledge that no landlord could raise the rent and force them from their property. Weeding on his hands and knees, Josep dug his fingers into the warm pebbled clay, feeling its welcome grittiness under his nails. *This earth.* How wonderful to own it, from the sun-baked growing surface to however deep a man wanted to dig! It didn't matter that this ground gave sour wine instead of wheat. To have it was to possess a slice of Spain, to own a piece of the world.

Late in the afternoon he moved inside and began to set the house to rights. He took the dirty dishes and utensils outside and scrubbed the filth and the mould from them, first with handfuls of sand and then with soapy water. He wound the French clock, checking the

time from Nivaldo's clock at the store and estimating the
few minutes it took him to walk home. Then he swept
the floor, the packed earth that had been polished by a
century of Alvarez feet. Tomorrow, he told himself, he
would scrub his clothes in the Pedregós, along with the
soiled clothes Donat had abandoned. He was aware of
his own body stink. The air wasn't warm, but he needed
the luxury of a full wash. When he returned the broom,
he noticed that the wooden handles of the tools were dry,
and he took the time to give them a careful oiling. Only
then, as the sun was sinking, did he allow himself to take
the thin bar of brown soap and make his way toward the
river.

When he passed the Torras place, he saw that it was
still tended, but poorly. The vines, many as yet unpruned,
looked as if they sorely needed fertilizer.

The next vineyard was the one that had been Ferran
Valls's. Four large, twisted olive trees bordered the road,
their old roots as thick as Josep's arm. A little child was
playing between the roots of the second tree.

The boy watched him as he approached. He was a
handsome fellow, blue-eyed and dark-haired, with thin,
knobby arms and legs that were browned by the sun.
Josep saw that his hair was too long, almost as long as a
girl's.

He stopped and cleared his throat. "Good afternoon.
I suppose you are Francesc. I am Josep."

But the boy sprang to his feet and scuttled away behind the trees. He ran lopsided; there was something
wrong with his legs. By the time Josep passed the last
tree, allowing him to look deeper into the vineyard, he
could see the child's ragged progress toward a figure
working in the rows with her hoe.

Maria del Mar Orriols. They had called her Marimar.
The girl he recalled as Jordi's lover, now a widow, he
thought, feeling strange.

When the boy pointed, she stopped her activity and
stared out at the man in the road. She looked stockier
than he remembered, almost like a man except for the

work-stained dress and the kerchief around her head. "Hola, Maria del Mar!" he called, but she made no reply; obviously, she didn't recognize the figure in the road. He stopped and waited for a moment, but she didn't walk forward to speak with him, nor did she give him any signal that would invite him to approach.

In a moment he waved and continued toward the river, and at the end of her property a curve in the road took him toward the bank of the Pedregós and out of her sight.

4

The Saint of Virgins

*E*verywhere he looked in Santa Eulália, Josep saw Teresa Gallego. There was one year's difference in their ages. When they were little, Teresa was just another of the many children who ran about the village street and started working on the land while still very young. Her father, Eusebi Gallego, rented a hectare and made a questionable living raising white grapes. Josep had always seen her about, but she didn't register in his consciousness, even in such a small village, until she was seven years old. Compact for her age but quick and strong, she was the mascot of the Castellers of Santa Eulália. The young favorite of the community, she was the child everyone knew would have been chosen—if only she had been a male!—to be the peak of the human structure of castellers wearing green shirts and white pants, who on public occasions celebrated God and Catalonia by raising themselves toward the sky, standing on one another's shoulders.

Some said the castellers reenacted Christ rising into heaven. While musicians played old songs on drums and traditional Catalan oboes called grallas, a quartet of barrel-chested strong men took their places. Wrapped in suffocatingly tight sashes to give support to their backs and bellies, they were surrounded by hundreds of eager volunteers, the crowd pressing in on them, propping them, holding them in place with dozens of hands to provide a firm baixos, a base. Four additional strong men climbed atop the bottom four, their bare feet on the lower men's shoulders. Then four more climbed up, and four more on top of them. And so on, until there were eight layers of men, each layer lighter than the preceding one because it would have to bear less weight. The upper levels were youths, and the last to ascend the castell was the small boy who was the anxaneta, the pinnacle.

Little Teresa Gallego was strong and nimble as a monkey, by far a better climber than any boy in the village. She attended every practice of the castellers because her father, Eusebi, lent his invaluable strength in the fourth layer of men. Though a female could not be the pinnacle, little Teresa was admired and loved, and sometimes she was allowed to climb to the fifth row during rehearsals, over four bodies as if each were a ladder, stepping on calves, buttocks, backs, outstretched arms, and shoulders, until she stood on her father. She climbed carefully and smoothly, making no frantic moves that would cause the castell to sway, but often it swayed anyway and shuddered while she climbed. A quick escape command yelled from the coach below could send her sliding down again over all the backs and legs as the castell trembled and twisted. Once in a practice climb it broke beneath her, and she fell to earth, a small piece of human fruit dropping among the thudding, hard adult bodies. There were minor injuries from the fall, but God protected her from harm.

Though she was acknowledged to be the best child climber, when there were splendid times of public success during the castellers' scheduled appearances at festivals, always it was a slower and less accomplished boy who clambered upward and achieved completion as the ninth layer, stepping across a final back to raise one arm in victory as he became the pinnacle, like the cherry on a tall layer cake, while the crowd cheered wildly. In those moments, Teresa stood on the firm earth and gazed upward in frustration and longing, as the music of the drums and the grallas sent shivers through her, and the entire human castell triumphantly unfolded itself earthward in victory and in perfect order, layer by layer. She climbed in practice for only two years. By the middle of the second season her father began to show early signs of flagging health and had trouble carrying his weight in the tower. He was replaced and Teresa stopped going to the castellers' drills. She became less cute as she grew older, and she stopped being everyone's darling, but Josep continued to study her from afar.

He had no idea what made her so interesting. He watched her change from a child as she grew tall and strong. The year she turned sixteen she was small-breasted, but her body was womanly, and he began to stare when he thought he wasn't noticed, gazing quickly at her legs when she tucked the hem of her skirt into her waistband to keep it from the vineyard dirt. She knew he was watching her, but they never spoke.

Then on Santa Eulália's Day that year, they both found themselves by the blacksmith shop, watching the church procession.

There was controversy about the saint's day, because there were two saints named Eulália—Santa Eulália, patron saint of Barcelona, and Santa Eulália of Merida—and people couldn't agree from which of them the village took its name. Each of the saints was a martyr who had died in agony for her faith. The day of Eulália of Merida was December 10, but the village celebrated on February 12, the saint's day observed by Barcelona, because they were closer to Barcelona than to Merida. Some of the villagers eventually merged the estimable powers of both saints in their minds, making *their* combined Santa Eulália more powerful than either of the other two. Their village's Eulália was the patron saint of a number of things—rain, widows, fishermen, virginity, and the prevention of miscarriages. For most of the important problems of life, one could pray to Santa Eulália.

Fifty years earlier, residents of the village had noted that the remains of one of the Eulálias were entombed in the Barcelona Cathedral, while worshipers in Merida had relics of their Santa Eulália in the basilica of their church. The villagers of Santa Eulália had wanted to honor their saint too, but they had no relic, not even a single bone from a finger, and they pooled their meager funds and commissioned a statue of her for their church. The sculptor they hired was a maker of gravestones, a man of limited talent. The statue he made was large and cumbersome, with a disapproving face that was homely enough to be human, but the statue was painted in bright colors and the village was proud of it. Every Santa Eulália's Day, the women dressed their saint in a white robe adorned with many bright-ringing little bells. The strongest men of the region, including those who served as the base of the human tower, would jostle the statue onto a square platform made of stout timbers. While the men at the front of the platform walked forward with grunts and groans, the men at the rear walked backward; they moved slowly and staggeringly from one end of the village to the other and then twice around the plaça, the bells on the statue tinkling as if in saintly approval. Children and dogs chased each other in the platforms's wake. Babies bawled, the dogs barked, and Santa Eulália's progress was marked by a wave of applause and cries of pleasure from the crowds of people who had come in their church clothes, some of them from considerable distances, to join in the festivities and pay homage to the saint.

Josep was acutely aware of the girl near him. They stood without speaking, his eyes fixed determinedly at the building on the other side of the narrow street in order not to look at her. Perhaps she was as bewitched as he. Before they awoke to the fact that the saint approached, Eulália was almost upon them. The street was very narrow at that point. There were only a few centimeters of clearance on both sides of the saint's platform, which sometimes ground alarmingly against the stone walls of buildings until the men carrying it could make the tiny correction needed for a clean passage.

Josep looked ahead and saw at once that beyond the blacksmith shop the street was wider but already was occupied by a crowd of onlookers.

"Senyoreta," he said warningly, the only time he spoke to her.

In the wall of the blacksmith shop there was a shallow niche and, taking the girl by the arm, he pushed her into it and pressed in after her just as the platform reached them. Had they still been on the street, the ponderous weight would have crushed and ground. As it was, he could feel the edge of the platform move the fabric of his trousers at the back of his thighs. If the platform had been jostled, injury still might have occurred.

But he was scarcely conscious of the danger. He was pressed against the girl's body—so close together—amazingly aware of every sensation.

For the first time he examined her face, at close range and without being forced to look away after two seconds. No one would ever mistake her for one of the world's famous beauties, he told himself. Yet to him, somehow her face was better than that.

Her eyes were of ordinary size, a soft brown color; her lashes were long, her eyebrows heavy and dark. Her nose was small and straight with thin nostrils. Her lips were full and the upper lip was chapped. Her teeth were strong and white, rather large. He smelled the garlic she had had for lunch. She had a very nice chin. Beneath her jawbone on the left side there was an almost-round brown mole that he wanted to touch.

Everything he saw, he wanted to touch.

She didn't blink. Their eyes were locked; there was no other place to look.

Then Santa Eulália had passed them. Josep stepped back. Without a word the girl slipped away from him and fled down the street.

He stood there, not knowing where to gaze, certain that everyone in the vicinity was staring at him accusingly for having pressed his hardened maleness against the purity of such a female. But when he raised his shamed eyes and glanced about, he saw that no one looked at him with any interest or appeared to have noticed anything, and he hurried away from there also.

For weeks after that he avoided the girl, unable to meet her eyes. He thought it was inevitable that she would never want to have anything to do with him. He sorely regretted that he had gone to the blacksmith shop on the Santa's day, until one morning he and Teresa Gallego met at the well in the plaça. While they were drawing water, they began to talk.

They looked directly at one another, and they spoke for a long time, quietly and seriously, as befit two people who had been brought together by Santa Eulália.

5

A Thing Between Brothers

*E*xactly a week after Josep's return, his brother, Donat, came to the masia with his woman, Rosa Sert, his face a curious mixture of welcoming and foreboding. Donat had always been stocky, but now there were dewlaps under his jowls and already his belly was swollen like rising dough. Josep saw that soon Donat would be a really fat man.

His older brother, a fat semi-stranger who lived in the city.

They both exchanged kisses with him. Rosa was short and plump, a pleasant looking woman. She was watchful but smiled at him tentatively.

"Padre said you were gone for a soldier, probably in the Basque country," Donat said. "Wasn't that the purpose of that hunting group, to train you to be a soldier?"

"It didn't turn out that way."

Josep offered no explanations, but he told them about his four years of work in Languedoc. He poured a taste, the last from the wineskin he had brought from France, and they complimented the vin ordinaire, though it had long since lost its edge.

"So you're working in a cloth factory? Is the work all right?"

"I like it enough. There's money twice each month, whether there is hail or drought or any other calamity."

Josep nodded. "Steady money is good. And what is your job?"

"Helper to a worker who keeps watch over the spools that feed the looms. I'm learning things. If the thread or yarn breaks, we rejoin it with weavers' knots. Before the spools run out of thread, I replace them with fresh spools. It's a big mill, lots of looms, driven by steam. There is opportunity to advance. I hope some day to be a mechanic of the looms or the steam engines."

"And you, Rosa?"

"I? I examine the cloth and mend faults. Take care of stains and such. Sometimes there is an imperfection or a tiny hole, and I use needle and thread to fix it so it can't be seen."

"She's very skilled," Donat said proudly, "but they pay skilled women less than unskilled men."

There was a momentary lull.

"So what shall *you* now do?" Donat asked.

Josep knew they would have noted at once that the FOR SALE sign was gone.

"Grow grapes. Make wine for vinegar."

"Where?"

"Here."

They were both looking at him with horror. "I earn less than two pesetas a day," Donat said. "I will be on half-pay for two years, while I learn the trade, and I am in need of money. I'm going to sell this land."

"I am going to buy it."

Donat's mouth was open and Rosa's lips were pressed tight, making her mouth a worried line.

As patiently as possible, Josep explained. "Only one person is willing to buy this land—Casals, who would pay piss-money for it. And of the alcalde's piss-money, one-third would come to me, as the younger son's share."

"Padre always made it clear. The entire vineyard was to go to me!"

Padre had always made that clear. "The land was to go to you unbroken because only one family can survive on it by growing grapes and making vinegar wine. But

Padre didn't leave the land entirely to you so you could *sell* it. As you know. As you well know. As you absolutely and positively *know*, Donat."

They glared at one another, and it was his brother who looked away.

"So the rule must apply: two-thirds to the eldest son, one-third to the younger son. I will pay you a good price, a better price than Angel Casals. From that sum we will deduct one-third, because I won't buy what I already own."

"And where will you get the money?" Donat asked too quietly.

"I'll sell my grapes, as Padre always did. I'll make payment to you every three months, until the entire sales price is paid."

The three sat silently, looking at one another.

"I saved most of my wages, four years of hard work in France. I can give you the first payment at once. You'll get extra money every three months for a long time. On top of what the two of you earn, it will make things easier for you. And the land will stay in the Alvarez family."

Donat looked at Rosa, who shrugged. "You must sign a paper," she said to Josep.

"Why a paper? This is a thing between brothers."

"Still, there is a proper way to do it," she said, sounding determined.

"Since when do brothers need a paper?" Josep asked Donat. He allowed himself to become very annoyed. "Why should brothers give good money to a law merchant?"

Donat was silent.

"It is the way to do such a thing," Rosa insisted. "My cousin Carles is a lawyer, he will provide the legal paper for us for very little money."

They gazed at him stubbornly, and now it was Josep who looked away and shrugged.

"Very well. Bring me the God-damned paper," he said.

They were back the following Sunday. The document was crisp and white, important looking. Donat held it as if it were a snake and handed it over to Josep with relief.

He tried to read it, but he was too nervous and irritated; the words on the two pages swam before his eyes, and he knew what he must do.

"Wait here," he said curtly, and he left them sitting at what he still thought of as his father's table.

Nivaldo was in his apartment above the grocery, his newspaper, *El Cascabel*, spread out before him. On Sundays he didn't open the grocery until the church service let out, when the worshipers came in to buy staples to last them for the week. His bad eye was closed, and he squinted fiercely at the newspaper with his good eye, the way he read anything. He always reminded Josep of a hawk.

Nivaldo was the smartest man Josep had ever met. Josep felt he could have been or done anything. He had once told Josep he couldn't remember ever having been in a schoolroom. In the same week in 1812 in which the British had forced Joseph Bonaparte to flee from Madrid, Nivaldo had fled the sugar fields of his native Cuba. Twelve years old, he stowed away on a boat bound for Maracaibo. He had been a gaucho in Argentina and a soldier in the Spanish army—from which, Padre once revealed, Nivaldo had deserted. He had served on sailing ships. From enigmatic things he had said from time to time, Josep felt sure he had been a privateer before settling down as a storekeeper in Catalonia. Josep didn't know where Nivaldo had learned to read and write, but he did both well enough to teach Josep and Donat when they were young, giving lessons at his little table, which were interrupted anytime someone came into the shop for a hunk of chorizo or a few slices of cheese.

"What is happening, Nivaldo?"

Nivaldo sighed and folded *El Cascabel*. "This is a bad time for the government's army, one of its worst defeats, two thousand troops taken prisoner by the Carlists after a battle in the north. And there's trouble in Cuba. The Americans are giving weapons and supplies to the rebels. The Americans can practically piss on Cuba from Florida, and they won't be happy until they own it. They can't stand to see a jewel like Cuba being run by a country as

far away as Spain." He folded *El Cascabel*. "So what's on
your mind?" he asked, somewhat grumpily, and Josep
held out the lawyer's paper.

Nivaldo read it through in silence. " . . . Ah, you're
buying the vineyard. That's very good." He started anew
at the beginning and studied it again. Then he sighed.
"You have read this?"

"Not really."

"Jesús." He handed it back to Josep. "Read it carefully. And then read it a second time."

He waited patiently until Josep had done so, and
then he took the paper. "Here." His splayed forefinger
pointed out the paragraph. "Their lawyer says if you
miss a single payment, the land and the masia revert to
Donat."

Josep grunted.

"You must tell them this part has to be changed. If
they must squeeze you, it should at least say that you
won't forfeit the land unless you've missed three payments in succession."

"To hell with them. I'll sign the damned thing as it is.
It makes me feel dirty to bargain and squabble with my
brother over our family land."

Nivaldo leaned over and grasped Josep's wrist hard,
and looked into his eyes. "Listen to me, Tigre," he said
gently. "You aren't a child. You are not a fool. You must
protect yourself."

Josep felt like a child. "What if they won't accept a
change?" he asked sullenly.

"They surely will not. They expect you to haggle. Tell
them if ever you are late with a payment, you agree to
add ten percent to the sum of the next payment."

"You think they will accept that?"

Nivaldo nodded. "I believe they will."

Josep thanked him and got up to leave.

"You must write in that change, and you and Donat
must sign your name next to the changed part. Wait."
Nivaldo got the wine and two glasses. He took Josep's
hand and shook it. "I give you my blessing. May you
have only good fortune, Josep."

Josep thanked him. He downed the wine quickly, the way wine never should be drunk, then he returned to the masia.

Donat guessed that Josep had consulted Nivaldo, whom he respected as much as his brother did, and he was not inclined to argue with the requested change. But, as Josep expected, Rosa objected at once. "You have to know that you must pay without fail," she said severely.

"I do know," he growled. When he countered with the offer of the ten percent penalty, she thought for a long and painful moment before she nodded.

They watched while he laboriously wrote out the changes and then signed both copies of the agreement twice.

"My cousin Carles the lawyer told us that if there were changes, he must read them before Donat signs," Rosa said. "Will you come to Barcelona to collect your paper?"

To pay us our money, Josep knew that she meant. He had no desire to go to Barcelona. "I have just walked home from France," he said coldly.

Donat looked embarrassed. He clearly wished to mollify his brother. "I'll return to the village every three months to collect your payments. But why don't you come to visit us next Saturday night?" he said to Josep. "You can pick up your signed copy of the paper, give us the first payment, and we will have a real party. We will show you how to celebrate in Barcelona!"

Josep was fed up. He wanted only to have them out of his sight, and he agreed that he would come to see them at the end of the week.

When they were gone, he continued to sit at the table in the silent casa, as if stunned.

Finally he got up and went outside and began to walk the vineyard.

It was as if suddenly he had been transformed into the eldest son. He knew he should feel excitement and joy, but instead he was made leaden by doubt.

He walked up and down the plantings of vines, studying them. The rows were not as carefully spaced as the immaculate rows at the Mendes vineyard, and they were curved and contorted like snakes instead of bring reasonably straight. They had been planted carelessly, a jumble of varieties—his eyes picked out small and large groups of Garnacha, Samso, and Ull de Llebre, all mixed in among one another. Generations of his forebears had made wine from them, to be turned into a raw, indifferent vinegar. His ancestors hadn't cared about varieties, so long as they grew black grapes that gave sufficient juice.

That's how they had survived. He should be able to survive in the same way, he told himself. But he was troubled; it seemed to him that his change of fortune had happened too easily. Would he be able to meet the challenges of this responsibility?

He wasn't supporting a family, he told himself, and he had few personal needs save for the simplest of foods. But there would be expenses for the vineyard. He wondered if he could afford to buy a mule. Padre had sold his mule when his two sons became old enough to do a man's work. With three men in the vineyard, they could handle the work without having to fuss with the care of an animal.

But now he had only his own labor, and a mule would be a godsend.

Over the years, all of the easily useable land had been planted with vines, but as he walked, he saw the last of the late afternoon sun still striking the top of the hill that composed the rear border of the property. Only half of the slope was planted with vines; the steepness was very close to the angle Leon Mendes had told him was more than forty-five degrees. That was too steep to work with a mule, but Josep had spent many hours planting and tending vines in France, working with hand tools on similarly steep hills.

Most of the older vines were Ull de Llebre. But one section of the hill was planted with Garnacha, and he climbed to where the vines were beautiful and aged,

perhaps a hundred years old, with gnarled lower por-
tions as thick as his thighs. There were a handful of hard
raisins clinging to the dried tendrils, and when he picked
and ate them, he found them still full of lingering flavor.

He went higher, several times going down on one
knee as his feet failed to gain sufficient purchase on the
roughness of the hill, here and there pausing to pull gorse
and weeds. A lot of vines could be planted here! He could
considerably increase the production of grapes.

He realized that perhaps he had learned some things
that his father hadn't known. And he was willing to work
like a farm animal, and to experiment in ways his father
wouldn't have tried.

That night he would begin to sleep in his father's bed.

He understood that what had occurred was miracu-
lous, as important to him as the day the king and General
Pedro Pablo de Aranda had given the land to Sergeant
Jose Alvarez. In that moment all doubt left him, and he
was flooded with the happiness that had been eluding
him. Filled with thanksgiving, he sat on the warmed earth
of the slope and watched as the sun smeared the horizon
with redness before disappearing between two hills. In a
short time, dusk settled on the small, vine-filled valley of
Santa Eulália, and night began to fall on his land.

6

A Trip to Barcelona

*O*n Saturday morning Josep hoed and dug for two hours, breaking the ground along a poor row where very old Ull de Llebre vines were scraggly and the hardpan earth chipped like rock. But he stopped working while the day was still early, not knowing how long it would take him to reach the textile mill where Donat worked. He made his way to the Barcelona road; the long walk from France was still fresh in his memory, and he had no desire to go to the city on foot. Instead he stood and waited for a likely vehicle, allowing several private coaches to pass; then, sighting a large wagon laden with new barrels and pulled by four huge draft horses, he held up his hand and pointed down the road.

The driver, a red-cheeked man built as generously as his horses, pulled on the reins long enough for him to clamber aboard and affably wished him a fine morning. It was a fortunate ride. The horses clopped briskly, and the driver was an even-tempered soul content to spend the time of day in lazy conversation that shortened the trip. He said he was Emilio Rivera, whose cooperage was in Sitges.

"Fine barrels," Josep said, glancing at the load behind him. "Bound for winemakers?"

Rivera smiled. "No." He did not sell to winemakers, he said, though he supplied barrels to the vinegar trade.

"These are slated for fishfolk on the Barcelona waterfront. They fill my barrels with hake, bream, tuna, herrings . . . sometimes sardines or anchovies. Not very often with eels, for mostly they sell their entire catch of eels fresh. I do like young eels."

Neither of the men mentioned the civil war; it was impossible to tell whether a stranger was a Carlist conservative or a government-supporting liberal. When Josep admired the horses, the conversation turned to draft animals.

"I'll be looking to buy a strong young mule soon, I think," Josep said.

"Then you must come to the horse fair in Castelldefels, which will be held in only four weeks. My cousin Eusebio Serrat is a buyer of horses, mules, and such. For a small fee he will help you select the best offered there," the cooper said, and Josep nodded thoughtfully, tucking away the name in his head.

Rivera's horses moved well. It was not long after midday when they reached the place where the textile factory was located, just outside the walls of Barcelona; but, since Josep had arranged to meet Donat at the mill at five o'clock, he rode beyond the mill village with Senyor Rivera. As he jumped from the cooper's wagon at the Plaça de la Seu, the bells in the Cathedral tower were sounding the news that it was two o'clock.

He strolled through the basilica and vaulted galleries, and ate his bread and cheese on a bench in the cloisters, throwing a crust to a gaggle of geese grazing beneath the medlars, magnolias, and palm trees of the Cathedral garden. Then he sat outside on the stone steps, enjoying the thin sun that warmed the cool air of early spring.

He knew he was a short walk from the neighborhood where, according to Nivaldo, Teresa's husband had a shoe repair shop.

He was nervous about the possibility of meeting her in the street. What could he say to her?

But she did not appear. He sat and watched the people entering and leaving the Cathedral—priests, members of the upper classes in fine clothes, nuns in several different habits, working people with worn faces, children with dirty feet. The shadows were lengthening as he left the Cathedral and made his way through narrow streets and courtyards.

He heard the mill before it came into his sight. At first the roar was like a distant surf that filled his ears with dull and muffled sound and left him uneasy and strangely apprehensive.

Donat embraced him, happy and eager to show Josep where he worked. "Come," he said. The mill was a large presence of flat red brick. In the entryway the roar was more insistent. A man in a finely-cut black jacket and gray waistcoat looked at Donat. "You! There is a bale of spoiled wool near the carders. It is rotten and cannot be used. You will dispose of it, please."

Josep knew his brother had been working since four a.m., but Donat nodded. "Yes, Senyor Serna, I will attend to it. Senyor, may I present my brother, Josep Alvarez? I have finished my shift and am about to show him our mill."

"Yes, yes, show it to him, but then dispose of the bad wool . . . Is your brother seeking employment then?"

"No, senyor," Josep said, and the man turned away dismissively.

Donat paused at a crate filled with raw wool and showed Josep how to take some of the material and stuff it into his ears. "To protect against the noise."

Despite the ear plugs, sound burst over them as they went through a set of doors. They entered a balcony overlooking the vast concrete floor on which limitless rows of machines raised a clacking pandemonium that pounded against Josep's skin and filled the hollows within his body. Donat tapped his arm to gain his attention.

"Spinners . . . and . . . looms," he mouthed silently. "And . . . other . . . things . . ."

"How . . . many?"

"Three . . . hundred!"

He led Josep and they swam through the sea of sound. Donat's gestures indicated how draymen poured coal directly from delivery wagons into a chute that dropped it close to two boilers into which four half-naked stokers shoveled fuel without pause, creating steam that ran the great engine powering the looms. Down a brick corridor was a room where the raw wool was taken from bales and sorted for quality and staple length—Donat signified that the longer lengths were better—before being fed onto mechanized tables that shook the wool to allow dirt to sift through a screen onto a container below. Scouring machines washed the fleece and shrank it, and carding machines straightened the fibers and prepared them for spinning. In the carding room, Donat smiled at a friend and touched his arm.

"My . . . brother."

His co-worker smiled at Josep and took his hand. Then the man touched his own face and turned away. It was a workers' signal, Josep would learn, indicating that a boss was watching. He could see the overseer—seated behind a table on a small raised platform in the center of the room—looking sharply at them. Next to the overseer a large sign proclaimed

WORK IN SILENCE!

SPEAKING DOES NOT ALLOW YOU TO DO
PERFECT WORK!

Donat quickly led him from the room. They followed the path of the wool through the many processes that led to the spinning of the yarn and thread and the weaving and dyeing of the cloth. Josep was dizzied by the noise and the combined stinks of raw wool, machine oil, coal lamps, and the sweat of a thousand active workers. By the time Donat proudly instructed him to stroke the finished rolls of richly colored fabric, Josep was trembling, and eager to do or say anything that would allow him to get away from the ceaseless, conglomerate screaming of the machines.

He helped Donat dispose of the rotting bale of wool in a dump behind the factory. The sound of the machines followed, but he was grateful to be away from them.

"Can I have a bag of this stuff? I believe I can use it."

Donat laughed. "Why not? This stinking mess is no good to us. You can have as much as you can bear away." He filled a cloth sack with the wool and smiled indulgently when his strange brother carried it as they walked from the dump.

Donat and Rosa lived in the mill village, in a tiny "cheap house," so called because workers rented them from the company inexpensively. His was one in many rows of identical houses. Each house had two miniscule rooms—a bedroom and a combination kitchen and sitting room—and shared an outhouse with a neighbor. Rosa greeted Josep warmly and at once produced the two copies of the sales agreement. "My cousin Carles the lawyer approves the changes," she said, and watched narrowly as her husband signed both papers. When Josep accepted one of the papers and handed Rosa the notes that were his first payment for the land, she and Donat beamed.

"We will celebrate," Donat declared, and hurried away to buy the ingredients of a feast. While he was gone, Rosa left Josep alone in the house but returned very quickly, accompanied by a buxom young woman: "My friend Ana Zulema, from Andalucia." Both women had clearly prepared for the occasion and wore almost identical dark skirts and starched white blouses.

Donat returned very quickly with food and drink. "I went to the company store. We also have a company church and a company priest. And a company school for small children. You see, all that we need is right here. We never have to leave." He laid out spiced meat, salads, bacallá, breads, olives; Josep saw that he must have spent most of the first payment on food. "I bought brandy, and vinegar made by the people that used to buy from Padre. Maybe this very bottle of vinegar was made from Padre's grapes!"

Donat drank deeply of the brandy. Even when he was at home, he couldn't seem to stop talking about his work. "It's a new world here. The workers in this mill, they are from all over Spain. Many came from the south, because there are no jobs there. Others had their old lives torn up in the war craziness—houses ruined by the Carlists, crops burned in the fields, food stolen by soldiers, children starving.

"There is a new start here, such a fine future for them and for me, with the machines! Are not the machines wonderful?"

"They are," Josep said, but hesitantly, because the machines intimidated him.

"I shall be an apprentice only until I've been with the mill for two years, and then I'll be a weaver." Life wasn't easy for mill workers, Donat admitted. "The rules are hard. One has to be discreet about spending time in the outhouse when that is necessary. There is no meal break, so I bring a piece of cheese or a little meat in my pocket and eat it while working." The mill ran twenty-four hours a day, two long shifts, he said. "It stops only on Sundays, when the machinery is oiled and repaired. That's the work I wish to do, some day."

When the four of them finished the bottle of brandy, Donat yawned, took his wife's hand, and announced it was time for bed.

Josep had been drinking brandy too, and his head swam. He found himself lying next to Ana on the pallet Donat had unfurled for him on the floor. Beyond the thin wooden door Donat and Rosa were making love noisily. Ana giggled and moved closer. She had strongly perfumed face powder. When they kissed, she moved her leg over his body.

It was several months since Josep had been with Margit in Languedoc, and his body felt weak with the strength of his need for release. Ana tried to pull him to her; but he was having a nightmare vision of this stranger, pregnant; a hasty marriage in the company church, a job for him as a company peon in that roaring, clacking hell.

"Josep?" she said eventually, but he forced himself to pretend he was asleep, and soon she got up and went out of the house.

He lay awake all the night, wanting her back, sullen and ashamed that he had let her go. He listened to the fury of the machines, burdened with worry over the debt he had incurred to his brother and sister-in-law. Before dawn he left the pallet, took the sack of wool from where it had been left outside the door, and began to walk toward home.

It was late afternoon before he reached Santa Eulália. He had had five separate rides, walking in between each one. He was tired, but he went at once to the row in the vineyard where he had worked on impacted earth the day before. He spread generous handfuls of the wool in wide circles around each of the Ull de Llebre vines and then dug the material into the thin soil. He felt that the wool, already rotting, might feed some elements that could help the vines. At any rate, the springy wool loosened the soil and would make it possible for water and air to find their way to the roots. He worked until the sack was empty and was sorry he hadn't carried more of the wool home. Perhaps, he thought, he might convince Donat to bring him another bag.

As dusk fell, he went into the old stone house that suddenly seemed solid and dependable and got chorizo and a hunk of bread and a wine skin. He climbed halfway up the ridge and sat on a rock and ate his evening meal and sprayed the sour wine into his mouth. The evening felt crisp and clean, and in a few weeks the air would be perfumed with the smell of green, growing things.

When he had been a small boy, Nivaldo had told him that deep in the ground beneath his father's land there lived a village of little furry creatures, neither man nor animal—the Small Ones. It was the occupation of these creatures to bring moisture and sustenance to the hungry and thirsty roots of his father's vines, Nivaldo had told him, and their destiny was to produce grapes from the vines regularly, year after year. Often as Josep went to sleep at night, fearful but fascinated, he had pictured them—little, burrowing figures like young children with fur and sharp-nailed hands they used to dig, communicating with squeaks and grunts, laboring, laboring within the dark earth.

Now he spilled a little wine into the ground, a sacrifice to the Small Ones, and as he watched, an owl moved past in the sky. For a fleeting moment it was silhouetted against the full moon, the feathers at the tips of its wings like spread fingers. Then it was gone. Everything was so quiet that he could hear the silence, and at that moment, with tremendous relief, he knew he had made a wonderful bargain with Donat and Rosa.

7

Neighbors

*H*e was walking slowly along his rows, enjoying the sight of the pale bumps and eager tendrils on the awakening vines and looking for snails or any sign of blight that would call for treatment with sulfer.

He heard Maria del Mar Orriels from her own vineyard.

"Francesc. Francesc, where are you?"

At first she called out every couple of minutes, but soon she was shouting more frequently from the road, annoyance in her voice: "FRA-A-AN-CE-E-ESC!"

Josep saw the little boy peering at him from the end of the row of vines, like an imagined garden imp.

The child hadn't come from the direction of the road. Josep knew he must have walked from the back of his mother's land, through the Torras holding, and then onto Josep's vineyard. There were no fences. Little more than the width of one person separated a grower's plantings from his neighbors; they all knew very well the boundaries of their properties.

"Hello there," Josep said, but the boy didn't answer.

"I'm walking my rows. Learning to know my vines again. Taking care of business, you see?"

The child's large eyes never left Josep's face. He was dressed in a threadbare but carefully mended shirt and trousers, undoubtedly sewn by his mother out of the best parts of overused adult garments. One of the knees of his trousers was earth-stained, and there was a small tear over the other knee.

"Frannn-ce-e-sc! Fra-a-nn-ce-e-scc!"

"He's here. He's up here with me," Josep shouted. He reached down and took the small hand. "We'd best bring you to your mama."

Francesc seemed no different from any other country child, but once they started to walk his pronounced limp was painful for Josep to experience. His right leg was shorter than the other. With every step of the shorter leg, his head was deeply drawn to the right, then it was pulled erect again with the next step of his left leg.

They met his mother halfway to the road. He had never known her well, but he saw she was discernibly different from the girl he remembered. Older, harder, with a guarded wariness in the eyes, as though she expected bad news or nastiness at any moment. She had good posture. Her body seemed ripe and large, her long legs hidden in a soiled black skirt, muddy at her knees; some recent strenuous effort had crazed her hair and left her flushed and sweaty. When she knelt by the child he saw a dark wet circle on the back of her work shirt, between her shoulder blades.

She took Fransesc's hand. "I told you to stay on our land while I worked. Why did you not do that?" she asked her son severely.

The little boy smiled.

"Hello, Maria del Mar."

"Hello, Josep."

He was afraid she would ask him about Jordi. Jordi was dead; the last time Josep had seen him, Jordi's throat had just been cut. But when Del Mar looked at him, her eyes were unquestioning and impersonal.

"I'm sorry if he bothered you," she said.

"No, he's a fine boy. He's welcome anytime . . . I'll be working my father's land now," he said, aware that by now everyone in the village must know that he had become the owner.

"I wish you good fortune," she said quietly.

"Thank you."

She addressed her son again. "Well, you know better than this, Francesc. You must stay nearby when I'm working." She nodded to Josep, took Francesc by the hand, and led him off. Josep noted that despite her impatience she did not walk fast, allowing for the boy's hindrance, and he found himself moved as he watched them walk away.

He sat with Nivaldo that afternoon, drinking coffee and brooding. "Our women didn't wait very long for us, did they?"

"Why would you expect that they would?" Nivaldo said reasonably. "You left without telling them you weren't coming back. You never sent word to anyone after that, even just to say you were alive. Everyone in the village came to believe you were gone for good."

Josep knew the old man was right. "I don't believe any of us could have sent word. I couldn't. There were . . . reasons."

Nivaldo waited a moment in case more information was forthcoming. When it wasn't, he nodded.

If anyone should understand, it was Nivaldo; there were things in Nivaldo's own life that the old Cuban couldn't talk about.

"Well, what's done is done," Nivaldo said. "There's a limit to how long a man and woman can stay apart and still be a couple."

Josep didn't want to talk about Teresa, but he couldn't help a bitter observation. "Maria del Mar certainly lost little time in marrying."

"God, Josep! She had to figure out some way to survive. Her father was long gone and her mother was sick with the consumption. They barely earned their food, as I'm sure you remember."

Josep did.

"Her mother died soon after you left. She had nothing but that healthy body and a little kid. Lots of women would have gone to some city and started selling it out of a park. She chose to accept when Ferran Valls offered to marry her. And she's got big balls, that girl, she labors like a horse. Since Ferran died she grows those grapes all by herself. She's a better worker than most men, but she's had it hard. Lots of folks think it's fine for a woman to be a worker in the fields, but they see a female who's her own boss, trying to run her own business—they can't stand that, the jealous shits call her a greedy bitch.

"Clemente Ramirez, who buys for the vinegar company, he pays her less than he pays for wine made by a man. I've tried talking to him, but he just laughs. She can't just switch and sell her grapes elsewhere. Even if she could connect to another company, she knows they would cheat her in the same way. A woman without a husband is at their mercy. She's got to take whatever they give her, so she can feed the boy."

Josep was thoughtful. "I'm surprised she hasn't married again."

Nivaldo shook his head. "I don't think she wants anything from any man, if you catch my meaning. Ferran was already old when they married. I'm sure he mostly wanted a strong worker, free labor. After he died she took up with Tonio Casals and he lived in her house most of last year. He kept on working for his father and never did anything in her vineyard. Tonio's the kind who does mean things to his mules and his women. She must have soon seen that he'd be a terrible example for the little boy, and finally she got rid of him.

"So think about it. First, Jordi got her pregnant and left her. Then Ferran took her in only because she can work and work. And then Tonio Casals . . . Almost for certain he mistreated her. With that kind of a past, I imagine she considers it a blessing to be without a man, don't you?"

Josep did.

The way it sometimes does, summer drove spring away with a burst of very hot weather. The high heat continued for five weeks, forcing bud break and then searing the blossoms, foreshadowing another season of drought and a light harvest. Josep roamed the vineyard, watching the plants closely. He knew that in their constant search for moisture the old vines had sunk meandering roots. The deep roots helped them survive, but after a time some of the vines began to develop flaccid shoot tips and yellowed basal leaves, signs of intense stress.

Then he awoke one morning to thunder and a world awash. The rain slashed without pause for three days, followed by a return of heavy warmth. The tough grapevines survived, the heat and the rain combining to produce fresh buds and then a profusion of new flowering that would become a heavy crop of extra large fruit. Josep knew that if the weather was the same in Languedoc, Leon Mendes was full of gloom, for the large, vigorously growing grapes would be inferior in flavor and character, poor stuff from which to fashion wines. But what was bad news in Languedoc was good news in Santa Eulália, where increased bulk and weight of the grapes meant more wine to sell to the vinegar and brandy companies. Josep knew that the weather had made it possible for him to realize income from his first season as proprietor of the vineyard, and he was grateful. Still, he was intrigued to note that in the row of old Ull de Llebre plants where he had dug in raw wool to aerate the hard soil, the vines were full and dense and laden with clusters. He couldn't resist treating the fruit of just that one row of vines as he knew Mendes would have done, thinning it and taking some of the leaves, so the essence of each plant would be concentrated in the grapes that were left.

The lush weather and the moisture had caused the weeds to flourish as well, and soon the spaces between the rows were overgrown again. Cultivating the vineyard by hand would be an unending task. The horse show in Castelldefels had come and gone, and Josep had resisted the urge to buy a mule. Slowly but surely, his little hoard of money was depleting, and he was aware that he must conserve his funds.

But Maria del Mar Orriels had a mule. He forced himself to go to her vineyard and approach her.

"Good morning, Marimar."

"Good morning."

"The weeds are fierce, no?"

She stared at him.

"If you let me use your mule to pull my plow, I'll turn your weeds under as well as my own."

She thought for a moment and then agreed.

"Good," Josep said. She watched while he went and fetched the animal. He started to lead the mule away, but she held up her hand.

"Do mine first," she said thinly.

8

A Social Organization

*T*here was a time when he and Teresa Gallego had been inseparable, when everything had been clear to them, the world and the future plain to contemplate, like the routes on a simple map. Marcel Alvarez had seemed strong as stone; Josep had thought Padre would live a long time. He knew vaguely that when Padre finally did die, Donat would take over the vineyard, and he was dimly aware that then he would have to find a way to earn his own living. He and Teresa would find some way to marry, have children, do hard labor to earn their bread, and then die as everyone must, Jesús protect us! There was nothing complicated about it. They understood very well what was possible in life, and what was needed.

The villagers became accustomed to seeing them together whenever they weren't working in the vineyards for their fathers. It was easier to maintain perfect propriety during the daylight hours, when all the eyes of the village witnessed them. At night, under the cover of darkness, it was more difficult; the call of the flesh was stronger. They began by holding hands while they walked, a first erotic touching that made them want more. The darkness was a private chamber, allowing him to embrace her, to give her clumsy kisses. They pressed together so each could learn of the other by the tactile imprint of thigh and breast and groin, and they kissed a great deal as time went by, and grew very familiar.

One night in August when the village was panting under hot, heavy air, they went to the river and, shedding their clothes, sat hip to hip in the gently flowing water and explored one another with thrilled wonder, touching everywhere, hairiness, nakedness, muscle and curve, soft creases of skin, hard horn of toenails, scratches and calluses left by hard labor. She nursed him like a child. He discovered and gently touched the dam, proof of her innocence, as though a spider had entered and woven within her a virginal web of thin warm flesh. The most unworldly of lovers, they enjoyed the forbidden newness but simply did not know very much about what to do. They had seen animals joined, but when he tried to emulate that act, Teresa became adamantly angry and afraid.

"No! No, I would not be able to look at Santa Eulália!" she said wildly.

He moved her gripping hand until enough seeds to populate a village burst from him and floated away down the Pedregós River. It was not the grand sensual destination that, they knew instinctively, lay somewhere beyond the horizon. But they recognized that they had passed a milestone, and for the time being they were satisfied to be unsatisfied.

Their burning quickly dissolved their complacence about the future. He knew the answer to their dilemma was an early marriage, but in order to accomplish that, he would have to find employment. In a rural village of tiny agricultural plots it was not possible, for almost every farmer had heirs, and younger sons who would compete savagely with Josep in the unlikely event that a job opportunity should appear.

He yearned to escape from this village that kept him a prisoner without hope, dreamed of finding some place where he would be allowed to work eagerly and with all his strength to make a life.

Meantime, he and Teresa found it difficult to keep their hands from one another.

Josep grew irritable and red-eyed. Perhaps his father noticed and spoke to Nivaldo.

"Tigre, I want you to come somewhere with me tomorrow night," Nivaldo told Josep.

"Go where?"

"You'll see," Nivaldo said.

On the following evening they walked together a league from the village, into the country to a deserted lane and a small lopsided structure of plastered stone. "The house of Nuria," Nivaldo said. "I have been coming to her for years. Now she is retired, and we visit her daughter."

Inside, they were greeted amiably by a woman past middle age, who paused in her knitting long enough to accept from Nivaldo a bottle of wine and a bank note.

"Here is my friend Nivaldo, therefore it is the fourth Thursday. So . . . where is Marcel Alvarez?"

Nivaldo cast a veiled glance at Josep. "He cannot come tonight. This is his son, my friend Josep."

The woman looked at Josep and nodded.

"Child?" she called.

A younger woman opened the cloth separating the two rooms of the little house. Seeing Nivaldo sitting next to her mother and Josep standing awkward and alone, she crooked a finger. Josep was pushed by Nivaldo's hand in his back.

The small room behind the curtain held two sleeping mats. "I am Renata," the girl said. She had a squat body, long inky hair, a round face with a large nose.

"I'm Josep."

When she smiled he saw that her teeth were square and wide, with several gaps. She was about his age, he thought. For a moment they stood and looked at one another, and then she skinned out of her black dress in one swift motion.

"Well. Take it off. Everything. More enjoyable, yes?"

She was an ugly and amiable girl. Her fat breasts had very wide nipples. Conscious that others behind the curtain at the door could hear everything, Josep disrobed. When she lay on the rumpled bed and opened her short legs, he could not look at the dark patch. She smelled faintly of onions and garlic, like Nivaldo's stew to which had been added lye soap. She guided him inside deftly and everything was over almost at once.

Afterwards, Nivaldo took his turn in the little room, joking with Renata and roaring with laughter, while Josep sat and listened and watched the mother. As Nuria knitted, she hummed hymns, some of which he recognized.

When they were walking home, Josep thanked Nivaldo.

"For nothing," Nivaldo said. "You're a good fellow, Josep. We know it's hard to be a second son, with a sweet girl to drive you mad, and no employment."

They were quiet for a moment. Josep's body felt easier and released, but his mind was still troubled and confused.

"Important things are beginning to happen," Nivaldo said. "There is going to be another civil war, a big one. Since Queen Isabella fled to France, Carlos VII has been assembling an army, a militia that will be formed into regiments wearing red berets. The movement has the support of people throughout Spain and in the Church, as well as many soldiers and officers in the Spanish army."

Josep shrugged. He had little interest in politics. Nivaldo knew that and looked at him sharply.

"This will affect you," he said. "This will affect all of Catalonia. One-hundred-and-fifty years ago, Philippe V," he said, and paused to spit, "Philippe V outlawed the Catalan language, revoked the Catalan constitution and did away with the fuero, the charter that established rights and privileges and home rule in Catalonia. Carlos VII has pledged to restore the fueros to Catalonia, Valencia, and Aragon.

"The Spanish army is preoccupied with the uprising in Cuba. I think Carlos has an excellent chance to prevail. If he does, the militia could be the national army of the future and would offer a good career.

"Your father and I . . ." Nivaldo said carefully, ". . . we have heard that a man is coming to Santa Eulália, a wounded officer who is being sent to the country to recover. While he is here, he will seek out young men who can be made into good Carlist soldiers."

Josep's father had told him his future would have to be with the Church or the army. He had never wished to be a soldier, but on the other hand he had no desire to be a priest. "When is he coming, this man?" he asked cautiously.

Nivaldo shrugged.

". . . If I were to enter for a soldier, I would leave the village. I would go elsewhere to serve, no?"

"Well, of course. I have heard the militia regiments are forming in the Basque country."

Good, Josep told himself morosely. He hated the village, which offered him nothing.

". . . But not at once. Acceptance must be won. This man . . . he will work with a group of young men and select only the best of the lot to become soldiers. He seeks young men who can be taught to pass on to other soldiers what they themselves have learned. I am confident you could qualify. It is an opportunity, I think, because if one enters an army early in its existence, and it goes on his record that he was chosen in such a way—on the basis of merit—advancement in rank could come quickly.

"The Carlists don't wish to call attention to the recruitment," Nivaldo said. When the youths train in Santa Eulália, they will come together as if to attend a friendly gathering."

"A friendly gathering?"

Nivaldo nodded. "They are calling it a social organization. A group of hunters," he said.

PART TWO

The Group of Hunters

Village of Santa Eulália
Catalonia
April 3, 1870

9

The Man

*F*or several weeks that seemed a longer time nothing changed, and finally Josep couldn't stop himself from speaking to Nivaldo. "This man who is supposed to come here. Has something happened? Is he not coming?"

Nivaldo was opening a small barrel of bacallá. "I think he will come. One must be patient." The good eye shot a glance at Josep. "Have you decided then? You wish to go for a soldier?"

Josep shrugged and then nodded. He had no other prospects.

"I was a soldier myself for several years. There are a few things to keep in mind about that life, Tigre. Sometimes it is boring work and men turn to drink, which dooms them. And dirty women congregate about soldiers, so one must beware of the pox. 'Do not bite at the bait of pleasure till you know there is no hook beneath it.'" He grinned. "Some wise man wrote that. Some Alemany, or an Ingles." He broke off a tiny piece of codfish and nibbled to make certain it was sound.

"One other warning. You shouldn't reveal that you're able to read and write, because surely then they will name you a clerk, and low rank clings to a clerk like stink to a swine. Let the army teach you to be a fighting soldier, for that is the way to advance, and tell them you can read and write only when that is an advantage. I think one day you could become an officer. Why not? After that, anything would be possible for you in life."

Sometimes Josep daydreamed, seeing himself in a formation of many men, wearing a sword, urging troopers to charge. He tried not to think of less pleasant possibilities—such things as having to fight other human beings, hurting them, killing, perhaps receiving painful wounds or losing his own life.

He couldn't understand why Nivaldo called him Tigre. He was very much afraid of so many things.

There was work to be done in the vineyard. All of the large vats had to be scrubbed, as well as assorted barrels, and a small section of stonework in the casa needed to be repaired. As usual, when a job involved either hard or unpleasant labor, Donat turned up missing.

That evening he and his father sat with Nivaldo in the grocery.

"He is here," Nivaldo said. "The man."

Josep felt his eyes widen. "Where is he?"

"He will be staying with the Calderons. Sleeping in that old shed of theirs."

"Since Nivaldo has had experience in the army," Josep's father said, "I asked him to speak to the man for us."

"We have already talked," Nivaldo told Josep. "He is willing to allow you to try. He'll meet with some local youths tomorrow morning, in a clearing in the forest behind the Calderon vineyard. At the time of the early Mass."

It was still dark the next morning when Josep reached the Calderon vineyard. He made his slow way through the rows to the end of the vines. He had not the slightest idea where to go from there, so he stood where the vines ended and the fringe of the forest began, and he waited.

A voice came from the dark. "What is your name?"

"Josep Alvarez."

The man appeared next to him. "Follow me."

He led Josep down a narrow path in the woods to a clearing.

"You are the first to arrive. Now, go back to where I found you. You will guide the others in."

They began arriving at once:

Enric Vinyes and Esteve Montroig, almost simultaneously.

Manel Calderon stumbling from his house, rubbing his eyes.

Xavier Miró, whose morning chorus of farting Josep heard before he saw him.

Jordi Arnau, too sullen in his half-sleep even to offer a greeting.

Clumsy Pere Mas, who tripped on a root as they entered the clearing.

Guillem Parera, smart and quiet and watchful.

Miquel Figueres, grinning nervously.

The boys had known each other all their lives. They squatted in the clearing in the gray rising light and watched the man who sat calm and unsmiling on the ground, his back held straight. He was of medium height and dark-complexioned, perhaps a man of southern Spain, with a thin face, high cheekbones, and a hooked nose as challenging as a hawk's. His black hair was cut short, and his spare body looked hard and strong. The youths were aware of cool, appraising eyes.

After Lluis Julivert arrived—the ninth boy to join the group—the man rose. He had obviously known how many to expect. He walked to the center of the clearing, and Josep now saw what he hadn't observed while following him in the dark: he walked with a slight limp.

"I am Sergeant Peña," he said and turned as another youth entered the clearing. He was tall and skinny, with a bush of wiry black hair, and he carried a long musket.

"What do you want?" the man named Peña asked quietly.

His eyes stayed on the firearm.

"Is this the group of hunters?" the thin youth asked, and some of the boys began to laugh, for they saw it was dim-witted Jaumet Ferrer.

"How did you know to come here?"

"I was setting out on my hunt when I met Lluis and asked where he was bound. He said he was going to a meeting of a group of hunters, so I decided to follow him, for I am the best hunter in Santa Eulália."

They laughed at him again, though what he said was true. Handicapped from birth, unable to comprehend many skills, Jaumet Ferrer had taken to hunting eagerly and well at an early age, and people were accustomed to the sight of his scarecrow figure returning from a hunt with a brace of birds, half a dozen pigeons, or a fat hare. Meat was expensive, and the village wives were always happy to take his game in exchange for a small coin.

Sergeant Peña reached out a hand and took the musket, a very old smooth-bore rifle. In some places the barrel had been worn down to blue metal but he saw that the weapon was cleaned and very well cared for. He observed the dullness in the boy's eyes and heard the innocent confusion in his voice.

"No, young man, this is the not the hunting group. Are you extremely good at mathematics?"

"Mathematics?" Jaumet looked at him in bewilderment. "No, I do not comprehend mathematics, senyor."

"Ah. Then you would not like this, for this is the mathematics class." He held out the musket to the boy. "So you must return to your hunt, eh?"

"Yes, I must do that, senyor," Jaumet said seriously, and taking the musket, he walked out of the clearing to the sound of more laughter.

"Be silent. Frivolity will not be tolerated."

The sergeant didn't raise his voice, but he knew how to address men.

"Only intelligent young men can do our work, for it takes a working mind to receive an order and to carry it out. I am here because our army requires good young men. You are here because you need an occupation, for I am aware there is not a first son in this group. I understand your situation very well. I myself am the third son of my family.

"You are being given an opportunity to earn selection to serve your fatherland, perhaps even to do great things. You will be treated as men. The army does not want boys."

To Josep's ear, the sergeant's Catalan was diluted by an accent from elsewhere; perhaps Castile, he thought.

Sergeant Peña asked them to state their names and listened as each did so, gazing at them intently.

"We will meet here three times a week, Monday, Wednesday, and Friday mornings, while it is still dark. The training will take many hours, and the work will be difficult. I shall temper your bodies for the rigors of military life and prepare your minds to allow you to think and act like soldiers."

Esteve Montroig spoke up eagerly. "Will you be teaching us to fire guns and the like, then?"

"Whenever you speak to me . . . You are Montroig? Esteve Montroig. You will address me properly as 'Sergeant.'"

There was a silence. Esteve gazed at him, confused, and then realized what he was waiting for.

"Yes, Sergeant."

"I shall not entertain idle or stupid questions. This is a time when you must learn to obey. *To obey!* Without question. Without hesitation or the slightest delay. Do you understand me?"

"Yes, Sergeant," they answered hesitantly, in an uneven chorus.

"Listen carefully. A word that you must wipe from your mind for all time as a soldier is *why?* Every soldier of every rank has someone above him to whom he owes instant obedience without question. Let the person giving you the orders worry about the why.

"Do you understand me?"

"Yes, Sergeant!"

"There is much to learn. Get on your feet now."

They followed behind him in a casual column down the path through the woods to a wider trail that led into the country. That was where he ordered them to run, and they began light-heartedly, since they were young and high-spirited. They were all farm boys; their bodies were already conditioned by physical work, and most were in good health, so some of them smiled as they ran with long, bouncing strides.

Guillem made comic faces at Sergeant Peña's back and Manel hid his laughter, letting a single snort escape.

But in their daily life they seldom had reason to run more than a few meters, and soon their breathing became ragged.

Pere Mas, who was built like Donat with a fleshy body, fell to the end of the line almost at once and presently was left behind. Their thudding feet rose and fell without cease and clumsily, so that they got into each other's way. Now and again they jostled one another as they ran, and Josep began to feel a stitch in his side.

Their smiles disappeared as their breathing became labored.

Eventually, the sergeant ran them into a field and allowed them to flop down on the ground for a very brief time, while they gasped in silence in their sweaty work clothes.

Then he stood them in a rank facing him and taught them how to dress their line so it was straight from beginning to end.

How to snap to attention at once when ordered.

How to address him in strong unison when asked a group question that required a "YES, SERGEANT!" or "NO, SERGEANT!"

Then he ran them again—hawking and spitting and gasping—back to the forest clearing behind the Calderon vineyard.

Pere Mas came in walking, long after the others. His head was pounding and his round face was flushed. He attended the hunting group only on the very first day.

Miquel Figueres came to one more meeting, but he confided to Josep with joy that he was going to live in Girona, to work on the chicken farm of an uncle who did not have sons. "A miracle. I prayed to Eulália and God damn it, she gave me a miracle, truly a miracle."

Envious, most of the others also prayed to the saint— Josep did, long and hard!—but she turned a deaf ear, and after that, nobody quit. None of the others had anywhere else to go.

10

Strange Orders

*A*ll through that hot August of 1869 and into the month of September, the members of the hunting group sweated and toiled for the taciturn, watchful stranger. They watched him in return, careful not to stare. The sergeant's mouth was a straight slash between thin lips. They quickly learned it was better for them when the corners of the mouth didn't turn up. There was never humor in his rare, inscrutable smile, which appeared only when they performed in a way he considered truly contemptible, after which he worked them without mercy, running them so far, marching them so long, drilling them so hard, and making them review their errors so often, that the mistakes that had engendered the smile and disgust finally disappeared.

He was twice their age, yet he could outlast them when running, and he was able to march for hours without showing fatigue, though he had an injury. They had seen his leg when everyone took to the river after a long sweaty march. There was a bullet hole above his knee like a puckered belly button, which he must have received long ago, since it was fully healed. But on the outside of the thigh they saw the wound that made him limp, a long ugly scar that looked new enough to be still healing.

He sent them on missions, strange errands, sometimes alone, sometimes in groups—with terse instructions that were always bizarre.

"Find nine flat rocks the size of your fist. Five of the rocks must be gray and contain black mineral markings. Four must be perfectly white with no blemishes."

"Find healthy trees and cut two dozen billets of live wood, seven of oak, six of olive wood, the rest of pine. Then peel them of bark. Each piece must be perfectly straight and twice as long as Jordi Arnau's foot."

One morning he sent Guillem Parera and Enric Vinyes to an olive grove in search of a key, which he said could be found at the foot of one of the trees. There were nine rows of olive trees, twelve trees to a row. They began at the first tree; on their hands and knees they made slow, painful circuits about the base of the trunk, widening the circle each time as they scrabbled with their fingers in the soil and detritus until they were certain the key hadn't been hidden there.

Then they went on to the next tree.

More than five hours after they began, they were crawling around the second tree in the fifth row. Their filthy hands were scratched and sore, and two of Guillem's fingers were bleeding. He told Josep later that nibbling at his mind was the disturbing thought that the sergeant might have buried the key a little deeper than their fingers were probing; perhaps it was under 15 or 20 centimeters of earth, beneath one of the trees they already had inspected.

But at the moment when that fear was strongest, Guillem heard Enric call out. Enric had overturned a small rock, and beneath it was a small brass key.

They wondered what lock the key had been fashioned to fit, but when they carried it back, they knew better than to ask Sergeant Peña. He accepted it and dropped it into his pocket.

"He's a crazy son of a bitch," Enric told Josep when the day's training was done, but Guillem Parera shook his head.

"No, the things he has us do are difficult, but they're not impossible or crazy. If you think about it, there's a lesson attached to every assignment. The assignment about finding the special rocks and the assignment about the pieces of wood—*Pay attention to the smallest details.* The assignment about finding the key—*Keep trying until you are successful.*"

"I think he's getting us accustomed to obey without thinking. To follow any command," Josep said.

"No matter how peculiar the order?" Enric asked.

"Exactly," Josep said.

Josep soon realized that he had neither talent nor aptitude for soldiering, and he felt certain that soon this would also become obvious to the driven, quiet man who was training them.

Sergeant Peña took them on forced marches in the dark of night and under the onslaught of the noonday sun. One morning he led them into the river, and they followed him in the water for mile after mile, stumbling over rocks, pulling the nonswimmers through pools. The youths had grown up along the river and knew it intimately for the few miles near the village, but he took them farther than they had ever been, finally taking them into a small cave. The grotto entrance was a bushy opening not easily seen, yet Peña led them to it without hesitation, and it struck Josep that the sergeant had been there before.

Wet and exhausted, they flopped down on the rock floor. "You must always be on the alert for places like this," Peña told them. "Spain is a land of caves. There are many places to give you concealment when others are trying to find and kill you—a dark hole, a hollow tree, a stand of brush. You can even hide in a dip in the ground. You must learn to make yourself small behind a rock, to breathe without making sound."

That afternoon he showed them how to crawl up to a sentry and take him from behind, how to pull his head back to extend his neck, and then how to cut his throat with a single slash.

He made them practice the technique, taking turns being the sentry and the stalker. They used short sticks instead of knives, the end always pointed away, so that what moved over the "victim's" throat was the side of a fist. Still, when Josep had Xavier Miró's head back and his neck exposed, for the briefest moment of weakness he could not bring himself even to simulate the throat-slitting.

To add to his nervousness, he saw that the cool, calculating eyes had caught the hesitation, and the mouth was *smiling*.

"Move your hand," Peña said.

Humiliated, Josep drew his hand across Xavier's throat.

The sergeant smiled. "What is hardest about killing is to think about it. But when it is necessary to kill— *necessary* to kill—then anyone can do it. Killing becomes very easy.

"Never fear, you will like war, Alvarez," he said, again showing the bitter little smile, as if able to read Josep's mind. "A young man with hot blood in his balls loves war, once he gets a little taste of it."

Josep sensed that despite the words Sergeant Peña had recognized that his balls did not contain blood of the necessary heat and was watching him.

Later, as they sat in the woods, basted in their own sweat after the final run of the day, the man talked to them.

"There will be occasions during a war when the army advances beyond its department of supply. When that happens, soldiers must live off the land. They must either obtain food from the civilian population or starve . . . Can you understand that, Josep Alvarez?"

"Yes, Sergeant."

"Within the next week, I want you to bring two chickens to our meeting, Alvarez."

"Chickens . . . Sergeant?"

"Yes. Two chickens. Hens. Fat ones."

"Senyor. Sergeant. I have no money to buy chickens."

The man regarded him with lifted eyebrows. "Of course you do not. You will take them from a civilian, find them in the countryside as a soldier sometimes must do."

The sergeant studied him. "Do you understand the order, Alvarez?"

"Yes, senyor," he said miserably.

11

The Visitors

$\mathcal{T}$he next morning Marcel Alvarez and his sons began the harvesting of their vineyard, cutting the plump dark bunches of grapes and filling basket after basket, which they emptied into two good-sized tumbrels. Josep loved the musky, sweet scent and the heft of the juice-filled bunches in his hand. He threw himself into the work, but his exertions didn't bring him peace of mind.

Jesús. From whom must I steal those chickens, those two fat hens?

It was a terrible question. He could name offhand half a dozen villagers who raised chickens, but they did so because the eggs and meat were precious. They needed the birds to feed their families.

Mid-morning, he was diverted from his worrying when two neatly-dressed Frenchmen came to the vineyard. In courteous, strangely Frenchified Catalan, they introduced themselves as Andre Fontaine and Leon Mendes of Languedoc. Fontaine, tall and very slender, with a carefully tended goatee and a full head of hair like spun grey iron, was the wine buyer for a large vinegar-producing cooperative. His companion, Mendes, was shorter and portly, with a pink balding scalp, a round clean-shaven face, and serious brown eyes warmed by his smile. Since his accented Catalan was better than Fontaine's, he did most of the talking for the pair.

He was a winemaker himself, he revealed. "My friend, Fontaine, is a bit short of good grapes this year," Mendes said. "As you may have heard, we had two disastrous hailstorms in Southern France this spring. You did not have the same misfortune, I believe?"

"By the grace of heaven, no," Marcel said.

"Most of the grapes in my own vineyard were undamaged, and the Mendes vineyard will make a vintage this year as usual. But some of the farmers in the vinegar cooperative have lost a lot of grapes, and Fontaine and I have come to Spain to buy young wine."

Marcel and his sons continued to work while their visitors stood with them and talked companionably.

Fontaine took a small folding knife from his waistcoat pocket and cut a bunch from an Ull de Llebre vine, and then a Garnacha. He tasted several of the grapes from each bunch, munching judiciously. Then, his lips pursed, he glanced at Mendes and nodded.

Mendes had been watching Josep, noting the swift sure way that he filled his basket with fruit and emptied it, again and again. "Dieu, this boy works like a perpetual motion machine," he called to Marcel Alvarez. "I would dearly love to have a few workers such as this one!"

Josep heard and drew a deep breath. When Miquel Figueres had been summoned to work on his uncle's farm in Girona, he had told Josep gratefully that it was a miracle that allowed him to escape the unemployment in Santa Eulália. Could this plump little man in his brown French suit be a similar miracle, a source of a job for Josep?

One of the small wagons was bountifully filled, and Marcel looked to his sons. "Best bring this one to the press," he called.

The visitors pitched in and helped the Alvarez men push the tumbrel filled with grapes to the small plaça.

"The press is used by the community?" Mendes said.

"Yes, we share its use. My father and others built this beautiful large press more than fifty years ago," Marcel said proudly. "*His* father had built a granite cistern for stomping the grapes. It exists still, behind our shed. I keep supplies in it now. You have your own press in Languedoc?"

"Actually, no. We tread our grapes. Treading produces a softer wine with maximum flavor, because the foot doesn't break the pips and release bitterness. So long as we have feet we shall use them on our grapes, though it costs. It takes extra hired help and friends to tread the grapes from our eighteen hectares," Mendes said.

"Easier and cheaper to do it this way. And one is not required to wash his feet," Marcel said, and the visitors joined in his laughter.

Fontaine lifted one of the bunches. "They still have their stems, monsieur. Would you be willing to remove them if I should request it?" Fontaine asked.

"The stems do not hurt anything," Marcel said slowly. "After all, senyor, you only want a wine that will become vinegar. Same as us."

"We make a very special vinegar. Very expensive to buy, actually. To make such a special vinegar, one requires special grapes . . . If we were to buy from you, I would be prepared to pay for the extra effort of destemming."

Marcel shrugged and then nodded.

When they reached the press with the tumbrel, the two Frenchmen stared as Josep and Donat began to shovel in bunches of grapes.

Fontaine cleared his throat. "It is not necessary to wash the press first?"

"Oh, it has been washed this morning, of course. Since then, it had received only grapes," Marcel said.

"But there is something already in it!" Mendes cried.

It was true. A vomitous yellow sludge of broken fruit and stems still lay at the bottom of the press tub.

"Ah, my neighbor, Pau Fortuny, has been here before me and has left me a small gift of white grapes . . . It is no problem, it all makes juice," Marcel said.

Fontaine saw that Donat Alvarez had found half a basket of white grapes left behind by the sloppy Pau Fortuny and had added these grapes to the press as well.

He glanced at Mendes. The smaller man understood his look at once and shook his head regretfully.

"Well, my friend, we wish you good fortune," Mendes said, and Josep saw that the Frenchmen were preparing to leave.

"Senyor," he blurted.

Mendes turned and looked at him.

"I would like to work for you, senyor, and help you make wine at your vineyard in . . . in . . ."

"My vineyard is in the country, near the village of Roquebrun, in Languedoc. But . . . work for me? Ah, but I am sorry. I fear that would be quite impossible."

"But, senyor, you said . . . I heard you say . . . that you wished you had someone like me to work with your grapes."

"Well, young man . . . But that was only a manner of speaking. A way to offer a compliment."

The Frenchman's eyes were on Josep's face, and what he saw there visibly embarrassed him and made him regretful. "You are an excellent worker, young man. But I already have a crew in Languedoc, deserving local people from Roquebrun who have worked for me a long time and are trained in my requirements. You understand?"

"Yes, senyor. Of course. Local people," Josep said.

He was aware of his father and Donat gazing at him, and he turned to the tumbrel and resumed shoveling grapes into the press.

12

Foraging

*D*uring the remainder of the harvest Josep returned to hard, practical thought, uncontaminated by childish hope or dreams of miracles.

Where was he to get two hens?

He told himself that if he must steal, it should be from a wealthy man whose family wouldn't suffer because of the crime, and he knew of only one rich man who raised chickens.

The alcalde. "Angel Casals," he said aloud.

His brother looked up.

"What about him?" Donat said.

"Oh . . . He . . . rode past on their mule, inspecting the village," Josep said.

Donat went back to cutting bunches of grapes. "Why do I care?" he said.

It would be dangerous. Angel Casals had a rifle of which he was proud, a long weapon with a mahogany stock that he kept oiled and polished like a gem. While Josep was still a small boy, the alcalde had used the rifle to kill a fox that had been trying to get at his chickens. The children of the village had stroked the corpse; Josep remembered clearly the beauty of the animal, the perfect softness of the lustrous red-brown coat and the silky white fur of the stomach, the yellow eyes fixed in death.

He was certain Angel would fire at a thief just as readily as he had fired at the fox.

The chicken theft would have to occur in the middle of the night, when everyone else in the village was deep in the sleep of honest working people. Josep thought he would be all right after he had gained concealment in the chicken house. The birds would be accustomed to the alcalde's sons coming into the henhouse to collect eggs; if he moved slowly and quietly, the chickens shouldn't make much of a fuss.

It was the time just before entering the henhouse that was the heaviest problem. Angel had a large, black mastiff, vicious and a barker. The safest way to deal with the dog would be to kill him, but Josep knew he could not kill a dog any more than he could slit a man's throat.

And the dog scared him.

For several days he ate only part of his chorizo when he had his dinner, gathering a modest collection of meat in one of his pockets, but he quickly realized it would not be enough. After the finish of the harvest, when he and Donat had taken the barrel containing the juice from the last batch of grapes and added it to one of the age-blackened fermenting vats in his father's shed, Josep walked to the grocery and asked Nivaldo if perhaps he had some salchicha so spoiled he would not be able to sell it.

"What do you want with rotten sausage?" Nivaldo said grumpily, and Josep told him it was needed for an exercise in woodcraft dreamed up by the sergeant, which required the baiting of animal traps. The old man took Josep to the storeroom where he kept a variety of salchichas, a whole row of large sausages hung on strings from a beam to cure, some of them whole, some already cut and partially sold off—morcilla made with onion and paprika, lomo with and without red pepper, salchichon, sobresada. Josep pointed to a piece of lomo that looked decidedly green on the cut end, but Nivaldo shook his head. "Are you serious? That is excellent slow-cured pork. Cut off the end and the rest will be beautiful. No, this stuff is all too good to throw away. But you wait

here," he said, and threaded his way between a mountain of beans in sacks and a box of wrinkled potatoes.
Josep heard him grunting behind the bean mountain as
he moved bags and boxes, and eventually he returned
holding a long piece of . . . something, mostly covered in
a white growth.

"Uh, will ...the animals ...you know,*want* it?"

Nivaldo closed his eyes. "Will they want it?
Blood sausage made with rice? This is too good for
them, mor-cilla that has been forgotten and aged too
long. It's just what you're looking for, Tigre."

When Josep was a boy, a cur bit him, a skinny yellow
mutt owned by the Figueres family. Whenever he passed
their vineyard, the dog leaped out at him, barking
madly. Terrified, he tried to intimidate the animal by
shouting at it and staring with false menace into the
dark little eyes that seemed to him the incarnation of
evil, but that only made the dog wilder. As it came at
him one day, snarling, he kicked out in his fright and
sharp teeth closed on his ankle, drawing blood when he
yanked his leg away. For two years, until the dog died,
Josep avoided going near the Figueres vineyard.

Nivaldo had counseled him. "One should never
gaze into the eyes of another man's dog's. A dog sees a
stranger's stare as a challenge, and if he is a fierce dog,
he responds by attacking, perhaps even wanting to take
your life. One should look at a dog only briefly, glance
away without fleeing or showing fear, and speak to the
animal softly and soothingly."

Josep had no idea if Nivaldo's theories worked, but he
considered them as he rubbed the blood sausage as hard
as he could with handfuls of grass, removing a lot of the
white bloom. He cut the sausage into small pieces, and that
evening as dusk fell on Santa Eulália, he walked to the
village plaça, past the Casals' vegetable field. The chicken
house was at the far end of the field, the rich soil of which
was manured but not ploughed. The dog, at-tached to the
rickety structure by a very long rope, lay

dozing in front of the henhouse like a dragon guarding a castell.

The alcalde's casa was within easy eyesight of the chicken coop, little more than half the length of the field away.

Josep walked aimlessly until the full darkness of night had fallen; then he returned to Angel Casals's field.

This time, keeping an eye on the lantern light in the window of the house, he walked slowly across the field heading straight for the dog, which soon began to bark. Just before he was close enough to see the animal, the dog came at him, held back only by the limitations of his rope tether. The alcalde, resting from his farming and mayoral duties, should be sound asleep, as should his sons, but Josep knew that if the barking continued, someone would come from the house.

"There, there, be quiet now, there's a good shit-dog. I've just come to pay you a little visit, you monster, you stupid asshole, you ugly beast," he said in a friendly tone Nivaldo would have approved, taking a piece of morcilla from his pocket. When he tossed the lump, the dog shied to the side as if a stone had been thrown, but the ripe scent of the blood sausage called. The piece was swallowed at a gulp. Josep threw another, which was eaten just as quickly. When he turned and walked away, the barking began again but it didn't last, and as he left the field, the night became quiet.

He went back again, after midnight. By that time the moon was high, and he would have been detected if anyone had cared to look, but the house was dark. This time the dog barked again in the beginning, but he seemed to be waiting for the two pieces of morcilla Josep fed him. Josep sat on the ground just beyond the end of the tether. He and the dog looked at one another. He talked to the beast very quietly and mindlessly for a long time, about grapes and the bodies of females and saint's days and the size of the animal's member and itchy balls and the lack of rain, then he gave the dog one more piece of sausage—a small one, he had to make his supply last—and he went home.

He returned to the alcalde's field twice the next evening. The first time the dog barked twice before Josep began to talk. When he came the second time, the dog was waiting for him silently.

On the following evening, the dog didn't bark at all. When it came time for Josep to leave, he moved toward the dog until he was well within biting range, speaking slowly and steadily. "You good old thing, you homely beautiful ugly beast, if you want to be my friend, I want to be yours . . ." He took a piece of blood sausage and held it out, and at the abrupt movement the creature growled, a low ugly sound. Then in a moment the great black head moved over his hand. First he felt the wet snout and then the thick tongue, wet and tickling and rough, like a lion's tongue moving over his palm, lapping up every bit of the blood sausage scent.

His late night departures had been noticed. Josep knew from the sly little smiles he saw in the morning that his father assumed he was sneaking away to be with Teresa Gallego, and he said nothing to contradict the belief.

That night he waited until the French clock had issued two of its gentle, asthmatic chimes before leaving his sleeping mat and walking quietly out of the house.

He drifted through the darkness like a spirit. In two or three hours the village would begin to waken, but at that moment the entire world was asleep.

Even the dog.

There was no lock on the poultry house—the people of Santa Eulália did not steal from one another—only a little stick through two small iron rings kept the door closed. He was inside in a moment.

It was warm and smelled strongly and sharply of bird shit. The upper half of one wall was wire mesh through which the low moon sent pale glimmer. Most of the chickens were sleeping, dark lumps in the moonlight, but several birds scratched and pecked in the straw on the floor. One glanced at Josep and clucked inquiringly, but soon lost interest.

Some of the chickens were on raised shelves against one wall. Josep thought those must be layers on nests, and therefore hens. He didn't want to get a sharp-spurred rooster by mistake. He knew that any flurry of action or sound could turn into a disaster of noise—clucking, crowing, the barking of the dog outside. His hands stole down to one of the nests. As his right hand clamped tight around the chicken's neck to shut off any squawk, his left pressed the bird into his body to prevent the wings from beating. Trying not to think of what he was doing, he twisted the feathered neck. He expected to hear something like a crack when the neck broke, but it was more a crackling, like the rapid snapping of many little bones. For a few moments the hen struggled, feet pushing to break from his grasp, wings fluttering against him, then as he continued to twist as if trying to rip the head off, the chicken quivered and was dead.

He set it back in its nest and tried to quiet his breathing.

When he took the second bird, things went almost as before, but with an important difference. His pulled the chicken against his chest instead of his abdomen, which bent the wrist of his right hand into an angle that restricted movement, so that he could twist only a limited distance that proved not enough to break the bird's neck. He could do nothing but hold fast to the chicken and continue to squeeze the feathered neck, so tightly that almost at once his fingers began to hurt. The hen struggled, strongly at first, and then more weakly. Her wings pulsed against him, fluttered. More feeble still, ah Déu, he was squeezing the future from this creature! He could realize the departure of life, feel the last bit of indistinct existence moving up the neck against his squeezing iron hand like a bubble rising in a bottle. Then it was gone.

He risked taking a swift new hold of the neck and twisted firmly, though that was no longer necessary.

When he left the poultry house the big black dog was standing there in front of him, and Josep cradled the hens in one arm like a baby and took the remainder of the sausage from his pocket, seven or eight pieces that he cast to the alcalde's dog.

He walked away on legs that were powerless and trembling, a murderous thief in the black night. Around him, everyone—his father, his brother, Teresa, the village, the whole world—slept in innocence and rectitude. He felt he had somehow crossed a chasm and been changed, and the meaning of Sergeant Peña's assignment was suddenly clear.

Go kill something.

When the group of hunters assembled in the morning, they found him in the clearing mending two small fires over which the cooked hens sizzled on greenwood spits hung from Y-shaped stakes.

The sergeant took in the scene judiciously, but the boys were delighted.

Josep cut up the chickens and distributed largesse, burning his fingers slightly in the hot fat.

Peña accepted a drumstick.

"Nicely crisped skin, Alvarez."

"A little oil rubbed on, Sergeant."

"Quite so."

Josep took one for himself and found the meat delicious. All the youths ate and they relaxed, laughing and chewing, enjoying the unexpected treat.

When they were finished, they wiped their greasy hands on the forest floor and sprawled on the ground and against tree trunks. They were full of well-being, belching and complaining about Xavier's farts. It felt like a holiday. They would not have been surprised if the sergeant had passed out sweets.

Instead, he told Miquel Figueres and Josep to follow him. He led them to the shack where he was staying and gave them boxes to carry back to the clearing. The wooden boxes were each about a meter square and surprisingly heavy. At the clearing the sergeant broke open Josep's box and from it took bulky packets wrapped in heavy oiled cotton and bound with rough jute cord.

When each youth had received one of the packets, Peña ordered them to take off the cord and unwrap the oilskin. Josep untied the cord carefully and put it into his pocket. He discovered that beneath the outer wrapping were two more layers of oilskin.

Within the third wrapping—inside *each* of the third wrappings, waiting to be discovered like a nutmeat—there was a gun.

13

Guns

"*I*t's a proper soldier's piece," the sergeant said, "the Colt .44. Lots of these to be found now, left-overs from the Americans' civil war. It blows a nasty hole, and the weight isn't bad for lugging it about—a curly hair more than a kilogram.

"If this was a single-shot gun, it would be a pistol. This weapon gives you six shots loaded into a cylinder that rotates, so it's a revolver. You comprehend?"

He showed them how to remove the small wedge in front of the chambers, which allowed the barrel to be broken away from the frame for cleaning. The box Miquel had carried proved to contain rags, and soon the youths were busily engaged in rubbing away the greasy film that had been protecting the guns.

Josep worked the cloth against metal that had been used and cleaned and used again, many times, until almost half of the blueing had been worn off by the hands of others. He felt an uneasy instinct that this was a gun that had been fired in combat, a deadly tool that had wounded and killed men, and he feared it far more than he had been afraid of Angel's dog.

The sergeant passed out more supplies from Miquel's box: to each youth, a stocking filled with black powder; a heavy sack of lead balls; an empty little leather tube, closed at one end; a small wooden bowl of lard; a cleaning rod; a sack of tiny objects shaped like drinking cups but smaller than the nail of Josep's little finger; and two strange metal tools, one ending in a sharp point. All these things, and the guns, were placed in cloth bags. Wearing the bags hung from their necks on rope straps, the youths were led away from the clearing behind the Calderon vineyard. In their work clothes instead of uniforms they still seemed awkward and unmilitary, yet carrying the guns made them feel powerful and important. The sergeant took them an hour's march away from the village to another forest clearing, where the sound of firing would not raise comment and alarm.

Once there, he showed them how to pull back the hammer of the gun until it reached a stop and was half-cocked, so that the trigger was locked into a safety position and couldn't be pulled.

"It takes the explosion of thirty grains of black powder to send a lead ball out of the barrel," the sergeant said. "When you are under fire, you have no time to be measuring grains of powder or dancing a slow sardana, so . . ." He held up the leather measuring tube. "You quickly pour powder into this sack, which holds the correct amount, and from the sack into an empty chamber of the gun. Next you place the lead ball into the chamber and pull down the loading lever to pack it into the powder firmly. A dab of grease over the powder and ball, then these little cups—the caps that explode when struck by the hammer of the gun—are placed over the bullet and powder, using the capping tool. You can spin the cylinder by hand and load each chamber, one by one.

"In combat, a soldier must be able to load all six chambers in less than a minute's time. You must practice this again and again. Now each may begin to load his own gun," he said.

They were slow and clumsy and felt doomed. Peña walked among them as they went through the process, and he made several men unload a chamber and repeat the loading. When he was satisfied that each of the guns was properly armed, he took his knife and made a slash mark on the trunk of a tree. Then he stood six or seven meters away from the tree, raised his own gun and fired six rapid shots. Six holes appeared in the trunk of the tree. Several of the holes were touching and there were no more than two finger-widths between any of them.

"Xavier Miró. Now, you try," the sergeant said.

Xavier took his place facing the tree, his face pale. When he lifted the gun, his hand was trembling.

"You must hold the gun firmly yet apply only the lightest pressure on the trigger. Think of a butterfly landing on a leaf. Think of a fingertip barely teasing a woman."

Words did not work with Xavier. His finger jerked against the trigger six times, the gun bucked and tossed in his nerveless hand, and the balls sprayed into the undergrowth.

Jordi Arnau was next and didn't do a great deal better. One of the balls landed in the trunk of the tree, perhaps by accident.

"Alvarez."

Josep went to face the target tree. When he extended his arm the hatred he already felt for the gun made his arm rigid, but he heard the sergeant's words again in his mind and thought of Teresa as he caressed the trigger. With each report, smoke and fire and sparks sprang from the barrel as if Josep were God, as if his hand hurled lightning to go with the thunder. Four new holes appeared in the group that had been made in the tree by Sergeant Peña's shooting. Two other holes were located no more than three centimeters from the grouping.

Josep stood, unmoving.

He was amazed and shamed by the sudden knowledge that there was a bulge in his trousers that could be observed by the other youths, but no one laughed.

Most disturbing of all: when Josep looked at Sergeant Peña, he saw that the man was studying him with watchful interest.

14

Widening the Range

"*T*he thing I remember the clearest about being a soldier was the other soldiers," Nivaldo told Josep one evening in the grocery. "When we were fighting with people who were trying to kill us, I became very close to my companions, even the ones I didn't really like."

Josep could count Manel Calderon and Guillem Parera as his good friends, and he liked most of the others in the group of hunters well enough, but there were several of the youths with whom he had no desire to become close.

Like Jordi Arnau.

Teresa, who had become moody and querulous of late, had used Jordi to let Josep know where her desires lay: "Jordi Arnau and Maria del Mar Orriols are marrying soon."

"I know," Josep said.

"Marimar told me they are able to marry because presently Jordi will be a soldier. Like you."

"It isn't certain any of us will be soldiers. We must be selected. The reason Jordi and Marimar must marry quickly is that she is pregnant."

"She told me."

"Jordi has been boasting of it to everyone. He is very stupid."

"She is too good for him. But if he is not selected for the army, what shall they do?"

He shrugged grimly. Pregnancy wasn't a disgrace; many of the brides who walked down the aisle of the village church did so with heavy bellies. Padre Felipe Lopez, the village priest, did not aggravate such situations with recriminations; he would rather give a quick blessing and spend most of his time with his devoted and close friend, Josep's neighbor, Quim Torras.

But though a couple joined in a "necessary" marriage suffered few recriminations, it was madness to try to support a new family with no work to be had, and Josep knew that for the trainees in the hunting group, the future was in doubt.

The youths had no idea which of them might be chosen and which rejected, or how the selection process would work.

"There is something . . . *odd* . . . about it," Guillem said to Josep. "The sergeant has had a good chance to judge each of us by now. He has studied everyone closely. Yet he has eliminated no one. It must have been quickly apparent to him, for instance, that Enric is always clumsy and the slowest in the group. Peña doesn't seem to care."

"Perhaps he is waiting until the end of the training, and then he will choose those who will be allowed into the army," Manel said.

"I think he is a strange man," Guillem said. "I would like to know more about him. I wonder where and how he got his wound."

"He doesn't answer questions. He is not a friendly person," Manel said. "Since he lives in our hut, my father has invited him to our table, but he always eats alone, then he sits alone outside the hut, smoking long, skinny black cigars that stink like piss. He drinks a lot, and he has money. Every night my father has to buy him a full pitcher of brandy from Nivaldo's barrel."

"Perhaps he needs a woman," Guillem said.

"I think he goes to a woman nearby," Manel said. "At least, sometimes he doesn't spend the night in the hut. I see him coming back, early in the morning."

"Well, she should do a better job. She should learn to do things to put him in a better humor," Guillem said, and the three of them laughed.

They had five sessions of firing the Colt revolvers, each session preceded by practice in loading the weapons and followed by practice in cleaning them. They grew faster and more adept but never fast enough to suit Sergeant Peña.

At the sixth firing session, the sergeant ordered Josep and Guillem to hand him their Colts. When he had received them, he drew other guns from a sack.

"These are for you two alone. You are our marksmen," he said.

The new gun was heavier than the other and felt formidable and important in Josep's hand. He was ignorant about firearms, but even to him it was apparent that this gun was different from the Colt. It had two barrels. The top one was long and similar to the Colt's barrel, but directly beneath it was a second barrel, shorter and fatter.

The sergeant told them the gun was the LeMat revolver, made in Paris. "It has nine revolving chambers instead of six, firing the balls from the upper barrel." He showed them that the top of the hammer had a pivoting striker that was rotated to fire the lower, larger barrel, which could be filled with small shot to spray a wide target area. "In effect, the lower barrel is a shotgun, sawed off," Peña said.

He said he expected them to learn to load all nine chambers in the same time it now took them to load six.

The LeMat felt similar to the Colt when the upper barrel was fired. But when Josep fired the lower barrel for the first time it felt as though a giant had placed a palm against the muzzle and pushed it back, so that his shot went wide, spraying the upper branches of a plane tree with bits of lead.

Guillem had the advantage of having observed him, so he used two hands when he fired the shotgun barrel himself, extending his braced arms as he pulled the trigger.

They were amazed at the wide area of fire from the lower barrel. It left holes in the trunks of four trees instead of one.

"Remember this when you fire the LeMat," the Sergeant said. "There is no possible excuse to miss with this gun."

15

The Sergeant

𝒩obody saw the newcomer arrive on his black horse. On a Wednesday morning, when the hunting group drifted toward the clearing in the woods, they observed that the horse was tied to the shack, and when the sergeant emerged from the shack to join them, with him was a middle-aged man. The two were a study in contrasts. Peña, tall and fit, wore soiled work clothes, ragged in places. He had a dagger in a scabbard tied to the calf of his left leg above the top of the boot, and there was a large gun on his hip in a leather holster. The newcomer was shorter than the sergeant by a head, and stocky. His black suit was wrinkled from riding but well-cut of a beautiful material, and he wore a derby that was the finest hat Josep had ever seen.

Sergeant Peña did not introduce him.

The man walked alongside Peña as he led the group to the more remote clearing where they did their firing, and the newcomer watched as each of the youths shot in turn at targets on a tree.

The sergeant asked Josep and Guillem to fire for a longer period than the others; when each of them had fired all chambers and both barrels of the LeMat twice, the stranger spoke quietly to the sergeant, who told them to reload and fire again. While they did so, Peña and the stocky man stared without speaking.

Afterwards the sergeant told the group to be at ease. He and the visitor walked away, the stocky man talking urgently in low tones, and the youths were content to loll on the ground.

When the two men returned, Peña marched the group back to the woods behind the Calderon property. While the youths prepared to clean their weapons, they saw the sergeant salute the civilian, not self-consciously as they were prone to do, but in a single fluid motion so practiced it appeared be almost careless. The other man seemed startled by the gesture, perhaps even embarrassed. He nodded curtly and then touched his fine black hat and got on his horse and rode away, and none of the youths ever saw him again.

16

Orders

*I*n the next weeks the December weather turned cold and wet, the rain a mist so fine that it added little moisture to the soil. Everyone put on an extra layer of clothing against the rawness and found jobs that could be done inside. Josep swept and dusted the house and then sat at the table and put keen edges on the machetes, hoes, and spades with a small-toothed file.

Two weeks after the stranger's visit the rain stopped, but when the hunting group assembled in the woods, no one sat on the wet ground.

It was the day after Christmas; most were still in a holiday mood and had already been to the early Mass.

Sergeant Peña stunned them with an announcement.

"Your training while living in Santa Eulália is now at an end. We'll leave here tomorrow morning to take part in an exercise. After that, you will become soldiers.

"You won't need your guns. Oil them and give them a light coating of grease, and wrap them in triple layers of oilcloth, as they were wrapped when you received them. Make a second small packet of your ammunition and gun tools in triple layers of the oilcloth I'll give you. I suggest that you bury both packets somewhere where water doesn't collect, for if the exercise is cancelled we would return here and you will need the guns."

Jordi Arnau cleared his throat and dared a question. "All of us are to go to the militia?"

Sergeant Peña smiled his smile. "All of you. You have each done well," he said sardonically.

That evening Josep greased the gun and buried it still unassembled. Repós en pau, rest in pieces. The driest earth he knew was a little sandy patch in the rear of the adjoining Torras vineyard, a meter beyond the end of his father's property. Their neighbor, Quim Torras, was a bad and lazy farmer, who spent so much of his time with Father Lopez that their friendship was a scandal in the village. Quim worked his vineyard soil as little as possible, and Josep knew he wouldn't disturb the earth of this neglected dry corner.

His family took the news of his impending departure with visible astonishment, as if they had never really believed the hunting group would lead to anything. Josep could see relief on Donat's face; he had always been aware that it had not been easy for Donat to have a younger brother who was so clearly a better worker. His father gave Josep a heavy brown wool sweater he had owned less than a year. "Against the chill," he said gruffly, and Josep took it gratefully to wear under his winter jacket. It was only slightly too large and it contained the faint smell of Marcel Alvarez, a comfort. Marcel also went into the jar behind his clock and came up with a small bundle of bills, eight pesetas, which he pressed into Josep's hands "for some emergency."

When he went to the grocery to say goodbye, Nivaldo gave him money too, six pesetas. "Here is a little present of the season—Bon Nadal. Buy yourself an experience some night and think of this old soldier," he said and embraced Josep for a long moment.

Josep found all the leave-takings difficult, but it was hardest to deal with Teresa, who turned pale at his words.

"You will never return to me."

"Why do you speak that way?" Her grief magnified his own fear of the unknown future and turned his regret into anger. "This is our chance," he said roughly. "There will be money from the militia, and I'll come back for you when I can, or send for you. I'll get word to you as soon as I am able." He found it impossible to realize he was leaving everything about her: her goodness, her presence and practicality, her musky secret flavor, and the tender voluptuousness of the thin bloom, like baby fat, that graced her shoulders and breasts and haunches. When he kissed her she responded wildly, trying to devour him, but his cheek was wet with her tears, and when his hand reached to claim her breast, she pushed him from her and ran off into her father's vines.

Early the next morning Peña showed up at the Calderon vineyard with a pair of two-wheeled carts hooded over by basket frames on which painted canvases were stretched, one new and blue and the other a faded and patched red. Each covered wagon was drawn by two mules, harnessed in line, and held two short wooden benches behind the driver with enough room for four passengers. Peña sat in one of the carts with Manel, Xavier, and Guillem, after loading the other cart with Enric, Jordi, Josep, and Esteve.

Thus they departed from Santa Eulália.

The final sight Josep had of his village through the flaps of the wagon canvas was a glimpse of Quim Torras. Instead of working on his scraggly vines, which needed all the help they could get, Quim was straining to trundle the fat priest, Padre Felipe Lopez, across the bridge in his barrow, both of them convulsed in laughter.

The last Santa Eulália sound Josep heard was the hoarse and guttural barking of his good friend, the alcalde's dog.

17

Nine on a Train

$\mathcal{B}$y the time the carts rolled to a halt at the railroad station in Barcelona, the youths were famished. Peña herded them into a workingman's café and bought them bread and cabbage soup, which they consumed eagerly, enjoying almost a holiday feeling in the excitement of the sudden change in their routine. On the station platform afterwards, Josep nervously watched the approach of the locomotive, which bore down on them like an incredibly loud, cloud-belching dragon. Of all the youths only Enric had been on a train before, and they filed into a third-class carriage with wide eyes. This time Josep shared one of the slatted wooden seats with Guillem, and Manel sat in one of the seats in front of them.

As the train shuddered and lurched back into motion, they were warned by the conductor not to open the windows lest sparks and sooty smoke from the locomotive blow back into the car, but the weather was cool, and they were content to keep the windows closed. The clacking of the wheels and the swaying of the car soon became unremarkable, and the youths stared for rapt intervals as the landscape of Catalonia rolled past.

Long before darkness began to shut out the world, Josep had grown tired of peering beyond the face of his friend Guillem, who had the window seat. Peña had brought bread and sausage onto the train and eventually fed them. Soon the conductor came in and lighted the gas lamps, which sputtered and threw across the car flickering shadows that Josep studied until overcome by the mercy of sleep.

Tension had exhausted him more than a hard day of work could have done. He awoke at intervals in the course of the uncomfortable night, the last time to see an inhospitably dark day as the train jolted into motion following a stop in Guadalajara.

Peña distributed more sausage and bread until his supply was gone, and they washed it down with train water that tasted of coal and gritted in their teeth. All else was boredom until three hours beyond Guadalajara, when Enric Vinyes looked out and gave a shout, "Snow!"

Everyone in the cars crowded to the windows to peer at white flecks dropping from a gray sky. They had seen snow only a few times in their entire lives, and then for the briefest of periods before it melted. Now it ceased falling before they tired of watching it, but three hours later, when the train pulled into Madrid and they disembarked, there was a thin white layer on the ground.

Peña obviously was familiar with the city. He led them from the railroad station, away from the broad boulevard and stately buildings and into a warren of old narrow streets that twisted darkly between stone apartment houses. In a small plaza there was a market, and Peña drew two food-sellers away from an open fire long enough to buy bread, cheese, and two bottles of wine. Then he led his charges down a nearby alley to a doorway that opened into an unlit, battered foyer with a staircase wide enough for only one person at a time. They climbed to the third floor, where Peña knocked three times at a door marked by a small sign: *Pension Excelsior*.

The door was opened by an elderly man, who nodded when he saw Peña.

The room into which the hunting group was led was too small for the comfort of so many people, but they sat on the beds and the floor. Peña divided and dispensed bread and cheese and then disappeared, to return a short

time later with a steaming kettle and a tray of cups. He
poured several fingers of wine into each cup and filled it
with hot water, and the chilled youths drank the mixture
eagerly.

Peña left them, and they sat in the grimy pension and
waited as the hours of the long, strange afternoon slowly
passed.

The light outside the windows had begun to fade
when Peña returned. He stood in the middle of the room.
"Listen closely," he said.

"Now you have a chance to show your usefulness.
This evening, a man who is a traitor to our cause will be
apprehended. You will help to capture him."

They regarded him in nervous silence.

He reached under one of the beds and pulled out
a box that proved to contain long sulfur matches with
thick heads. He handed some to Josep, along with a small
square of sandpaper on which to strike them. "You must
keep these in your pockets, where they will not become
wet, Alvarez. We'll go to where the man will enter a carriage, and we'll follow the carriage as it moves away. If
the carriage should turn a corner, we'll enter the new
street too, and at every turn you will light a match." He
struck one, which produced an acrid stink.

"When I give a signal, the group will move to sur-
round the carriage so he can be taken. Guillem Parera
and Esteve Montroig, each of you must grasp a bridle
and prevent the horses from continuing.

"If we should become separated, make your way to
the railroad station, and I will pick you up there. When
the event is over, you will receive a commendation, you
will be taken to join a regiment, and your military careers
will commence."

Soon he led them from the pension, down the stairs
again and out into the narrow streets. The snow had
drifted down thinly all day, off and on, and now flurries
of feathery bits fell more steadily. In the plaza marketplace the accumulation had extinguished the fire, and the

vendors had left for the day. Josep stared at flakes blazing whitely against Peña's raven-black hair. Following after the sergeant, the hunting group made its way through the weirdly-pearled world.

Soon they were out of the old neighborhoods and crossing avenues lined with great structures. On a boulevard, Carrera San Jerónimo, Peña stopped before a large and imposing building. Near the entrance, men in pairs and small groups stood under the flickering light of a gas lamp and talked quietly. The doorman gave the youths only a passing glance as they gathered around Peña.

The heavy door of the entrance was wedged open, and through it Josep could hear male voices. Someone was delivering an address, his voice rising and falling. Now and again, when he paused, there were shouts; it was impossible for Josep to know whether they were expressions of agreement or of anger. Once there was a collective groan; twice there was laughter.

The hunting group waited, growing colder in the falling snow while almost an hour crept by.

18

The Spy

*I*nside the building, men roared and applauded.

An elderly woman hobbled forward into Josep's vision, grey-haired, wrapped in two ragged shawls, with small dark eyes in a face like a wrinkled brown apple. Taking careful steps, she approached the men nearest her and held out a basket.

"Alms . . . Alms . . . A bit of food for me in God's mercy, señor . . . Mercy in the name of Jesús!"

Her quarry shook his head as if warding off a fly, turned his back and continued to talk.

Undaunted, the old woman went to the next group, held out her basket and made her plea. This time she was rewarded with a coin and paid for the charity with a blessing. For a while Josep watched her limping her way toward him like an old wounded animal.

Two men came out of the building.

"Yes," Peña said quietly.

One of them was obviously a gentleman, a man of middle age, neat-bearded, wearing a fine-looking heavy cape against the weather and a formal high hat. He was short and stocky but erect and proud of bearing.

The other man, walking half a step behind, was much younger and plainly dressed. Which of the two was the traitor? Josep was bewildered.

"A carriage, Excellency?" When the gentleman nodded, the doorman stepped into the pool of light beneath the gas lamp and raised his arm. A carriage detached itself from the line of vehicles waiting down the street, and its two horses pulled it to the front of the building. The doorman moved to open the carriage door, but the plainly dressed man was there before him. Clearly a servant, he bowed his head as the other man climbed in, and then he closed the door and went back into the building.

Josep watched in awe. The carriage was richly appointed and seemed enormous. He could scarcely see its occupant through the two high, narrow windows. Nearby, a man coughed and lit a match, holding it up before lighting his pipe. Startled, the doorman cast a quick glance and went to the seat of the cab, whispering something as the driver leaned down to hear him. Then he knocked lightly on the carriage door and opened it.

"My great apologies, Excellency. There appears to be something wrong with an axle. If you will pardon the nuisance, I shall get another carriage for you at once." If the man inside answered, Josep could not hear it. While the passenger disembarked, the doorman hurried to the row of carriages, and soon a second conveyance was there, even more ornate than the first but narrower and with deeper windows. Before the gentleman entered the new vehicle, Josep saw his exhausted eyes and drawn features; his cheeks were swarthy and powdered, causing his face to appear as artificial as the one on the statue of Santa Eulália.

Now two men came from the building and approached the carriage. They were well dressed. Gentlemen, obviously. One of them opened the door of the carriage. "Excellency?" he said quietly. "It is done as you asked of us."

The man inside said something muffled, and the other two entered the carriage, closing the door behind them. They sat opposite the first occupant, the three heads close together. Those watching from the outside had fallen silent but could hear almost nothing, for the men in the carriage did not raise their voices.

They spoke for a long time, almost half an hour, Josep estimated. Then the door opened, and both of the men withdrew and went back inside the building.

Almost at once the servant who had ushered the gentleman into the coach returned, this time accompanied by a second servant. He knocked discreetly, waited for permission, and then opened the door. They got in with a word to the driver, who nodded.

Traffic was light because of the weather, but the horses moved away slowly, unaccustomed to the snow on the cobblestones.

Peña and the hunting group had little trouble keeping up as they followed the carriage down the Carrera San Jerónimo. They passed the departing beggar woman and left her behind. When the horses pulled the carriage around the first corner and entered the Calle de Sordo, Josep obeyed his instructions. His hand trembled when he struck the match and held it high, a sputtering circle of yellow.

They followed the plodding horses down to another turn, onto the Calle de Turso, where Josep struck a second match.

This was a narrower street and darker except for a single pool of light beneath a lamp.

Beyond the lamplight two shapes loomed, a pair of coaches moving slowly down the dark, street side by side. Then they stopped, blocking the way.

"Now," Peña said, just as the carriage moved into the light.

Guillem and Esteve leaped into the road and seized the bridles of the horses while the hunting group surrounded the coach. From two coaches and the darkness on the other side of the street other figures emerged, and several came around to where Josep stood staring into the startled face of the man within the carriage. The driver of the blocked coach was standing, and he had begun flailing at Esteve with his whip.

Agents of the militia, Josep thought as he saw the newcomers, three of them with drawn handguns, and he took a step back so they had a clear course to the coach door.

But instead they held out their guns.

A series of flat, coughing reports.

The man in the coach had turned to look out the window and presented a wide target; he jerked as he was struck in the left shoulder, touching the place with his left hand. His right hand came up as though in protest and Josep saw part of his ring finger fly away. Then another bullet hit him in the breast, leaving a small dark bite in his cloak like the hundreds of holes the hunting group had shot into their target trees.

It shocked Josep to recognize the bitter realization in the man's face.

Someone shouted "Jesucrist!" and screamed, a long, feminine sound. At first Josep thought it came from a woman, then he realized that the voice was Enric's. And suddenly everyone was running into the darkness, and Josep ran too, over the snowy ground away from the shying horses and the pitching carriages.

PART THREE

Out in the World

Madrid
December 28, 1870

19

Walking in Snow

$\mathcal{H}$e fell once in the cold wet and got up and ran again until his breath was labored, and finally he stopped and leaned against a building.

In a while he resumed flight, walking now instead of running, but still in terror. He had no idea where his feet were carrying him, and he was startled, as he passed under a street lamp, when a voice came from the darkness.

"Josep. Wait."

Guillem.

"What happened, Guillem? Why did they shoot the poor bastard? Why didn't they just arrest him as we were told they would?"

"I don't know. Well . . . it didn't happen just the way Peña predicted, did it? Perhaps Peña can explain. He said to go the railway station if anything happened."

"Yes, the station . . . Do you know how to find it? I haven't the slightest idea where we are."

"I think it's somewhere in this direction . . ." Guillem said helplessly.

They plodded for a long time before Guillem admitted he was as lost as Josep. Soon they came to a hack stand, and when Josep asked one of the carriage drivers how to get to the railway station, they learned they had been walking north instead of south.

The man gave them long, complicated directions, and they turned and began to retrace their steps.

Above all they did not want to go back to the vicinity of the attack, and this required a detour, during which both Josep and Guillem forgot some of the details of the directions they had been given. Cold and weary, Josep pointed to a nearby sign that announced a small café called the Metropolitano. "Let's ask in there."

Inside, even the low prices on the chalkboard intimidated them; they had little money. But each ordered a coffee.

Their arrival interrupted an argument between the large and burly proprietor and his elderly waiter.

"Gerardo, Gerardo! The goddam lunch dishes! They were never washed! You expect to serve food in dirty dishes?"

The waiter shrugged. "Not my fault, is it? Gabino did not show up."

"Why did you not get somebody else, you stupid shit? The fiesta, without a dishwasher! What do you expect me to do now?"

"Perhaps the dishes, señor?" The waiter shrugged again, bored.

When he served their coffee, Guillem asked him how to find the railroad station.

"You are west of the railroad. You must walk down this street and take the second right. Six or seven blocks down you will see the railroad yards. The shortest way from here is to go right through the yards to the rear of the station."

As they drank the coffee eagerly for its heat, he added a cautionary note. "It is safe to cross the railroad property so long as you are not idiots who would walk on the tracks."

It had stopped snowing by the time they reached the railroad yards, but there were no stars. They walked among the coal bins and woodpiles. The white-coated boxcars seemed like sleeping monsters. Soon they saw the gas lamps of the depot area, and they followed a path to it, along a deserted train. When they peered around the end of the locomotive, Josep said, "There's Peña. And, look, there's Jordi."

Peña was standing next to a waiting carriage with two men and Jordi Arnau. Peña spoke briefly to Jordi and opened the door of the coach. At first Jordi seemed ready to enter, but he saw something inside that made him draw back, and one of the men began to push him.

"What the hell?" Josep said.

Three more men approached the carriage and stood watching as Jordi turned and raised his fist.

The man nearest him pulled a knife and moved it in a way Josep couldn't believe, into Jordi's throat, and across.

It could not be happening, Josep thought, but Jordi was on the ground, in the yellow lamplight his blood black against the snow.

Josep felt faint.

"Guillem, we have to do something."

Guillem gripped his arms. "There are too many of them, and more coming. Shut up, Josep," he whispered. "Shut up."

Two of the men picked Jordi up and threw him into the carriage. Far to the left, Josep saw that another group of men had surrounded Manel Calderon.

"They have Manel."

Guillem drew Josep back. "We have to get away from here. Now. But don't run."

They turned and walked wordlessly, back through the train yards. A high, cold sliver of moon had appeared, but the night was still black. Josep was trembling. He strained his ears, dreading to hear the sound of shouts and running feet, but none came. When they were almost out of the yards, he dared to speak.

"Guillem, I don't understand what is going on . . . What is happening?"

"I don't understand what's happening either, Josep."

"Where shall we go?"

But Guillem shook his head.

They walked past the Metropolitano Café, but then Guillem put his hand on Josep's arm and turned back. Josep followed him inside, where the elderly waiter was wiping one of the tables with a wet rag.

"Senyor . . ." Guillem said. "May we speak with the owner?"

"Señor Ruiz." The waiter pointed with his chin. In the back room, they found the proprietor standing over a battered copper tub, his arms buried in water.

"Senyor Ruiz," Guillem said. "Would you like to hire us as your dishwashers?"

The man's red face was oily with sweat, but he tried to hide the sudden eagerness in his eyes. "How much?"

The bargain was quickly struck. Meals, a few coins, and permission to sleep on the floor after the last patron had left. The proprietor wiped his arms, rolled down his sleeves, and fled into the kitchen. A few seconds later, Guillem and Josep had taken his place at the sink.

They settled into the routine willingly, Guillem washing the dishes in hot water and dropping them into a cold-water rinse, Josep wiping down the clean dishes and stacking them.

The water didn't stay hot very long, and they had to continually add boiling water from three big pots over the grill in the fireplace and then replenish the supply in the pots with water from the small pump in the sink. The café did a good business. They kept exchanging clean dishes for more stacks of dirty ones. From time to time, when the tub could hold no more water and the mixture had become cold and terrible with grease, they would empty the dishwater into the alley behind the café and start afresh. The small back room was hot, and each of them removed several layers of clothing.

Josep kept seeing Jordi, reliving the terrible moment. In a little while he spoke. "They were getting rid of witnesses."

He could not disguise the fear in his own voice.

Guillem stopped working. "You really think so?" He sounded ill.

"Yes."

Guillem looked at him palely. "I do too," he said, and then he reached into the water for another dish.

Several hours after midnight, Gerardo, the old waiter, brought them bowls of goat stew and half a loaf of bread, only slightly stale, and watched them wolf it down.

"I know why you went to the railroad," he said.

They regarded him silently.

"You want to jump a train, get a free ride. Isn't that right? Listen to me, you cannot hop a train in Madrid. My cousin Eugenio works for the railroad, and he has told me they have guards with clubs, and they check each car before leaving the yard. You would be beaten and thrown into jail. What you need to do is climb into a freight car when the train has stopped somewhere outside of the city. That is the way to do it."

"Thank you, senyor," Josep managed.

Gerardo nodded loftily. "A small word to the wise," he said.

They slept next to the comfort of the dying fire. It was cool in the café when the fire died, but they had full stomachs, and it was far better to sleep on the filthy floor than it would have been to be outside in the rawness of winter,

The next day, they swept the floor clean and emptied the fireplaces of ashes, before Gerardo came to the café in midmorning, and he rewarded them with a good breakfast. "The boss wants you to stay a few more days and help us out," he said. "Ruiz says if you stay until after the eve of the new year, he will show his appreciation."

Josep and Guillem looked at one another. "Why not?" Josep said.

They gratefully spent the next two days and nights as the dishwashers of the café, aware that the back room was the perfect place to hide. Despite the fact that the noise of the patrons reached them during peak hours, only Gerardo entered into their domain, and they left it only to visit the outhouse or to discard the used dishwater in the alley.

On New Year's Eve, Gerardo brought them each a block of turrón, the hard kind made with whole toasted almonds. As the cathedral bells began their sonorous pealing, they paused in their work and gnawed the confection.

Then, with the taste of sugar, egg white, and honey still in their mouths—as the people in the café joined in the general tumult—they resumed washing the dishes.

That night when Gerardo and Ruiz had followed the patrons from the little café, Guillem found a copy of a newspaper abandoned under one of the tables. He couldn't read or write, and he carried the newspaper to Josep at once. By the light of two candles, Josep examined it.

La Gaceta, published the day before.

"Well? . . . *Well?*" Guillem demanded.

Josep was trembling. "God, Guillem! Oh. My God, my God . . . Do you know who he is?"

Guillem stared at him speechlessly.

"*He is Juan Prim.*"

"Juan Prim . . . No. Juan Prim, the president?"

"The president. General Juan Prim."

"Is he dead?" Guillem asked faintly.

"He is alive. He is wounded, but they did not succeed in killing him."

"Ah, thanks to God. Josep, we are blest!"

"The head of the government council of Spain, Guillem! And they shot him. And he is a good man, General Prim, always for Spain, always for the people. No, Jesús! Does it mention the Carlists?"

"No. Madre, they have his whole life. Prominent in the movement that led Queen Isabella to abdicate and flee to France . . . former captain-general of Puerto Rico, hero of the war with Morocco . . . Born in Reus, twice a grandee, a marquis, and a count.

"Does it say he was shot by the militia?"

"No. Guillem . . . It says he was shot by unknown assassins who were assisted by a group of accomplices."

Guillem stared.

"Do you think they were members of the militia, Guillem? The attackers?"

"I don't know. A man like that. The *president!* He would have big enemies, don't you think? But who knows if they were from the militia or . . . whatever? Probably Peña is not truly a sergeant. Perhaps he is not truly a Carlist."

"Probably he is is not truly named Peña," Josep said quietly.

20

News

*O*n the following day, the second day of 1871, "Perhaps," Guillem said, "we should stay here a while longer."

Josep was amenable. He was still in shock, and he liked the safety of the place and the certainty of food and warmth. But it wasn't to be.

"Ruiz is going to pay you off," Gerardo said. "He has hired the daughter of his brother to work here with us. Paulina." He shrugged. "She is a slut but also a very good worker, and Ruiz has such a large family. He was determined to employ a relative."

Gerardo had a proposition for them, however.

"Two nice young men, obviously Catalans. And interested in returning east, perhaps?" When they nodded, he beamed.

"A man named Dario Rodríguez is a long-time patron of this café. He makes hams. *Such* hams!" He kissed his fingertips. "For years we have bought and served them. Tomorrow he goes to Guadalajara, delivering his hams to restaurants and groceries along the way. I have spoken to him. In exchange for some labor on your part, he will take you with him and deliver you at La Fuente. La Fuente is a way station of the railroad, a place where the trains stop briefly to take on fresh water and coal. A freight train is due there tomorrow evening at ten minutes past the hour of nine. My cousin Eugenio says it is an excellent place to board a freight car, since there are no disagreeable guards with clubs at La Fuente."

It seemed a very welcome opportunity to Josep and Guillem.

Early the next morning, modestly enriched by Ruiz and blessed with a gift from Gerardo—a sack containing pork sausages, bread, and two large slices of somewhat old potato and egg tortilla—they clambered onto Darío Rodríguez's meat wagon. Rodríguez, as burly as Ruiz but more affable, laid out the rules:

"You'll ride in back with the hams. At each stop, I'll call out the number of hams to be delivered. If the order is for a single ham, you'll take turns. If more than one, both of you shall carry them."

So they departed from Madrid, seated in a cleared spot on the wagon bed, wedged between heavy pig haunches, and blanketed by their thick, rich smell.

It was almost dusk when Rodríguez dropped them off at the La Fuente train yard, a smaller version of the railroad yard in Madrid.

Josep nervously noted several men standing in the shadows of some of the detached cars, but nobody came forward to challenge them as they moved behind one of the cars themselves.

Waiting was difficult. Finally, just as darkness was settling over the yard, there was the monster-sound of the approaching train. Unsure of themselves, they hesitated when it groaned to a stop, until they saw other men running to the train, pulling open doors.

"Come on!" Guillem said; he grunted with effort as he ran, and Josep followed.

Each freight car seemed to have a padlock on the door as they ran past.

"Here's one," Josep said at last. The door protested when they pulled it open. In a moment they were inside, and the door screeched again as they shoved it closed.

"Everyone must have heard that," Guillem muttered. They stood in silent desperation in the perfect dark, waiting for guards with clubs.

Nobody came.

In a moment there was a hard jerk as the car moved and stopped. Then it moved again, and this time it kept on moving.

The freight car strongly disclosed the nature of its last cargo.

"Onions," Josep said, and Guillem laughed.

Josep moved cautiously around the car's perimeter, holding onto the swaying walls, making certain they shared the darkness with nobody else. But the car was empty of other people as well as of onions, and he felt a great sense of relief when he was back at Guillem's side.

At midday they had eaten free bowls of lentil soup in a restaurant kitchen where they had left hams, so Josep still clutched the sack of food Gerardo had given them. In a little while they sat and ate, beginning with the sausages and the hardened bread. The tortillas had broken apart, but they savored every crumb; then they lay back on the vibrating floor.

Josep farted.

". . . Well . . . not as bad as Xavier Miró's," Guillem said judiciously.

"Nothing is as bad as Xavier's."

Guillem's laughter was strained.

"I wonder where he is."

"I wonder where all the others are," Josep said.

They were worried that guards might inspect the train in Guadalajara, but when they reached there just before midnight, no one bothered the car door during the few long minutes the train sat at the station. Eventually the train jolted forward again and moved on, rattling and swaying, the noise and motion making a strange rhythmic music that at first kept Josep awake and finally lulled him into sleep.

He awoke to the squealing of the door being moved back by Guillem, daylight diluting the dark. The train was clacking along at good speed, through open farm country. Guillem pissed through the door, no people or animals in sight except for a large bird hanging in the sky.

Josep felt rested but very thirsty, and hungry again; he regretted not saving some of Gerardo's food. He and Guillem sat and watched farms, fields, forests, villages appear and disappear. A long nervous stop in Zaragoza, then Caspe . . . smaller pueblos, open fields, crops, sandy wastes . . .

He whistled. "Big country, no?" he said, and Guillem nodded.

Bored, he slept again for three or four hours. It was afternoon when Guillem shook his shoulder and woke him.

"I just saw a sign, five leagues to Barcelona."

Gerardo had warned them that most likely in Barcelona there would be guards checking all the freight cars.

They waited until the train was in a slow, labored climb up a long incline and jumped from the open door with little difficulty. They stood and watched the train move away, and then they began to walk along the tracks in the direction the train had gone. Half an hour later they came to a sandy road that began to run parallel to the rails, easier walking.

The sign on a neglected olive tree said *La Cruilla, 1 league.*

A hot sun made the weather mild, and soon they unbuttoned their heavy jackets and then took them off and carried them. La Cruilla turned out to be a village, a cluster of whitewashed houses and a few shops that had sprung up where another dirt lane crossed the tracks and the road they had been following. There was a café, and they were very hungry. When they sat at a table, Josep ordered three eggs, tomato bread, and coffee.

The woman who served them asked if they would like ham, and he and Guillem both grinned but didn't order any.

Josep spotted a newspaper at a nearby table and went to it at once. It was *El Cascabel*. He began to read it on the way back to their table, walking very slowly, stopping in his tracks twice. "Ah . . . Ah . . ."

"What is it?" Guillem said.

The story was on the first page of the paper. It had a black border around it.

"He died," Josep said.

21

Sharing

*J*osep read every word of the news story aloud to Guillem in a low voice hoarse with tension.

The newspaper said that President Prim had been one of the men responsible for the overthrow of Queen Isabella, the reinstatement of a monarchy, and the election by the Cortes of a member of the Italian royalty—Amadeus, Prince of Savoy and Duke of Aosta—as the new king of Spain.

Amadeus I had arrived in Madrid to assume his throne only hours after the death of General Prim, his principal supporter. On the new monarch's orders, General Prim's body was to lie in state for four days of public mourning, and in the presence of the corpse Amadeus had taken an oath to obey the constitution of Spain.

"The Guardia Civil is said to be close to making arrests of several persons thought to have been participants in the assassination," Josep read.

Guillem groaned.

They ate their food without tasting it and then wandered off without destination, two people in a shared bad dream.

"I think we should go to the Guardia, Guillem."

Guillem shook his head grimly. "They will not believe that we were merely dupes. If they have not captured Peña or the others, they will be happy to blame the murder on us."

They walked in silence.

"Perhaps they were Carlists. Who knows? We were chosen because they wanted stupid country boys to fashion into killers," Josep said. "Desperate, unemployed peons who could be trained to do whatever they ordered."

Guillem nodded. "Peña selected us to be his marksmen, you and I. But then they decided we weren't to be trusted. So other persons were found to fire at that poor bastard and kill him, while we were deemed just smart enough to hold a horse and light a match," he said bitterly.

"We can't return to the village," he said. "Peña's people—the Carlists or whatever they are—may be looking for us. The police may be searching for us! The army, the militia!"

"Then what shall we do? Where can we go?" Josep said.

"I don't know. We had best think," Guillem told him.

By the time dusk approached, they were still trudging aimlessly along the road next to the train tracks, in the general direction of Barcelona. "We must find a place to spend the night," Josep said.

Fortunately the weather was mild, but it was winter in northern Spain, which meant that the air could become raw and chill without notice. "The important thing is to be protected in case the wind starts to blow," Guillem said. Presently they came upon a large stone-lined culvert that ran under the road, and they agreed it was a suitable site.

"We'll be fine unless there is a downpour, in which case we'll drown," Josep said, for the conduit was designed to funnel the waters of a stream beneath the road and the tracks, but years of drought had caused the stream to vanish. Inside the big pipe, the air was still and warm and there was an accumulation of soft, clean sand.

It took only a few minutes to collect a pile of driftwood from the riverbed. In Josep's pocket he still had several matches from the handful Peña had given him, and very quickly they had a small, brisk fire making satisfactory snapping noises and shedding warmth and light.

"I am going to go south, I think. Perhaps Valencia or Gibralter. Maybe even, Africa," Guillem said.

"All right. We'll go south."

". . . No, I'd best go south alone, Josep. Peña is aware we are close friends. He, and the police, will be looking for two men traveling together. One man can blend into any background more easily, therefore it will be safer for each of us to travel alone. And they'll be searching for us close to home, so we must go far away from Catalonia. If I go south, you should go north."

It sounded like good sense. "But I don't believe we should split up," Josep said doggedly. "When two friends travel together, if one of them runs into trouble, the other is there to help."

They regarded one another.

Guillem yawned. "Well, let's sleep on it. We can talk some more in the morning," he said.

They lay on either side of the fire. Guillem soon was asleep and snoring loudly, while Josep lay awake, from time to time placing another piece of wood on the fire. Their pile of branches had almost disappeared by the time he finally drifted into sleep, and soon the blaze had become a small circle of ashes with a glowing heart.

The fire was cold and grey when he awoke, and so was the air.

"Guillem?" he said.

He was alone.

Guillem was off somewhere taking a piss, he thought, and allowed himself to drift back into sleep.

When he awoke again, the air was warmer. Sunshine streamed into the end of the culvert.

He was still alone.

"Hey," he called. He clambered to his feet.

"Guillem?" he called.

"GUILLEM?"

He went outside the culvert and clambered up onto the road, but he could see no living creature in either direction.

He called out to Guillem several more times, feeling dismay growing within him.

Spurred by a sudden thought, he reached into his jacket pocket and experienced relief when he felt the roll of bank notes that had been given to him by his father and Nivaldo.

But . . . it felt different.

When he took it from his jacket and counted the bills, he saw that seven pesetas—half his money—was gone. Stolen from his pocket!

By his *friend*.

Nearly faint with rage, he lifted his fist and shook it at the heavens.

"SHAME! BASTARD! ROTTEN BASTARD!"

"FU-UCK YOU, GUILLEM!" he screamed.

22

Alone

$\mathcal{H}$e returned to the culvert for no reason, like an animal crawling back into its den, and sat in the sand next to the ashes of the dead fire.

He had depended heavily on Guillem. Guillem hadn't known how to read or write, but after Nivaldo, Guillem Parera was the smartest person Josep knew. Josep remembered how Guillem had stopped him from stupidly wandering back to Sergeant Peña at the Madrid railroad yard, and how Guillem had known immediately that the scullery sink at the Metropolitano Café would be a safe haven for them. Josep didn't feel smart, and he didn't know if he could survive alone.

As he transferred the thin roll of pesetas from his pocket to his sock, he thought about the fact that Guillem could easily have stolen all his money instead of half, and it dawned on him that Guillem had made a contest of their troubles.

It was as if Guillem spoke to him.

We start off from here equal in money. See which of us can do better.

It made him angry again and overrode his fear, so that he was able to abandon the temporary safety of the culvert. Blinking against the warm sunlight, he scrambled back up to the road and began to walk.

In less than a league he came to a place where the train tracks heading east into Barcelona were crossed by tracks going north and south. Though it bothered him to admit it even to himself, Guillem had been right about several things in their disagreement of the previous evening. He could not go back to Santa Eulália. It would be dangerous for him to go to Barcelona, dangerous even to remain in Catalonia.

He turned left and followed the new tracks north.

He felt justified in taking Guillem's advice now; after all, he told himself, he had paid for it.

He didn't know where trains would stop or where they could safely be boarded, but when he came to a long, steep hill, he climbed the incline until he was near the top, then he lay down beneath a tree and waited.

Less than an hour later he heard the faint rumbling and clacking, the distant animal howl of the whistle, and he waited with rising hope and expectation. The train's motion became ever slower as it climbed the hill, just as he had hoped. By the time it reached him he could have boarded easily, but the train was made up entirely of passenger cars and thus was of no use to him.

From the windows of car after car, people in crowded third-class coaches looked at him as they passed on the way to lives far more secure than his.

Less than an hour later he heard train sounds again, and this time it was what he had been waiting for, a long line of freight cars. As they went past, he saw a car with the door partially open, and he ran alongside and easily lifted himself onto the bed.

When he rolled into the dark interior and got to his feet, he would have settled for the scent of onions, for this car was stale with the old odor of urine. Probably that was one of the reasons guards wielded their clubs when they caught riders, he thought. Then somebody quietly said "Hola."

"Hola."

As Josep's eyes adjusted to the interior dimness, he saw the speaker lying in the gloom, slight and slim, with a small dark beard.

"I am Ponc."

"Josep. "

"I go only as far as Figueres."

"I am staying on the train. I'm going to France to seek work. Do you know a likely town?"

"What kind of work have you done?"

"Everything in a vineyard."

"Well, there are so many vineyards." The man shook his head. "But hard times everywhere, also." He paused thoughtfully. "Do you know the Orb valley?"

"No, senyor."

"I have heard times are better there, a valley with its own climate, warmer than Catalonia in the winter, perfect for grapes. *Many* vineyards there. Perhaps with employment, eh?"

"How far away is this valley?"

The other shrugged. "Maybe a five-hour ride from the border. The train goes directly to it."

"This train?"

The man snorted. "No, these tracks end well before the border. Those who think of such things in Madrid built our Spanish train rails wider than the rails of France, so that if the Frenchies should decide to invade, they can't simply move in troops and guns on the railroad. You must walk to Portbou, cross the border there, and jump another train in France."

Josep nodded, tucking the information away.

"You should know that they search every car at the border. You must be careful to leave this train about one-quarter of an hour—no more!—after it passes through the town of Rosas. After you see a big white water tower, the train slows on an upgrade. That's when you leave."

"I am greatly obliged."

"For nothing. However, just now I wish to sleep, so no more talk."

Josep settled himself against the wall of the car, close to the open door. Under different circumstances he could have slept himself, but he was nervous. With the toe of his right shoe he nudged the seven pesetas in his left sock, making certain the money was still there. He kept his eyes fixed on the recumbent lump in the darkness that was his fellow traveler, as the train slid over the crest and, rocking and clacking, began to pick up speed on the descent of the hill.

23

Wandering

*T*hree hours later, he left the train without incident and walked down a winding road that eventually brought him to the sight of the Mediterranean, shining and dazzling in the warm sunlight. He went past a dozen beached fishing boats and soon was in the central plaça of Portbou, where he found that Friday was market day. His empty stomach was growling as he strolled past braziers on which chicken, fish, and pork sizzled and filled the air with the most delicious of aromas.

Finally he bought a large bowl of spicy chickpea stew, which he ate slowly and with great enjoyment, sitting with his back against a stone wall.

Near him an old woman offered a pile of blankets for sale, and when Josep finished the stew, he returned the wooden bowl and went to her stand. He touched a blan-ket and then hefted it, feeling its soft thickness almost with reverence. When he shook it open, he saw it was quite large, wide enough to cover two people. A warm blanket like this would make all the difference to some-one forced to sleep outside.

The old woman studied him with the experienced eyes of a trader. "The finest wool, and from the loom of the best weaver, my daughter. A genuine bargain. For you . . . one peseta."

Josep sighed and shook his head. "Fifty centimos?" he said, but she shook her head scornfully and held up her hand to stay any negotiation.

He turned away, then stopped. "Perhaps sixty?"

The wise eyes reproached him as she shook her head again.

"Do you know someone, then, who needs a good worker?"

She shook her head. "There is no employment here."

So he walked away. When he was out of her sight he took the coins from his pocket and assembled 75 centimos. Presently he approached the old woman again and held out the money.

"It is all I have to spend. Absolutely."

She sensed a final offer and her talon-like hand grasped the cash. She counted it and sighed, but she took it, and when he asked for a piece of rope that he glimpsed behind the blankets, she gave it up. Making a roll of the blanket and tying the rope to each end, he fashioned a sling and settled it over his shoulders.

"Grandmother, where is the border station?"

"Follow the road through the town, and it will take you to the station. Half a league."

He looked at her and decided to take the plunge. "I don't wish to cross the border at the station."

She smiled. "Of course you do not, my handsome young man. Few sensible people do. My grandson will show you the way. Twenty centimos."

Josep walked a distance behind the small skinny boy, whose name was Feliu. It was part of the agreement that he would pay the coins at once and that they would not walk together. They went through the town and into the countryside beyond, always within sight of the sea on the right. Presently Josep saw the border station, a wooden gate across the road, manned by uniformed guards interrogating travelers. He wondered if they had been given his name and description. Even if they had not, he couldn't go through the station, for they would demand papers and proof of identification.

Feliu continued to walk toward the station, and with growing alarm, Josep followed. Perhaps the old woman and the child were leading him straight into arrest, in return for the money from him, and more from the guards whenever they delivered a smuggler.

But at the last moment Feliu turned left into a small dusty lane that ran inland from the road, and when Josep came to the lane, he turned into it as well.

They walked only a few hundred meters down the lane before Feliu stopped, picked up a stone, and threw it off to his right. It was the arranged signal, and the boy went away at a swift walk without looking back. When Josep reached the place where Feliu had thrown the stone, he saw a narrower lane that ran along the edge of a winter-fallow onion field, and he turned into it. Unharvested onions poked green fingers through the earth, and he salvaged several of the bulbs. They were strong and bitter when he ate them as he walked.

The onion field was the last cropland he saw, the small valley turning into thickly forested hills. He walked for almost an hour before he came to a place where the trail became a fork, splitting into two paths.

There was no directional sign, and no Feliu or any other person from whom he could seek advice. He took the path on the right, and at first he saw no difference in the trail that threaded between the hills. Then it became gradually apparent to him that the trail was growing narrower. Sometimes it seemed to disappear, but each time he would see ahead of him marks worn by travel between trees, and he would hurry to pick up the way again.

And then the path disappeared for good.

Josep moved on through the forest, believing that he would discover the route in a few paces, as he had done previously. When finally he conceded there was no sign of any path through the woods, he tried to retrace his steps to go back over the trail he had followed from the fork, but though he searched hard, he couldn't find the way he had come.

"Shit," he said aloud.

For a while he moved aimlessly through the woods, but he saw no footpath. Worse, he had lost all sense of direction. Finally, coming upon a trickling brook, he decided to follow it. Houses were often built near a water source, he reasoned; perhaps he would come to a house.

It was hard, traveling through the small trees and overgrown brush. He had to crawl under and over fallen trees and circle around cliffs. Several times he passed deep, rocky chasms, all twisted earth and ragged rock. His arms became scratched by brambles, and he grew short of breath and by turns cranky and fearful.

But finally the brook entered a wooden pipe, a long hollowed log.

And the pipe ran under a road.

It was a good highway, deserted at the moment but—it led somewhere! Feeling vastly relieved, he stood in the middle of it and noted signs of life, the ruts made by wagon wheels, and hoof marks in the dust. To stroll on the road unimpeded was a luxury after fighting all the brush and the trees. He walked only a while, perhaps ten minutes, before he came to proof of his presence in France, a sign nailed to a tree.

VILLE de ELNE

    11 km

In small letters at the bottom of the sign it said,
Province de Roussillon

24

Fellow Travelers

$\mathcal{H}$e found the railroad tracks in Perpignan, a city with imposing buildings, many of them medieval and colored a dusky red from the narrow bricks used in their construction. There was a neighborhood of fine houses next to squalid sections of narrow littered streets hung with washing, the warrens of gypsies and other poor people. It also had an imposing cathedral in which Josep spent a night sleeping on a bench. The following day he spent an entire morning stopping in shops and cafés to inquire about the possibility of work, each time without success.

In the early afternoon he followed the railroad tracks out of the city to a likely spot and then waited. When the freight train appeared, the ritual felt natural. He picked a car with a partially open door, ran along, and hoisted himself inside.

As he got to his feet, he saw there were already four men in the car.

Three of them were clustered around a fourth man on the floor.

Two of the standing men were big, with large, round heads; the third was of medium size, thin, and rat-faced.

The man on the floor was on his hands and knees. One of the large men, whose trousers were lowered, gripped the back of the kneeling man's neck in one hand, while the other hand was underneath, lifting the bared buttocks.

In that first second, Josep saw them as a tableau. The standing men stared at him in astonishment. The man on the floor was younger than the others, perhaps Josep's age. Josep saw that his mouth was open and his face contorted, as if he were screaming silently.

The one holding the younger man didn't drop him, but the two others turned toward Josep, who also turned . . .

And leaped out the door.

It was not a jump for which he had prepared. He was already unbalanced when his feet touched the ground, and it was as if the earth leaped up at him, hard. He went to his knees and then smacked down on his stomach and slid on cinders, the fall knocking the wind from his body so that for a short, frightening time he had to struggle for air.

Then all he could do was lie there in the dirt as the cars clattered past.

The whole train went by him and away as he mentally cursed Guillam for leaving him alone and vulnerable. First he lost the noise of the locomotive, and then the clacking sounds softened and faded into distance.

25

Stranger in a Far Land

*A*fter that, he gave no thought to riding the trains but began a frozen, dreamy meandering northward on foot, asking for work wherever he went. He became accustomed and inured to rejection, almost not hearing the expected refusals. His hopes ceased to be centered on self-support and a sound future and instead quickly became fixed on meeting his daily need for food and a safe place to sleep. Every day he felt more like an alien. When he had entered the province of Roussillon, people had spoken Catalan almost as they did in Santa Eulália, but as he moved north, he heard more and more French words and expressions in the language. After he crossed into the province of Languedoc, he could still understand others and be understood, but his accent and halting speech marked him at once as an émigré.

People readily accepted his Spanish money, but he was driven by the cold understanding that he had to stretch his few pesetas, and he never considered paying for lodging. He sought out cathedrals, which were apt to be open to worshipers all night, offering him gloomy illumination and a bench to stretch out on. He slept in several large churches as well, though he found that many churches were locked at night. In one church the pastor took him to the parish house the next morning and fed him gruel, while in another a furious young priest woke him, shaking his shoulder roughly, and ordered him into the darkness. When he had to, he wrapped himself in the blanket and slept on the ground in the open, but he tried to avoid this, having a lifelong fear of snakes.

He made an early decision to buy only bread, seeking out bakeries that were likely to sell stale baguettes cheaply. The loaves quickly became hard and tough as wood, and he sawed pieces off with his knife and gnawed bread like a bone as he walked.

On a street in the city of Béziers he was brought up short by the sight of a large group of dull-eyed men wearing clothing that bore the wide stripes of prisoners. They were chained at the ankles, so they shuffled and clanked when they walked, and they used shovels, mauls, and heavy hammers, some of them smashing rocks to produce small stony pieces that others spread and firmed into a roadbed.

Uniformed guards carried large shotguns with a greater range than anything Josep had fired with the hunting group; he thought that a blast from such a weapon could cut a man in half. The hard-eyed guards seemed bored, while their prisoners, constantly under their gaze, worked steadily but deliberately, faces blank, their upper bodies active, but moving their feet as little as possible because of the thick chains.

Josep stood and watched them, transfixed. He knew something like this would be his fate if he were caught.

It was while sleeping that night in the Cathédrale de St. Nazaire, in Béziers, that he began having the dream. Here was the great man entering the coach; Josep saw his features clearly. Here was the hunting group trailing the carriage along dark, snowy boulevards; whenever they turned onto a new street, Josep struck a match. Then one of the shooters stood next to him, firing, firing, and Josep saw the balls impacting, sinking into the flesh of the horrified man in the carriage.

Josep was shaken awake by an old man whose prayers had been interrupted by his groans.

That day he moved beyond Béziers into the mountainous countryside. In rural places food could be bought only in small groceries, which often didn't have any kind of bread, so he had to buy cheese or sausage, and his money seemed to melt. Once, a small dirty inn gave him permission to wash dishes and paid him with three meager sausages and a plate of boiled lentils, but he was always tired and hungry.

Each day merged with the next, and he became confused, walking in whatever direction his feet took him. Eleven days after crossing the border he had only one peseta left in his sock, a wrinkled bill with one corner missing. Finding work before having to spend that last peseta became the most important thing in his life.

At times he became dizzy from lack of adequate food, and he felt a growing terror that hunger finally would cause him to snatch something for which he couldn't pay, a baguette or a piece of cheese, the inevitable desperate theft that would put the chains on his ankles and the stripes on his back.

The sign had two directions on it, an arrow pointing east that read *Béziers, 16 km.*, and an arrow pointing west that read *Roquebrun, 5 km.*

He knew that village name.

He recalled the two Frenchmen who had come to Santa Eulália to buy bulk wine. One of them had said he came from the village of Roquebrun.

It was the man who had liked the way Josep worked. Fontaine? No, that was the name of the taller man. The other man was shorter, stocky. What was his name?

Josep couldn't remember.

But half an hour later, it came to him and he said it aloud.

"Mendes. Leon Mendes."

He saw Roquebrun before he came to it, a village nestled comfortably on the slope of a small mountain. As Josep drew nearer, he saw that it was surrounded on three sides by a loop of river, which eventually he crossed on a hump-backed stone bridge. The air was mild and the foliage was strongly green. The river banks were lined with orange trees. The village was clean and well-kept, with winter-blooming mimosa everywhere; some of the feathery flowers still looked like pink birds, but most had already aged into small blizzards of white.

A man in a leather apron was sweeping the cobblestones in front of a shoe repair shop, and Josep asked him if he knew Leon Mendes.

"Of course I do."

The cobbler said the Mendes vineyards were located in the valley plain, a bit more than a league outside of Roque-brun. He pointed out the lane that would take Josep there.

The winery was as well-maintained as the village, three good-sized outbuildings and a residence, all of stone and each with a tile roof. The home and one of the outbuildings were softened by ivy, and the land that stretched from the house—two steep hillsides and a flat valley—was all in grapevines.

He knocked, perhaps too timidly, for no one answered. He was trying to decide whether to knock again, when the door was opened by a middle-aged woman with white hair and a round red face.

"Oui?"

"I would like to see Leon Mendes, if you please, Madame."

"Who are you?"

"Josep Alverez."

She regarded him coolly. "Please to wait."

In a few moments he came to the door exactly as Josep remembered, a small plump man, neatly—perhaps even fussily—dressed, hair perfectly combed. He stood at the door and looked at Josep inquiringly.

"Monsieur Mendes, I am Josep Alvarez."

There was a long moment.

"Do you perhaps recall me, monsieur? Josep Alvarez? Son of Marcel Alvarez of Santa Eulália?"

"In *Spain?*"

"Yes. You visited our vineyard in the fall. You told me I was a very good worker, an excellent worker. I asked you for employment."

The man nodded slowly. He didn't invite Josep in, instead coming outside himself and closing the door firmly behind him. He stood on the wide, flat stone that served as the front step of the house, eyes veiled.

"I do remember that. Now I remember you. I told you I had no work for you. Did you come all this distance in the expectation that appearing here would cause me to change my mind?"

"Ah, no, monsieur! I—I had to leave, you see. I assure you I am here . . . really by chance . . ."

"You had to leave? Then . . . you . . . made a *mistake,* did something wrong that forced you to flee?"

"No, monsieur. I did nothing wrong . . ."

Another long moment.

"I did nothing wrong!"

His hand closed on the small man's arm, but Leon Mendes did not flinch or step back.

"I witnessed others doing something wrong. I saw something very bad, a crime, and those who committed it *knew* I had seen. I had to leave for my life."

"Truly?" Mendes said softly. He removed Josep's hand from his arm and took a tiny step toward him. The stern, dark eyes seemed to bore into Josep's.

"Are you a good person then, Josep Alvarez?"

"I am!" Josep cried. "I am. I am . . ."

Suddenly, to his horror, to his great and overwhelming shame, he was weeping hoarsely and wildly, like a small child.

It seemed to last years . . . forever. He was dimly aware that Leon Mendes was patting his shoulder.

"I believe that you are," Mendes said gently.

He waited for Josep to gain control.

"First, I would guess that you must have food at once. Then you will be allowed to sleep. And finally . . ." He wrinkled his nose and smiled. "I shall give you a piece of the strongest brown soap we can find, and the river contains a great deal of water for rinsing."

Two mornings later, Josep stood on the steep slope of one of the hills. He had a new landlady, an attractive widow whose late husband had owned the worn but clean work clothes Josep now wore, though they were too large for him at the waist and too short at both the ankles and the wrists.

He had a pruning knife at his belt and a hoe in his hand, and he was studying the long rows of grapevines. The earth here was redder than his father's but just as stony. Leon Mendes had told him the stubs of the pruned vines could be expected to send out leaves and tendrils earlier than his father's plants, because of the milder climate of the Orb valley. He knew they were not varieties of grapes that were familiar to him, and he was impatient to see the differences in the leaves and the fruit.

He felt newly made.

It was not only due to the fact that he was fed and had slept well, he thought. Strength came to him directly from the soil, as it had in Santa Eulália. He was standing in a vineyard under the benevolent sun doing familiar things that he did well, and sometimes—if he didn't hear anyone speaking their Frenchy language, or dwell on the fact that there were no furry Small Ones feeding these vines under the rose-colored loam—he could relax long enough almost to be able to imagine that he was home.

PART FOUR

The Alvarez Land

Village of Santa Eulália
Catalonia, Spain
October 2, 1874

26

Painted Vines

*T*he first autumn after Josep returned home he felt a new gladness as the leaves on the vines of Santa Eulália began to change. It didn't happen every year, and he didn't know what triggered the transformation—the warm Spanish afternoons of late fall coupled with cooler nights? Certain combinations of sun, wind, and rain? Whatever it was, it happened again that October, and something within him responded. The Ull de Llebre leaves were suddenly a variety of hues from orange to bright red, the shiny green leaves of Garnacha turned yellow with yellow-brown stems, and the Samso leaves became a richer green with red stems. It was as if the vines were defying their coming death, but for him everything was part of a new beginning, and he walked the rows gripped by a quiet excitement.

His first crop on his own land was larger and heavier than usual for his father's crowded vines, many of the grapes half as big as a man's splayed thumb and darkly purple, and all the varieties bursting with juice from too much rain at exactly the wrong times. That the fermented juice would be less than wonderful didn't matter to growers who sold their new wine cheaply and in bulk. Business at Nivaldo's grocery was good, and the people Josep met in the village seemed to smile more than usual, and walk with a spring in their step.

Josep talked with Quim Torras about pooling their labor for the harvest, and his neighbor shrugged. "Why not?"

After much reflection and indecision, he also ventured beyond Quim's to the Valls vineyard, and made the same proposition to Maria del Mar. It took only a moment for her to agree, and Josep knew from her eagerness and from the way her face cleared that the prospect of harvesting and crushing the grapes without help had burdened her.

So the three of them picked their berries as a team, cutting cards to see the order in which the crops would be taken. Quim won with the jack of hearts, Maria del Mar got the nine of spades, and Josep the seven of diamonds, giving him the most risk that a late storm with hail or pounding rain could ruin his fruit before it could be pressed.

But the weather held, and they began to take Quim's grapes. Though all three of them had equal amounts of land, Torras had the lightest crop. He was a poor and lazy husbandman. Weeds choked his vines, and he always had something to do that prevented him from using his hoe—walking and playing games with his good friend Father Ricardo or wading in the river to see how low the water was becoming or sitting in the plaça and arguing about how to fix the unsightly door of the church. Half his vines were Garnacha, very old vines that produced small black grapes. When Josep took some to allay his thirst, he found their flavor deep and delicious, but he saw Maria del Mar masking her scorn when she looked at them. The three neighbors ignored the choking wildness of weeds; they cut the bunches of grapes and then muscled too few tumbrels of fruit to the communal press, but Quim was satisfied.

Maria del Mar's vineyard looked even better than it had when Ferran Valls had worked it, though her late husband had been a good worker. Josep had plowed her lanes with the mule, and Maria del Mar's hoeing had kept the rows mostly free of weeds. She had a large grape crop, and they worked hard to bring it in. Francesc was too young to remember much about the previous year's harvest, and he hovered about them, watching everything. Several times his mother spoke to him sharply.

"The boy is fine, Marimar. I like it that he's here," Quim Torras told her, flashing his easy smile as he emptied his filled basket into the tumbrel.

But she didn't smile in return. "He must learn not to get underfoot."

She didn't baby Francesc, but Josep had watched her hugging the child and talking to him tenderly. He thought she did very well, raising the little boy without a father while at the same time working hard and constantly.

A short time later, when Quim went off to his outhouse, Josep turned to her.

"I hear the wine buyer cheats you."

Straightening up from bending over a laden vine, she looked at him without expression.

Josep stumbled on. "So. When Clemente Ramirez comes to Santa Eulália with his empty vinegar barrels, I'd like to tell him I've bought the Valls land as well as my father's vineyard. That way, he'll have to pay the regular rate for your wine."

"Why do you want to do that?"

He shook his head and shrugged. "Why wouldn't I?"

Her eyes stared directly into his, making him uncomfortable.

"I want nothing in return," he said roughly. "Not money, or . . . anything. Clemente is mean. It would give me satisfaction to make him pay."

"I am as good a grower as any man!" she said bitterly.

"Better than most. Anyone with eyes can see how hard you work, how well you do."

"All right," she said finally, and turned away.

He felt curiously relieved as she resumed working, but a simple word of gratitude would not have been misplaced, he thought sourly, and went back to work himself.

Rain fell for a few hours two mornings later when they began to harvest Josep's crop, but it was gentle moisture that beaded the grapes and made them more beautiful.

The three neighbors cooperated smoothly, by now familiar with each other's individual work rhythms. Though
accustomed to working alone, Josep almost regretted it
when all his bunches had been squeezed by the big press
and the juice was safely within the old fermenting vats in
the shed behind his casa. He thanked his neighbors and
told himself that he and the Small Ones had made a very
good beginning.

When Ramirez and his two helpers showed up with
their big wagon filled with barrels, the wine buyer was
clumsy with words of sympathy and effusive with congratulations to the new owner of the vineyard.

Josep thanked him. "Actually, I've taken over the Vall
vineyard as well."

Clemente cocked his head and stared, his lips pursed.
"Ah . . . You and *she* . . . ?"

"No, I've *bought* the vineyard."

So . . . where shall she go?"

"She'll go no where. She'll continue to grow grapes
here."

"Ahhh. So she will work for you?"

"That's it."

Clemente looked sideways at Josep and smiled. He
opened his mouth to say more, but he caught something
in Josep's face.

"Well," he said, "I'll empty these vats first. They'll
take several trips, and then we'll get to the Valls vineyard. Best to start pumping wine, eh?"

At midday, he and his men were seated in the shade
of his wagon, chewing bread, when Josep passed nearby.
"Did you know you have a rotted place in one of your
vats?" he called cheerfully.

"No," Josep said.

Clemente showed him, several slats in the aged oaken
vat. The rot had been easy to overlook, since the wood
was mostly blackened with age.

"Might get away without leakage for another season
or two."

"I hope so," Josep said bleakly.

Maria del Mar was busy with her vines when they arrived at Vall's. She nodded at them and continued to work.

When Ramirez had taken the last of the wine from her vats, he directed his horses to the side of the road, and he and Josep leaned against the wagon and settled up, Josep doing the mathematics several times before accepting the bundle of bank notes.

Several hours later, when he returned to the Vall winery, Maria del Mar was still on her knees midway down a row of vines.

Josep was careful about separating her share of the money correctly. She did not watch and accepted the bills in a silence that he took as further proof of her anger and coldness, so he muttered a goodbye and went away.

The next morning, when he left the casa to begin his day's work, he almost stumbled over something that had been left in front of his door. It was a large, flat dish filled with potato tortilla still warm from the fire, so freshly made he could smell the onions and the eggs. A piece of paper, weighted down by a small stone, rested on the clean cloth in which the tortilla was wrapped.

One side of the paper was an old receipt which showed that for 92 centimos her late husband had purchased a narrow-bladed rake from a farm store in Vilafranca.

In the center of the reverse side there were three words done in the cramped, lopsided hand of a woman who rarely needed to write.

WE THANK YOU

27

Winter

*O*ne January morning he was carrying buckets, three in each hand, to be scrubbed in the river, when he saw Francesc sitting in the sun at the front of his mother's property.

The little boy's face brightened. "Hola, Josep!"

"Hola, Francesc. How are you this morning?

"I am fine, Josep. I am waiting for the olives to ripen so I may climb my trees again."

"I see," Josep said gravely. Growers of early-bearing varieties had been picking olives since November or December, but these were late bearers. The large trees bore heavily only every six or seven years, and this year there was a meager crop of olives colored light green to mature purple-black, olives for eating and not for oil. Maria del Mar had stretched cloths beneath each tree to catch the olives that ripened and fell away, and she would use a stick to beat down those that remained on the tree. It was an efficient way of harvesting them when they were ready to be cured in salt or brine, but it struck Josep that the ripening process must be gallingly slow to a little boy aching to climb again.

"May I sit with you for a while?" he said on sudden impulse, and when Francesc nodded, he set down his buckets and sank to the ground.

"I need these trees. I must practice climbing, for I hope some day to be the anxaneta of the Castellers," Francesc said seriously.

"The pinnacle," Josep said, wondering whether such an ambition was realistic, given the boy's misshapen hip. "I hope you get your wish." He cast a look for Maria del Mar, who was nowhere in sight. "And what does your mother think of your idea?"

"She says all things are possible, if I practice very hard. And meantime, my job is to watch the olives."

"These trees are slow to drop them, eh?"

"Yes. But they are good trees to climb."

It was true. The trees were very old and oversized, with thick trunks and contorted limbs. "These are very special trees. Some people think olive trees this old were planted by the Romans."

"Romans?"

"Romans were people who came to Spain a long time ago. They were fighters, but they also planted olives and grapes and built roads and bridges."

"Long time ago?"

"Very long ago, almost back when Jesús was alive."

"Jesús Crist?"

"Yes."

"My mother told me of him."

"Did she?"

"Josep, was Jesús a padre?"

He smiled and opened his mouth to say no, but when he looked down at on the small face he was baffled by the extent of his own ignorance. 'I don't know," Josep said, and reached out wonderingly and touched the boy's face. He was a skinny little boy but there was baby fat at that place, just above the jawbone.

"Would you like to come to the river with me? Why don't you ask your mother if you may go to the river to help me wash out my pails," he suggested, and smiled to see the how fast the hobbling boy could run.

In a very short time Francesc was back. "She says no, no, no," he said soberly. "She says I must watch the olives. That is my work."

Josep smiled at him. "It's good to have work, Francesc," he said, and he collected his buckets and went off to the river to clean them.

One morning he met Jaumet Ferrer returning from a hunt, carrying two plump partridges he had just killed, and they paused to talk. Jaumet was just the same as Josep remembered, a good-natured, slow-minded boy who had become a good-natured, slow-minded man.

Jaumet asked him no questions. He gave no sign he was aware that Josep had been away from the village for an extended time. They chatted about the partridges, which were destined for the Sunday table of Senyora Figueres, and about the weather, and Jaumet smiled and went on his way.

Both Jaumet and the overweight Pere Mas had been interested in the hunting group but had been unfit to undergo the training.

How fortunate they had been!

That evening Josep brought to the grocery a pitcher of the new wine he had retained for his own use when Clemente Ramirez had emptied his vats. While Nivaldo cooked eggs with peppers and onions, they sipped the wine without joy, for it had been insipid stuff to begin with and heat already had turned it sour.

"Ech," Josep said.

Nivaldo nodded judiciously. "Well, not wonderful wine, but . . . a cash crop. You have money to pay your brother and Rosa, money to allow you to work on next year's vintage, money to buy food. Speaking of which, I must tell you, Tigre, you eat like a stupid animal. The only time you have a decent meal is when you come to me. Otherwise, you keep yourself alive with chorizo and old bread and a bite of cheese. You are my best customer for chorizo."

Josep thought of the potato tortilla, which had given him two good meals. "I'm a working man with no woman in the house. I have no time to waste on complicated meals."

Nivaldo snorted. "You should find yourself a wife. But I'm a man who lives without a woman, yet I cook. A man doesn't require a woman to make a decent meal. A sensible man catches a fish, shoots a bird, learns to cook for himself."

"What has happened to Pere Mas? I don't see him in the village," Josep said, to change the subject.

"No," Nivaldo said. "Pere has found work in a mill that produces cloth, like Donat. In Sabadell."

"Oh." Josep found he was almost as lonely in Santa Eulália as he had been in the Languedoc. The first sons of the village were busily entrenched in their lives. Of his own generation of younger sons, his closest friends were gone.

"I never see a man come to Maria del Mar's house."

"I don't think there has been anyone since Tonio. Who knows? Perhaps she is hoping Jordi Arnau may come back to her."

". . . Jordi Arnau is dead," Josep said.

"You're certain?"

"I'm certain, though I didn't tell her that. I couldn't go into it."

Nivaldo nodded, not judging him. "Still, she is aware that some people come back," he said thoughtfully. "You came back, didn't you?" he said, and took another sip of the sour wine.

28

Cooking

*J*osep's first winter as a landowner began with dull weather, and the glow of satisfaction at getting in his own crop dwindled and disappeared. The vines had lost most of their handsome leaves and become dry, brittle skeletons, and it was time to begin the serious pruning. He walked the vineyard and looked at it critically. He saw that already he had made mistakes, and he concentrated on learning from them.

For example, the vines he had so smugly planted on the bare section of steep hillside, thinking he was more imaginative and more clever than his father and his forebears, had dried up and died in the burning summer's heat, because—as Padre must surely have understood!—at that spot the insubstantial layer of top-soil sat on impenetrable rock. To survive there, the vines needed to be irrigated, and both the river and the well in the village were too far away to make that practical.

Josep wondered what else his father had known about the land that he had failed to absorb while coming of age.

He had no inclination to become a hunter himself, but the next time he met up with Jaume he recalled Nivaldo's lecture about his need to eat better.

"Can you get me a rabbit?" he asked, and Jaume smiled his slow smile and nodded. He came to the casa the next afternoon with a young rabbit he had shot in the neck, and he seemed pleased by the coins Josep gave to him in return. He showed Josep how to skin and dress the animal.

"How do you like to cook them?" Josep asked.

"I fry them in lard," Jaume said, and departed with a bonus, the head and the pelt. But Josep remembered how his father had dealt with rabbit. He went to the grocery and gathered garlic, a carrot, an onion, and a long, red picant pepper. Nivaldo raised his eyebrows as Josep paid him.

"Doing some cooking, are we?"

Back home, he drenched a cloth in his sour wine and scrubbed the little carcass inside and out, then quartered it. He placed the pieces into a pot with wine and olive oil, added half a dozen crushed garlic cloves, and cut the vegetables into the pot before setting it above a small fire to simmer.

When he ate two of the pieces hours later, the meat was so tender and good he felt sanctified. He sopped up the spicy gravy, allowing it to soften chunks of stale bread until they became semi-liquid and luscious, so that he almost sucked them down.

When he was finished eating, he carried the pot to the grocery, where Nivaldo was chopping up a cabbage for the stew.

"Something for you to taste," he said.

While Nivaldo ate, Josep read *El Cascabel*.

Despite himself, the events that had enmeshed him had resulted in making him more interested in politics and the monarchy. He always read the newspaper carefully, but he almost never found the kind of information he was looking for. Soon after he had returned to the village, *El Cascabel* had published a story about General Prim on the fourth anniversary of his assassination. The article had revealed that following the murder several people had been taken into custody, but after questioning them, the police had let them go.

Nivaldo chewed and swallowed busily. "I haven't read the paper yet. Is there anything of interest?"

"There is still bitter fighting. We may be thankful it has not come nearer to us. In Navarre, the Carlists attacked a force and seized arms and artillery pieces and took three hundred prisoners. Déu!" He rattled the newspaper. "They nearly captured our new king."

Nivaldo looked over at Josep. "So? What was King Alfonso doing with the troops?"

"It says that he attended Sandhurst, the British military college, and he will take an active part in quelling the civil war."

"Oh? That is interesting," Nivaldo agreed. He ate the last bit of meat, and to Josep's satisfaction he began to suck the bones.

Francesc was left to amuse himself alone much of the time while Maria del Mar labored nearby, and frequently he appeared at the Alvarez vineyard to follow after Josep like a shadow. At first they rarely had conversations; when they did, it was always about simple things, the shape of a cloud, the color of a flower, or why weeds were not allowed to prosper and grow. Most often Josep worked in silence, and the little boy watched raptly, though he had seen his mother doing similar tasks again and again in her own vineyard.

When it was clear that Josep was reaching the end of a task, the boy always spoke the same words.

"What do we do now, Josep?"

"Now, we hoe some weeds," Josep would say.

Or, "We oil the tools."

Or, "We dig up this rock."

Whatever his reply, the child would nod as though giving his permission, and they would move to the next chore.

Josep suspected that as well as the need for company, Francesc was drawn to the sound of a man's voice, and at times he spoke comfortably and softly about things the boy was too young to absorb, the way a person may sometimes talk to himself while working.

One morning he explained why he was transplanting wild rosebushes in front of and behind each row of grapevines. "It's something I saw in France. The flowers are beautiful but they also do a job, they give warning. The roses aren't as strong as the vines, so if something goes wrong—if a problem develops with the soil, for example—then the roses will show signs of the trouble first, and I can think about how to fix it before it hurts the vines," he said. The boy soberly watched until the transplanting was finished.

"What do we do now, Josep?" he asked.

Maria del Mar grew accustomed to the fact that when she did not see her son at home, he most likely could be found at the Alvarez vineyard. "You must send him home when he becomes a bother," she told Josep, but he meant it when he replied that he enjoyed Francesc's company. He sensed that Maria del Mar harbored a resentment toward him. He didn't understand the reason, but he knew the distrust made her hesitate to accept any favors from him. He had settled into an identity as her neighbor, a relationship which each of them seemed to accept.

Nivaldo was right, he told himself. He needed a wife. There were widows and unmarried females in the village. He should begin to pay attention until he found a woman who would share the work of the vineyard, keep the house, cook him real meals. Give him children, share his bed . . .

Ah, share his bed!

Lonesome and wanting, he walked into the country one day, to the lopsided house of Nuria, but the house was deserted, the door left open to the wind and any animal or bird. A man spreading fertilizer in a nearby field told him that Nuria had died two years before.

"And the daughter, Renata?"

"Set free by the mother's death. Gone away." He shrugged.

The man said he raised beans in the field. "The soil is thin, but I have plenty of goat-shit from the Llobets. You know their farm?"

"No," Josep said, suddenly interested.

"Llobet goat farm. Very old farm." He smiled. "Very big, many goats, they are drowning in goat shit, old goat shit, new goat shit, piled in their fields. No place to store it any more. They know that in the future they will have a lot more goat shit. A *lot*. They kiss your hands when you take away a load."

"Where is the farm?"

"An easy walk south, over the hill."

Josep thanked the bean grower, whose information, he knew, was a stroke of fortune, better for him than if he had found Nuria and Renata still living in the house.

29

Hinny

On the rare occasions when Padre had found a source of fertilizer, he had borrowed a horse and wagon to carry it home, but Josep didn't have the kind of relationship with his father's friends that allowed for such presumption. He knew he couldn't go on using Maria del Mar's mule indefinitely, and his first successful harvest had given him the cautious courage to spend some money, so one morning he made his way to Sitges and sought out the cooperage of Emilio Rivera. The barrel factory was a long low building with peeled logs stacked in the yard. Near the stacks he found the red-faced barrel-maker, Rivera, and an elderly worker with whom he was quartering logs, using steel wedges and heavy mauls. Rivera didn't remember Josep until he was reminded of the morning when he had been kind enough to give a stranger a ride to Barcelona.

"I told you I needed to buy a mule, and you told me about your cousin, a man who is a buyer of horses?"

"Oh, yes, my cousin, Eusebio Serrano. Lives in Castelldefels."

"Yes, in Castelldefels. You spoke of a horse fair there. I was unable to go there then, but now . . ."

"The horse fair is held four times a year, and the next one is in three weeks time. It is always held on a Friday, market day." He smiled. "Tell Eusebio I sent you. For a small fee he will help you buy a good mule."

"Thank you, senyor." But Josep lingered.

"Something else?" Rivera said.

"I'm a wine-maker. I have an old fermentation vat in which two of the staves are rotting and must be replaced. Can you make that kind of repair?"

Rivera looked pained. "Well . . . but you cannot bring the vat to me?"

"No, it is large."

"And I'm a busy cooper, with orders to fill. If I were to go to you, it would be too costly." He turned to the worker. "Juan, you can begin stacking the quartered logs . . .

"Besides," he said, turning back to Josep, "I can't spare the time."

"Senyor . . . ," Josep hesitated. "Do you think you might advise me how to make the repair myself?"

Rivera shook his head. "No chance. You need long experience for that. You wouldn't be able to get it tight enough, and it would leak. You can't even use planks from sawn logs. The planks have to come from logs like these, split with the grain so the wood is impermeable." He saw Josep's face and set down the maul. "Here's what we can do. You tell me exactly how to find your place. Some day when I happen to be in your area, I'll drop by and do the repair on your vat."

"It must be fixed by autumn, when I crush my grapes."

Or I am lost. He said it silently, but the cooper seemed to understand.

"That gives us months. I'll probably get there in time."

The word *probably* made Josep uneasy, but he realized there was nothing else he could do.

"Can you use some good second-hand barrels, 225 liters? Used to contain herring?" Rivera said, and Josep laughed.

"No, my wine is bad enough without stinking of herring!" he said, and the cooper grinned.

Castelldefels was a medium-sized town that had become a large horse fair. Each place Josep looked there were four-legged animals surrounded by knots of talking men. He managed not to step in the horse dung that was everywhere, its stink sharp and heavy.

The horse fair started badly for Josep. He spotted a man limping away from him. His walk appeared familiar, and so did the man's body structure, and the shape of his head, and the color of his hair.

Josep's fear was so strong it surprised him.

He wanted to flee, but instead he forced himself to circle the group of horse traders the limping man had joined.

The fellow was the wrong age by fifteen years. He had a jovial red complexion and a large, coarse nose.

His face looked nothing like Peña's.

It was a while before Josep calmed. He wandered through the fairgrounds, lost and anonymous in the crowds, and eventually he regained control of himself.

It was fortunate that it took him a good deal of time and inquiry to track down Eusebio Serrano.

He marveled that Serrano and Emilio Rivera were related, for in contrast to the bluff, workmanlike Rivera, his cousin was an assured and dignified aristócrato in a fine gray suit and dressy hat, his snowy shirt adorned with a black string tie.

Nevertheless Serrano listened to Josep politely and with close attention and quickly agreed to guide his purchase in return for a modest fee. Over the next few hours they visited eight mule-sellers. Though they closely examined thirteen animals, Serrano said he could recommend only three of them for Josep's consideration.

"But before you decide, I want you to see one more," he said. He led Josep through the mass of men, horses, and mules to a brown animal with three white stockings and a white muzzle.

"A bit larger than the others, isn't he?" Josep said.

"The others are properly mules, out of female horses bred by male donkeys. This one is a hinny, out of a female donkey bred by an Arab stallion. I've watched him from the time he was born, and I know him to be gentle and able to outwork any two horses. He costs a bit more than the others we've seen, but I recommend that you buy him, Senyor Alvarez."

"I must buy a wagon as well, and I have limited funds," Josep said slowly.

"How much money do you have?"

Serrano frowned when Josep told him. "I think it would make sense to put most of it into the hinny. He's real value. Let us see what we can do."

Josep watched as Serrano engaged the hinny's owner in a congenial conversation. Senyor Rivera's cousin was friendly and quiet. There was none of the loud dickering that Josep had heard between other buyers and sellers. When a figure was mentioned by the dealer, Serrano's face looked politely regretful, and then there was renewed calm conversation.

Finally Serrano came to Josep and told him the man's lowest price—more than Josep had planned, but not a great deal more. "He'll throw in the harness," Serrano said, and he smiled when Josep agreed.

Josep handed over the pesetas, and a receipt was written and signed.

"There's something else I can show you," Serrano said and led Josep away to the section where equipment dealers displayed wagons and carts and plows. When he stopped before an object at the rear of one of the displays, Josep thought he was joking. The wooden bed sat flat on the ground. Once it had been a wagon of the kind he wanted, a rough hauling cart with low walls. But there was a long open space in the bed where a wide plank was missing, and the splintered plank next to that had two wide cracks.

"Just needs a couple of boards," Serrano said.

"It has no axles or wheels!"

He watched as Serrano made his way to the dealer and spoke with him. The dealer listened and dispatched two of his assistants.

In a few minutes Josep heard a loud screeching, the sound of an animal in pain. The assistants reappeared, each of them bent over and pushing an axle attached to two wagon wheels that protested shrilly as they were turned.

When the men brought the two sets of wheels closer, Serrano reached into his jacket and took out a pocket-knife. Snapping it open, he scraped the axle and then nodded. "Surface rust. Good sound metal underneath. It will last for years."

The total price was within Josep's budget. He helped a group of men lift the battered bed and bolt the axles fast and then watched them grease the wheels.

In a short time the hinny was between the shafts, and Josep sat on the seat, holding the reins. Serrano reached up and shook his hand. "Bring it to my cousin Emilio. He'll fix it for you," he said.

Senyor Rivera and Juan were working in the yard when Josep arrived at the cooperage. They walked to the wagon and inspected the ruined bed.

"Is there anything concerning your vineyard that is not broken?" Rivera said.

Josep grinned at him. "My faith in mankind, senyor. And in you, for Senyor Serrano said you would fix my wagon."

Rivera looked annoyed. "He did, did he?" He motioned to Juan to follow him, and they went away.

Josep thought they had deserted him, but in a little while they came back carrying two thick planks. "We have boards that are bad for barrels, but good for wagons. I give a special price to all my old and treasured customers." Juan measured the spaces and called out the numbers, and Rivera quickly cut them to size. Juan drilled the bolt holes, and they bolted the planks fast.

Soon Josep left the cooperage driving a sound wagon that he felt could carry any load, the wheels turning with only the softest grating sound, and the responsive hinny sweet and easy in the traces. His spirits rose. There was a difference between being a boy riding in a wagon loaned to his father as an act of charity and being a man driving his

own wagon. It was, he thought, similar to the difference between being an unemployed youth with no prospects and
a vineyard owner busily working his own land.

He was unhitching the wagon and introducing the
hinny to the shading shelter beneath the overhung roof at
the rear of the house, when Francesc appeared.

The boy watched him for a while.

"Is he yours?"

"Yes. Do you like him?"

Francesc nodded. "He is like ours. His color is
different and his ears are a little longer, but mostly he is
like ours. Can he be a padre?"

Josep scratched his chin. "No, he can't be a padre."

"No? My Mama says ours can't be a padre either.
What is his name?"

"Well . . . I don't know. Does yours have a name?" he
asked, though he had been plowing with Teresa's mule
for months

"Yes. The name of ours is Mule."

"I see. Well, why don't we name this one Hinny?"

"That's a good name. Can you be a padre, Josep?"

"Hah . . . I believe I can."

"That's good," Francesc said. "What do we do now,
Josep?"

30

A Knocking

*E*arly the next morning he drove the wagon into the countryside, searching for the Llobet goat farm. He heard and smelled the farm long before he could see it, led by the mass bleating and a faint, bitter whiff, both of which became pronounced as he approached. As he had been told, there was manure ready for the taking, and the farm's proprietors were eager for him to do so.

At the vineyard, he unloaded the manure into the barrow and used a shovel to scatter it along the rows. It was aged and crumbly, fine stuff that wouldn't burn his vines, but despite the plentitude of his supply, he spread only the thinnest layer. His father had taught him that it was good to nourish the plants, but even a small excess of fertilizer could ruin them, and he had heard Leon Mendes say that grapes required "a bit of adversity to build their character."

At the end of a single workday he had fertilized his entire vineyard, and the following day he hitched Hinny to the plow and blended the manure into the dirt. Then he adjusted the plowshare so it would turn a ridge of soil against the lower portion of each vine as he plowed; frost came to Santa Eulália some winters, and his plants would be protected until warmer weather.

Only then, at last, Josep was able to devote himself to the pruning he loved, and as winter settled in, he was warm and secure in the feeling that he was making progress.

In the middle of a February night a banging wakened him from dreamless sleep, and when he stumbled down the stone steps in his underwear, Maria del Mar was outside the door with wild eyes and crazy hair.

"Francesc."

A three-quarter moon made the world a jagged mixture of shadow and spilled light. Josep ran to her house the shortest way, through his vineyard and then Quim's. Inside her house he went up stone stairs similar to his own and found the little boy in a small bedroom. Maria del Mar arrived behind him just as he knelt over Francesc's sleeping pallet. The boy's head and face were very hot, and Francesc began to quiver and thrash his limbs.

Maria del Mar made a strangled sound.

"It's a convulsion, from the fever," Josep said.

"Where did it come from? He seemed happy, ate a supper. Then he threw up his food and was sick all at once."

Josep watched the quivering child. He hadn't the slightest idea what to do to help him. There was no physician to be summoned. An animal doctor lived half an hour away and sometimes treated humans, but he was a grim joke; people said that every time he was consulted, the horse died.

"Get me wine and a cloth."

When she brought them, Josep removed Franscesc's sleeping shirt. He soaked the cloth in the wine and began to bathe the boy, who lay like a skinned rabbit. He poured some of the wine into his cupped hand and massaged Francesc, pulling his hands over Francesc's arms and legs. The small, skinny body with its deformed hip filled Josep with sadness and trepidation.

"Why are you doing that?"

"I remember my mother doing it to me when I was sick." He gently but briskly massaged Francesc's chest and back with the wine and then wiped him dry and put his shirt back on. Francesc appeared to be sleeping normally, and Josep tucked the blanket around him.

"Will it happen again, the shaking?"

"I don't know. I think that sometimes it does. I remember Donat had convulsions when we were little boys. We both had fevers several times."

She sighed. "I have coffee. I'll go and make some."

He settled down next to the pallet. Francesc made a small noise twice, not moans, just quiet protests. By the time his mother returned, the second convulsion had begun to shake him, somewhat stronger and longer than the first, and she put down the coffee cups and picked up the little boy, kissing his face and head, holding him tightly and rocking him until his tremors passed.

Then Josep bathed him with the wine again and massaged him, and this time Francesc became submerged in sleep, with the total stillness of a cat or dog dozing by the fire with no restlessness or sounds.

The coffee was cold, but they drank it anyway and sat and watched him for a long time. "He's going to be all sticky and uncomfortable," she said, and she got up and went away, coming back with a bowl of water and more cloths. He watched her bathe her son and dry him and then change his shirt. She had long, sensitive fingers with dusky nails that were short and clean. "He can't sleep on this sheet," she said, and she went away again and he could hear her in the next room, taking the sheet from her own bed. When she was back he picked up Francesc, who didn't waken, and held him while she put her sheet on the pallet. He put the boy down again and she knelt and tucked the blanket about him, and then lay down next to her son. She looked up at Josep.

Thank you, she mouthed silently.

"For nothing," Josep whispered. He watched them for a moment and then, understanding that from then on he was an intruder, he murmured a goodnight and went home.

That day he waited for Francesc to come down to him through the vineyards, but the boy didn't come.

Josep worried that he may have taken a turn for the worse, and that evening he walked the Vall house and knocked on the door.

It took Maria del Mar a little time before she responded to the knock.

"Good evening. I just wondered how he is doing."

"He is better. Come in, come in."

He followed into the kitchen.

"The fever is gone, and the shaking. I kept him very close at hand all day, and he napped several times. Now he is sleeping as usual."

"That's good."

"Yes." She hesitated. "I was about to make a new pot of coffee. You want coffee?"

"Yes, please."

The coffee was in a clay jar on a high shelf. She went up on her toes and started to stretch for it, but he was one step behind her, and he reached up and took down the jar. As he handed it to her she turned; and without thought or plan, Josep kissed her.

It wasn't much of a kiss, having been a surprise to each of them. He waited for her to shove him away and tell him to leave her house, but they looked at one another for a long moment. This time, knowing fully what he was doing, he kissed her again.

This time she kissed him back.

A few seconds later they were kissing frantically, their four hands were exploring, their breathing was loud.

In a little while they sank to the floor. He must have made some kind of sound. *"Do not wake him,"* she whispered fiercely, and he reassured her and went on with what he was doing.

They sat at her table and drank the chicory-tasting coffee.

"Why didn't you come back to Teresa Gallego?"

He waited for a moment. "I couldn't."

"Oh? She went through hell, waiting for you. You can believe me."

"I'm sorry I caused her pain."

"Are you? And what kept you from her, senyor?" Her voice was thin but controlled.

"I can't tell you that, Maria del Mar."

"Then let me tell you." The words seemed to spring out of her.

"You were lonely. You met a woman—perhaps a lot of women, and they were prettier than she is, perhaps they had better faces, or better—" She shook her shoulders. "Or maybe it was just that they were close at hand. And you said to yourself, that Teresa Gallego, she is far away in Santa Eulália, and really, Teresa is nothing much. Why should I return to her?"

At least now he knew what it was about him that she resented. "No. It wasn't that way at all."

"No? So. Tell me how it was."

He took a sip of his coffee and looked at her. "No, I won't," he said quietly.

"Look, Josep. I ran to you last night because you are my closest neighbor, and you helped my son. I thank you for that. I thank you so much. But what just happened . . . I ask you that you forget it forever."

He felt quick relief; that was what he wanted too, he realized. She was like her coffee, too bitter to enjoy.

"All right," he said.

"I want a man in my life. I've had bad ones, and I think next time I deserve a good one, who will treat me well. I think you are dangerous, the kind of man who can just disappear, like smoke."

He saw no reason to defend himself to her.

"Do you know if Jordi is still alive?" she asked.

He wanted to tell her Jordi was dead. She deserved to know, but he realized it would lead to too many other questions, too many dangers.

He shrugged. "I've a feeling he's not." It was the best he could do.

"I think if he were alive he'd have come back to see the child. Jordi had a warm heart."

"Yes," he said, perhaps too drily.

"He didn't like you," Maria del Mar said.

I didn't like him either, he wanted to tell her, but when Josep looked at her he knew he was seeing raw wounds, and he stood and told her gently not to allow anything to keep her from coming to him again if Francesc needed him.

31

Old Debts

*I*n a couple of days Francesc was visiting him again with regularity, looking as energetic as ever. Josep liked the child, but the situation was awkward. He and Maria del Mar were carefully friendly in the presence of others, but he believed that Clemente Ramirez had spread the word that they were connected, and the village took note that he was spending a lot of his time with her son.

The village was quick to jump to conclusions, right or wrong.

One evening as Josep walked to Nivaldo's, he passed Tonio Casals lounging before the church with Eduardo Montroig, Esteve's older brother. Josep thought that Eduardo was nice enough but far too serious for someone who was not an old man. Eduardo rarely smiled, and at the moment, Josep thought, he appeared particularly uncomfortable as Tonio lectured him about something in a loud and truculent voice. Tonio Casals was a big and handsome man, like his father, but there the similarity ended, because he was often an ugly drunk. Josep had no desire to join in their conversation, so he wished them both a good evening and would have passed.

Tonio smiled. "Ah, the prodigal. How does it feel to plow your own land again, Alvarez?"

"It feels good, Tonio."

"And how does it feel to plow a woman better men have broken in, eh?"

Josep took a moment to keep himself in check. "Once you get past the tiny used bit, it's truly wonderful, Tonio," he said pleasantly.

A big fist smacked into the side of his mouth as Tonio flung himself at him. Josep hit back in a fury with two fast, hard punches, his left fist striking into the side of Tonio's jaw, his right fist solidly finding the place under the other man's left eye. Tonio went down almost at once, and to Josep's later shame he drew back his foot and kicked the fallen man. And spat at him, like an enraged small boy.

"Ah, Josep, no, no!" Eduardo Montroig said, placing a cautionary hand on his arm.

They looked down at Tonio. Josep's mouth was bleeding and he licked his lip. He told Montroig of his reason for deceiving the wine buyer. "Eduardo, Maria del Mar and I. We are just neighbors. Please tell people that."

Eduardo nodded seriously. "Maria del Mar is a good sort. Oh, Déu. This one is disgusting, no? When we were younger, he was such a good fellow."

"Shall we try to take him home?"

Montroig shook his head. "You go along. I'll fetch his father and his brothers." He sighed. "Unfortunately, they are very accustomed to taking charge when Tonio is like this," he said.

The next morning Josep was pruning his vines when Angel Casals came to the vineyard.

"Good morning, Alcalde."

"Good morning, Josep." Breathing heavily, the alcalde took a large red handkerchief from his pocket and mopped his face.

"Let me get you some wine," Josep said, but the older man shook his head. "Too early."

"Then . . . some water?"

"Water would be good, if you please."

Josep went into the house and came out with two cups and a cántir. He gestured respectfully toward the bench by the door, and the two of them sat and drank.

"I'm come to make certain you're all right."

"Oh, I am fine, Alcalde."

"Your mouth?"

"It's nothing, just a mark of my shame. I shouldn't have hit him at all, for he was drunk. I should have walked away."

"I doubt that would have been possible. I've talked to Eduardo, and I know my son Tonio. I apologize in his name.

"My son . . . For him each swallow of brandy is a plague. It takes only a little taste, and his soul and his body cry for more, but little more than a sip and, sadly, he becomes crazy and acts like a beast. It is his cross to bear, and his family's."

"I'm all right, Alcalde. I hope I didn't cause him real injury."

"He will be all right also. He has a swollen eye. He looks a lot worse than you do."

Josep's lips hurt as he smiled ruefully. "I suspect that if ever we fight while he is sober, the results will be sad for me."

"You will not fight him again. He is leaving Santa Eulália."

"Oh?"

"Yes. Since he is unable to perform a first son's responsibility to our farm, each day he remains here reminds him of his weakness. I have a lifelong friend, Ignasi de Balcells, who has olive groves in the village of Las Granyas. For many years Don Ignasi was the alcalde of that village. Now he is a justice of the court there, and as well he serves as the alguacil, the director of the regional jail. He has known my son all of Tonio's life and loves him. Ignasi is accustomed to dealing with the weaknesses of men, and he has offered to take Tonio into his own house. He will teach him to grow olives and make oil, and Tonio also will work in the jail. And we devoutly hope, he will learn to discipline himself."

The alcalde smiled. "Between the two of us, Alvarez . . . my friend Ignasi has an incentive to succeed with my son. He has an unwed daughter, a good girl but nearly beyond the age of marrying. I wasn't born last week. I think Ignasi will try to reform Tonio into a son-in-law."

"I hope it works out well for him," Josep said awkwardly.

"I believe you, and I thank you." Angel Casals looked about, casting an approving glance at the neatly pruned vines, the recently planted rose bushes, the soil plowed and banked against the rows. "You're a *farmer*, Josep Alvarez," he said."Unlike one I could name who is not a farmer but a butterfly, a damn papallona," the alcalde added thinly, looking beyond Josep's land to the tangled and nondescript vineyard of Quim Torras.

Josep kept his silence. It was well known that the alcalde was an angry denouncer of Quim's relationship with the village priest, but Josep didn't want to discuss either Quim or Father Lopez with Angel Casals.

Casals rose from the bench and so did Josep. "Another moment, Alcalde, if you please," he said.

He went into the house and came out with some coins that he placed into Angel's hand.

"And . . . this is for?"

"Payment for two hens . . ."

Angel cocked his head.

". . . That I stole from you five years ago."

"The hell you say," Angel said fiercely. "Why did you steal from me?"

"I needed the chickens badly, and I had no money to pay you."

"So why do you pay me now?"

Josep shrugged and told the truth. "I can't stand even to walk past your damned henhouse."

"What a sensitive thief it is!" The alcalde looked down at the coins. "You have paid too much," he said sternly. He reached into his pocket, found a small coin, and handed it to Josep.

"An honest thief must not cheat himself either, Alvarez," he said, and his loud laughter spilled over.

32

The Intruder

*L*ate in February the first pale yellow-green buds appeared, and as winter turned to spring, Josep spent long days working in the vineyard, finishing the pruning and pulling the banked soil away from the base of the vines. By April the small tender leaves were open, and soon after that the sun turned warmer and more ardent, and flowers made the vineyard heady with their scent.

His father had always said that grapes would be ready for picking one hundred days after the flowers appeared. The blossoms attracted the insects that pollinated them and made grapes possible, but the green vines attracted destructive animals as well.

Francesc was with him the morning Josep discovered half a dozen plants lying in ruins, uprooted and chewed. The damage was done in the rear of his property, near the base of the ridge. There were tracks in the soil.

"Be damned," he whispered and had to stop himself from saying worse in front of the child.

"Why are the vines broken, Josep?"

"Wild pig," he told the boy.

Quim Torras had lost vines, too—eight vines—though Maria del Mar had not.

That evening Josep sought out Jaumet Ferrer and asked him to hunt down the pig before it damaged more of the vineyards.

Jaumet came and squatted on his heels near the wasted vines.

"The tracks were made by a boar, I think just one rascal. All the sows and . . . ah . . . you know, the young ones?"

"Shoats," Josep offered.

"Shoats." Jaumet tasted the word. "Sows and shoats bunch together. The boars wander off alone. This one probably stays close to the river because of the dryness. He went for the roots of your vines. Pigs will eat anything. Dead meat. A live lamb or a calf."

Josep asked Maria del Mar to keep Francesc home and in her sight for a while.

Jaumet came before dawn with his long hunting rifle and patrolled their vineyards all day under the hot sun. After dusk when it became too dark to see, he went home.

He returned before dawn the next morning, and the morning after that. But he told Josep that the following day he was going to hunt rabbits and birds. "The wild pig may never bother you again," Jaumet said.

"Or," he said carefully, "he may."

The following morning Josep left the casa very early, and as he entered the vineyard he heard animal noises among the vines deep in the plantings. Seizing a rock in each hand, he ran. He made too much sound, for he reached the invaded row just in time to see the back and the long tasseled tail as the boar darted into Quim's vines.

He threw both rocks and ran after it, shouting senselessly, but lost it almost at once. When he ran into the Vall vineyard, he startled both Maria del Mar and Francesc, who had seen nothing of the animal.

Maria del Mar frowned as she listened to his description of the boar.

"He can *cost* us. So what shall we do? Call Jaumet again?"

"No. Jaumet can't stay among our vines permanently."

"Then, what?"

"I'll think of something," Josep said.

He remembered exactly where to dig for the two packets he had buried in the neglected sandy corner where Quim's land touched his own, and he found them remarkably unharmed by the rare rains that had drained past them through the porous soil. He brushed the packages carefully until they were free of the coarse sand and then brought them into the house and cut the cords and unwrapped them on the table. The outer layer of wrapping was browned by contact with soil minerals, but the two inner layers of oilcloth appeared absolutely unmarked and in excellent condition, and so did the contents of both packets. The parts of the LeMat revolver were covered with so much grease that it took him until very late that night to wipe them free, using every available rag that he owned and then sacrificing an old shirt, a bit ragged but still wearable. He tore it up, and he had only one square left when the assembled gun lay in front of him denuded of grease, freshly oiled, clean and shiny and scaring him because he had hoped never to see it again.

He laid out the contents of the second packet and loaded the cartridges very slowly and carefully, at first uncertain that he remembered exactly how it was done, pouring the powder from the stocking into the leather measuring sack and from the sack into one of the empty chambers.

The gun and the act of loading brought him to memories he preferred to avoid, and for a time he had to stop because his hands were trembling, but he placed a lead ball into the chamber and pulled the loading lever to drive it into the powder, dabbed a bit of grease over the powder and ball, and used the capping tool to set a percussion cap over everything. Then he moved the cylinder by hand and loaded all the other chambers except two, because he found there was only enough powder in the stocking to provide seven loads.

He tidied up the table and placed the LeMat on the mantel next to his mother's clock. Then he went upstairs and lay awake in the bed for a long time, afraid that if he slept he would dream.

33

Cracks

*F*or almost a week the vine-destroying boar was the subject whenever villagers spoke with one another, but the wild pig didn't appear again, and soon it was replaced in their conversations by heated arguments about the door of the church, which was dented, battered, and gouged. Local legend said that it had been ruined by the musket-butts of Napoleon's soldiers, but Josep's father had talked knowingly about a village alcoholic and a hand-held rock. A long and jagged crack also marred the wood, a surface opening that didn't harm the structural intergrity of the door but was threatening to split the village community. Parishioners had attempted several times to fill the fissure with putties made of various ingredients, but the break was too wide and deep, and every unsightly attempt had failed. The church had enough money to buy a new wooden door, and some felt this should be done, while others were unwilling to empty the church treasury lest a more important emergency should arise. A small minority, led by Quim Torras, thought that a priest with Padre Lopez's sensibilities deserved a more elegant door on his church. Quim proposed an artistic door with carvings in a religious motif, and he urged that the village begin to raise funds.

One morning Josep was going to the well for water when he met Angel Casals.

"So. What do *you* think about the church door?"

Josep rubbed his nose. In truth, he had given little consideration to the church door, but the thought of any unexpected drain on his meager cash alarmed him. People said that for years Angel had watched over a small village fund, never making public the amount of money in the village treasury, never wanting to spend a centivo because no emergency was ever large enough for him to touch the fund.

"I wouldn't care for a tax to raise the money, Alcalde."

"There will be no tax to support the church!" Angel growled. "No one wishes to pay it. One may as well try to squeeze wine from a stone."

"I don't think we need the kind of door that graces a cathedral. We have a very nice country church. It needs a plain wooden door, stout and good-looking. If it were up to me I would spend some of the money for lumber. We should be able to fashion a suitable door and still leave the church a portion of its funds."

The alcalde looked at him with interest. "You are right, Alvarez, you are right! Do you know where to buy proper lumber?"

"I believe I do," Josep said. "At least I can make inquiries."

"Then please do so, Josep," Angel said with satisfaction.

Late the following afternoon, when the sun had moved low in the sky and Josep's body was signaling that soon it would be good to end a long day of labor, he heard the dreaded noise.

He stopped the pruning at once and froze. He listened . . .

Listened, and the sound came to him again, an energetic snapping of vegetation that caused him to move at once to the house. The LeMat hadn't been touched since he had placed it on the mantel. He took the revolver into the vineyard and moved down the rows as quietly as he was able, hearing the sound louder now. He held the revolver pointed forward, ready to fire but telling himself not to shoot too quickly, lest the sound was being made by Francesc, or perhaps by Quim.

But in the next moment he saw the boar, larger than he would have thought from the glimpse he had had earlier.

The boar had thick black-brown fur, unlike any domestic pig. His body was bulky and dense, the head scarily huge in proportion, and the legs were short but wide and looked strong. The animal stared, seemingly fearless but wary, his eyes small and dark above the flatness of the black leather nose.

It's just a pig, Josep told himself.

Tusks!

Josep saw the tusks clearly, two small ones pointing downward from the corners of the upper jaw, two longer ones rising from the corners of the lower jaw, perhaps twelve or fifteen centimeters long, curving to wicked points. The boar gave a coughing grunt and tossed his head up with a long thrust. Josep knew that was how it would fight, using the tusks to disembowel.

The boar lurched sideways to flee, and Josep was suddenly perfectly cold and cruel.

He led the animal only slightly, his arm rigid and controlled, and his finger barely caressed the trigger. The roar was loud. He saw the bullet punch into fur just behind the right shoulder, then the boar stopped and turned and took one running step toward Josep, who fired two more shots from the revolver, straight at him.

Three shots.

(*Flat, barking reports. The man in the stalled carriage, doom already in his face, twisting and grimacing as the bullets found his body. Horses bucking, carriage thrashing. Enric screaming shrilly, like a woman. Running, everyone running.*)

He had forgotten the puff of smoke that appeared with every shot, and the smell of something burning.

The wild pig veered off and ran straight into the only cover, a clump of brush at the foot of the ridge. Suddenly it was very quiet. Josep stood there, trembling and staring at the stand of tall growth into which the animal had disappeared.

Time passed slowly, perhaps half an hour spent with his eyes nervously fixed on the stand of brush, his gun at the ready. But the boar didn't come out.

Presently Jaumet was there with his rifle.

"I heard the shots." Jaumet studied the bright spilled blood that led into the brush stand. "Best we wait."

Josep nodded, drawing great relief from his presence.

The two of them stood, watching.

They waited for perhaps an hour, but nothing happened.

"Together," Jaumet whispered finally, gesturing with his rifle. Rifle and pistol pointed, the two of them walked to the thicket.

Josep's heart was pounding. He pictured the boar about to charge out at them as Jaumet parted the foliage.

But nothing was there.

The trail of blood on the underbrush led to the base of the ridge, and they could see an opening under an overhang of rock and earth. Jaumet signaled a retreat.

"Some kind of den. He's in there."

"Do you think he's alive?"

Jaumet shrugged.

"It will be dark in a couple of hours." Josep was worried. If the wounded boar still lived and got away from them during the night, it could be very dangerous.

"We need a pole," Jaumet said.

Josep went to the house and got the axe. He walked to the river and cut and trimmed a young tree.

Jaumet nodded when he saw the pole. He set his rifle against a vine and motioned Josep to follow him to the den.

"Be ready," he said and squatted before the opening. He poked the pole into it, prodded and jumped back. Then he laughed and returned and pushed the pole again and again.

"Rascal is dead."

"Are you certain?"

Jaumet reached into the opening and began to pull, grunting with the effort.

Josep held the LeMat pointed at the carcass as it began to emerge from the hole, first the hooved rear legs and the tail, then the bristly haunches.

They stared at the bloody wounds.

The boar was indisputably dead, but somehow he looked unconquered and fierce, and Josep still feared him. His teeth were green and appeared to be very sharp. One of the lower tusks was cracked like the split in the church door, the break running from the sharp point all the way into the boar's flesh.

"That tusk must have pained him," Josep said.

Jaumet nodded. "Their meat is good, Josep."

"It's the wrong season to be butchering. Everybody's too busy in the vineyards. I am myself. And if tomorrow's warm . . ."

Jaumet removed his long knife from its scabbard. Josep watched as he made a long diagonal cut across the back of the pig, and two vertical cuts, and then peeled away a large flap of skin and a layer of fat. Beneath it he cut out and removed two generous square pieces of pink meat.

"The lomo, the best part. One piece for you, one for me."

The bloody remains, with two gaping holes in its back, looked badly used. But by the time Josep placed the meat inside the house, Jaumet had found two shovels among the tools and was waiting for him to select a spot on the property where it was all right to dig.

Josep gave his piece of meat to Maria del Mar, who—at first—didn't seem terribly happy to receive it. She had put in a full day of hard work herself and was not enthusiastic about the necessity to cook the pork at once, before it could spoil. But she was also relieved that the threat of the boar had been removed, so her thanks were sincere.

"You will come tomorrow and eat it with us," she said, not quite grudgingly.

So the next evening he sat at table with Maria del Mar and Francesc. She had stewed the lomo with root vegetables and dried plums, and he admitted to himself that the result was even better than what he could do with a rabbit.

34

Wood

One evening as he walked through Santa Eulália, he saw a group of boys laughing, shouting insults at one another, tussling on the ground like animals. They were youths teetering on the edge of young manhood, still children in many ways, and too soon those who were not first sons would face unemployment, the rough ways of the world, and the problems of dealing with the future.

That night he dreamed of village boys challenging each other and carrying on—but these were *his boys*, Esteve with his crooked smile; sullen Jordi; earnest, round-faced Xavier; Manel laughing at Enric as he pinned him to the ground; smart Guillem watching everyone quietly. When he awoke, he lay in his bed and wondered why all of them were gone—why they would be boys forever—while he had survived to worry about ordinary things.

He was working within view of the road that afternoon when, to his surprise and great pleasure, Emilio Rivera drove up in a small wagon pulled by a single horse.

"Ah, so you had business nearby?" Josep said after they had exchanged greetings, and Rivera shook his head. "It was the beautiful weather of spring," he said sheepishly. "I tasted the warm sea breeze and knew I couldn't stay inside the cooperage. What the hell, I thought, I'll ride up into the pretty hills and fix that vat, the one that's troubling young Alvarez."

When Josep ushered him to the vat in question, Rivera examined it and nodded. In the wagon he had brought some oak boards, split with the grain and already nicely tongued and grooved. Soon, while Josep returned to his work on the vines, from the shed at the rear of the house came the comforting sounds of sawing and hammering.

It took Rivera several hours of labor before he came out into the vineyard and declared the vat repaired and guaranteed to be unleakable. Considering the trip and the amount of work the man had done, Josep steeled himself for bad news when he asked what he owed, but the answer left him grateful and clearly in Rivera's debt. He wished it were possible to cook the cooper dinner in gratitude, a rabbit or a chicken, but instead he did the next best thing, and soon the two of them were seated at Nivaldo's small table, drinking sour wine with the grocer and eating great bowls of his stew.

"There is something I'd like to show you," Josep said when they had finished, and he took Rivera next door to examine the ill-used entrance to the church.

"What would it cost for wood to replace this door?"

Rivera groaned. "Alvarez, *Alvarez*! Have you a single profitable project to bring to me?"

Josep grinned. "Some day, perhaps. I should have plied you with a bit more wine before showing you this door."

"You say you want only the wood? You'll do the work yourselves?"

"Just the wood."

"Well, I have some good oak boards. They'll cost more than the rough plank you got for your wagon. These will have to be nicely planed, so they can be sanded and stained to make a handsome door . . . But I'd keep the price of the wood down, for a church."

"How would I go about putting the boards together?"

"How would you *put them together. . . ?*" Rivera stared at him.

He shook his head. "Well, for a little more money, Juan could cut squared channels into the sides of the boards, and he could make wooden strips, called splines, that are twice as wide as the channels are deep.

"You coat a channel with glue and tap the spline into it. Next, you coat the channel in the side of another board, and you fit that board onto the exposed part of the spline, carefully tapping until the edges of the boards are tightly joined."

Josep listened attentively.

"Then you put the boards in some nice, big clamps and leave them overnight, until the glue has dried."

"Big clamps?"

"Big, tight clamps. You have someone in the village who owns big clamps?"

"No."

They regarded each other in silence.

". . . You own clamps such as that?" Josep asked.

"Big clamps are very expensive," Rivera said dourly. "I don't allow mine to be taken out of the cooperage." He sighed. "Look. Damn it to hell. I'll be using the clamps myself for the next two weeks. But if you show up at my shop two weeks from tomorrow . . . By *yourself*—By Déu, do not bring a committee from the church into my cooperage! I won't need to use the clamps for that week and I'll allow you to work quietly, alone in a corner. You can assemble and finish the door yourself. Juan and I will keep an eye on you, so you don't get into a shit of trouble, but otherwise you won't bother us. Agreed?"

"Oh . . . agreed, senyor," Josep said.

For the next two weeks he labored in his vineyard with new purpose, for he needed to complete the bulk of his work before he could spend his time on the door.

On the day specified he rode Hinny down from the highlands and was at the cooperage by mid-day.

Rivera greeted him gruffly, but by then Josep was accustomed to his personality. Rivera had cut lengths of string to the measurements of the old church door before he had left Santa Eulália, and he had five nicely planed and channeled boards waiting for Josep, as well as four splines and a receipt for Josep to give to the church. The cost of the boards was reasonable, but when Josep had stacked them on the table in the promised corner, he examined them anxiously, realizing that if they should be ruined by his lack of skill, he would be responsible for their expense.

Yet Emilio Rivera had not left him too much he could ruin. It took him surprisingly little time to join the first two boards, following Rivera's instructions precisely, placing a battered block first on the spline and then on the second board to absorb the shock of the tapping hammer without marring the wood. Rivera ignored him, but Juan checked his work quickly and then showed him how to set the heavy clamps that were necessary to hold the boards together under pressure while the glue dried, and Josep left the cooperage while there were still several hours left in the afternoon.

With new knowledge of how long he needed to spend each day making the door, he was able to work five or six hours in the vineyard before leaving for Sitges. This meant that it was almost dusk before he could leave the cooperage and ride Hinny back onto the road to the south, but it was worth it to get the extra few hours with the vines, and he found it pleasant to ride back to the village through the darkness and cool night air.

On the third evening, as he left Sitges, his route took him through a section of small houses along the waterfront. Most were the homes of fishermen, but in front of one house women stood and spoke soft invitations to passing men.

He was sorely tempted but repelled, for most of them were hard-looking, unattractive females whose garish cosmetics could not disguise how pitilessly they had been used by life. So he had ridden past one of the women before something about her features struck a chord of memory, and he turned Hinny and came back to her.

"Lonely, senyor?"

"Renata? Is it you?"

She wore a wrinkled black dress that clung to her, and a dark kerchief knotted about her head. She had lost weight and her body appeared more seductive but she looked older than her age and terribly tired. "Yes, I am Renata." She peered at him. "Who is it, then?"

"Josep Alvarez. From Santa Eulália."

"From Santa Eulália. You wish my company, Josep?"

"Yes."

"So come in here, amor meu, to my room."

She waited while he tethered Hinny to a rail in front of the neighboring house, then he followed her up a flight of urine-scented stairs. A burly man in a white suit sat at a table at the top of the stairs and nodded to Renata as they passed.

The room was small and dirty—a sleeping mat, an oil lamp, soiled clothes heaped in two corners.

"I had been away for years. When I returned I went looking for you, but you were gone."

"Yes." She was nervous. Speaking rapidly, she told him what she was going to do to give him pleasure. It was obvious she didn't remember him.

"I came to your mother's house to see you, with Nivaldo Machado, the grocer of Santa Eulália."

"With Nivaldo!"

He had started to disrobe and saw her reach for the lamp. "No. Leave it on, if you please, the way it was then," he said.

She looked at him and shrugged. Hiking the hem of her dress up around her hips, she sank to the mat and waited for him.

"Won't you at least remove the head scarf?" he said, bothered but half joking, and reaching down, he pulled it from her head as her hand moved too late to prevent him.

The front half of her scalp was bald, shiny with sweat, while the hair of the other half was matted and patchy, like dried turf.

". . . What is it?"

"I don't know. Some little illness you can't catch from being with me this once," she said sullenly. She reached to undo his trousers, but he moved away.

On her legs, a blotchy rash.

"Renata . . . Renata, I'll wait." He took another step back and saw her face dissolve and her shoulders begin to shake, though she made no sound.

"Please . . ." She looked at the door.

"He gets so cross," she whispered.

Josep reached into his pocket and took out whatever money was there, and her hand closed over it. "Senyor," she said, wiping her eyes, "this thing will not last long. I don't think it is the pox, but even if it should be, the pox goes away after a month or two, and then one is all right. One is perfect again. You will come to see me after it is gone?"

"Of course. Of course, Renata."

He went out of the room and down the stairs, and when he remounted, he kicked Hinny into a trot until they were well beyond the town.

35

Changes

*W*hen the joining of the door was completed, Josep worked hour after hour sanding the wood until it was a smooth, unbroken surface. He stained it a deep rich green, the only color Emilio Rivera had to offer him, and then finished with three coats of varnish, each layer burnished with fine-grit sandpaper until the final coat glowed and felt like glass.

He carried the finished door home in the wagon on a bed of blankets. Once it was safely in the village unmarred, he allowed the men of the church to assume responsibility for hanging it, which they did with dispatch, utilizing the bronze brackets taken from the old door.

He was reimbursed for the cost of the wood, and a small dedication ceremony was held. Padre Felipe accepted the door and gave thanks with a blessing, and the alcalde spoke warmly of Josep's contribution of his time and energy, which embarrassed him.

"Why did you do that?" Maria del Mar asked him the next day when she met him on the road. "You don't even go to Mass!"

He shook his head and shrugged, unable to explain it to her, just as he was unable to explain anything to her.

To his astonishment, the answer to her question suddenly came to him. He had not done it for the church.

He had done it for his village.

Five days after the new door was dedicated, two middle-aged clerics came into the village in a carriage pulled by a pair of horses. They entered the church and were inside with Padre Felipe Lopez for half a day; then they emerged alone and went into the grocery with the driver. The three men ate bread and sausage and drank well water before getting back into the carriage and riding away.

That evening, Nivaldo told Josep about the priests' brief visit, but neither of them learned anything more for three more days, when Padre Felipe said goodby to several people and, after twelve years of service as pastor of the village church, left Santa Eulália for all time.

The gossip spread quickly and astounded the village. The riders had been monsignors from the diocesan Office of Vocations in Barcelona. The prelates had come to tell Padre Felipe that he had been summarily transferred, reassigned to become confessor to the congregation of religious women at the Convent of the Royal Barefoot Nuns, in the diocese of Madrid.

For only five days the church was without a pastor, and then one afternoon a tired old horse pulled a hired hack across the bridge, carrying a thin, saturnine priest in a wide-brimmed black hat. When the priest left the carriage, his eyes, behind the thick lenses of spectacles, slowly inspected the plaça before he carried his bag into the church.

The alcalde hastened to the parish house to call as soon as he heard of the arrival, and subsequently Angel went to the grocery and reported to Nivaldo and several customers who were present that the new priest was Padre Pio Dominguez, a native of Salamanca, who came to Santa Eulália after a decade of being an associate pastor in Girona.

That Sunday those who attended Mass found it strange to see that the black-robed figure consecrating the Eucharist was a tall and slender stranger instead of the familiar sight of the rotund Padre Felipe. In place of Padre Felipe's alternately jolly and unctuous style, the new priest spoke sparely, his homily a puzzling story of why the Madre Maria one day had sent an angel into a poor family's home to bring everyone the love of Jesús in the form of a jug of water that turned into wine.

It was a Sunday morning like any other Sunday morning, except that a different priest stood by the door as everyone left the church. Surprisingly few people in Santa Eulália appeared to care.

Over the next week the alcalde accompanied Padre Pio into all of the homes, calling upon the village families one by one. They reached Josep on the third day, when he was midway through the afternoon's work. Nevertheless, he broke off what he had been doing and invited them to sit on the bench. He served them wine, watching the priest's face as he took his first sips. Padre Pio drank manfully, but Josep took approving note that he did not try to compliment the terrible stuff.

"I think it would be a blessing, Padre, if the Madre or the Lord could once in a while turn our wine into water," Josep said.

The priest didn't smile, but something flickered in his eyes. "I do not believe you were in the church on Sunday, senyor."

It was not an accusation, merely a statement of fact.

"No Padre, I was not."

"Yet you refer to my homily?"

"In this village, each bit of news is shared and received like good bread."

"It was Josep who made our church's new door," Angel said. "A handsome door, is it not, Padre?"

"Handsome, indeed. An excellent door, and your labor, a generous contribution." Now the priest smiled. "I hope you remember that your church door opens wide." He drank all of his wine and stood. "We will allow you to return to your work, Senyor Alvarez," he said, as though he could read Josep's mind.

Angel motioned with his chin toward Quim's property. "Do you know when he will return? We tried at his house, but no one answered our knock."

Josep shrugged. "I don't know, Alcalde."

"Well," Angel told the priest distastefully, "you will no doubt see a lot of him, Padre, for he seems to be a very religious man."

Josep liked to walk at night along the rows of vines among which he spent his days working. That was why he was at the familiar edge of his vineyard in the darkness that night, when he heard the unfamiliar sound. For a panicked moment he supposed it was another boar, but he knew at once it was raw sobbing, a human noise, and he followed it off his own property.

He almost stumbled over the body in the weedy growth.

"Ahh, my God . . ." The words sounded so wounded.

Josep knew the hoarse voice.

"Quim?"

The man continued to sob. Josep could smell the brandy, and he knelt to him.

"Come, Quim. Come on, old friend, let me take you to the house." Josep raised Quim with difficulty. Half dragging and half supporting, he moved toward his neighbor's casa, Quim's legs loose and unhelpful. Inside the house, Josep fumbled in the dark until he got the oil lamp lit, but he made no attempt to get Quim upstairs. Instead he went by himself to the fetid upper room and came down with the sleeping pallet, which he spread on the kitchen floor.

Quim had stopped weeping. He sat with his back to the wall and watched dully as Josep assembled and lighted a small fire and set the pan of cold coffee, perhaps days old, on the grate. There was a chunk of hard bread in the breadbox. Quim took the bread when Josep handed it to him and held it in his hand, but he didn't eat it. When the coffee was hot, Josep poured some into a cup and blew on it until it was drinkable, then he held it to the other man's mouth.

Quim took a sip and groaned.

Josep knew the coffee must be terrible but didn't remove the cup. "Just another swallow," he said, "with a bite of the bread."

But Quim was weeping again, silently this time, his face turned away.

In a few moments he sighed and scrubbed at his eyes with the fist still holding the bread. "It was goddamned Angel Casals."

Josep was confused. "What was?"

"Angel Casals, that piece of filth. It was Angel got Padre Felipe transferred."

"No! Angel?"

"Yes, yes, the alcalde, the ignorant, dirty old bastard couldn't stand to look at us. We knew."

"You can't be certain," Josep said.

"I'm certain! The alcalde wanted us out of his village. He knows someone who knows somebody else who is high up in the church, in Barcelona. That's all it took. I've been *told*."

"I'm sorry, Quim." But Josep was unable to offer healing or even comfort. "You must try to pull yourself together. I'll drop by tomorrow and knock on your door. Will you be all right if I leave you alone?"

Quim didn't answer. Then he looked at Josep and nodded.

Josep turned to leave. Stopped by a vision of Quim knocking over the light and spilling flaming oil, he picked up the lamp. In the entry he extinguished it and set it safely out of the way. "Goodnight then, Quim," he said, and after a moment he closed the door on the silent darkness.

In the morning he went early to the grocery and bought bread and cheese and olives and left the food and a jar of fresh water on Quim's doorstep. On his way home he passed the place where he had found his sodden abutter spilling his grief among the vines. Nearby, Josep discovered the broken pieces of an empty brandy bottle that had struck a stone when it was thrown, and he picked up the pieces gingerly before he allowed himself the welcome relief of his own work.

36

A Talk with Quim

*J*osep loved to see what the advent of summer did to his vines. In Languedoc he had pruned varieties of grapes that were not as robust as the grapes native to Spain, French vines that had to be supported on expensive wire strung to posts along each row. On his own land Josep pruned as the Spanish vines had always been prepared by his family, so that each became self-supporting, shaped like a strong green vase with its branches reaching for the sun.

In contrast to his carefully tended vineyard Quim Torras's land was a jungle, the vines poorly hacked or ignored, the weeds rampant and tall. Quim seemed to be avoiding Josep, perhaps out of embarrassment. Nivaldo told Josep that his neighbor was eating evening meals more or less regularly at the grocery. Twice, Josep met him in the lane and paused as if to talk, but Quim hurried by, his eyes red and his glance averted, and both times Josep saw that his walk was unsteady.

So Josep was surprised but pleased late one evening when Quim knocked on his door and appeared to be serious and sober. Josep greeted him warmly and ushered him inside. He offered bread and chorizo and cheese, but Quim shook his head and thanked him faintly.

"There is something I need to discuss."

"Of course."

Quim appeared to be searching for the proper way to begin. Finally, he sighed and blurted the words. "I am leaving Santa Eulália."

"Going away, Quim? For how long?"

Quim smiled faintly. "For always."

"What?" Josep looked at him in concern. "Where are you going?"

"I have a cousin in San Lorenzo de El Escorial, a fine woman to whom I'm devoted. She has a laundry in San Lorenzo, doing washing for nobles and the wealthy, a good business. She is growing old. Last year she urged me to come and live with her, to help her operate the laundry. At that time I told her I couldn't go. But now . . . "

"Are you allowing Angel to run you out of our village?" Josep got along well with Angel, but he didn't admire his treatment of Quim.

Quim dismissed the idea with a wave of his hand. "Angel Casals is of no importance." He looked at Josep. "San Lorenzo is not close to Madrid, but it is not too far, and I will be able to meet with Father Felipe on occasion. You see?"

Josep saw.

". . . And what will become of your vineyard, Quim?"

"I shall sell it."

Josep thought he understood. "You desire me to deal with Angel for you?"

"Angel? He's no longer looking for land for Tonio. Besides, that bastard never will own my land."

"But . . . there is no one else."

"There is you."

Josep didn't know whether to laugh or cry. "I have no money to buy your land!" Surely Quim must realize that, he thought in annoyance. "It takes every penny I have to make the payments to my brother and his wife," he said bitterly. "After I sell the grapes, I have little left for luxuries like food. Wake up, man!"

Quim looked at him stubbornly. "Work my land the way you work your own, sell the grapes. I won't make life difficult for you. I need a little money now, and a little money when you harvest the first crop of grapes from my land, just so I can get started in San Lorenzo. After that, whenever you have a bit to spare, send it to me. I don't care if it takes you many years to pay me for the vineyard."

Josep was frightened by this new complication, sensing danger. He wished Quim had never knocked on his door.

"Are you drunk, Quim? Are you certain you know what you are doing?"

Quim smiled. "I am not drunk. Ah, I am not." He patted Josep's arm. "It is not as though I have my choice of many buyers," he said quietly.

Josep had learned something from Rosa. "We must have a paper. We must each sign."

Quim shrugged. "So, bring me a paper," he said.

37

Rites of Passage

*H*e sat at his table for most of the night, the oil lamp throwing yellow light and dark shadows crazily about the room as he shifted about in his chair, reading and restudying his copy of the agreement that had allowed him to buy his land from Rosa and Donat.

Finally he got ink powder, a dull pen nib in a wooden holder, and two pieces of folded paper, all taken from a small box in which his father had put them away, who knew how long ago. One of the pieces of paper had started out white, and the other was brown and somewhat wrinkled; he didn't care which he would give to Quim and which he would keep. He placed a little of the black powder in a cup, added water, and stirred it with a stick of dried vine until it became ink.

Then he began to copy most of the document that had been prepared by Rosa's cousin, the attorney. Josep was not an experienced scribe. He clutched the pen almost desperately. Sometimes the point of the nib caught in the surface of the paper, sending a little spray of ink next to the word he was writing. Several times he neglected to brush the dipped nib against the rim of the cup to release excess ink, which left fat, black blots on the paper, twice obliterating half a word, so that he had to cross out the remaining letters and write the word again. Long before he was half through transcribing the first copy, he was sweating and exceedingly cranky.

He spent a long time thinking about a fair price for Quim's land. The Torras vineyard had been neglected and poorly tended by several generations of growers, and it didn't seem fair to Josep that the tract would be worth as much as his family's carefully husbanded piece. At the same time, he knew that Quim was letting his vineyard go to him under terms that were incredibly generous. In the end, he valued the Torras land as equal to the price he had paid for his father's property, without the fraternal discount he had demanded and received from Donat as his right, and he copied the first agreement verbatim except for four changes. The names of buyer and seller were different, the date was different, and he omitted any mention of the frequency with which payments would be made, or any indication that there would be a penalty for missed payments.

Quim couldn't read. Josep read the document to him slowly, in a voice that was too loud. From time to time he stopped and asked if Quim had any questions, but there were none. Quim had learned to print his own name, and when Josep had finished he picked up the pen, dipped it in the ink, and scrawled the letters on both copies.

Josep signed also, and then he counted out the first payment and handed it over. The transaction seemed unreal and perhaps unjustified; he felt guilty, as though he were bilking his neighbor of the Torras family property.

"Are you certain, Quim? We can still tear this up and call it off."

"I'm certain."

Josep gave Quim the contract written on the white paper and kept the copy on the brown paper for himself.

Two days later, he harnessed Hinny and drove Quim to Sitges, where Quim would take an ox-pulled diligéncia west. The coach made many stops and was far slower than the train, but it was also much cheaper. It was owned and driven by an old friend of Quim's, Jonatán Cadafalch, to whom Quim introduced Josep. "When you wish to send me a message," he said—by which Josep knew he meant, *when you wish to send me a payment*—"give the message to Jonatán, and he will see that it reaches me."

Quim and he had never been close, but Josep was curiously moved when they said goodbye. Quim was a bad and careless farmer and a sot, but also a good soul, a merry spirit, a forgiving and easy neighbor, a link to his childhood and to his father. They exchanged a long, tight abrazo.

Then Quim gave Jonatán his bag and climbed into the diligéncia, along with another man and a pair of elderly nuns. Jonatán clambered onto his seat, took the reins, cracked his whip, and the oxen pulled the carriage away.

When Josep returned home, he saw to Hinny's comfort and then went into the vineyard.

It was strange.

A paper signed, a little money handed over, and the invisible boundary between the Alvarez vineyard and the Torras vineyard had disappeared.

Yet he knew that in his mind the boundary would always remain, fainter and no longer forbidding, but a marking off place between his father's land . . .

. . . And his own new land.

He ventured into what used to be his neighbor's vineyard and studied the morass of wild growth with new dismay. It was one thing to note with dispassionate disapproval the neglect of someone else's crop and quite another to face the realization that he now owned responsibility for the rampant weeds that were sucking food and moisture from the vines.

Quim had simply walked away leaving multiple problems, his tools dull and needing oil, his house a stinking mess, his vines fighting for light and air.

Josep would have to deal with everything, but he knew his priority. In his own toolroom he found his father's scythe and a file, and he sharpened the blade until it was dangerous to test it with his finger.

Then he took off his shirt and carried the scythe into Quim's vineyard. In a moment he began the shearing, the blade brought high, his arms swinging it down to hiss as it cut, lifting as it passed through, pulling it back high again to make another arc. Josep mowed smoothly . . . swing . . . swing . . . swing. He marched forward slowly and steadily, leaving behind him a cleared space between the rows of vines.

The next day he harnessed Hinny to the plow and turned over and broke up the soil in the mowed areas. Only then was he able to get to the most laborious work, ripping out by hand the grasses and weeds that had crowded in close to the vines. Slowly, the plants emerged as he pulled and pulled, and he was struck by the fact that so many of them were old. Most of the grape farmers he knew replaced their vines about every twenty-five years—when, in human terms, they were middle-aged and past the years of their greatest grape production. His father had replaced plantings in the rows that were easiest to reach, willing to keep old vines on the hard to work places, the slopes and difficult corners. Quim's family had seldom replaced a plant. Josep estimated that some of the vines he freed from the weeds were a hundred years old. Although they still produced small grapes with a wondrous depth of flavor, the vines were gnarled and crooked, like bleached driftwood logs that had been cast up on the beach—old men lying there to bake in the sun.

It took him several more days of hand weeding before he reached the outer limits of the vineyard. When he paused to pull a kerchief from his pocket and wipe his wet face, he looked back with satisfaction at a vineyard transformed, plantings no longer attacked by a jungle.

He glanced over into the neighboring vineyard at the matching neatness of the Vall property. Neither Francesc nor Maria del Mar was in sight. The day before he had seen Maria del Mar pausing at her work to watch him, and they had waved. She would be itching to know why he was tending the Torras vines and worried to think that Quim had met with a calamity. He knew that the next time they saw one another, she would walk over to him and ask. He wondered how she would feel to learn they were abutters.

Now the world of his labor had been doubled, and he quickly became accustomed to walking the long rows without pausing when he reached the end of the Alvarez vineyard and entered what he would forever think of as the Torras piece.

As the days grew longer and hotter and the grapes formed and grew, he knew that he had best deal with Quim's abandoned house before the anxious harvest season crept up on him.

The house was a disaster.

He hauled trash—a basket full of fermented and spoiled grain from the attic, filthy clothes, blackened rags not worth washing, two stinking sleeping pads. All of it went into a pile that he sprinkled with oil and set afire. He sharpened Quim's cutting tools and oiled the handles of hoes, shovels, and rakes. He salvaged whatever he could: a pair of barrels that appeared to be sound, broken shards of wood that could feed his fire in the winter; a basket full of nails, screws, two awls, a thimble, and one rusted hinge; a large sack half-filled with corks; a small copper cooking pot and a rusted iron fry pan; and thirty-one bottles of different shapes and design, some of them still crusted with the river mud from which Quim had salvaged them. Then he found a box containing seven dusty wine glasses. When they were washed he saw that they were old and beautiful, made of a fragile green glass. One of them was badly cracked, and he threw it away. The other six he treasured.

When Quim's casa was empty, he left the door and the windows opened wide for ten days and then started using the house as a combination toolroom and warehouse. It was handy being able to go a short distance to get whatever he needed while he was working in the Torras piece.

In Sitges to buy a bag of sulfur, he met up on the street with Juan, the elderly worker at Emilio Rivera's cooperage, and he paused politely to pass the time of day. Juan spoke of the busyness of the work at the cooperage, the heat of the season, the lack of rainfall. He peered at Josep.

"Emilio tells me you are not married."

Josep peered back at him.

"I have a niece. Married only six years, and now six years a widow. Juliana."

Josep cleared his throat. "Children?"

"Alas, no children."

"Er . . . How old?"

"Still young. Strong. Can *bear* children, you understand! Can help a man in his work. A very good worker, Juliana . . . I have told her about you."

Josep looked at him dumbly.

"So. Would you like to see her?"

" . . . Well. Why not?"

"Good. She is a waiter in a café, very near here. I will buy you a wine," Juan said grandly.

Josep followed him nervously.

The café was a workingman's place and crowded. Juan led him to a scarred table and in a moment touched his hand.

"Psst."

Josep registered that she was older than he was, with a voluptuous body that had begun to sag, and a pleasant, good-humoured face. He watched her exchanging badinage with four men at a nearby table. She had a high, coarse laugh.

As she turned toward them, Josep felt a rising panic.

He tried to tell himself that this was an opportunity. That he had wanted to meet new women.

She greeted Juan warmly with two kisses, calling him
uncle. He performed the introduction gruffly: "Juliana
Lozano. Josep Alvarez."

She smiled, made a little dip of a bow. When they
ordered wine, she left at once and brought it. "You like
white bean soup?" she asked Josep.

He nodded, though he wasn't hungry. But she hadn't
been talking about the café menu. "Tomorrow night.
I give you white bean soup, yes?" She grinned at him,
warm and easy, and he grinned back.

"Yes."

"Good. The house across the street, second floor," she
said. "The middle door."

Clouds hid the moon the following evening. The
street was poorly lighted by a flickering streetlamp, and
the stairway of her house proved to be even darker. Carrying a long pa as his share of the dinner, he went up the
stairs in semi-darkness to a narrow corridor and tapped
at the middle door.

Juliana welcomed him with good cheer, accepted the
bread, broke it with a couple of twists, and placed it on
the table.

He was seated without ceremony and served the
spicy bean soup at once, which both of them ate with en-
thusiasm. Josep complimented her on her cooking, and
she smiled. "I brought it home from the café," she said,
and they both laughed. They talked sparingly of her uncle Juan, Josep relating to her the kindnesses Juan had
shown to him at the cooperage.

Presently, even before he moved to kiss her, Juliana
led him to the bed as matter-of-factly as she had served
him the soup.

Before midnight he was making his way home again,
his body lighter and released but his mind curiously
burdened. It had been, he thought, rather like eating a
piece of fruit that had proved to be edible and without
fault but was undeniably less than sweet, and he rode
hunched and brooding as he and Hinny made their way
over the road leading back into the countryside.

38

Harvesting

*J*osep understood the puzzlement of some of the villagers. He had left Santa Eulália a jobless boy. When he returned, he had gained control of his father's vineyard, and now he had the Torras property as well.

"Are you able to work both pieces of land by yourself?" Maria del Mar asked him doubtfully.

He had given it thought. "If you and I continue to work together to harvest our crops, as we did before, I'll hire somebody to pick the grapes from Quim's vines. One picker should be enough, since the Torras crop will be much smaller than either of ours," he said, and she agreed.

He had his choice of every village youth who wasn't a first son, and he chose Gabriel Taulé, a quiet, steady boy of seventeen years, who had three older brothers. Known to everyone as Briel, the youth looked stunned when Josep approached him with the offer of work, and he accepted eagerly.

Josep scrubbed his wine vats and then turned to the tanks located under a roof extension at the side of Quim's casa. What he saw when he began to clean them disturbed him, for two of the containers had areas that reminded him unpleasantly of the rotted section he had been forced to have Emilio Rivera replace on his own vat. But he told himself that it was no use worrying about problems if

one was not certain they existed, and he washed the vats
with water and a sulfur solution and prepared them to
accept the juice of the grapes.

As the summer turned into the autumn, and the
bunches of grapes on the vines became heavy and
purple-black, Josep walked among the rows every day,
sampling and tasting—now the warm spiciness of a small
grape from an old Garnacha vine; now the fruity, complex
promise of an Ull de Llebre; now the acid tartness of one
of the Sumolls.

He and Maria del Mar agreed one morning that the
grapes had reached the time of perfect ripeness, and he
summoned Briel Tauré and gave him Hinny and the
tumbrel to use on the Torras piece.

He and Maria del Mar and Quim had worked well
together, but Josep found that it was even better to work
alone with her, because they thought alike about the tasks
and harvested well in tandem, talking rarely. He had
hitched her mule to his wagon. The only sound was the
snick! snick! snick! of their sharp knives as they severed
bunches from the vines and dropped them into their
baskets. They toiled under a radiant sun, clothing soon
plastering against their bodies and showing dark, intimate patches. Fransesc hovered, fetching an occasional
cup of water for one of them from the clay cántir kept in
the shade under the wagon, limping after the wagon to
the press, or perching on the back of the mule.

Sometimes Briel, alone and lost in the reverie of work,
would allow himself a burst of song in a loud off-key
chant, more a yawping and shouting than a singing, and
at first when this sound reached them, Josep and Maria
del Mar exchanged wry smiles. Having the large wagon
was a luxury; even though Maria del Mar and Josep each
cut faster than Briel, the youth filled the small tumbrel
quickly. Each time he did so he shouted, and Josep was
forced to drop his knife and hasten to help him muscle
the fruit-filled tumbrel to the press.

Josep was aware that during his frequent trips to the press with grapes from the Torras piece, Maria del Mar continued to work in her own vineyard alone, a contribution of her time and energy that was over and above the terms of their working agreement. He felt he must make it up to her, and at the end of the day, when he had sent Briel home and Maria del Mar had unhitched the mule and left to make her son his supper, Josep continued to work stolidly by himself in her vineyard.

An hour later, when she came out of her house to throw the gathered crumbs from her table to the birds, she saw Josep still bent over a vine and wielding his knife.

She walked to him. "What are you doing?"

"My share of the work."

When he looked at her, he saw that she was stiff with anger.

"You insult me."

"How do I do that?"

"When I needed help to get a fair price for my work, you provided it. You said then that you did what any man would have done, your exact words. But you don't allow yourself to accept even the slightest help from a woman."

"No, it's not that way."

"It is exactly that way. You disrespect me in a way you wouldn't do to a man," she said. "I want you out of my vineyard until tomorrow."

Josep felt his own anger. Damn the female, he thought, she was twisting things, confusing him, as usual.

He was disgusted, but he was tired and dirty and had no heart for stupid quarrels, and he cursed silently, flipped his basket into the wagon, and went home.

The next morning for a brief time things were awkward between them, but the rhythms of the shared work soon drove away the irritated words they had exchanged the evening before. Josep continued to break off and leave whenever Briel signaled that he needed help, but he and Maria del Mar functioned together very well, and he was pleased with their harvest of her grapes.

It was midmorning when Briel made his way to Teresa's vineyard, and Josep knew at once from his face that something was wrong.

"What?"

"It is the vat, senyor," Briel said

When Josep saw the tank, his heart sank. It wasn't gushing, but a steady ooze of grape juice made wet tracks down the exterior of the container. There were six vats in a line on the shady side of Quim's house, and he studied them and then pointed to the one that looked least suspicious, though there was little to differentiate them. "Use that one," he said.

Late in the afternoon, while he was working, he spotted Clemente Ramirez driving his great wagon down the lane to the river to rinse out his barrels.

"Hola, Clemente!" Josep called.

He raced to intercept the wagon and lead Clemente to inspect the offending vats.

Ramirez examined the wooden tanks carefully and then shook his head. "These two are gone." He pointed. "Repairing them would be to throw good money after bad. This other vat Quim Torras can use for a few more years yet, I think.

"I can come tomorrow and take the juice from here early, and they'll ferment it at the vinegar plant. Of course, that means I must pay Quim a bit less for it, but . . ." He shrugged.

"Quim is gone."

Clemente was visibly impressed to learn that Josep now owned the Torras land as well as the Alvarez vineyard. "Jesucristo, I must treat you well, for at this rate you will end up a great landowning lord and our governor."

Josep did not feel like a lord and a governor as he returned to work. He had known that it would take several seasons before he could build up his yield from the Torras piece. Now his return from this year's harvest would be even less than he had anticipated, and Clemente's assessment of the vats was the worst possible news.

New vats were very expensive.

He had no money for new vats.

He cursed the day when he had listened to Quim's pleas and agreed to buy his vineyard. He was a fool to have taken pity on a neighbor who was a raddled old drunkard and a failed and miserable farmer, he told himself bitterly, and now he was afraid that before he had truly begun as a grower of grapes, he had been ruined by Quim Torras.

39

Troubles

*I*n a fog of dull despair, Josep finished the harvest in four more days, forcing himself not to think of his problems. But the day after all the grapes had been picked and pressed, he rode Hinny to Sitges and found Emilio Rivera at his midday meal in the cooperage, his ruddy face expressing pleasure as he spooned garlicky hake-with-cider into his bearded mouth. Emilio motioned him to a chair, and he sat and waited uncomfortably for the older man to finish eating.

"So?" Emilio said.

Josep told him the entire story: Quim's departure, their agreement, and the disastrous discovery of the rotted fermentation vats.

Emilio watched him gravely.

"So. Too far gone to be fixed?"

"Yes."

"Same size as the one I repaired for you?"

"The same size . . . How much would two new vats cost?"

When Emilio told him, he closed his eyes.

"And that's my best price."

Josep shook his head. "I don't have it. If I could get the vats replaced before next year's harvest, I could pay you for them then," he said.

I *think* I could pay you then, he amended silently.

Emilio pushed away the empty soup bowl.

"There are things you must understand, Josep. It's one thing for me to give you a hand in fixing a wagon, or to help you replace a door for a church. I did those things gladly because I saw that you are a good fellow, and I like you. But . . . I'm not a rich man. I work hard for my living, as you do. Even if you were my sister's son, I would not be able to use prime oak to make two large vats for you without receiving any money. And," he added delicately, "you are *not* my sister's son."

They sat unhappily.

Emilio sighed.

"Here is the best I can do for you. If you pay me now for one of the tanks—in advance, so I can use your money to buy the wood—I'll build both vats for you, and you may pay me for the second one after next year's harvest."

Josep nodded in silence for a long time.

He tried to thank Emilio as he rose to leave. The cooper waved him away, but came after him before he had reached the door.

"Wait a moment. Come with me," he said, and led Josep across the cooperage and into a crowded storeroom. "Do you have any use for these?" he asked, pointing to a pile of casks, less than half the size of regular barrels.

". . . Well, I could use them. But—"

"Fourteen of them, one hundred liters each. Made two years ago for a man who wanted them for anchovies. He died, and they've been here ever since. Everyone wants 225-liter barrels. Nobody's willing to take 100-liter barrels off my hands. If you can use them, I'll add a little something to your bill."

"I don't really *need* them. I can't afford them."

"You can't afford to refuse them, either, because I'm practically giving them to you." Emilio picked up one of the small barrels and thrust it into Josep's hands. "I said a *little* something. It will be a very little something. Get them the hell out of here before you leave," he said brusquely, trying to sound like a man who was accustomed to striking hard bargains.

It was three more weeks before Clemente Ramirez came back and took the rest of Josep's wine. After Ramirez paid him, Josep gave Maria del Mar her share and immediately made the trip to Sitges to give Emilio the cash advance they had agreed on.

He had a brief contest with his conscience regarding the second payment to Quim Torras. It was Quim, after all, who had gotten him into the financial trouble that made it difficult for him to sleep at night. But the older man had made it clear that he needed the money to accomplish the changes in his life, and Josep knew that it had been his own responsibility to examine the tanks and the house before he had agreed to take over the vineyard.

It bothered him to turn the payment over so trustingly to Quim's friend, Jonatán Cadafalch. The coachman was, after all, a stranger to Josep; but Quim had claimed him as a friend, and Josep, seeing no alternative, found Cadafalch at the stage station.

He counted the money into Cadafalch's palm and then gave him a receipt he had written out for the transaction. He also handed over a few extra pesetas. "Please ask Quim to sign the receipt and bring it back here with you," Josep said, "and I will give you an additional payment when I return for it." Cadafalch glanced at him keenly but then grinned toothily to show he understood Josep's position. Taking no offense, he stuffed the money and the receipt carefully into a leather bag, and wished Josep a good day.

That night Josep sat at his table and placed his money before him. First he separated from the small pile the payments he would have to make to Donat and Rosa before next year's harvest, and then, a smaller amount for supplies and food.

He saw that what was left was meager and inadequate for any other real emergency that might arise, and he sat for a long time before sweeping the money into his cap in disgust and making his way to his bed.

The following afternoon he sat on his bench and prepared to taste the wine he had retained for his own use out of this season's pressing, in the hope that a miracle had taken place to make it wonderful. When he had worked in Languedoc, Leon Mendes had regularly insisted on an exercise following every new vintage. Each of his workers was given a cup of the wine, and with each sip would announce in turn some subtle flavor detected in mouth or nose.

"Strawberry."

"Fresh-cut hay."

"Mint."

"Coffee."

"Black plums."

Now Josep sipped his own wine and found it already spoiled, sour and unpleasing, tasting of strong ashes and the acidity of spoiled lemons. Also tasting of disappointment, though his expectations had not been high. As he poured the rest of the cup back into the pitcher, the first note of the churchbell drifted into his consciousness, loud and startling.

Another note followed. And another.

A slow, solemn tolling, telling the villagers of Santa Eulália that life was hard and fleeting and sad, and that that one of their own had left their community of souls.

He did what he had done all his life at the sounding of the death toll; he walked to the church.

The church door would have a first small hole marring its finish, for the mortality notice was tacked to it. Several people had already read the notice and turned away. When Josep reached it he saw that the new priest, in a fine, legible hand, had written of the death of Carme Riera, Eduardo Montroig's wife.

Carme Riera had had three miscarriages and a fourth pregnancy in the three-and-one-half years of her marriage. On that quiet November morning she had begun to bleed without pain and presently she gave birth to a two-month-old speck of bloody tissue, after which the clear fluid leaking from her turned into a gentle red flow. That had happened the second time she had lost a child, but this time the flow of blood didn't stop, and she had died late in the afternoon.

That evening Josep went to the Montroig home, which was the first of the four houses located in the plaça, just beyond the church. Maria del Mar was among other people who sat quietly in the kitchen, lending their presence.

Two candles shedding yellow light at her head and two more at her feet, Carme lay on her own bed, which had been transformed into a bier by drapes of black cloth that the church kept for successive use in houses of misfortune. She was five years younger than Josep, who scarcely knew her. She had been a somewhat attractive girl with squinting eyes and a heavy bosom from early girlhood, and now her hair was washed and combed, her face white and sweet. She looked as though at any moment she might yawn. The small bedroom was crowded with her husband and several relatives who would sit with her all night, and with a pair of plañideras, old women who had been hired to weep for her. After a while Josep made room for others to view her and returned to sit stiffly in a room that at times seemed loud with whispers and hushed voices. Maria del Mar had already gone. Space was limited and chairs were few, so he did not stay overly long.

Josep was saddened. He liked Eduardo and found it hard to look at the grief that contorted Montroig's solemn, long-jawed face and robbed it of its usual serious serenity.

The following morning, no one worked. Most of the villagers walked behind the coffin as it was carried the short distance to the church for the first funeral conducted in Santa Eulália by Padre Pio. Josep sat in a back row throughout the long Requiem Mass. By the time the priest's calm and sonorous voice recited the rosary in Latin, and the words of the prayer were repeated by the choked voices of Eduardo and Carme's father and her sister and three brothers, Josep's troubles had become very small.

40

What the Pig Knew

$\mathcal{H}$is first work of the cleanup that always followed the harvest was to disassemble the two defective vats. He took them apart as carefully as once they had been put together, probably by a Torras ancestor who had enjoyed far more skill than Josep did. That man had used very few nails, and Josep took great pains not to bend them when he pulled them free of the wood. He straightened any nail that did bend and saved each of them, because nails like these—bits of steel hand-forged to be hard and efficient, like a farmer's life—were expensive.

As he freed the boards, he separated them into two piles. The boards that were riddled with rot would be cut up for firewood, but a number of boards were sound and he stacked them separately, the way he had seen Emilio stack wood at the cooperage, with small sticks of wood keeping them apart from one another so air could keep them dry.

In less than a day, the two failed tanks were gone, and he was free to begin the labor he loved best, walking behind the plow to steer the blade while Hinny pulled it through the stony soil.

He had almost finished ploughing the Alvarez piece, when he passed the patch of brush and thistle into which the boar had plunged after he had shot it. He realized he should do some work there, clean up the volunteer undergrowth and plow the soil so he could plant a few more vines; and while he was about it, he would pack soil firmly into the space below the overhang, so no wild creature could ever take refuge there again and threaten his grapes.

He went to work with the scythe on the brush, which gave him sufficient resistance, so that by the time it was cut, he was happy to pause. He remembered that the hole had been large enough to hide the entire pig, and he realized he would have to shovel a lot of dirt and pack it into the space.

He got down on his knees, bent his head, and peered, but he could see only the first few feet, where daylight spilled into it. Beyond that, there was darkness.

A coolness reached out to his face.

The pole that Jaumet had used to poke at the dead pig was lying on the ground. When Josep pushed it under the overhang, it went all the way in.

Something strange: when he lifted his hand as high as he could in the dark space, and flexed his wrist, he could point the pole downward, farther than he would have expected. When he rested his wrist in the dirt and moved the stick so it pointed upward, the point of the stick moved a considerable distance too.

"HOLA!"

He heard the hollowness of his voice.

Hinny, still in harness and attached to the plow, brayed in protest, and Josep forced himself away from the hole in the ridge to unharness the animal and see to its comfort, which gave him a little time to think. The hole in the ridge was exciting and interesting and frightening, all at once; he wanted to share it with somebody, perhaps Jaumet. Then he knew that he must not turn to Jaumet every time he had a problem he didn't wish to face himself.

He went to the toolroom and found a lantern, made certain it contained oil, turned up the wick and struck a match, and carried the lighted lantern through the bright sunlight to the bottom of the ridge. When he lay on his stomach and pushed it into the opening, it threw light a good distance forward.

The natural overhang was about twice as wide as Josep's shoulders and it ended a little more than an arm's length from his face. Then a roundish hole began and went in for perhaps a meter.

And beyond that, there was a dark, wider space.

Probably there was enough room for him to wriggle into the hole, pushing the lantern before him. He told himself that the boar had been as wide as he was, and thicker. But the thought of getting stuck in the narrow dark place, alone and without help, chilled him.

There were some rocks visible in the overhang, but mostly it seemed to be composed of stony soil from which a variety of weeds sprang. Josep went to the house and brought back an iron bar, a bucket, a mattock, and a shovel, and he began to dig.

When he had made the hole wide enough to enter on his hands and knees, he paused at the opening, holding the lantern forward, and peered at . . . what?

He forced himself to crawl inside.

Very quickly, the ground made a slight drop. As he went forward, the floor was covered with rocks, but he was able to stand shakily.

It wasn't a cave. The lantern revealed a place more confined than his little bedroom, not even big enough to be called a grotto—a small, rocky bubble in the shallow hill, the size of a large fermentation vat. The wall to his left was of greyish stone and rose in an arch.

The light of the lantern played crazily as he turned, trying to see, realizing there could be wild things here. Snakes.

Standing there, in a little natural box in the earth, it was possible to believe that small, furry creatures might live here when they were not tending the roots of grapevines.

He turned, reentered the hole and crawled back into the world.

Outside, the air was softer and warmer, and dusk was beginning to fall. Josep stood and regarded the hole in wonder, and then he blew out the lantern and put the tools away.

That night he slept for a few hours and then lay awake for hours and thought about the hole in the hill. As soon as the earliest morning light began to dilute the darkness, he hurried out to make certain it hadn't been a dream.

The opening was still there.

The little bubble in the hill was too small to be of any real use to him.

But it was a good place to begin. And he took its discovery to be a message that he should start working.

He returned to the house and brought out the tools, and then he studied the ridge above the opening with new eyes. It was unremarkable until he reached eye level, where a large boulder, longer than a man but thin and flat, stretched perpendicular, a natural support for the soil that would be above the doorway. He began to excavate the earth beneath the stone ridge, conscious of the fact that a door would have to be wide enough to admit his wheelbarrow.

He worked first with the mattock and was engaged with shoveling away loose soil, when Francesc wandered into sight. They greeted one another, and the boy sat on the ground and watched him work.

"What are you doing now, Josep?" Francesc said finally.

"I'm digging a cellar," Josep said.

PART FIVE

The Blood of the Grape

Village of Santa Eulália
Catalonia
January 12, 1876

41

Digging

*I*t soon became a topic of conversation in Santa Eulália that Josep Alvarez was spending his time digging into the ridge. His neighbors were only mildly interested, though a few thought he was becoming odd, and they smiled when they caught a glimpse of him in the village streets.

Winter was the time for cleanup and pruning. The vines on the Torras piece needing careful remedial work, and Josep gave it to them; still, on most days he managed to find a few hours to work with the pick and shovel, and when all his vines had been nicely pruned, he became a fulltime digger. It was always cool but not cold in the hole, and forever nighttime, so that he dug near a sputtering lantern that cast yellow light and black shadows.

Nivaldo looked upon the project darkly.

"When you start burrowing deep, you can get killed by spoiled air. There are bad vapors and . . . what do they call them . . . miasmas? Like poison farts from the bowels of the earth, if you breathe them, you die. You should get yourself a little birdie in a cage to keep you company in there, the way miners do. If the bird dies, you run like hell."

He had no time to bother with birds. He was a digging machine, exhausted when he flopped onto the bed, often still in his gritty digging clothes, his sweaty stink in his nostrils. A warm day was a blessing, for he could grab a proper bath in the river and perhaps scrub some laundry. Otherwise he washed from a bucket whenever he became disgusted by his own raw smell.

The cleared space within the hill began to take shape. It seemed more like a passageway into the ridge than a proper cellar, which he would have chosen to be formed as a square or a wider rectangle. But he dug along the rock wall and the narrow rock ceiling he had found in the original little bubble that had been his starting point, the pig's haven. The left wall of rock went forward, retaining its slightly curved shape, similar to a long segment of a tube in which the right side had been jaggedly removed. The width of his tunnel was determined by the fact that when he dug beyond the edge of the narrow rock ceiling, there was just dirt. He wasn't a miner; he knew nothing about shoring up the huge heaviness of earth above his head, so he simply dug the soil away from the existing ceiling and left wall of rock, and followed them forward. Slowly, a tunnel began to take shape, a little higher than Josep's head and somewhat wider than it was tall, the left wall of rock curving up and into the rock ceiling, and the right wall and floor composed of the dirt of the hill.

In Nivaldo's newspaper, one evening, Josep read a story about a man convicted of assault and robbery. The criminal was a Portuguese man named Carlos Cabral, a pimp who seduced young women and kept them in a bawdy house in Sant Cugat.

Josep remembered Renata, her misery and disease in the whorehouse in Sitges, and recalled the man of whom she had been terrified, a burly man in a soiled white suit, who had sat outside of her room.

His imagination began to nibble at him. Nivaldo had said that the man who had married Teresa Gallego and taken her away was a repairer of shoes.

Name of Luis Mondres, something like that.

Nivaldo had said he wore a white suit and smoked Portuguese cigars.

Well, so what?

Suppose, Josep thought . . .

Suppose this shoe repairer, this Luis, was similar to the pimp in the newspaper, who had married four women in order to make them whores. Suppose this Luis had married Teresa in order to take her to a house like the one in Sitges. Suppose even now, Teresa Gallego might be in a room like Renata's room.

He forced himself to put it from his mind.

But sometimes, while digging like a mole in the ridge, or lying in bed in a sleepless moment, his memory drifted to Teresa.

He recalled how innocent she had been. The thought haunted him more than once that perhaps, by not being able to return to her, he was responsible for some terrible existence in which Teresa now lived.

42

The Swap

$\mathcal{A}$t one point in the tunnel, as Josep dug he discovered that the wall of rock made a sharp turn left for an arm's length and turned right again for a similar distance, leaving an indentation about a meter wide and half again as deep. He at once labeled the indentation in his mind as "the wine closet," because from the moment of its excavation he could visualize it as a space that should be lined with shelves full of hundreds of bottles.

But after the "closet," the rock wall and the supporting stone ceiling ended, and that fact, for Josep, determined the final dimensions of the cellar—a space about as long as a railroad car and only a little wider.

He had spread about half of the spoil from the excavation along the surface of the lane to the river, but he had carefully saved all the stones and small rocks of desirable size for wall-building, and now he got a barrow-load of clay from the river and started to line the earthen rear and right walls with a surface of stonework, which he thought would be a proper way to finish a cellar. But that project did not go far, because he was aware that the winter was coming to an end.

Soon heat would find its way into the cool space he had worked so hard to achieve, unless he could find a good way to block the opening in the hill.

One morning he entered the church and waited until Padre Pio came forward to greet him.

They exchanged amenities, and Josep proceeded at once to the point of his visit.

"What has become of the old door of the church, Padre?"

"The former door? It's in the storeroom."

"I would like to buy it."

Padre Pio regarded Josep reflectively in the small silence that followed. "No, it is not for sale," he said finally.

"Oh . . . You're saving it for something?"

"Saving it? No, not really . . . I might be willing to trade for it."

Josep began to feel annoyance toward this priest. He had nothing to trade, and he maintained his silence.

"If you are willing to make a confession and bring your presence to my Mass each Sunday morning, I'm willing for you to take the door."

Josep felt awkward. "I don't have . . . a true faith, Padre." By now, he knew, the priest must have learned much about his early history, including his having been reared by the village's two most determined heretics, his father and Nivaldo. "I'm not a believer."

"I don't ask that you believe. Only that you confess and come to Mass."

Josep sighed. He needed the damned door.

He nodded sourly.

"Then we have made a bargain," the priest said, and taking Josep's hand, Padre Pio shook it briskly. He took his long purple stole from a hanger on the wall, slipped it about his neck, and led Josep to the confessional at the rear of the church, which he entered from his side.

Josep pushed through the red velvet curtain into the narrow dark space and knelt, his knees finding the reclinatorio. In the thin light from the crack in the curtain he could make out the half wall topped by a metal screen with pinprick holes, behind which Father Pio's unseen hand slid open a small inner screen.

"Yes, my son. You wish to confess?"

Josep took a breath, and welling up from the memory of his frightened boyhood, the words spilled. "Bless me, father, for I have sinned."

"How long is it since you have last made confession?"

". . . Many years," he said.

"Well?"

". . . I have done things with women."

"You have committed the act outside of the sacrament of marriage? A number of times?"

"Yes, Padre."

The priest helped him. "Have you also had impure thoughts?"

"I have, Padre."

"How often have you had these thoughts?"

". . . Every day."

"Repeat after me. 'O my God, I am heartily sorry I have offended thee and I detest all my sins . . .'"

Josep did so through his dry throat.

". . . because I dread the loss of heaven and the pains of hell . . ."

". . . but most of all because they offend thee, my God, who are good and deserving of my love."

". . . I firmly resolve, with the help of thy grace, to confess my sins, to do penance, and to amend my life."

Josep finished like a drowning man.

"When you go to your home, recite twenty-five Paternosters. Be thoughtful and penitent, my son. I absolve you from your sins in the name of the Father and of his Son and of the Ghost who is holy. Pray that your sacrifice may be accepted to God.

"Let us now leave the confessional."

On the other side of the red velvet, blinking against the light, Josep saw Padre Pio removing his stole.

"Do you have your wagon outside?"

"Yes, Padre," he said, startled.

"I will help you carry the door," Padre Pio said.

He used some of the planks from the dismantled vats to make the doorframe. Fastening it to the hillside was a challenge. On one side of the entrance he nailed the wood of the frame into a pair of thick old tree roots, and on the other side he drove spikes into a crack in a boulder. The heavy old door was fine for his purpose, once he had used his saw to make it narrower and shorter. The disfiguring cracks did not go all the way through the surface, and the general battered condition of the wood, bizarre in a church door, was fine in the covering of a hole in a hill. In the trash he had cleaned from Quim's house was a rusted door hinge, and he picked up another hinge at the Sitges market, longer and narrower than Quim's hinge, but complete with matching rust. Well-oiled and installed, the odd pair of hinges worked with only an occasional squeal to alert the Small Ones whenever Josep entered their world.

That Sunday he bathed from a bucket in the early morning chill and then put on clean clothing and made his way to the church. He sat in the rear row. He was aware that some of the people at the Mass observed his presence with interest. On the other side of the church, Maria del Mar saw him and looked away. Francesc smiled and waved vigorously until his mother's hand clamped onto his arm.

To Josep's surprise, it was pleasant to be there. He seldom had an opportunity to sit in one place and rest. Now the sonorous sounds of the prayers, the scripture reading, the psalms, and the hymns, became a blanket of sound that comforted him into unthinking peace. The priest's sermon on the words of Sant Francesc Xavier lulled him into brief sleep; when he opened his eyes, he saw Maria del Mar's cold glance and the grinning face of his young friend, the saint's namesake.

Eduardo Montroig, mourning band on his shirtsleeve, came around with the basket for the offering, and Josep dutifully added his coin. Soon people sank to the kneeling benches, and Padre Pio put on his white stole and began to make his way through the congregation to place the Host into waiting mouths. "This is my body. Take it and eat."

Josep quickly made his escape.

Communion had not been part of the bargain, he told himself piously.

43

Thirst

Josep knew exactly the grapes he wanted to use, small dark grapes, dense with flavor, borne each year by undefeated vines that were four times as old as he was.

He had never counted the buds on a vine until he got to France, but now as his vines came to life, he checked them and found that most of them produced about sixty buds, except the very old ones, which produced about forty.

Leon Mendes had limited his vines to fifteen or twenty buds, and Josep began stripping his oldest vines down to that number. Maria del Mar came to fetch her son and paused. "What are you doing?" she said, disturbed because every time he rubbed off a bud, she knew he was throwing away three bunches of grapes.

"The fewer the buds, the more strength and flavor goes into the grapes. In the grapes that are left, even the pips ripen. I'm going to make wine."

"We already make wine."

"I want to make *wine*, good wine that people will want to drink. If I can do that and sell it, I can make more money than I can by selling garbage wine to Clemente."

"And what if the wine doesn't turn out to be good? What a chance you're taking, wasting so many grapes! You're a second son who has managed to get two sections of land, but still you don't know how to be content," she said severely. "Why do you torture yourself with grand dreams, with digging a cellar? Do you forget that you're a peasant? That all of us in Santa Eulália come from peasants? Why can't you be satisfied with what you have, with our life?" She didn't wait for his answer but went to where Francesc was playing in the shade, took his hand, and led him away.

Josep continued to strip buds from his vines. Her words rankled, but he knew she was wrong. He had no pretensions; he just wanted to make good wine.

Still . . . when he thought about it, he knew it was more than that. If the wine turned out to be bad, perhaps he could learn how to make a good vinegar. He faced the fact that he hungered to be able to do work that resulted in making something that was good.

A fine day, a day of soft, warm winds and scudding clouds that gentled the sun, was spoiled for the village by the death of one of its old men. Eugenio Rius, skin-and-bones, bent, and whitehaired, had been a fixture on the shaded bench in front of the grocery, where he had been napping when his heart stopped. As always when one of its own died, the village turned out to attend his funeral Mass.

Eugenio Rius had been a member of the Village Council. By law, the Council was composed of two councilors and the alcalde. Three years before, when another councilor, Jaume Caralt, had died, Angel Casals had neglected to see him replaced, but with the passing of the only remaining councilor, the alcalde knew he would have to hold an election for two new members and report the results to the governor's office in Barcelona.

Angel didn't like having to bother himself with such events, which called for planning and exertion, and at once he saw the wisdom of choosing two candidates who were likely to develop wisdom with the passing years, yet who were young and energetic enough to serve for a long time.

The first person he approached was Eduardo Montroig—sober, earnest, of pleasant demeanor, a leader of the village castellers and a hard worker for himself and for the church, and for the second seat on the Council he turned to another of the younger landowners, Josep Alvarez, who had acted well in the matter of the church door.

Josep was startled and somewhat amused. Though flattered—he could not remember anyone ever choosing him for anything—he had no wish to accept Angel's nomination. With two sections of land, an unfinished cellar, and plans to try to make credible wine, he had no wish for more responsibilities, and he hesitated, trying to decide on a diplomatic way to decline.

"It is necessary. The village will be grateful for your service, Josep," Angel said.

It gave Josep further pause, because implicit in the remark was the knowledge that their neighbors would be hurt by a resident's refusal to help the village. Coming soon after Maria del Mar had accused Josep of forgetting his origins, it left him with only the ability to thank the alcalde for the honor.

Angel declared June 1 to be the date of the election. By law only literate males who were landowners could vote. The alcalde knew exactly who was in that select group and spoke to each of them. On June first, seventeen men, one hundred percent of the eligible voters of the village of Santa Eulália, including Josep Alvarez and Eduardo Montroig, scrawled the names of the only two candidates Angel told them about as they entered the church.

The two new councilors took comfort in the knowledge that the Council almost never met, and that, by mutual understanding, any meeting would last only long enough for them to agree to decisions made by Angel Casals.

That summer was a good one for grapes, the long days filled with golden heat, the nights made cool by breezes that played among the shallow hills. Josep was alive to the changes that were taking place in his ripening grapes. His awareness that something strange was happening to the water in the village well occurred very gradually. At first it was the faintest gaminess that he felt in the back of his throat when he paused in his work and slaked his thirst.

Then when he drank he began to detect a more decided tang, almost a fishiness.

By the time the water began to stink, most of the people in the village were racked by a flux that kept them in the outhouses, weak and gasping from the terrible cramps.

A steady line of villagers began to pass Josep's vineyard, following the lane to the Pedregós River with bottles and jars, taking drinking water from the river as the original settlers of Santa Eulália had done before they had dug the village well.

The alcalde and the two councilors took turns peering down the well, but it was ten meters deep and all they saw at the bottom was darkness. Josep tied a lighted lantern to a rope and they peered at it as he let it down.

"... Something floating," he said. "Do you see it?"

"No," said Eduardo, whose vision was bad.

"Yes," Angel said. "What is it?"

They couldn't tell.

Josep continued to stare down. It didn't look any more frightening than the hole in the hill. "I'll go into the well."

"No, it will be easier to send down a strong boy," Angel said, and he chose Briel Taulé's younger brother Bernat, who was fourteen years old. They looped a good rope under Bernat's arms, set him inside the well, and began to pay out the rope slowly and carefully.

"No more," he called up to them after a while, and they held the rope at that level. Bernat had carried down a bucket, and the rope began to move and twitch in their hands like a line with a hooked fish, and then his hollow shout came up again.

"I have it!"

When they hauled him up the stink was very strong, and when he held out the bucket they saw a moving mass of maggots in a bundle of soaked white feathers that once had been a dove.

The three of them sat on the bench in front of the grocery.

"We have to empty the well of the spoiled water, pail by pail. It will take a long time," Angel said.

"I think it's a bad idea," Josep said reluctantly.

The other two looked at him.

"The same thing could happen again. The well is our only real source of water. The river can't be depended on for good drinking water at times of flood or drought. I think we should cap the top of the well to protect the water, and install a pump."

"Too much money," Angel said at once.

"How much money does the village have?" Josep asked.

". . . A little. For emergencies only."

"This is an emergency," Josep said.

The three of them sat in silence.

Eduardo cleared his throat. "Exactly how much *does* the village have, Alcalde?"

Angel told them.

It was not a great deal, but . . . "It's probably more than enough. If it is, I think we should order a pump," Josep said.

"I do also," Eduardo said. He spoke softly, but his voice was firm.

Angel glanced at each of them sharply. He struggled with the rebellion for only a moment and then surrendered. "Where can we get a pump?"

Josep shrugged. "Perhaps Sitges. Or Barcelona?"

"It was your idea. You go," the alcalde said crankily.

The next morning, the hottest day of the year descended on Santa Eulália. On such a day work would produce huge thirsts, and as Hinny trotted down the

Barcelona road Josep found himself hoping that the river water would stay clean.

In Sitges he wasted no time but went directly to the cooperage, to his unfailing source of good advice. "There is no place in this little fishing town to buy a pump," Emilio Rivera said. "You must go to Barcelona." There one could arrange for a water pump, he said. "One company does business just behind La Boqueria, but they are no good, don't bother with them. The best company is called Terradas, located in the Barri Gótic, on the Calle Fusteria."

So Josep continued on to Barcelona and entered the Gothic Quarter. He found the Terradas Company in a workshop littered with machinery and smelling of metal, lubricating oil, and paint. A sleepy-eyed man behind a tall desk listened to his story, asked the width and the depth of the well, did some computations on paper, and then slid the paper to him with an encircled figure that Josep read with relief.

"When can you install it in Santa Eulália?"

The man made a face. "We have three crews, and they are all busy."

"You must understand," Josep said. "An entire village without water. In this weather . . ."

The man pulled a leather-bound journal to him, opened it and turned pages. "A bad situation. I do understand. I can deliver the pump and install it three days from now."

They shook hands, sealing the order.

That accomplished, he was free to go home, but as he rode through the Barri Gótic, he found himself directing Hinny to Sant Doménech del Call, and when he found it, he rode slowly down the narrow street, studying the shops.

He almost passed the small tablet on the side of the building without reading it.

Repairer of Shoes. L. Montrés.

A tiny workshop on the shady side of the street, with an open door because of the heat.

So. The shop, at least, was real.

Josep moved Hinny past the next couple of doorways, dismounted, and tethered him to a post. He walked to the bakery opposite it and pretended to study the breads, and when he could, he cast a casual glance through the open door of the cobbler's shop.

Luis Montrés, if it was he, was seated at his bench, trimming leather slivers from a new sole on a shoe. Josep noted a scruffy, unkempt beard, half-closed eyes, a calm brown face concentrated on his task. He was not wearing a white suit, but work clothing under a ragged blue apron, and a limp brown cap. As Josep watched, he placed a line of small tacks between his lips and then removed them quickly, one at a time, to bang each into the shoe with a fast, strong hammer stroke.

Uneasy lest he be discovered staring, Josep moved away.

He went back to Hinny, and as he turned, he saw a woman come around a nearby corner carrying a basket. She walked down Sant Doménech and approached the small shop, and it took him a long moment to realize it was Teresa Gallego.

Josep moved back to where he could glance into the shop and watched her remove the man's midday meal from the basket.

Montrés set aside his work and began to eat as an older woman came into the shop. Josep saw Teresa go behind the small counter and accept a pair of shoes. She talked briefly with the customer and then, as the other woman departed, showed the shoes to the eating man before she placed them on his shelf.

Teresa appeared calm and very different from the girl Josep had recollected. Older, of course. And heavier, grown rather plump in marriage; or perhaps, he thought, she was expecting a child. She looked . . . contented, he decided. He remembered touching her secret places and for some reason felt like an adulterer.

To his astonishment, he realized she was now a woman who was a complete stranger to him. Certainly she was not the sultry creature of his dreams.

Presently the man in the shop finished eating. Josep saw that Teresa was placing things back into her basket and soon would leave, and in a panic he returned to Hinny. He mounted and rode away at a walk, fleeing slowly in order not to call attention to himself.

Outside the city, he stopped several times to allow the hinny to rest and graze. Josep was calm and contented, for now he knew that his imagination had lied to him. Whatever might befall Teresa Gallego in her future, he had seen enough to know that he had not ruined her life, and it was as though he could allow himself, finally, to close a door he had long kept open a tiny crack.

By the time he reached Sitges, it was evening. Both he and the hinny were very tired and Josep decided that it would make sense to sleep there that night and finish the trip the next morning. It occurred to him, with a sudden raw, horny surge, that he might share Juliana Lozano's bed, though he hadn't contacted her after their single experience, and he rode to the café where she worked and tethered Hinny to a post.

Inside, it was crowded and noisy but he found a table. Juliana saw him from the other side of the room and approached him with a smile.

"How are you, Josep? Good to see you!"

"And you. And you, Juliana!"

"We must talk. I have something to tell you," she said. "But first, let me bring you something."

"A wine," he said, and watched her ample hips move as she went to fetch it.

News to share? he thought uneasily.

By the time she brought the filled glass, he had had enough time to begin to feel worried. "What is it you have to tell me?"

She leaned forward and whispered. "I will be getting married."

"Really?" he said, and hoped that she mistook his relief for regret. "And who is your intended?"

"It is he," she said, and pointed to a table where three beefy men sat drinking. One of them saw her pointing finger, beamed, and waved.

"His name is Victor Barceló. He is a drover for the tannery."

"Ah," Josep said. He looked across the room at the other man and raised his glass, and Victor Barceló smiled broadly and raised his glass in return.

Josep ordered and ate white bean soup. Perhaps the thought of his thirsty village drove him to ask Juliana repeatedly to fill his water glass.

When finally he left the café, he led Hinny to the waterfront and followed a narrow path between several open beaches until he came to a cove in which small fishing boats had been pulled up on the sand. He tethered Hinny to a mooring ring and spread his blanket between two of the boats. He slept almost at once, awakening several times in the night to add his saltiness to the edge of the sea. No moon showed. It was quiet and warm and dark, and Josep felt comfortable in the world.

When the crew from Barcelona came to Santa Eulália, they worked swiftly and efficiently, three men who knew their job. They made short work of the windlass, the rope, and the wooden well structure; then one of the men went down into the hole to make certain the mechanism was seated properly in the water. After that, the piping was installed in sections and rose to poke up above the ground like a growing thing.

The mechanics had brought a stone slab to cap the well. It had a hole drilled in its center just large enough to accept the pipe. Some of the same strong men who hauled and shoved the saint's platform at festivals were now chosen to assist at the most delicate moment of the installation. They had to hold the heavy slab over the well while a pipe was pushed through the hole in the stone and threaded onto the well piping, and then lower the slab along the pipe without damaging it.

The aboveground housing and the long steel handle came painted a deep blue. Once it was installed, the mechanics demonstrated how the handle had to be raised and lowered several times to raise water into the chamber. The first stroke produced a mechanical sigh, the second an indignant squawk, and finally a smooth-running gush.

Initially, of course, the water was foul. First the councilors took turns purging the well, and then several others pumped. From time to time the alcalde put his hand into the stream from the spout and sniffed it, and each time he frowned.

Finally when he smelled his hand, he turned toward Josep and raised his eyebrows. Eduardo and Josep captured some of the water in their cupped hands and sniffed it.

"Perhaps a little more," Eduardo said, and Josep took his place at the pump. Presently he picked up a cup, held it under the spout, and brought it to his lips to taste it tentatively. Then he drained the cup of sweet cold water, rinsed it, and held it out to the alcalde, who drank and nodded his head, beaming.

Eduardo had the cup to his lips and was drinking as villagers crowded about them, waiting their turn to get water, and thanking the alcalde.

"I made up my mind this must never happen again. I will always take care of you," Angel Casals said modestly. "I am so happy to have found a permanent solution to the problem."

Over the cup's rim, Eduardo's eyes met Josep's. Eduardo's face remained as bland and serious as ever, but by the time he stopped drinking, his eyes were sharing an enjoyable fellowship with Josep's.

44

Towers

Eduardo Montroig's house was on the plaça, and each morning as soon as he awoke, he hurried outside to prime the pump. Josep drifted into an easy friendship with him, though they didn't spend much time together because they both worked hard, long days. Eduardo was not pompous, but his face bore an expression of solemn responsibility that made him a natural leader. He was the cap de colla of the village castellers—the captain and coach of the troupe—and he recruited his fellow councilor into its ranks. Goodwill warming his homely, long-jawed features, he appeared shocked when Josep required more than a single invitation to join.

"But we need you! We need you, Josep."

Where Josep was needed, it turned out, was in the fourth tier. He remembered from his youth that it had been to the fourth tier that Eusebi Gallego, Teresa's father, had climbed.

He had doubts, but he went to a practice and found that building a human castell began with ritual.

The members of the troupe wore a uniform—bare feet, baggy white trousers, billowy blouses, headscarves bound tightly to protect the ears. They helped each other into black sashes called faixas. Each sash was long, more than three meters; the helper pulled it straight out, very taut, while the climber held the other end against his body and then whirled like a top, round and round, until he was bound into a tight corset of fabric that gave rigid support to his spine and back and offered a good handhold to other climbers.

Eduardo spent long hours plotting the tower on paper, assigning each position based on the climber's individual strengths and weaknesses, constantly analyzing and making changes. He insisted on music at all the practices, and the grallas shrilled as he signaled the climbers to start.

Soon he called, "Let's go, four," and Josep, Albert Fiore, and Marc Rubió climbed up and over the backs of the first three layers of men.

Josep couldn't believe it. When he ascended to his place the castell was only half built, yet he felt he was as high as a bird could fly. For a split moment of terror he teetered, but Marc's strong arm kept him in place, and he regained his balance and his confidence.

Another moment and they held each other tightly while others climbed over them in turn, and Briel Tauré's feet and weight settled onto Josep's shoulders.

It was in the fifth layer that the trouble occurred, Josep feeling it first as a ripple from above, then a lurching that threatened to pull his hand away from Marc's shoulder, and finally a tearing away of the hands that had steadied him. He felt Briel's toenails rasp his cheek and heard Albert's gutteral groan, "Merda," and they all went down together, bodies falling on other bodies.

He lay for a brief unpleasantness with someone's moist armpit on his face, but everyone quickly disentangled, cursing or laughing, according to their personalities. There were many bruises, but Eduardo soon established that there were no serious injuries.

What a strange pastime, Josep thought. But even as he did so, he recognized a new truth.

He had found something he was going to love to do.

On a warm Sunday morning Donat came to the village, and they sat on the bench near the vines and ate slightly stale bread and hard sausage.

Donat clearly thought that digging a cellar was a form of lunacy, but he was tremendously impressed by the fact that Josep had acquired their neighbor's land. "Padre would not believe it," he said.

"Yes . . . Well, but . . . I'm not going to make this quarter's payment to you and Rosa," Josep said carefully.

Donat looked at him with alarm.

"I am short of cash, but it will be just as we arranged in the contract. When I make the next payment, following the harvest, I'll also give you this payment as well, plus ten percent."

"Rosa will be upset," Donat said nervously.

"You must explain to her that it's to your advantage to wait for payment, since now you'll receive the additional penalty."

Donat became cold and distant. "You don't understand. You are not married," he said, and Josep couldn't argue with him.

"Do you have more sausage?" Donat asked peevishly.

"No, but come and we'll stop at Nivaldo's and get you a nice piece of chorizo that you can eat on the way home," Josep said and patted his brother on the shoulder.

45

Vines

*T*hat summer the weather was precisely what Josep would have ordered if it had been possible to do so, days of tolerable heat and cooler nights, and he spent long hours among the vines, wandering along the rows when his work was completed, haunting the old plants whose buds he had limited, inspecting everything as though his eyes could make the grapes grow better at every stage. The grapes on those vines came in very small. As soon as they darkened in color, he began to sample them, savoring flavors unripe but full of promise.

He did very little work in the cellar, intent on other projects. In July he emptied the stone cistern his great-grandfather had used to stomp his grapes, moving the things that had been stored in it—tools ands buckets and bags of lime—to Quim's house, and then scrubbing out the tank and rinsing it with water hauled from the river and warmed and mixed with sulfur. The cistern still was very serviceable, but the petcock that would allow him to drain the juice of trodden grapes was in bad shape and he saw it would have to be replaced. For several Fridays he attended the market in Sitges, looking for a used spigot, but finally he gave in and bought a new one of shiny brass.

It was mid-August when Emilio and Juan came to the vineyard in the cooperage's big wagon and Josep worked with them to unload two large vats made of new oak wood that smelled so good he couldn't believe they were his. They were the only new vats he had ever seen, and set in place next to Quim's house they looked even better than they smelled. He had paid Emilio for one of them, as they had agreed, and though that had left him with diminished cash and heavier debt, he was so excited that he took Maria del Mar aside and asked her to do him a favor. She hurried to Angel's farm and bought eggs, potatoes, and onions, and while the coopers sat with Josep and drank bad wine, she made a fire and cooked a huge tortilla that soon they all shared with great relish.

Josep was grateful to Emilio and Juan and liked their company, but he was impatient for them to leave. When finally they drove their wagon away, he hurried back to the Torras piece and stood before his new tanks for a long time, just looking at them.

With each passing day he was more anxious and uneasy, acutely aware of the risks he had taken. He studied the sky a great deal, waiting for nature to torture him with hail or pounding rain or some other calamity, but rain fell only once, a gentle soaker, and the days continued to be warm and the nights progressively cooler.

Maria del Mar enjoyed the autumn tradition they had established and wished to cut the cards again to see whose crop should be harvested first, but he told her he wanted to take her grapes before his, because the fruit on the old vines wasn't ripe enough. "We might as well wait until we can move onto my land and do my entire harvest," he said, and she agreed.

As usual, he enjoyed working with her. She was a ferocious worker with amazing energy, and sometimes he had to struggle to keep up as they moved along the rows, rapidly harvesting grapes.

He found himself enjoying her proximity and comparing her to other women he had known. She was prettier than Teresa and far more interesting. He allowed himself to admit that she was more desirable than

Juliana Lozano, or Renata, or Margit Fontaine, and so much easier to be with than any of those women, when she wasn't giving him hell about something.

When they finished pressing her grapes, Josep and Maria del Mar moved onto his land and harvested the grapes whose juice would go to the vinegar works, hauling them to the village press in the usual way. Most of that harvesting was done on the Alvarez piece, and he filled his own vats with the juice that would go to the vinegar company. Though many of the old Garnacha and Cariñena vines he had pruned of buds were on his family land, the oldest Ull de Llebre vines were on the Torras piece, and Josep roamed among them, picking a grape here and there and chewing judiciously.

"They are ripe," Maria del Mar told him.

But he shook his head.

"Not ripe enough," he said.

The next day, his verdict was the same.

"You're waiting too long. They will be overripe, Josep," Maria del Mar said.

"Not yet," he told her firmly.

Maria del Mar looked up at the sky. It was cloudless and blue, but they both knew how the weather could change, bringing a terrible rainstorm or a destroying wind. "It is as if you are daring God," she said in frustration.

He didn't know how to reply. Perhaps she was right, he thought, but "I think God will understand," he said.

Early the next day when he put an Ull de Llebre in his mouth and his teeth broke the thick skin, the juice in the single small grape flooded his mouth with flavor, and he nodded.

"Now we pick," he said.

He and Maria del Mar and Briel Taulé began to take the grapes in the first grey light, cutting bunches and spreading each basketful on a table in the shade and picking the individual berries, slow, fussy work. If the growth had been greener Josep would have asked them to destem everything, but the vines were so ripe he told them a bit of stem now and then would be a good thing. They carefully culled out any spoiled grape or bit of trash before pouring the beautiful dark treasure gently into the stone cistern.

They picked part of the crop in the coolness of early morning, and began to pick the rest in the late afternoon, working hard and fast throughout the early evening in order to beat the coming darkness. When all light failed just before ten o'clock Josep placed lanterns and torches around the stone cistern and Maria del Mar carried her sleeping son to a blanket Josep spread where she could see him.

They sat on the rim of the cistern and scrubbed their feet and legs and then they ventured into the tank. Josep had spent most of his life on this vineyard yet had never trod grapes until he had found his way to France. Now the wet feeling of the grapes popping under his naked feet was deliciously familiar, and he smiled to see the expression on Maria del Mar's face.

"What should we do?" Briel asked.

"Just walk," Josep said.

For an hour it was pleasant to stride in the tank in the cool air, back and forth, six paces the long way. The two men were shirtless, their trouser legs rolled high, and Maria del Mar's hem was pinned to her waist. After a time, it grew more difficult, their legs tiring, each step marked by the sucking sound of the sweet-smelling must that seemed to release their feet almost reluctantly.

To keep from impeding one another, they walked in a line. Soon Briel began to sing a song about a thieving magpie that stole olives from a farmer's wife. The rhythm of the music helped them walk, and when the youth's song was done, Maria del Mar began to sing tunelessly about the new moon shining on a woman who yearns for her lover. She didn't do the song well, but she was brazen and sang it through, several verses, and after that Briel sang again, another song about lovers, but not a romantic song as hers had been. He sang of a fat boy whose sexual excitement caused him to faint each time he prepared to make love. The beginning of the song was very funny, and the three of them were laughing, but Josep thought Briel was a fool and disrespectful to Maria del Mar.

"Enough singing, I think," he said drily, and Briel fell silent.

When Josep reached the end of the tank and turned, he saw that Maria del Mar was smiling at him just a bit mockingly, as if she could read his mind.

It was early morning before Josep thought the grapes thoroughly crushed. In the first gray light, Maria del Mar lifted her sleeping son and carried him home, but Josep and Briel still had work. A pailful at a time, they moved the trodden must to one of the new high oak vats. Then they hitched the hinny to the wagon and brought water from the river and carefully sluiced out the treading tank.

When Josep fell into bed the sun was high and he had only a few hours of sleep before they had to begin to pick the Garnacha.

On the third day, when they harvested the Cariñena, they were exhausted and Briel had a painful stone bruise on the ball of his left foot; by the time they began to tread grapes in the tank the youth was in pain and limping badly, and Josep sent him home.

Worse, Francesc could not sleep and was running about in the dark. Maria del Mar sighed.

"My son must sleep in his own house tonight."

Josep nodded readily. "There is less than half the volume of Cariñena grapes than we had of Ull de Llebre or Garnacha," he said. "I can mash them by myself."

Yet when she carried the little boy home, he faced the long night ahead with less than pleasure. The sky was moonless. It was very quiet; far away, a dog barked. The day had been slightly warmer but there was a cooling breeze that he welcomed, because he had been told that air movement carried natural yeasts into the tanks, helping the fermentation process turn the grape juice into wine.

Reaching down, he took a handful of the sweet mash and chewed as he began to plod. Overtired, he walked sullenly by himself in the satin darkness, his mind closing down so that he was barely conscious, his world diminished to six paces up, one pace across; six paces back, one pace across; six paces up . . .

A long time passed.

He wasn't conscious of her approach, but Maria del Mar was there, stepping carefully into the mash.

"He is finally asleep."

"You could have slept also," he said, but she shrugged.

They walked together in silence until they collided while making a turn.

"Jesús," he said. He reached out only to help but in a moment found himself kissing her.

"You taste like a grape," she said.

They kissed again for a long time.

"Marimar."

His hand spoke to her and she gave a slight shudder.

"Not here in the must," she told him. When he helped her out of the tank, he was no longer tired.

46

Small Sips

The next morning, after the juice and the must had been stored, they sat at her table. Josep knew just enough about coffee to recognize that her brew was bad, but nevertheless they drank several cups as they talked.

"After all, it is a natural need," Maria del Mar said.

"Do you believe the need is the same for a woman as for a man?"

"The same?" She shrugged. "I am not a man, but . . . a woman has a great need also. Did you think otherwise?"

He smiled at her and shrugged. "You have no one at the moment, nor do I," Josep said. "So . . . It's good we are able to give one another comfort. As friends."

"Only, not too often," she said shyly. "Perhaps we should wait until the need builds very strongly, so when finally we are together . . . Well . . . You understand?"

He looked at her dubiously and sipped his coffee.

Maria del Mar went to the window and peered out.

"Francesc is climbing his trees," she said.

They agreed it was an opportunity. Because, after all, it might be some time before it would happen again.

Now Josep allowed himself to become extremely nervous, because he had placed his livelihood in nature's hands and had to wait for the mysterious process by which grape juice was transmuted into wine. There were

several vital things he had to do to help things along.
Everything in the must that wasn't juice—the skins, the
seeds, and the stems—were repeatedly buoyed up to the
surface of the liquid to become a cap, and the cap soon
dried. Every few hours Josep drained off liquid from the
bottom of the tank and climbed a ladder so he could pour
the juice over the floating solids, and now and again he
would use a rake to push the cap down, mixing it with
the body of the liquid.

He did these things over and over again, throughout
the day, and sometimes when he awoke in the middle
of the night, he would go to the tanks and perform the
rituals in the dark, almost in his sleep.

The weather stayed cool, slowing what was happening to the grape juice, but when a week had passed, Josep
began drawing a few ounces from each vat twice a day
and tasting it.

He was moody and skittish, poor company, and
Maria del Mar left him alone. She had always lived with
grapes, and no one needed explain to her that now timing was everything. If Josep should interrupt the process
too soon, it would mar the coloration of the wine and its
ability to age, and if he waited too long, it would become
poor, flat stuff. So she hovered in the background and
sternly kept Francesc in his own vineyard.

Josep waited, each day interminable, wetting the caps
and punching them down, tasting samples again and
again, the sips revealing to him the growing strengths in
the juices and their differences.

When the pressings had been in the vats for two weeks,
the sugars in the juice had become alcohol. If the weather
had been hot the Ull de Llebre mash would have grown
too strong, but cool temperatures had kept the alcohol
moderate, and the sweetness that remained was fresh and
appealing. The Ull de Llebre lacked acidity but his Garnacha was tart and lively, while the Cariñena had a green,
almost bitter power that Josep knew was a necessary in-
gredient in any wine that could be expected to age well.

Fourteen days after he had placed the juice in the vats, he sat at his kitchen table early one morning with three filled bowls in front of him, and an empty bowl, a pitcher of water, a large glass, a very small glass, and a paper and pen.

He began by half-filling the small glass with Ull de Llebre and pouring it into the large glass, to which he added a similar measure of Cariñena and another of Garnacha, mixing them with a spoon. Then he took a sip, swished it around in his mouth at length, and spat it into the empty bowl. He sat reflectively for a moment before he rinsed his mouth with water and made a note of his reaction to the blend.

He forced himself to wait, to allow his mouth to lose the taste of the sampling, going outside and busying himself with small jobs, and then came back and blended and sampled another combination, this time mixing only Garnacha and Cariñena.

Every few hours he would taste another blending, reflect on it, and make a brief note, each time replacing the wine in the bowls so that overexposure to the air would not give him false information.

By the morning of the seventeenth day of fermentation, he knew the wines were ready and that he would place them in barrels that afternoon. Three sheets of paper on his table held his notes, but he knew many more combinations were possible. To begin the day he made a new mixture, sixty percent Ull de Llebre, thirty percent Garnacha, and ten percent Cariñena. He took a sip, swirled it in his mouth, and spat it out.

He sat for a moment, and then he made the same mixture and repeated the exercise.

He waited a bit longer before repeating exactly what he had just done twice, with a single exception—the third time he could not bring himself to spit.

Other mixtures had shown promise, but this wine seemed to fill his mouth. Josep closed his eyes, tasting the same flavors of berries and plums he had found in previous samples. But also black cherries, a lick of stoniness, a whiff of sage, a sniff of the wood of the vat. Scents he remembered, and tiny traces of sweetness and tartness that he was meeting for the first time. This mixture had a new wholeness, and he allowed it to play softly along the lining of his cheeks, slip under his tongue and slide over it, so that a little trickled down his throat and teased warmly.

When he swallowed, the drink bloomed fully as it went down, so that he sat and closely studied his rising pleasure. The taste played on and on in his mouth after the liquid was gone.

The scents rose into his nose and stayed, and Josep began to tremble as though something bad had happened, as though he were full of fear, as though he were not newly realizing that he had made *wine*.

He sat late at the table, just looking at the wine as if by studying it in the bowl he could learn secrets and wisdom. It was rich and dark, scarlet-red, the color gifted by the thick grape-skins that had soaked for two-and-a-half weeks in the fermenting juices.

He thought it beautiful.

And was tormented by an overwhelming need to show it to someone.

If only he could fill a bottle with this wine and present it to his father, he thought . . . Perhaps he should bring it to Nivaldo.

But he poured wine into his coffee-stained cup and carried it through the rows of vines to Maria del Mar's threshold, where he tapped carefully, lest he waken the child.

Finally she opened the door, blinking crankily, her eyes concerned and her hair wild from the pillow, and he followed her to the oil lamp on her table before he gave her the cup, because he wanted to see her face as she drank.

47

Like a Brother

*J*osep made a small, hot fire and held each of the empty 100-liter barrels over it in turn, searing and toasting the interiors as he had seen winemakers do it in France. The blended wine filled all fourteen of the small 100-liter barrels, as well as two of the four 225-liter barrels that he owned. From time to time he would have to take wine from one of the large barrels and top off the small casks, for the new oak drank liquid like a thirsty man, and air in the barrels would spoil the wine. After the three large vats were drained, Josep and Briel took the must to the village press and squeezed out another half-barrel of wine. Added to some of the unblended wine from the trodden grapes, the second pressing gave him nearly a barrelful of ordinary wine that didn't have the quality of the blend but still was far better than any of the wines his father had made.

He and Briel had just begun carrying the barrels into the cellar when Donat came walking in from the road, and Josep greeted his brother easily but with some inner wariness, because he knew the purpose of the visit.

"Let me give you a hand," Donat said.

"No, you sit and rest. You've come a long way," Josep told him. In fact, even the larger and heavier barrels were best handled by one man at each end, and a third man would only get in the way. But Donat trailed after them as they lugged a cask, examining the details of the cellar.

"This cellar has been a fair amount of work. Wouldn't Padre be amazed to see it in his hill!"

Josep smiled.

Donat pointed to the half-finished stone lining of the earthen wall. "I could give you a hand with that work if I could get away from the job for a few days."

"Oh, no thank you, Donat, I enjoy the work with the stones. I just do a little bit now and again," Josep said.

His brother dawdled and watched as they carried in the rest of the barrels, then the visit took a good turn, when Josep drew a pitcher of the blended wine and they carried it to Nivaldo's.

The old man was impressed by the wine and was visibly pleased to have the brothers with him, and the three of them spent several hours sitting companionably over the drink and several bowls of Nivaldo's stew. Nivaldo gave Donat a cheese to carry back to Rosa.

Josep and his brother walked back to the casa through the still coolness of the evening.

"Peaceful," Donat said. "A good old village, isn't it?"

"It is."

He made up the sleeping pad with a blanket and a pillow, and Donat, feeling the wine, settled into it at once. "Goodnight, Josep," he called warmly.

"Sleep well, Donat."

Josep washed and dried the pitcher, and by the time he went upstairs he heard the familiar sound of his brother's snores.

In the morning they ate bread and hard cheese, and then Donat belched, pushed back from the table, and stood. "Might as well get on the road for the early traffic, so someone can give me a ride."

Josep nodded.

"So, the money."

"Ah, the payments? I don't have the money yet."

Donat's face reddened.

"What do you mean? You told me, 'Two payments, after the harvest.'"

"Well, I've made the wine. Now I'll sell it and get the money."

Donat looked at him. "Who will you sell it to? And when?"

"I don't know yet. I'll have to learn that. Don't worry, Donat. You've seen the wine and tasted it. It's like money in your pocket, plus ten percent."

"Rosa will have a crazy fit," Donat said heavily. He found the chair and sat down again. "It's a hard thing for you, isn't it, making the payments?"

"This is a difficult time," Josep said. "I've had unexpected expenses. But I can do it. You just have to wait a little while for your money, that's all."

"I have been thinking about something that could make things easier for you . . . I'd like to come back to the village. I want to be your partner."

They regarded one another.

"No, Donat," Josep said gently.

". . . Then, how is this? You have two pieces of land. You give one of them—I don't care which one—to Rosa and me, to settle your debt with us. It could be good, Josep, living next to one another. You want to make us some nice wine, I'll help you, and we could each of us work together, sell our main wine for vinegar, brothers making a living."

Josep forced himself to shake his head. "What's happened to your plans?" he asked. "I thought you loved working at the mill."

"I'm having trouble with a foreman," Donat said sullenly. "He picks on me, makes life a misery. I'll never get a chance to become a mechanic. And the damn machines are destroying my hearing." He sighed. "Look, if I have to, I'll just work for you for wages."

Something within Josep shuddered as he remembered what it had been like, always squabbling, always having to do Donat's share as well as his own.

"It wouldn't work out," he said, and he saw his brother's eyes harden.

"I'll give you some of the second pressing to take home," Josep said, and busied himself washing out a bottle and finding a cork.

Donat came with him to the wine. "We're not good enough to be given your best?" he said roughly.

Josep felt guilty. "Yesterday I wanted you to taste the blend, but I won't be drinking it myself, or giving it away," he said. "I need to sell it so I can give you your money."

Donat placed the filled bottle in his sack and turned away.

What did his grunt mean? Cheap bastard? Thank you? Goodbye?

As Josep stood and watched his brother moving slowly down the path to the road, it seemed to him that Donat walked like a tired man treading grapes.

48

The Visit

*T*he Castellers of San Eulália had not met during most of the autumn, but as soon as the grape harvest was complete, Eduardo assembled his climbers.

Josep was glad to attend the practice, though he didn't understand why he liked it. He wondered what makes men want to stand on one another's shoulders, as high as they can build a tower with human flesh and bone instead of stone and mortar, and enjoy doing it again and again.

Inevitably, the time always came when a mishap would be caused by someone's momentary lapse, a second of strayed attention, a careless movement, a desperate swaying followed by a mass plummeting to earth.

"A fall need not happen," Eduardo told his castellers, "if everyone knows exactly what he must do, and he does it precisely the same way, time after time. Listen to me, and we shall have nothing but success. We need strength, balance, courage, and good sense.

"I want you to climb and descend in silence, quickly, with spirit, not a second wasted, everyone taking care of himself.

"But, if you should fall . . ." He paused, wanting them to listen hard. "If you should fall, try not to fall out and away from the tower, because that's where injuries lurk. Fall into the base of the castell, where your drop will be broken by the pinya and the folre."

At the very bottom of the castell, the strong men who bore the brunt of its weight were surrounded by a large crowd that pressed in on them and formed the pinya, the bulk. On the shoulders of the pinya stood a crowd of other people, the folre, or cover, also pressing forward to add more support to the second and third layers of climbers.

Josep thought the pinya and the folre were like a great rootball lending strength to the shaft of a tree that rose skyward.

He had quickly learned the nomenclature. A structure with three or more men per level was a castell. With two men per layer, it was a tower, with one man per layer, a pillar.

"We have an invitation," Eduardo told them. "The Castellers of Sitges have challenged us to a contest of castell-building, three men to a layer, to be held in their marketplace the Friday after Easter Sunday—the Sitges fishermen against the Santa Eulália grape-growers."

There were murmurs of approval and some quick applause, and Eduardo smiled and raised a cautionary hand. "The fishermen will be very strong competition, because they grow up constantly balancing themselves on boats tossed by the sea.

"I have given a great deal of thought to how we can build our best castell eight tiers tall."

Eduardo had already designed the castell on paper, and he began to call out names; as his name was called, each climber took his assigned position, and the castell began to rise slowly and raggedly.

Josep was assigned one of the places in the fourth tier, and he participated as the castell was assembled and disassembled three times, with Eduardo studying the climbers and making several changes and substitutions.

During a break period Josep noted that Maria del Mar and Francesc had arrived. She stood with Eduardo, their heads close and their faces serious as they spoke, and finally Eduardo nodded.

"Climb on me," he called to Francesc, and turned his back to him.

Francesc began to run unevenly, and something caught in Josep's throat. The boy looked bad as he scuttled like a crab. But he gained momentum and threw himself at Eduardo's back and clawed to his shoulders.

Eduardo was satisfied. Turning, he caught Francesc and ordered the first four layers of the tower to climb again so the boy could be tested.

When Josep was in position, he could no longer see Francesc. People were chatting as they stood in clumps and relaxed, but the drums and the grallas began to play lustily, as if this were a performaßnce before royalty instead of an opportunity to evaluate a very young climber.

In a few moments he felt small hands clutching his trousers, and the child was on him like a small ape. Francesc's arms circled his neck and he felt the boy's breath.

"Josep!" a joyful voice said into his ear.

Then Francesc quickly climbed down again.

On Saturday afternoon Josep was moving a barrowload of gravel from the cellar excavation to be spread on the road when he noted a trap approaching, pulled by a grey horse and containing a man and a woman.

As it neared him, he saw that the woman was his sister-in-law, Rosa Sert. The man was someone he had never seen before. Rosa gave a little wave as the driver turned the horse into the vineyard.

"Hola," Josep called and left what he had been doing.

"Hola, Josep," Rosa said. "This is my cousin, Carles Sert. The mill is servicing the machines, and I have a bit of time to be free of the job, and Carles wanted to take a day in the country, so . . ."

Josep looked at her without comment.

Her cousin Carles. The attorney.

He led them to the bench, brought cool water, and waited until they drank.

"You go on with your work," Rosa said, waving her hand. "Don't you bother about us."

So he got another barrow-load of gravel and went back to spreading it on the road. From time to time he glanced up to keep track of them. Rosa was walking the lawyer about the property. The man wasn't saying very much, but she did a lot of talking. They disappeared into the vines, and then they reappeared and went to the masia. They stopped to assess the house from afar and then made a complete circuit around it, peering.

"What the hell," Josep growled to himself, for the lawyer was shaking the door to see if it was built solidly.

Josep dropped the shovel and went to them.

"I want you to get the hell away from here. Now."

"No need to be unkind," the cousin said coolly.

"You've put the wagon before the mule. Your cousin can wait until I don't make the third payment before she takes possession. Until then, get off my property."

They went, not looking at him or speaking again. Rosa's mouth was set in a cool grimace, as if to indicate to Josep that he didn't know how to talk with civilized people. The lawyer flicked the reins, the grey horse moved them away, and Josep stood by the house and watched them disappear.

What do I do now? he asked himself.

49

A Trip to the Market

*J*osep had inherited thirty-one empty bottles that had been abandoned by Quim, but only fourteen of them were the correct shape and would hold three-quarters of a liter. He found four old bottles tucked away among his tools, and when he sent Briel Taulé through the village to see how many he could collect, Briel came back with eleven more. In all, twenty-nine were usable.

He scrubbed and rinsed them until they gleamed, filled them with the dark wine, and tapped in the corks very carefully. Marimar came to help him make the labels. The sight of the filled bottles had the strange effect of making both of them nervous.

"Where will you sell them?"

"I'll try to sell them in Sitges. Tomorrow is market day. I thought I'd take the boy with me, if that's all right," he said, and she nodded.

"Oh, he'll like that . . . What do you want me to print on these labels?"

"I don't know . . . Finca Alvarez? Bodega Alvarez? No, those sound too grand. Perhaps, Vinas Alvarez?"

She frowned. "They don't sound exactly right." She dipped the nib into the ink and the pen scratched as she drew some circles and a stem.

When she held up the label, he looked at it and shrugged. But he smiled.

JOSEP'S VINES

1877

Early the next morning he wrapped each bottle in several sheets of newspaper, old copies of Nivaldo's *El Cascabel,* and made a nest of ragged blankets to cushion the wine on the trip to Sitges. In a cloth sack he packed chorizo and bread, and it went into the wagon too, along with a bucket and two drinking cups.

It was still dark when he drove Hinny into the Valls vineyard, but Francesc was dressed and waiting for him. Maria del Mar stood, morning cup of coffee to her lips, and watched as they went away, the boy sitting next to Josep on the wagon seat.

Francesc was quiet, but he had never been beyond Santa Eulália, and his face showed his excitement. Very soon they entered territory that was new to him, and Josep saw that his eyes were everywhere, taking in the occasional masia, unfamiliar fields and vineyards and olive groves, three black bulls behind a fence, and the far-off sight of Montserrat reaching for the sky.

When the sun came out, it was very pleasant to sit in the wagon with the child as Hinny clop-clopped northward.

"I have to pee," Josep said presently. "Do you have to pee?"

Fransesc nodded, and Josep stopped by some pines. He lifted Francesc down, and the two of them stood next to one another at the side of the road, two males watering the gorse. It may have been his imagination, but Josep thought he saw a bit of swagger in Francesc's limping as they returned to the wagon.

The sun was well-up when they reached Sitges, and the market was already crowded with vendors, so Josep had to settle for an open space at the very rear, next to a stall that gave off the fine smells of broiling squid and prawns and garlicky fish stew. One of the two burly cooks was waiting on a customer, but the other ventured over to the wagon, a smile on his face.

"Hola," he said, peering at the newspaper-wrapped bottles. "What is it you are selling today?"

"Wine."

"Wine! Is it any good?

"Not merely good. *Special*."

"Ohhh . . . How much is this special wine?" the man said in mock dread.

When Josep told him, he closed his eyes and turned down his mouth. "That is twice as much as one has to pay for a bottle of wine."

Josep was aware this was true, but it was the price he would need to receive, while selling every bottle in order to be able to pay his debt to Rosa and Donat.

"No, it is twice as much as one has to pay for the ordinary wine of the region, which is mule piss. This is *wine*."

"Where is this wonderful wine made?"

"Santa Eulália."

"Santa Eulália? I'm a casteller of Sitges. We will soon compete with the castellers of Santa Eulália."

"I know. I'm a casteller of Santa Eulália."

"Truly." He grinned. "Ah, we shall mercilessly beat your natjas, senyor."

Josep grinned back. "Perhaps not, senyor."

"I am Frederic Fuxá, and that is my brother Efrén, serving the food. He is assistant to the leader of our team, and he and I are in the third tier of our castell."

Third tier, Josep marveled. This man and his brother were *large*. If they were third tier, what did the men of the first two tiers look like? "I'm in our castell's fourth tier. I'm Josep Alvarez, and this is Francesc Valls, who is in training to become our enxaneta."

"The enxaneta? Oh, that is a very important job. No one can win a castell competition without a very good little enxaneta to reach the very top," Fuxá said to Francesc, who smiled.

"Well, I wish you good fortune today," Fuxá said.

"I thank you, senyor. Are you interested in buying my wine?"

"It's too expensive. I'm a hard-working fisherman, Senyor Alvarez, not a wealthy winemaker from Santa Eulália," Fuxá said good-naturedly and returned to his stall.

Josep filled the bucket with water at the public pump and set it on the wagon bed.

"It will be your job to rinse the cups after somebody samples the wine," he said.

Francesc nodded. "What do we do now, Josep?"

"Now? We wait," Josep told him, and the boy nodded again and sat expectantly, holding a cup in each hand.

Time passed slowly.

There was a great deal of bustle in the interior lanes of the marketplace, but fewer people walked into the final row, where most of the spaces still were vacant.

Josep looked over to the food stand, where a heavyset woman was buying a serving of tortilla.

"A bottle of good wine, senyora?" he called, but she shook her head and walked away.

A few minutes later, two men bought squid and ate it while standing there.

"A good bottle of wine?" Josep called, and they sauntered to the wagon.

"How much?" asked one of them, still chewing.

When Josep told them, the man swallowed and shook his head. "Too high," he said, and he and his companion turned away.

"Have a taste before you go."

Josep unwrapped a bottle and reached for his corkscrew. He poured the wine carefully into each cup, about one-quarter the amount of a normal small serving of wine.

The men accepted the cups and drank, two slow swallows.

"Good," one of them said grudgingly.

His friend grunted.

They looked at one another.

"We might each take a bottle, give us a lower price."

Josep smiled but shook his head. "No, I can't."

"Then . . . " the man shrugged, and his companion shook his head as he handed the cups back.

Frederic Fuxá had been watching from his booth, and he winked grimly at Josep: *See? Did I tell you?*

"Now you can do your job," Josep said to Francesc, and the boy beamed and sloshed the used cups in the pail of water.

At the end of an hour they had given out four more samples but made no sales, and Josep was beginning to wonder if selling the wine in a marketplace was a plan that was going to work.

But the first two men who had sampled the wine wandered back.

"It was good but I can't be certain," one of them said. "I need another little swallow."

"Ah, I'm sorry. I am able to give only one sample to each customer," Josep said.

"But . . . afterwards we might buy your wine."

"No. I'm truly sorry."

The man looked annoyed, but his companion said, "It's nothing. I'm going to buy a bottle now."

The first man sighed. "I will take one also," he said finally.

Josep handed over two newspaper-wrapped bottles and accepted their money with unsteady hands, feeling the blood rushing to his face. He was accustomed to a lifetime in which his family produced wine that was picked up by Clemente in a fixed, unremarkable routine. But this was the very first time that someone had bought his wine as a matter of choice, paying their money to him because he had made a vintage they desired.

"Thank you, senyores. I hope you enjoy my wine," he said.

Frederic Fuxá had been listening from his booth and came to the wagon to congratulate Josep. "Your first sale of the day. "But do you mind if I give you some advice?"

"Of course not."

"My brother and I have been coming here nineteen years. We are fishermen. Everything we cook at the market we have taken from the sea ourselves. Everyone knows us, and we don't have to prove our seafood is fresh and good. But you are new to the market. People here don't know you, so what harm in giving someone a second sample of your wine?"

"I can only give away two of these bottles," Josep said. "I must sell every one of the rest of them or I am in terrible trouble."

Fuxá pursed his lips. As a businessman he understood the situation without another word.

"I would like to taste your wine myself, senyor."

Josep poured into both cups. "Take one to your brother."

Frederic bought two bottles and Efrén Fuxá, one.

Half an hour later, two men and a woman came to the food stand.

"Hola to the Bocabellas. How is it where you are today? Are you selling much?" Efrén asked.

"Not bad," the woman said. "How about you?"

Efrén pursed his lips and nodded.

"We hear someone is giving tastes of wine," one of the men said.

Frederic pointed at Josep's wagon. "Truly fine. We just bought it for our Easter wine."

They came over and claimed their samples. The woman smacked her lips. "Very nice. But our Oncle makes wine."

"Aaargh. Oncle doesn't makes wine you would drink when he's not with you," one of the men said, and the three of them laughed. They each bought a bottle.

Frederic watched them walk away. "That was a fortunate sale. They are cousins, vegetable farmers, an important family in Sitges, and born talkers. They take turns every market day to visit other vendors and exchange gossip. They'll mention your wine to a number of people."

In the next hour half a dozen people tasted the wine without buying. Then two venders came at the same time, and another arrived while the first two were tasting the wine. Josep had noticed that shoppers at the market tended to stop where there were already people, perhaps out of a human need to investigate something that others found desirable. That worked now, for a short line of shoppers gathered behind the vendors, and the line didn't disappear for several hours.

By midafternoon, when he and Francesc managed to eat their lunch of bread and chorizo, Josep had changed the rinsewater twice and finally had emptied the bucket. Despite his edict barring second helpings, he had used up the two bottles of sample wine while nine bottles remained unsold. But by that time word of mouth about the presence of a wine vendor at the market had done its work, and he sold his last bottle by late afternoon, several hours before the market's closing. He bought Francesc a victory plate of squid, and while the boy ate, Josep visited a vender of second-hand objects and found four empty wine bottles.

On the way home Francesc sat in his lap, and Josep showed him how to hold the reins. Francesc fell asleep while driving. For half an hour Josep drove with the skinny little form plastered against his chest, then Francesc woke long enough to be transferred, and for the rest of the trip home he slept on the blankets in the back of the wagon, next to the empty bottles.

That Sunday the attorney drove his gray horse into the vineyard again, and this time Donat was with him.

The attorney sat in the trap and did not look at Josep, who noted a leather case on the seat. Doubtless, he thought, it contained papers they would have served him while taking possession of the land for nonpayment.

His brother greeted him nervously. "Do you have the money, Josep?"

"I do," he said quietly.

He had the sum all counted out and waiting for them, and he brought from the house papers of his own, individual receipts for each of the two payments he had missed, and a third receipt for the payment due that day. He handed his papers to Donat, who read them quickly and handed them to the man in the trap. "Carles?"

The attorney read them. Undoubtedly he was disappointed, but his face was carefully without expression.

Donat's face, however, unmistakenly contained relief as he accepted and counted the money. Josep brought pen and ink, and Donat signed the three receipts.

"I'm sorry about all the fuss, Josep," he said, but Josep didn't reply.

Donat turned away and moved toward the trap, but then he stopped and came back.

"She is not a mean woman. I know it looks as though she is. It is only that at times she is overcome by our situation." Josep saw that Rosa's cousin did not like apologies; his disapproving face was no longer blank.

"Goodbye, Donat," Josep said, and his brother nodded and climbed into the seat next to Carles Sert.

Josep stood by his house and watched them go away. It was odd, he thought, how it was possible to feel good and bad at the same time.

50

A Decision

Eduardo Montroig took castelling competitions very seriously, and the atmosphere at the practice sessions of the Santa Eulália castellers grew very businesslike, with less bantering and more work to perfect balance, rhythm, and the precision of their tasks.

Eduardo had a good deal of information about the Sitges castellers, who were very experienced and accomplished, and he had become convinced that Santa Eulália could win the competition only if it could add something special to its castell. He designed a new element for their structure, which required more frequent and more vigorous practices for the village team, and he cautioned his castellers that it must be kept secret so it would be a surprise when it was unveiled in Sitges.

Maria del Mar brought her son to several of the practices, and then Josep suggested that he could bring Francesc, since he was going anyway, and she agreed gladly.

For Josep the high point of each practice was the moment when Francesc clambered over three tiers of men and ended up on his back long enough to whisper his name into his ear. Francesc dreamed of the day when he would be able to climb over many tiers of men and youths and reach the top of the assembled castell to raise his arm in triumph. Josep worried about him, because a small frail boy would be particularly vulnerable in the event that a castell should collapse. But Eduardo was bringing Francesc along slowly, and Josep knew that Eduardo was steady and sensible, a man who did not take unnecessary risks.

One day, without comment or fuss, Eduardo reached the end of his mourning period and removed the black bands from the sleeves of his clothing. He retained his calm dignity, but the people of the village noticed a change, if not a lightness than at least an easing of his personality, and they told each other wryly that soon Eduardo would be looking about for a new wife.

Several evenings later, Josep was pruning vines when he saw Eduardo walking down the road. He paused in his work with pleasure, for he enjoyed the prospect of a visit. But to his surprise, Eduardo merely lifted a hand in greeting and continued to walk past.

There was nothing on the lane beyond Josep's land except Maria del Mar's house and vineyard.

Josep busied himself with his vines, keeping an eye on the road.

He waited a long time. It was dusk when he saw Eduardo making his way back. Francesc was keeping him company as he walked down the lane, Josep observed.

"Bona tarda, Josep!" Eduardo called.

"Bona tarda, Josep!" Francesc echoed.

"Bona tarda, Eduardo. Bona tarda, Francesc," he answered heartily, his knife cutting too swiftly and almost blindly, doing damage to a perfectly sound vine.

He lay awake most of the night, staring into darkness.

Well, he must feel happy for Maria del Mar, he tried to tell himself.

Several times she had spoken to him about the kind of man she dreamed might some day come into her life. Someone who was gentle and who would treat her with kindness. A steady man who would not run away. Someone who was a good worker, someone who would be a good father to her son.

In short . . . serious Eduardo Montroig. Perhaps not a man with a sense of humor, but a good person and a community leader, a man with standing in the village.

In the morning Josep returned to his pruning chores, yet desperation and fury was rising within him as relentlessly as an ocean tide, and midmorning he dropped the knife and strode to her vineyard.

She was nowhere in sight on her land, and he struck the door.

When she opened it, he didn't answer her greeting.

"I want to share your life. In every way."

She looked at him with astonishment.

"I ... have the strongest feelings for you. The strongest feelings!" Now she understood, he saw. Her mouth quivered—was she stifling laughter at him, he thought, panicking—and she closed her eyes.

He went on, his voice breaking, no more able to control his emotions or his words than a bull in the midst of a clumsy charge straight at the point of the sword. "I admire you. I want to work with you every day and sleep with you every night. Every night, and never again to fuck as if we were each just doing a favor for a friend. I want to share your son, who also has my love. I will give you other children. I want to fill your belly with children.

"I offer you half of my two sections. They have debt, but both are valuable, as you know.

"I need you. Marimar, I need you and I want you to be my wife."

She was very pale. He saw she was summoning strength, gathering herself to destroy him. There was moisture in her eyes, but her voice was steady when she answered him.

"Oh, Josep ... Of course."

He had steeled himself for refusal, and at first he couldn't accept the words.

"You must calm yourself, Josep. Of course I want you. Surely you must know that," she said.

Her mouth trembled as she smiled at him, and for the rest of his life he would never be able to decide whether her smile of tenderness also contained the gleam of victory.

51

Plans

*H*e held both her hands in his, unable to let her go, and covered her face with the kind of kisses given to a woman by a cherishing father or brother. What such kisses said to her was new, which made them exciting, though when his mouth found hers there was no doubt that they kissed as lovers.

"We must go to the priest," she said faintly. "I want you somehow bound to me before you come to your senses and run far away." But her smile told him she wasn't worried over that possibility.

Padre Pio was not surprised when he learned they wanted to marry.

"Where were you baptized?"

He was pleased when they both told him it had been in the church he now served as pastor.

"Is there any need for haste?" he asked Maria del Mar, not dropping his gaze below her face.

"No, Padre."

"Good. Some in the Church believe that whenever it is possible, an engagement between rigorous Catholics should last a full year," the priest said.

Maria del Mar was silent. Josep grunted and shook his head slowly. He met Padre Pio's gaze without defiance but without timidity.

The priest shrugged. "When the marriage involves a widow, so long an engagement is not so important," he said coolly. "But we are already two-thirds into Lent. Easter Sunday is April 2. Between now and the end of Easter week we shall be in our most solemn period of prayer and contemplation—not a period in which I am willing to celebrate an engagement or a wedding."

"When shall you be able to marry us then?" Josep asked.

"I can post the banns after Easter week . . . Suppose we agree that you are to be married on the last Saturday in April?" Padre Pio said.

Maria del Mar frowned. "That brings us to the season when the springtime work in the vineyard is at its heaviest. I don't want us to leave work to be wed and then hurry back to the vines."

"When would you prefer?" Padre Pio asked.

"The first Saturday in June," she said.

"You understand that between now and then you two are not to dwell together or engage in relations as man and wife?" he said sternly.

"Yes, Padre," Maria del Mar said. "Is that date all right?" she asked Josep.

"If that is what you wish," Josep said to her.

He was experiencing something totally unfamiliar to him, and with a shock, he recognized it as joy.

But when they were alone again, they faced the fact that the waiting period was going to be difficult. They embraced chastely.

"June 2 is ten weeks away. A long time."

"I know."

She cast a glance at Francesc, playing with some round stones in the dust at their feet, and moved closer so she could speak into Josep's ear.

"I think Francesc could do well with a small one to keep his eyes on while we are working, no?"

"I agree. I would like to start another child at once."

As they looked at one another, he allowed himself thoughts he would not share with the priest.

Perhaps she was having similar thoughts. "I think that for now we should not spend a great deal of time together," she said. "It will be best if we limit temptation, or we will surely be carried away, and we must go to confession before the wedding."

He agreed reluctantly, knowing she was right.

"What is the word for when people of wealth place money into a business?" she said.

He was puzzled. "An investment?"

She nodded; that was the word. "The waiting will be our investment," she said.

Josep liked Eduardo Montroig and wanted to treat him with respect. He walked to Eduardo's vineyard that afternoon and told him quietly and plainly that he and Maria del Mar had been to the priest and had made plans to be married.

Eduardo was betrayed by the briefest of frowns, but he stroked his long chin, and his plain face was warmed by a rare smile. "She will make a fine wife. I wish both of you all good fortune," he said.

Josep told the news to only one other person, Nivaldo, with whom he drank a toast in honor of the news. Nivaldo was very pleased.

52

A Contest in Sitges

$\mathcal{T}$he Sunday following Easter, Josep and Marimar sat in church with Francesc between them, and listened to Padre Pio.

"I publish the banns of marriage between Josep Alvarez of this parish and the widow Maria del Mar Orriols of this parish. If any of you know just impediment why these persons should not be joined together in Holy Matrimony, you are to declare it.

"This is the first time of asking."

He had placed the banns on the church door and would read them for two more Sundays, after which they would be formally engaged.

After the service, while the priest stood at the church door greeting his congregants and Francesc sat on the bench in front of the grocery eating a sausage, Josep and Marimar stood in the plaça and received the good wishes, embraces, and kisses of their fellow villagers.

Josep used a steady diet of labor to fill his life during the long and impatient days of the engagement. He finished the vines and returned to his work in the cellar, completing three-quarters of the stone retaining wall by the first Friday in April, the day of the castelling tournament. He had haunted marketplaces and had found thirty more wine bottles. Washed, filled with dark wine, and labeled, they were wrapped in newspaper sheets and stowed on blankets in the back of the wagon, sharing the space with Francesc. Marimar sat next to Josep as he drove to the marketplace in Sitges.

It was the same trip as the one he and the boy had made once before, but there were notable differences. When they came to the grove of pines, Josep stopped the hinny, but this time he took Francesc into the trees so they could piss in privacy, and when they returned to the wagon, Marimar visited the sheltering privacy of the trees.

The trip was pleasant. Marimar was good, quiet company, and in a holiday mood. Somehow, her manner made Josep feel that he was already a family man, and he relished the role.

When they reached Sitges, he drove Hinny directly to the location next to the seafood stand of the Fuxá brothers, who greeted him warmly but with jovial descriptions of how they would annihilate the Santa Eulália castellers in the coming tournament.

"We've been waiting for you," Frederic said, "because we used up our wine during the holiday." Each of them bought two more bottles almost before Josep had positioned the wagon, and this time he did not have a long waiting period for other customers, as several other vendors came to buy wine and attracted a small group of shoppers to the site. Maria del Mar joined Josep in selling the wine, which she did as naturally as if she had been selling from a wagon all her life.

Most of the people of Santa Eulália had come to the marketplace. Indeed, a large number of villagers were either climbers or members of the pinya or the baixos, the crowds that supported the bottom two rows of the castell. Most of Josep's neighbors had come to witness or participate in the tournament, and they wandered by to watch as he sold the wine he had made in the village.

Several people he knew in Sitges had come to support their own team, and they stopped by the wagon to greet him and to be introduced to Francesc and Maria del Mar.

Juliana Lozano and her husband bought a bottle, and Emilio Rivera bought three.

Josep sold his last bottle of wine well before everything closed down for an hour so the castelling could take place. He, Marimar, and Francesc sat on the lip of the wagonbed and ate the Fuxás' fish stew while they watched the brothers help one another into their faixas.

After they had eaten, Marimar held the end of the faixa while Josep turned and turned, girdling himself into a support so tight it barely allowed him to breathe.

As they made their way through the crowd, the Sitges musicians began to play, and Francesc took Josep's hand.

Very soon a whining melody summoned the base of the Sitges castell and as soon as it was formed, their climbers began to mount.

Eduardo had been right about the nature of the competition, Josep saw at once. The Sitges climbers ascended without a wasted second or an unnecessary movement, and their castell rose with swift efficiency until the boy who was their enxaneta scuttled up as the eighth layer, raised his arm in triumph, and descended on the other side, the climbers behind him deconstructing the castell as smoothly as it had been raised, to applause and shouts of praise.

The Santa Eulália musicians, already in place, began to play. The grallas called Josep, and he slipped off his shoes and gave them to Francesc as Marimar wished him good fortune.

The Santa Eulália base formed quickly, and very soon it was Josep's turn. He climbed swiftly and easily, as he had done in practice so many times, and soon he was standing on Leopoldo Flaquer's shoulders, his arms about Albert Fiore and Marc Rubió, steadying them as they steadied him.

Then Briel Tauré was standing on his shoulders.

Fourth tier was not so high, yet it gave Josep a vantage point. He could not see Maria del Mar or Francesc, but in the space beneath Marc's arm he viewed upturned faces and beyond them people who moved around the perimeter of the crowd.

He saw a pair of nuns, one short, the other tall, in black habits with white wimples.

A wild-haired boy lugging a squirming yellow dog.

A fat man holding a long bread.

A straight-backed man in a grey suit, perhaps a businessman, carrying a broad-brimmed hat. Walking with a slight limp.

Josep knew that man.

And he knew the the sudden fear that coursed through his own body as he watched the familiar limp.

He wanted to run but couldn't move, captive and completely vulnerable, imprisoned there in the air.

His knees were suddenly without strength, so that he tightened his grip on his companions, and Albert looked at him. "All right, Josep?" Albert asked, but Josep didn't reply.

The man's hair seemed still jet-black but there was a small circle of bald flesh at the very top of his head . . . Well, seven years.

Then he was gone.

Josep bent his head as low as possible while still held in the embrace of the others, peering under Marc's arm, trying to keep the man in sight.

In vain.

"Something?" Marc asked sharply, but Josep shook his head and held on.

Now there was a murmur, and people were pointing upward, where Eduardo's surprise—an extra tier of climbers—was taking place, and then the enxaneta went skyward over Marc's back.

Josep knew when the boy raised his arm at the top as the ninth layer and started down, because there was a murmur from the crowd and applause.

It was Bernat Taulé, Briel's brother, in the seventh layer, who was a bit too eager to descend. Losing his balance, he grabbed at his nearest partner, Valentí Margal. Valentí held him, preventing a fall while the castell rippled for a moment and swayed. Eduardo had taught them well. They retained their balance, Bernat recovered and went down a bit slower than usual, and the castell finished its deconstruction without further incident.

When Josep's feet reached the ground, he didn't flee but instead, shoeless, he pushed through the crowd in the direction the man had taken, trying for another sighting.

For half an hour he searched the marketplace, but he did not glimpse Peña again.

He scarcely registered that the judges had been arguing. The Sitges team had performed flawlessly, raising eight levels, but the Santa Eulália team had successfully built and dismantled a castell with nine levels. In the end, the judges agreed to declare the contest a draw.

Most people appeared satisfied with the decision.

As they rode homeward, Francesc slept in the rear of the wagon, and Josep and Marimar spoke little. Josep felt numb as he directed the hinny. Marimar was content to travel comfortably with her child and her intended, after a satisfying and enjoyable day. When she spoke Josep answered briefly; he perceived she didn't think that strange, probably assuming he was gripped by the same contentment she felt.

The thought occurred to him that perhaps he was going mad.

53

Josep's Responsibility

$\mathcal{H}$e sat on the vineyard bench in the lemony sunshine of early spring with his eyes closed, forcing his mind to work, trying to reason his way out of thought-paralyzing panic.

One: Was he certain that the man he had seen was Peña?

He was. He was.

Two: Had Peña seen and identified him?

Reluctantly, Josep decided that he must assume Peña had seen him. He couldn't afford to believe in coincidence. In all probability, Peña had come to the Sitges competition in the hope of glimpsing him. Perhaps in some way he had learned that Josep Alvarez had returned to Santa Eulália, and he had needed to determine that this was the Josep Alvarez he had known and trained, the man he had been looking for, the only one of the village boys who had eluded him.

Eluded him *thus far*, Josep told himself in despair.

Thus far.

Three: So. Somebody was going to come for him.

Four: What were his options?

He thought about how terrible it had been to be sought, homeless, and drifting.

Perhaps he could sell his wine, get cash, and pay for travel in a passenger coach instead of a baggage car, he thought.

But he knew there was not enough time for that.

He couldn't ask Maria del Mar and Francesc to run away with him and share a fugitive's life. Yet if he left them behind, life would be desolate for him, and he cringed at the thought of what a new hurt and another abandonment might do to Marimar.

He was left with only one choice.

He remembered the lesson Peña had driven home to him: When it is necessary to kill, anyone can do it. When it is *necessary*, killing becomes very easy.

The LeMat was where he had placed it behind a sack of grain in the eaves of the attic. Only four of the nine chambers were loaded, and he had no more gunpowder. So the four shots and a sharp knife would have to serve.

To survive fear he turned blindly to hard labor, always the best medicine for him when he was faced with trouble. He worked without stopping, building another piece of the stone wall that covered the unfinished earthen side of the cellar, and then switching off in late afternoon to prune his vines. Always, he kept the Le Mat within easy reach, though he didn't expect Peña to march through the village and attack him in broad daylight.

At dusk the gathering darkness in the house allowed his fear to magnify, and he took the LeMat outside and climbed the ridge to a place where the pale moonlight enabled him to see the section of the lane that approached the vineyard. It was almost pleasant to sit there, until he realized that if someone came, he surely wouldn't take the lane. Anyone taught by Peña would be likely to circle around and come down the hill, and Josep turned and looked up the slope, feeling exposed and unprotected.

Finally he went back to the house for blankets and carried them into the cellar, spreading them next to the wine casks and near the wheelbarrow of river clay. He lay down with his head between the wheelbarrow shafts, but before long the stones in the floor pushed into his back, and the cellar was a chill bedchamber, fine for wine but inhospitable to human flesh. Besides, it occurred to him that should trouble come, it would not be good to face it like an animal cowering in a hole in the ground.

So he took the blankets and the gun and returned crankily to the house, where he entered his own bed and found limited and troubled sleep.

The quality of his sleep remained poor for the next two nights. In the small early hours of the third night he finally slept more deeply, to be awakened after a time by a banging on his door.

He struggled into his work trousers and, holding the gun, he went down the stone stairs as the French clock was chiming five o'clock, his normal rising hour. He tried to force himself to think clearly.

No assassin would knock, he told himself.

Was it Marimar? Perhaps the boy was sick again?

But he could not bring himself to open the door.

"Who is it?"

"Josep! Josep, it is Nivaldo."

Perhaps someone was behind Nivaldo, holding a weapon.

He unlocked the door, opened it a crack and peered out, but the sky was cloudy and it was still dark, so he could see but little. Nivaldo reached in, and his trembling hand clamped hard onto Josep's wrist.

"Come," he said.

Nivaldo shook his head and would not answer questions as they hurried down the lane and across the plaça. He stank of brandy. His key rattled against the lock before he succeeded in opening the door of the grocery.

When he scratched a match and lighted a lantern, Josep saw an empty brandy bottle on the counter, and then he saw at once the cause of Nivaldo's nervousness.

The man lay on the floor as if asleep, but the unnatu-ral angle of his head made it apparent that he wouldn't waken.

"Nivaldo," Josep said gently.

He took the lantern from Nivaldo and bent over the form on the floor.

Peña lay next to the overturned chair on which he had been sitting. He did not look like the prosperous businessman Josep had viewed in the Sitges market-place; he looked more like a dead soldier, dressed as Josep remembered him in threadbare workclothes and worn military boots of good leather, a sheathed knife on his belt. His eyes were closed. His head hung at an impossible ninety-degree angle, and one whole side of his neck was a large bruise colored the purple-black of Ull de Llebre grapes, with a torn-open wound of raw meat and clotted blood.

"Who did this?"

"I did," Nivaldo said.

"You? How?"

"With that." Nivaldo pointed to a heavy steel bar lean-ing against the wall. It had always been a part of the gro-cery; Josep had used it himself on occasion, when he had helped Nivaldo pry open a cask of flour or a crate of coffee. "No questions now. You must get him out of here for me."

"Where shall I take him?" Josep said stupidly.

"I don't know. I don't want to know, I don't want to know," Nivaldo said wildly. He was half drunk. "You must get him out of here now. I have to clean everything, set things right before people begin to come through that door."

Josep stared at him, befuddled.

"Josep. *Get him out of here, I said!*"

The wagon and the hinny would make too much noise. He hurried home. His wheelbarrow was in the cel-lar, full of clay, but the big wheelbarrow he had inherited from Quim was empty. The rusty wheels screamed when he moved it, and he was forced to spend precious mo-ments applying oil before he was able to push the barrow through the darkness to the grocery.

They wrapped Peña in a stained blanket, and then Nivaldo took his feet and Josep his shoulders. Death had made Peña stiff, and when they placed him on the barrow, his body was rigid enough to lie across the rim, where it would surely fall off. Josep pressed down on his waist, and despite the rigidity in the body, enough pliancy remained to allow the buttocks to fold into the cavity of the barrow.

Nivaldo went into the grocery and closed the door, and Josep pushed his burden away.

It was still quite dark, but throughout the village vineyard workers were already leaving their beds, and he was in an agony of concern lest he should meet someone who was up and about and ready to pass a few minutes in conversation. More than once they had witnessed Quim Torras joyously and noisily pushing his plump priestly lover in this wheelbarrow, around and around the plaça. He went past Eduardo's house, moving as fast as he was able, very conscious of sound. The oiled wheels no longer shrieked, but they were metal-bound, making a soft, rapid clacking on the cobblestoned plaça and, once beyond the paved area, sending loose stones skittering.

As he passed Angel's field, a cock crowed and the alcalde's dog, successor to the long-gone animal Josep had once coerced, began to bark wildly.

Shut up, shut up, SHUT UP . . .

He moved faster and finally turned into his own vineyard with great relief, but then he stopped.

What now?

The first grey light was still several hours away, but if he was to carry out this strange responsibility Nivaldo had thrust upon him, the body could not be buried shallowly or carelessly. Nor could he dig a grave when at any moment someone could venture down the lane to the river, or Marimar could come seeking him.

Somehow, he had to get Peña out of sight.

He moved to the cellar, opened the door, and pushed the wheelbarrow inside.

By the time he had found the lantern in the dark and scratched a match, he knew what was required.

He worked his hands under Peña's shoulders and dragged the body from the barrow. The yawning rent in the rock wall that Josep had thought of as a natural closet would never contain shelves of wine bottles now. Peña was a large, muscular man, and Josep grunted as he crammed him deep into the opening in a standing position, his back to the smooth rock wall, his loose head and upper chest touching a knobby rock thrusting out of the opposite, rougher wall of the fissure. The body was still bent at the waist but Josep was not interested in seeking its best appearance.

On the previous afternoon he had added water to the river clay in his own wheelbarrow, but in the lantern light he could see that the surface of the clay had dried and cracked. He kept a cantír of drinking water in the cellar and he poured its contents onto the clay and worked it with his shovel, blending the surface with the moister interior. Then he filled a bucket with clay and scooped some out with his trowel and dropped it at the edge of the opening in the wall. He found a good large stone and pressed it down on the clay and mated it with another stone, neatly using the trowel to scrape the excess clay that joined them, working as slowly and carefully as he had on the other areas of stonework in the cellar.

When he had laid five courses of stone across the bottom of the opening, the top layer was the height of Peña's knees, and Josep took Quim's barrow out of the cellar to a pile of excavation soil that he had intended to spread on the lane. As he filled the barrow, the first grey light was filling the sky,

When he was back in the cellar, he shoveled the stony gravel into the area behind the body. He pulled the body erect so that it no longer leaned on the wall, and positioned the fill, carefully working it around the legs and tamping it down firmly so that in death Peña stood, bent but like a planted tree held up by the soil around its roots.

Then he went back to laying stone.

The wall had almost reached Peña's waist when he heard the high clear voice just outside the door.

"Josep."

Francesc.

"Josep. Josep."

"Josep."

The boy was searching for him, calling.

He stopped working on the wall and stood and listened. Francesc continued to call, his voice quickly dwindling and then disappearing, and after a few minutes Josep resumed laying the stones.

As the wall grew, every meter or so Josep added the fill until it reached the top layer of stone, and packed it down. When the wheelbarrow was empty of gravel, he went outside gingerly and cautiously, but he was alone in the bright dazzle of mid-morning, and he filled the wheelbarrow with another load of gravel and returned with it into the cool, lantern-lit darkness.

He worked with methodical grimness as he raised the wall and filled the space, disregarding hunger and thirst. The dirt seemed to ascend the body like a slowly rising tide; it took a lot to fill a grave, even when the grave was turned on end. He tried not to look at Sergeant Peña. When he did look, he saw the head resting on the right shoulder, hiding the ugly bruise and the wound in Peña's neck. He didn't want to note the bald spot of middle age, or the few silver hairs; they made Peña too human, a victim. Under the circumstances, Josep preferred to remember him as a murdering bastard.

By the time he covered the shoulders, he was working more slowly, from a step-ladder. He added one more row of stones to the wall and then shoveled gravelly soil, the pebbles and dirt obliterating Peña's thinning black hair, forever hiding the bald spot. Josep buried the head, added several inches of dirt, and tamped it down.

The new wall was still a meter below the stone roof when he ran out of clay, but now he felt able to go for more with reasonable safety, since anyone wandering into the cellar would see nothing untoward.

Outside, he saw from the sun it was late afternoon. He had had neither food nor drink since the previous day, and as he pushed Quim's wheelbarrow down the lane past Marimar's vineyard, he felt lightheaded and dizzy.

At the riverside he knelt and washed his hands. They still tasted of clay as he drank and drank of the cold water, but he didn't care. He splashed water on his face and then took a long piss against a tree.

The clay bank was a short distance downstream from the end of the lane, but the riverside was blocked by a thick stand of brush. Josep slipped off his shoes and rolled up his trousers; then he pushed the wheelbarrow into the shallow water. He had to manhandle the barrow over some rocks, but soon he was loading clay into it.

On the way back, as he passed Marimar's vineyard, she stepped out from behind her casa and saw him pushing another load of clay or stones from the river, as she had seen him so many times before. She waved, smiling, and Josep smiled back but didn't stop.

On his own land he also got a fresh load of fill, and then he went back to work steadily and purposefully.

He paused only once. On impulse, he descended from his ladder and went to where the LeMat rested on one of the barrels. He took the gun and placed it atop the soil in the opening and added several shovelsful of fill.

When the last bit of soil had been crammed under the roof, he laid the top course of stones, scraped the clay binding neatly with his trowel, and climbed down from the ladder.

The rock wall began at the left of the door and ran until it became a stone wall, straight and true, where the closet opening had been. The stone wall ran under the rock ceiling for about three meters, turned right at the end to cover the width of the cellar, and then turned right again. The entire right wall was lined with stone except for a narrow unfinished section close to the door.

All the stonework matched, and the cellar seemed to exude innocence as Josep examined it in the light of the lantern.

"Now you can have him," he said aloud and shakily.

As he closed the door behind him, he didn't know if he had spoken to the Small Ones or to God.

54

A Conversation with Nivaldo

"*Y*ou're part of it too," Josep said.

Nivaldo looked at him. "You want stew?"

"No." Josep had eaten, slept, wakened, washed, eaten again. Slept again.

If you knew where to look, it was possible to see where the spilled blood had been scraped from the grocery's dirt floor. He wondered where Nivaldo had disposed of it. Buried it somewhere, perhaps. Josep thought if ever he had to rid himself of bloody dirt, he would drop it through the hole in the outhouse.

Nivaldo's eyes were bloodshot, but the trembles were gone. He looked sober and in control. "You want coffee?"

"I want information."

Nivaldo nodded. "Sit down."

They both sat at the little table and regarded one another.

"He came about one o'clock, the way he used to. I was still awake, reading the paper. He sat where you're sitting and said he was hungry, so I opened a bottle of brandy for him and told him I'd warm up the stew. I knew he was here to kill me." Nivaldo spoke softly and bleakly.

"I was afraid to use a knife on him, afraid to get in that close. I'm old and sick, and he was so much stronger than I am now. But I'm still strong enough to use the iron bar, and I went straight to it. I came up behind him just as he was taking a drink, and I swung it as hard as I could. I knew he wouldn't give me a second chance.

"Then I sat at this table and finished the bottle of brandy, and I was drunk and didn't know what to do, until I knew I had to go for you. I'm glad I finished him."

"What good did it do? Some other killer will come for us and do the job right," Josep said with bitterness.

Nivaldo shook his head. "No, nobody else is going to come. If he had brought other people into it, sent them to kill us, he'd have had to kill *them*. That's why he came alone. We were the last two men who could cause him trouble. He came to Santa Eulália to rid himself of you, but he understood I'd connect him to your death, and I knew just enough about him so he'd feel better if I was gone too."

Nivaldo sighed. "Actually, I don't know *that* much about him. When I met him, he said he was a captain, wounded in '69 while fighting under Valeriano Weyler against the Creoles in Cuba. Once when we got drunk together, he told me General Weyler looked after his army career now and then, because both of them had attended the Military School at Toledo. He definitely had been to Cuba; he knew a lot about the island. When he heard I came from Cuba, we got to talking politics. We ended up talking quite a bit."

"Was Peña his real name?"

Nivaldo shrugged.

"How did you two get together?"

"At a meeting."

"What kind of a meeting?"

"Carlist meeting."

"So he *was* a Carlist."

Nivaldo rubbed his face. "Well, a lot of Carlist soldiers and officers were given amnesty and taken into the government army after the first two civil wars. Some deserted and rejoined the Carlist forces; others stayed with the national army and worked for the Carlists from the inside. A few became political converts and spied on their old comrades for the government. At the time, I accepted Peña as a Carlist. Now . . . now, I don't know where he stood. I just know he came to the Carlist meetings. He was the one who gave us the information that for the third rebellion the Carlist commanders were going to put together a real army in the Basque country, and he let me know he was looking for likely young Catalan men to turn into soldiers to wear the red beret."

"Did you know his plans for the hunting group?"

Nivaldo hesitated. "Not exactly. I'm just a country grocer, somebody who did things when he told me to do them, but I knew he was training you for something special. When I read in the newspapers about General Prim's assassination and the group that had stopped his carriage, I got chills. The timing was just right. I was certain our Santa Eulália boys were involved."

Josep looked at him. "Manel, Guillem, Jordi, Esteve, Enric, Xavier. All of them, dead."

He nodded. "Sad. But they went to be soldiers, and soldiers die. In my time, I've known a lot of dead soldiers."

"They didn't die as soldiers . . . You just served us up to Peña, worthless meat. Why didn't you bring us into it, give us a choice?"

"Think about it, Josep. Some of you might have gone along, but maybe none of you. You were just clumsy young bulls, not a political thought among you."

"You believed I was dead too. How did that make you feel?"

"Heart-broken, you fool! But tremendously proud. Prim was so bad for the country. All right, he got rid of that royal bitch Isabella, a disgraceful queen, but he invited the Italian Amadeus to take over the throne. To think that you and I changed history and helped to get rid of Prim made me feel tremendously proud. Patriotic." The one good eye fixed him like a beam. "I gave Spain the person I loved most in the world, don't you know that?"

Josep was chilled and nauseated. "Jesús, I wasn't yours to give. You're not my father!"

"I was more father to you and Donat than Marcel ever was, and you know that's true."

He felt it was possible that he would begin to weep. "How did you get involved in something like this? You're not even Spanish, not even Catalan."

"Is that how you talk to me? I've been Spanish and Catalan twice as long as you have, you ignorant bastard!"

Suddenly Josep didn't feel like weeping. He met the fury in the single good eye.

"You can go to hell, Nivaldo," he said.

For three days he couldn't bring himself to enter the cellar. Then it was time to check the wine casks to see if they needed to be topped off, and he wasn't going to do anything to endanger the wine, so he went into the cellar and took care of his business. There was just the neatly made wall of stone where the enclosed space had been. On the other side of the wall—on the other side of three of the walls in that cellar—there was the vast, deep solidity of the hill, the earth. He told himself that the earth contained all kinds of mysteries that it was fruitless to dwell on, natural and man-made.

He had a need to finish the work on the cellar. He had used up all all the stones he had saved during the excavation, so he took Quim's wheelbarrow to the river and collected a load of nice stones. It took him less than half a day to complete the small section of wall that had remained uncovered.

Then he just stood there and examined the place—the ceiling and most of one wall of rock, as nature had made it and he had found it; the other walls that he had fashioned, stone by stone; and his wine barrels in a neat line on the dirt floor. He felt shameless satisfaction and also relief, knowing that it would never again be difficult for him to work there.

In a way, he thought, it was very similar to being able to eat the cherries that grew in the cemetery behind the church.

55

The Joining

*I*t rained very early and with just the right intensity that spring, and by May the air had softened so that it seemed to kiss his cheek, fresh but warm, as he left the house each morning and entered the green rows. A few days before the end of the month the real heat arrived. On the first Friday evening in June, Marimar told him to be careful not to eat from a pot, because everyone knew that eating from a pot would bring rain.

The next morning, the air was warm even while it was still dark, and Josep made his way down the lane and sat in the river and scrubbed himself clean. After he soaped his scalp he held his nose and lay back in the running stream with his eyes open, seeing the hopeful, glittery light of the rising sun beyond the watery bubbles. The river ran over his face as if it were washing away his old life.

Back in the house he dressed in his church trousers, blackened boots, and a new dress shirt, and despite the heat he put on the wide light-blue tie and the dark-blue jacket Marimar had bought for him.

Francesc came a bit early, jumping with excitement, and he held Josep's hand as they walked down the lane, across the plaça, and into the church, where they waited restlessly until Briel Taulé drove up with Josep's mule-drawn cart, carrying Marimar.

She had no dressmaking skills, but she had paid Beatriu Corberó, Briel's aunt, who was a seamstress, to make her a dark-blue dress that almost matched the color of Josep's jacket—blue was a color that would bring them luck, Maria del Mar thought. It was a sensible purchase she could wear for a long time on special occasions, a modest dress, high-necked and with plain, easy-fitting sleeves that widened at the wrists. A double track of small black buttons ran down the front of the shirtwaist, pushed forward by the ampleness of her breasts, and though she had laughed away Beatriu's suggestion that the costume should include a bustle, the skirt, narrowing from the waist to the knees, showed the natural beauty of her flanks before widening to its full length. On her head she wore a black straw bonnet with a tiny red cockade, and she carried a small bouquet of the white vineyard roses that Josep and Francesc had gathered the day before. Josep, who had never seen her dressed in any but common work clothes, was struck almost dumb by the sight.

The church filled rapidly; Santa Eulália was a village that turned out for funerals and weddings. Before the service began, he saw Nivaldo slip in—it seemed to him Nivaldo was limping—and take a seat in the last row of benches.

Standing before Padre Pio, Josep scarcely heard the intoned words, almost overcome by the realization of his great good fortune, but soon he was brought to attention when the priest took two candles and instructed each of them to light one. The tapers represented their individual lives, Padre Pio told them. Then he took the candles and gave them a third candle to light together, the symbol that they were joined. He extinguished the first two candles and announced that from that moment, their lives had been merged.

Then the priest blessed them and pronounced them husband and wife, and Marimar placed her bouquet at the feet of Santa Eulália.

As they walked up the aisle from the altar, Josep glanced at the place where Nivaldo had sat, and saw that the seat was already empty.

Marimar had prepared food in advance and had thought to spend the first day of her marriage in quiet contentment with her husband and son, but the villagers would not have that. Eduardo set off firecrackers in the plaça as they emerged from the church, and the crackling noises followed the wagon as Josep drove them home.

Four borrowed tables had been set up in Marimar's vineyard, already laden with the donations of their friends and neighbors—tortillas, salads, chorizo, and a myriad of chicken and meat dishes. Soon people began to turn into her path and gather around them. The castell musicians left their drums and grallas at home but two of them brought their guitars. Within half an hour the heat had driven Marimar into the house to exchange her fancy new costume for ordinary clothing, and Josep had rid himself of his jacket and tie and had rolled up his sleeves.

He watched her face, alternating excitement with joyous repose, and he knew that Maria del Mar was having the wedding for which she had yearned.

Their well-wishers came and left, some to come again. It was late in the evening before the last of them drifted away with final hugs and kisses. Francesc had long since fallen asleep, and when Josep moved him onto his mat, he was slumbering soundly.

They walked together to the bedchamber and shed their clothing. He left the lamp lit near the bed and they inspected each other with eyes and touching and wet kisses, and then fell on one another, quietly but with hunger. They were each aware that it was different this time; when she sensed his climax was near she held him, pressing him into her with her hands to prevent the with-drawal they had previously felt necessary.

It was an hour before he left her and went to check the sleeping child.

When he returned to the bed, he still wasn't ready for sleep, and she laughed softly as he turned to her and made love again slowly. It was a powerful joining, somehow made more intensely their own by their inability to thrash and shout, in complete silence except for the renewal of the rhythms of mating and one stifled groan, like the sound of a prolonged and jubilant dying, that didn't waken the boy.

56

Changes

$\mathcal{M}$aria del Mar had no great affection for the house to which Ferran Valls had brought her and her child after their marriage. It took very little time for her to move her belongings into Josep's masia. Her kitchen table was better than his, slightly larger and more strongly made, and they switched the tables. Admiring the French clock and the carved pieces in Josep's bedroom, she took no other furniture from the Valls house, carrying off only three knives, some dishes, a few pots and pans, and her clothing and Francesc's.

She left all her tools. When she or Josep needed a hoe or a spade, they would go to whichever one was closest to where they happened to be working. "We are rich in tools," she told him with satisfaction.

The changed patterns of their lives occurred naturally. The second morning after the wedding she left the house after breakfast and walked to her own vineyard and began to hoe weeds. In a while Josep came with his hoe and began to work nearby. In the afternoon they moved together to the Torras piece, to prune young bunches of grapes from a row he had not managed to reach when he had debudded vines earlier in the spring, activity he continued the following day while she moved into the Alvarez vineyard to work.

Without any discussion, working together and separately to do whatever needed to be done, they made the united bodega theirs.

Several days after his marriage, Josep went to the grocery. He knew he would have to continue to shop there. It was unthinkable to travel afar for food and staples, nor did he wish to stimulate gossip by allowing the village to observe any change in his relationship with Nivaldo. They exchanged evening greetings like strangers, and Josep placed his order. It was the first time he was buying food and staples for a family instead of for only one person, but neither he nor Nivaldo made a comment. He carried the things to his wagon as Nivaldo placed them on the counter—lard, salt, a bag of flour, a bag of beans, a sack of millet, a sack of coffee, a bit of candy for the boy.

He noted that Nivaldo's face was pale and pasty and his limping was more pronounced as he filled the order, but Josep didn't ask the older man about his health.

Nivaldo brought out a small waxed round of cheese from Toledo.

"Congratulations," he said stiffly.

A wedding gift.

It was on Josep's tongue to refuse it, but he knew he should not. Some small gesture would have been normal, and Marimar would think it strange if Nivaldo offered them nothing.

"Thank you," he forced himself to say.

He paid his bill and accepted his change with a nod.

On the way home he was torn by conflicting feelings.

Peña had been evil, and Josep was glad he was gone and no longer to be feared. But he was implicated deeply in the death of the man. He believed that if he and Nivaldo were discovered, their punishment would be shared. He no longer suffered terrible dreams about the murder of General Prim, but now he experienced other horrifying moments while awake. In his imagination he saw hordes of policemen descending on his vineyard, ripping open the walls of his cellar while Maria del Mar and Francesc witnessed his shame and guilt.

They garroted murderers in Barcelona, or hanged them from gallows erected in the Plaça Sant Jaume.

He skipped his selling trips to the Sitges market dur-ing the heat of the summer, not wanting to cook the wine in the hot sun, but he continued to bottle wine in the cool gloom of his cellar, and as the bottles accumulated on the dirt floor he realized the need for shelving. He had a good supply of salvaged lumber from the disassembled vats but not enough nails. Early one morning he rode Hinny through the darkness at a leisurely pace and spent a morning in Sitges culling old wine bottles, of which he bought ten, as well as buying ink powder and paper for more labels, and a bag of nails.

Passing an outdoor cafe, he saw abandoned on one of the tables a copy of *El Cascabel*, and at once he hobbled Hinny in a nearby patch of shade. He sorely missed having access to Nivaldo's newspaper, and now he ordered coffee and eagerly sat to read.

The news held his attention long after the coffee cup was dry. As he had known, the war had been over for a time, now. The Carlists had not persevered, and things seemed to have quieted down all across the nation.

There was still bitter fighting in Cuba.

Antonio Cánovas del Castillo, the prime minister, had formed a government in Madrid that was a coalition of the moderates of the conservative and liberal parties, oppressive to all its rivals. On his own he had established a commission that had drawn up a new constitution, subsequently ratified by the cortes and supported by the throne. Alfonso XII wanted to rule a stable constitutional monarchy, and that was what had been achieved. An editorial in the paper observed that while not everyone agreed with Cánovas, people were relieved to turn away from bloodshed and strife. Another editorial commented on the popularity of the king.

That evening as dusk fell, Josep stood in the village plaça with Eduardo and discussed some of the political changes. "Cánovas has pushed through a new annual tax on landowners and business people," Josep said. "Now farmers must pay 25 pesetas, and shopkeepers 50 pesetas, in order to be allowed to vote."

"One can imagine how popular that will be," Eduardo said drily, and Josep smiled.

Eduardo also had noticed that Nivaldo looked as though his health was poor, and he mentioned it to Josep.

"The older generation of the village is fast disappearing," he said. "Angel Casals suffers greatly these days. His gout involves both of his legs now, and it gives him terrible pain.

He looked at Josep uncomfortably. "I had an interesting talk with him a few days ago. He believes it is time for him to step down as alcalde."

Josep was shocked. Angel Casals was the only alcalde of San Eulália that he had known in his lifetime.

"It is forty-four years since he succeeded his father as alcalde. He would like to remain alcalde one more year. But he realizes his sons are not old enough or experienced enough to succeed him." Eduardo's face reddened. "Josep . . . he would like me to succeed him as alcalde."

"But that would be perfect!" Josep said.

"You would not be offended?" Eduardo asked anxiously.

"Of course I would not."

"Angel admires you greatly. He said he struggled for a long time, trying to choose between us, and that finally he arrived at me because I am older than you." Eduardo smiled. "Which, he hopes, may indicate that I may be a bit more mature.

"But Josep, we do not have to allow Angel to choose his successor. If you would like to be alcalde of the village, I would support you with the greatest contentment," Eduardo said, and Josep knew he was sincere.

He smiled at Eduardo and shook his head.

"He made me promise I would serve for at least five years," Eduardo said. "After that, he said, perhaps you would take a turn, or one of his sons . . ."

"I need you to promise me that you will serve at least forty-five years. I would like to remain on the village council for that long, for it is my pleasure to work with you," Josep said, and he and Eduardo embraced.

Their encounter lifted Josep's spirits. He was genuinely happy that Eduardo would become the alcalde. He had come to see that whether someone was the owner of a great mill or a small grower of grapes, the very food and flavor of life depended on whether there was a good alcalde, a competent governor, an honest cortes, and a prime minister and a king who were truly concerned about the condition and future of their people.

Josep built cellar shelving that was strong enough to support several hundred bottles of wine, but without any attempt to make a piece of attractive furniture. He shelved the bottles next to one another on their sides, and he loved the sight of the array, the dark wine gleaming richly within the glass in the lantern light.

One day he was working among the vines late in the afternoon when a horseman turned his mount into the vineyard from the lane.

"Is this Josep's vineyard?"

"It is."

"You are Josep?"

"I am."

Dismounting, the man announced that he was Bru Fuxá of the village of Villanueva. He was on his way to Sitges to visit his relatives there.

"The last time I visited my cousin Frederic Fuxá, whom you know, together we finished the last drops of a bottle of your beautiful wine, and now I would dearly like to buy four bottles as gifts for my cousins."

It was not an overly hot day, but Josep cast a worried glance at the sun. It was already was low in the sky, but still, heat and wine . . .

"Why don't you linger for a bit, relax with me for an hour? Then you can ride on to Sitges in the pleasantness of early evening, when cooling breezes blow along the Barcelona road."

Bru Fuxá shrugged and smiled, and tied his horse next to Hinny in the shaded overhang of the roof.

He sat on the vineyard bench and Josef brought cool water. The visitor revealed that he was an olive grower, and they talked companionably about the raising of olives. Josep brought him to inspect the old trees on the Vall piece, which Senyor Fuxá declared to be beautifully maintained.

When the sun was sufficiently down, Josep brought him into the cellar and carefully wrapped four bottles in part of his dwindling supply of old newspaper, and they stowed the wine in his saddle bags.

Fuxá paid and mounted. As he saluted and turned his horse, he flashed a smile.

"A beautiful bodega, senyor. A beautiful bodega. But . . ." He leaned forward. "It lacks a sign."

The next morning Josep cut a square piece of oak planking and fastened it to a short length of narrow post. He asked Marimar to do the lettering, not confident that he could perform with the required neatness. The result was a sign that was not at all fancy, bearing resemblance to the For Sale sign that Donat had erected and he had destroyed. But the new sign performed its function well, which was to tell a stranger exactly where it was that he had arrived.

JOSEP'S VINES

On a Wednesday afternoon, when ordinarily he would have pictured Donat among his loud and clacking machines, Josep went to the grocery to buy chorizo and saw his brother standing behind the counter wearing a white apron, measuring out flour to Senyora Corberó.

Donat turned to Josep as soon as Senyora Corberó was leaving.

"Nivaldo is ill. He sent for us yesterday. I knew that it meant he's bad off, and we came at once. Rosa is trying to nurse him, while I'm keeping open the shop."

Josep tried to think of something appropriate to say under the circumstances, but could not.

"I only need some chorizo."

"How much?"

"Quarter of a kilo."

Donat cut the chorizo, weighed the hunk, added another slice, and wrapped it in *El Cascabel,* everybody's wrapping paper, the merchant's friend. He took Josep's money and counted out the change.

"You want to go up and see him?"

". . . I don't think so, no."

Donat stared. "Why not? Mother of God. You're angry with *him*, too?"

Josep didn't answer. He picked up the chorizo packet and turned to leave.

"You don't like anybody, do you?" Donat said.

57

Extreme Unction

*I*t was the time of year when the grapes were beginning to fulfill their promise, gaining their color, beginning to taste as they should, the season when Josep was starting to pick a berry now and then and pop it into his mouth to see what progress was being made.

The season to study the sky, to worry about the prospect of too much rain or freak hail or continued drought.

He attributed his moodiness to the seasonal uncertainty about the fate of the grapes.

But Marimar returned from a walk to the plaça with Francesc to get water and said she had met Rosa. And Rosa had told her the priest had been with Nivaldo almost the whole day.

When Josep went to the grocery, he noted that Donat's eyes were reddened.

"He is very ill?"

"Very ill."

". . . May I see him?"

Donat shrugged wearily and pointed to the three steps leading to the half-story above the storage room, the space that served as Nivaldo's living quarters.

Josep walked down the dark hallway and paused at the bedroom. The old man lay on his back, staring at the ceiling. Padre Pio was bending over him, his mouth moving almost silently.

"Nivaldo," Josep said.

The priest did not appear to notice Josep but seemed to be in another place, speaking words so soft Josep couldn't make them out. Padre Pio held a cup in one hand and a tiny brush in the other. As Josep watched, he dipped the brush and with it made a tiny cross on Nivaldo's ear, another on his lips, and on his nostrils.

He peeled back the blanket, revealing Nivaldo's bowed back and hairy, skinny, legs, and applied the oil of unction to his hands and feet. Jesús, to his groin! "Nivaldo, it's Josep," Josep said loudly.

But the priest had reached up and closed Nivaldo's staring eyes.

Padre Pio's hand had to go back again to bring the lid down over the bad eye, and then the little brush made its final cross.

For years every person in the village had visited the grocery regularly, and most people thought well of Nivaldo. Even those who didn't hold him in high regard attended his funeral Mass and followed the casket to the burial ground.

Josep and Maria del Mar and Francesc walked to the gravesite with the crowd.

In the churchyard, he found himself standing next to his brother and Rosa. She looked at him a bit nervously.

"I'm sorry for your loss, Josep."

He nodded. "I am too."

"A pity, isn't it, that they couldn't find a gravesite for him closer to Padre's," Donat said to Josep in a low voice.

Why is it a pity? Josep wanted to snap. *Do you believe he and Padre will want to get together regularly to play draughts?*

He swallowed his sarcasm, but he was not in a mood to talk to them, and in a few minutes he left Donat and Rosa and wandered closer to where the burial was taking place.

His mind was in a turmoil; he had never been so weary, so confused. He wished he had been able to hold Nivaldo's hand as he died, mourned that he had not been wise enough to offer reconciliation and some small comfort. One part of him still seethed at the thought of the obsessed, scheming insurgent, the mad old man who had sent young men off to die, who had made other men's sons his personal gift to war. But the other part of him remembered clearly his father's charming, affection-ate friend who had told stories of the Small Ones to a little boy, who had taught him to read and to write, who had helped a clumsy youth to rid himself of the burdens of innocence. Josep knew *that* man had loved him all of his life, and he stood apart from Marimar and Francesc and wept for Nivaldo.

58

The Legacy

*W*ithin two days the entire village had heard that Nivaldo Machado had left his legal will with Angel Casals as executor, and a day later everyone knew that the grocery had been bequeathed to Donat Alvarez and his wife Rosa.

The news was accepted without surprise, and there was not a stir in the village until almost three weeks later, when Donat moved the bench from its longtime place next to the entrance of the grocery. The bench was now located on the plaça before the final few meters of the grocery's land, as close to the church as it could get with-out being in front of church property. Directly in front of the grocery Donat placed the small round table that had been Nivaldo's, and another round table slightly larger than the first, and chairs. Rosa told people that the out-door tables would remain bare except on holidays, when she would cover them with clothsssep was among those who grumbled.

"Nivaldo has barely grown cold. Could they not have the decency to wait a while before making changes?"

"They run a business and not a monument," Maria del Mar said. "I like the changes they have made. The grocery never has been so spotless. The place even smells better, now that they have cleaned out the storage area."

"It won't stay that way. My brother is a slob."

"Well, his wife is not. She is a strong and energetic woman, and both of them are working hard every day."

"You realize that both the bench and the tables are on the plaça, which is public property? They don't have the legal right . . ."

"The bench has always been on the plaça," Maria del Mar pointed out. "And I think it is nice to have the tables there. They liven up the plaça, give it a more festive appearance."

Evidently most of the people of the village agreed with her. When Josep walked to the plaça it quickly became ordinary for him to see one or both of the tables occupied with people having coffee or a plate of chorizo and cheese.

Within two weeks Donat had added a third table, and no one in the village came to the alcalde or the council with an objection.

At a rehearsal meeting of the Santa Eulália Castellers, Eduardo told Francesc that he was progressing nicely. After the first of the year, he said, Francesc would be allowed to climb to the sixth tier in practice, and after a while he would become the pinnacle.

Francesc was visibly exultant. When the time came for him to do his practice climb he ascended very quickly, and Josep felt the boy's arms around his neck. He waited for what had become ritual, his name being spoken into his ear, but instead he heard something different.

A word scarcely spoken, a breath, a sigh, a tiny puff of sound, like the ghost of a word borne on a breeze.

Padre.

That evening, when the three of them sat at the table in the kitchen for the evening meal, Josep looked at Francesc.

"There is something I would like to ask of you Francesc. A favor."

The woman and the boy gave him their attention.

"I would enjoy it very much if, instead of calling me Josep, you would begin to address me as Padre. Do you think that would be possible?"

Francesc was not looking at either of them. Instead, he was staring straight ahead, his color high. He had a mouthful of bread, and he was stuffing in even more as he nodded.

Maria del Mar looked at her husband and smiled.

59

Talking and Listening

*T*heir time for privacy, their most intimate and cherished moments of the day, came after Francesc was sound asleep, and one evening Josep led Maria del Mar out into the darkness, and they sat next to one another on the vineyard bench while he talked.

He told her of the group of unemployed youths she remembered well, boys with whom she had grown up. The boys of the hunting group. He spoke of the arrival of Sergeant Peña to the village of Santa Eulália.

He reminded her of the military training and the promises, and then he told her things she didn't know. She listened to the story of how the village boys had been used as pawns; how, all unknowing, they had helped those who had assassinated an unidentified politician for reasons they could not begin to comprehend.

He told her how he and Guillem had watched while her son's father had been killed.

"You're certain Jordi is dead?"

"They cut his throat."

She didn't weep; she had given Jordi Arnau up for dead for a very long time. But her hand gripped his very tightly.

He told her the details of his life as a fugitive.

"I'm the only one left," he said.

"Are you in danger?"

"No. The only two men who could have felt threat-ened by me are gone. Killed in the fighting," he added, a comfortable lie.

It was all he told her. He knew he would never be able to reveal anything else to her.

"I'm glad there are no more secrets between us," his wife said, and kissed him hard on the lips.

He hated it that there were dark areas he could never reveal to her.

He would make it up to her, he vowed, by never fail-ing to treat her with love and tenderness. He found the remaining secrets as burdensome as a hump on his back, and he yearned for someone to whom he could talk about them. Unburden himself.

But there was no one.

On a Saturday afternoon, not quite believing what he was doing but unable to resist, he opened the door of the church and stepped inside.

There were eight people already waiting, pious and faithful men and women. Some came every Saturday afternoon to be shriven, so that they might bring clean souls to the church on Sunday morning to accept the Eucharist.

The heavy red velvet curtains of the booth blocked sound, but in a sensitivity designed to make sure that their own perversities would remain private, those awaiting their turns sat in the last row of benches, as far from the confessional as possible, and Josep found a place among them.

When it was his turn, he entered the dimness and sank to his knees.

"Forgive me, Padre, for I have sinned."

"When was the last time you made confession?"

"Six . . . No, seven weeks ago."

"What is the nature of your sins?"

"Someone with whom I was . . . close . . . killed a man. I helped him."

". . . You helped to kill the man?"

"No, Padre. But I . . . disposed of the man's body."

"Why was the man killed?"

The question puzzled Josep; it didn't seem to relate to his confession. "He came here to murder my friend. And me, he would have killed me also."

"Then your friend killed him in order to defend his own life?"

"Yes."

"And perhaps to save your life? Maybe, even, to make it unnecessary for you to kill?"

". . . Perhaps."

"If that were so, his killing the other man could be seen as an act of love, could it not. An act of his love for you?"

This priest knows, Josep realized.

The priest perhaps knew more about Peña's death than Josep did himself. Padre Pio had spent almost a full day with Nivaldo before Nivaldo had died, shriven.

"Did you bury the body?"

Buried standing, Josep thought crazily, but undoubtedly buried. "Yes, Padre."

"So where is your sin, my son?"

"Padre . . . He was buried in unconsecrated earth. Without final rites."

"By now, the man has met his maker and has been judged. It is not in your power to see that everyone is given the last rites. I'm certain the police would look differently upon your actions, but I do not work for the police, I work for God and the Catholic Church. And I tell you there was no sin. You performed a corporal work of mercy. It is a holy obligation to bury the dead, so there was no sin, and I am unable to hear your confession," the priest said.

"Find peace, my son. Go home, and be tormented no more."

On the other side of the tin screen with its myriad of pinprick holes there was a soft but decisive *clack*, a sound of finality as the inner partition was slid closed, and Josep's attempt at confession was over.

60

The Guardia Civil

$\mathcal{M}$id-morning on the third Wednesday in August, Josep sat at one of the tables in front of the grocery and read a newspaper while his brother wiped down the other tables. They both looked up when three riders clattered over the bridge and into the plaça. All three had the look of men who had traveled under the copper sun. The first two horsemen, riding side by side, were officers of the Guardia Civil. Josep had seen the Guardia in Barcelona, always in pairs and carrying shotguns, daunting in their three-cornered patent leather hats, high-necked black tunics, snowy white pants and gleaming boots. These two wore the distinctive hats, but also dusty green work uniforms with dark, wet splotches at the armpits and in the middle of their backs, where each of them carried his shotgun on a leather strap.

They were followed by a man on a mule, and Josep saw that this was someone he knew.

"Hola, Tonio!" Donat called.

Angel Casals' eldest son flashed Josep a quick glance and gave Donat a nod but didn't answer. He sat straight and tall as he rode, as if emulating the two men in front of him.

Josep watched them over the newspaper, and Donat stood with the wet washcloth in his hand and followed them with his eyes as they stopped near the wine press and tethered their animals on the public rail. They went straight to the pump, and the officers took turns, each holding both firearms while the other drank, then they waited until Tonio had drunk his fill and had run water on his face and head.

"We're right here, so may as well start here," Tonio said. "It's that house, the first one after the church," he said, pointing. "This time of day, he could either be in the house or in the vineyard. We could take a look in the vineyard first, if that is your wish."

One of the officers took the shotgun off his back and wriggled his shoulders.

While Donat washed the table for the fourth time, Josep watched the three of them cross the plaça and disappear behind Eduardo Montroig's's house.

Two hours later Josep and Eduardo found Maria del Mar and Francesc among the rows of vines, and they told her about the visitors.

"Two officers from the Guardia, who brought along Tonio Casals to guide them," Eduardo said. "They asked me the strangest questions. Went through my entire house, looking for what, I don't know. That damn Tonio, my boyhood camarata, dug two holes on my property. I have two natural low spots in the vineyard and they told him to dig there.

"From my place they went to Angel's farm about half an hour ago. When Josep and I passed, just now, they were all standing around and watching while Tonio filled in a hole he had dug near the henhouse. Can you imag-ine? Digging in his own father's land? What are they searching for?"

Maria del Mar was facing the lane, and she peered past them now. "Oh. Here they come. They're coming *here*," she said.

"What are they seeking?" Eduardo asked again.

Josep willed himself not to turn around and look at them.

"I don't know," he said.

One of the Guardia was stockier than the other and a head shorter. Though he was visibly older, he had a full head of hair, and the younger man already had a circular patch of baldness at the back of his head. The two uniformed men were unsmiling but never rude, which somehow made them more menacing.

"Senyor Alvarez? Senyora? I am Corporal Bagés and this is Private Manso. I believe you are acquainted with Senyor Casals."

Josep nodded, and Tonio looked at him without speaking. "Hola, Maria del Mar."

"Hola, Tonio," she said quietly.

"We would like to have a little look about your property now, senyor. This is not objectionable to you?"

Josep knew it was not a real question. He could not withhold permission, and even if he could, it would be taken as a mark of guilt. One did not play with the Guardia. They had total legal power, and there were stories about damage, both physical and economic, that some policia committed in their zealous maintainance of peace.

"Of course," Josep said.

They began with the houses. The corporal dispatched the younger Guardia to go through the Valls house with Maria del Mar, while he himself searched the Alvarez house accompanied by Josep.

There were not many places in the small house that easily lent themselves to hiding things. Corporal Bagés stuck his head into the fireplace and peered up the chimney, and checked under the bed and moved Francesc's sleeping pad. The stone house was cooler than the outdoors, but it was warm in the attic, where the Guardia and Josep sweated as they shifted bags of grain and beans so he could inspect the places under the eaves.

"How long have you known Colonel Julián Carmora?"

Josep felt regret, because he had hoped he would never learn Peña's true identity. He did not want to think about Peña.

But he looked at the corporal in puzzlement.

"What was the nature of your relationship with Colonel Carmora?" Corporal Bagés asked.

"I'm sorry. I don't know anyone with that name."

The Guardia held his gaze. "You're very certain, senyor?"

"I am. I have never known any colonels."

"Ha, then you may be thankful for your blessings," the corporal said.

When they returned to the vineyard, Maria del Mar and Francesc were seated on the bench with Eduardo.

"Where is Private Manso?" the corporal asked.

"We went through one house together," Maria del Mar told him. "The other house, the one in the middle, is full of some of our tools, two plows, old leather harnesses—all manner of things. I left him going through everything very carefully. That house, right up there," she said, pointing, and the Guardia officer went off.

They watched him go.

"Did you learn anything?" Eduardo asked, and Josep shook his head.

In a moment, Tonio Casals appeared from between rows of vines and came to them.

He knelt before the child. "Hola, Francesc. I am Tonio Casals. Do you remember me? Tonio?"

Francesc studied the face but shook his head.

"Well, it has been a long time, and I knew you when you were very little."

"And you, Tonio, how are you these days?" Marimar asked gently.

"I am doing . . . fine, Maria del Mar. I am assistant alguacil of the regional jail outside of Las Granyas, and I like that work."

"Your father says you also work in the olive business?" Eduardo said.

"Yes. Well, but growing olives is just another form of farming. I am not fond of farming, and my boss is an unpleasant man . . . . Life is always partly difficult, no?"

Eduardo murmured an assent. "And do you work regularly with the Guardia?" he asked his old friend.

"No, no. But I know them all and they all know me, because at one time or another every Guardia officer brings prisoners to my jail or takes them away from it for questioning. Actually, I am thinking of trying to join the Guardia myself. It is difficult because many apply, and one must take classes and pass examinations. But as I say, I know many of the Guardia now . . . and the work is related to my experience at the jail. These two were aware that I am from Santa Eulália. When they were sent here, they invited me as their guide and assistant, so I can assure the village that they mean no harm."

"But Tonio," Marimar said anxiously, "why are they searching our land?"

Tonio hesitated. "You need not be concerned," he said.

Marimar made her eyes large. "Why did they ask me if I knew a certain colonel?" she whispered.

Tonio's face showed his pride in being an authority. He cast a glance to make sure the two Guardia officers were out of sight. "A colonel with a desk at the Ministry of War has gone missing. Corporal Bagés says he is a coming officer with a brevet rank of brigadier. Corporal Bagés says one day he may be a general."

"But . . . why do they search for him here?" Eduardo asked.

Tonio made a face. "The reason is meager. Among other papers found on his desk was a District of Catalonia list naming the members of the town and village councils. The listing of Santa Eulália, including the three names of its council members, had been encircled."

The village council. That is how he found me, Josep thought.

"That is all? A circle drawn on a list of villages?" Eduardo said incredulously.

Tonio nodded. "I laughed when they told me. I said that perhaps the colonel was planning his eventual retirement and considered settling in this little village to raise grapes. Or perhaps he planned to send troops hereabouts on training maneuvers, or perhaps, or perhaps, or perhaps. But they insisted on sending investigators, so I had to dig a hole in my own father's field! They overlook *nothing*, not the smallest detail. That is why they are so successful, that is why they are the best." He smiled at Marimar. "But be patient, and we will be gone very soon."

Presently Corporal Bagés returned. "Senyor," he said to Josep, "will you come with me?"

He led Josep to the door in the ridge.

"What is this?"

"My wine cellar."

"If you please," he said, and Josep opened the door and they entered into the darkness.

In a moment Josep had found a match and lighted the lantern and they stood in its flickering light.

"Ah," the Guardia said softly.

It was a sound of pleasure. "It is so cool here. Why do you not live in here?"

Josep forced a smile. "We don't wish to warm our wine," he said.

The corporal reached over and took the lantern. He held it high and examined the scene before him: the rock wall and ceiling, the stonework that began behind the rack of filled bottles.

He held the lantern close to the stonework and peered at it, studying, and Josep realized something with sudden dismay. The clay between the stones would show different colorations, according to the different periods of time they had been drying. The grout became a light gray in color after it dried, almost the shade of many of the rocks, while the clay was much darker when wet, with brown tones.

The two newest sections could be identified.

His heart was hammering. He knew exactly what would happen next. The corporal would study the clay and begin to remove the stones that had been laid most recently.

The man held the light close to the wall and took a step forward, and in that moment the door of cellar was opened and the other officer entered.

"I think we have something," Private Manso said.

The corporal handed Josep the lantern and went to his colleague. Josep heard the murmured words, "A sunken grave."

The door remained ajar, and warmth was pouring in.

"Senyores, please . . . *the door,*" he managed to say, but the two Guardia were not listening to him as they hurried out, and Josep extinguished the lantern and followed, firmly closing the door behind him.

It was not an extremely hot day for Catalonia, but the contrast with the cellar's coolness was dizzying.

He saw that everyone was gathered at the eastern rear edge of the Alvarez piece, even Angel Casals, who must have hobbled slowly from his farm. The alcalde looked done in and was leaning on Marimar for support.

There was the sound of digging and the soft grunts made by someone using a shovel.

As Josep drew near he saw that everyone was watching Tonio Casals, who stood in a wide hole of his own making.

Josep joined the others, a bubble of hysterical mirth rising within him because the situation was exactly as his fearful imaginings had pictured it, with his wife and son and friends and neighbors assembled to witness if disaster and disgrace came to him.

"Here is something," Tonio said.

He dropped his shovel and reached down to pull, tugging until there emerged from the earth two long joined bones to which shreds of dirt and matter still clung.

"I think it is a leg," Tonio said, a bit importantly, Josep thought. But quickly he gave a small scream, "Mare de Déu!," and cast the grisly object back onto the earth. "A cloven hoof! It is the leg of a demon!"

"No, senyor." Francesc's young voice rose, excited and shrill. "It is not a demon. It is a pig."

In the small silence, Josep watched Eduardo begin to tremble. Eduardo's shoulders shook and his serious face worked.

He groaned, a sound that could have been made by a primed pump, and then for the first time Josep saw and heard Eduardo Montroig really laugh. His laughter was soft and wheezing, like the barking of an asthmatic dog that had run a long way.

Almost at once others joined in—even the Guardia—seduced as much by Eduardo's helpless joy as by the situation, and Josep found it easy to surrender to the hysteria, and to the laughter that began all over again as Tonio stoically reburied the boar.

Josep didn't like the way the alcalde looked, and he led Angel to the bench and brought him cool water.

Tonio continued to ignore Josep but turned to Marimar. "I would like to taste your wine," he said.

She hesitated, seeking a way to avoid serving him, but Angel Casals spoke to Tonio brusquely. "I would like you to take me home now. I have hired Beatriu Corberó to cook us her summer paella with chorizo and vegetables, a village-style dinner for you and your friends, and I must see to things." So Eduardo helped the alcalde onto his son's mule, and Tonio led him away.

Light-headed, Josep filled a pitcher from the almost empty barrel of ordinary wine and served it in Quim's wineglasses to the two policia and Marimar and Eduardo.

The two Guardia officers did not hurry away. They drank slowly, complimented the wine, and allowed Josep to convince them it was fitting that they have another glass, in which he joined them.

Then they shook his hand and wished him a bountiful harvest, and they mounted their horses and rode away.

61

The Monsieur

$\mathcal{B}$y early September several people had sought out the bodega to buy wine, and when Josep noticed the rider turning into the vineyard from the lane, he thought it was another customer. But as he approached, he saw that the man was reining in his horse while he examined the sign.

And then Josep recognized the man's face, which bore the broadest of smiles.

"Monsieur, Monsieur," he called.

Monsieur Mendes can taste my wine! he thought at once and felt joy and terror.

"Senyor," Leon Mendes called back to him.

He was very pleased to be able to introduce Maria del Mar and Francesc to Leon Mendes.

He had spoken to Marimar at length about Mendes, and she knew what the Frenchman meant to her husband. As soon as the introductions were finished, she took Francesc by the hand and hurried to the Casals farm to buy a chicken and to the grocery for other ingredients, aware she would be spending the afternoon preparing a dinner.

Josep unsaddled the horse. When Josep had been in Languedoc, Monsieur Mendes had ridden a very good black Arabian mare. This one was a mare as well, but a swaybacked brown animal of dubious lineage, a livery horse Mendes had rented in Barcelona after leaving the train. Josep saw to it that it had water and feed. He set two chairs in the shade and brought his visitor wet cloths with which to bathe his face and hands to remove the dust of the road.

Then he brought a cántir and cups, and the two of them sat and drank water and began to talk.

Josep told Mendes the story of how he had assembled his winery. How his brother and sister-in-law had wanted to sell the Alvarez land and how he had bought it. He recounted how his love-haunted neighbor had thrust upon him the responsibility for the adjoining Torras piece, and how, when he and Marimar had married, they had merged their properties.

Mendes listened attentively and asked an occasional question, his eyes wide with pleasure.

Josep had tried not to pounce on the French winemaker before they had shared a decent period of welcoming, but he found he was unable to contain himself any longer.

"Perhaps a glass of wine?" he asked.

Mendes smiled. "A glass of wine would be very welcome."

He got two glasses and hurried to the cellar for a bottle. Mendes looked at the label and raised his eyebrows as he handed the bottle back to be uncorked.

"See what you think of this, Monsieur," Josep said as he poured. They made no move to drink to one another's health. Both were aware this was a tasting.

Mendes held up the glass to note the wine's color, then moved it in gentle circles and studied the thin, translucent tracks left on the glass as the dark liquid swirled. He held it to his nose and closed his eyes. He took a sip and held the wine in his mouth, breathing in through parted lips, pulling air over it and into his throat.

Then he swallowed and sat with his eyes closed, his face stony and serious. Josep could tell very little from his expression.

He opened his eyes and swallowed another sip. Only then did he look at Josep.

"Oh, yes," he said softly.

"It's very fine, as I'm sure you know. It's rich and fruity, isn't it, yet dry enough . . . Tempranillo grapes?"

Josep was exultant but he answered casually. "Yes, our Ull de Llebre. Plus Garnacha. And a smaller amount of Cariñena."

"It's full-bodied but elegant, and its spirit stays with you long after you swallow. If I had made this wine, I should be exceedingly proud," Leon Mendes said.

"In a way, you *did* make this wine, Monsieur," Josep said. "I tried to remember the way you went about it, every step."

"In that case, I *am* proud. Is any of it for sale?"

"Déu, of course."

"I mean to me, in bulk."

"Yes, yes, Monsieur."

"Show me your vineyard," Mendes said.

They walked together along the rows, now and then picking a grape to test the growing ripeness and discussing optimal harvest times. When they came to the door in the ridge, Josep opened it and brought his guest inside.

In the lantern light, Leon Mendes studied every detail of the cellar. "You dug this alone?"

"Yes." Josep told him about discovering the rock formation.

Mendes looked at the fourteen 100-liter casks, plus the three 225-liter barrels. "This is all the wine you have made?"

Josep nodded. "I had to sell the rest of my grapes for vinegar, in order to finance this."

"Did you make a second label?"

"Just one barrel." He kept a cup on the barrelhead for dipping, and now, to give Mendes a sample drink, he had to tilt the cask. "This is the dregs," he warned, but Mendes tasted the wine judiciously and pronounced it a perfectly good vin ordinaire.

"Well, let us return to our chairs in the shade," he said. "There is much we need to discuss."

"Have you sold any of your good wine?"

"Relatively few bottles to date, in the Sitges marketplace, from the back of my wagon."

When Josep told Mendes the amount he had charged, the older man sighed. "You have badly underpriced an excellent wine. Well." He drummed his fingertips on his thigh as he thought.

"I would like to buy eleven of your 100-liter casks. I will pay you twice the price you set when you sold the wine from your wagon." He smiled at the expression on Josep's face. "It is not generosity, it is the market price. In the years since you left Languedoc, phylloxera has raged. That little bastard of a flea has destroyed three-quarters of the vineyards of France. People are clamoring for drinkable wine, and prices are very high and ever rising. After paying for shipping and bottling, I shall sell your wine at an excellent profit.

"Selfishly, I wish I could take every drop you have made, but I'm leaving you enough to fill about 900 bottles, and you should use them to begin to develop a clientele in your own territory.

"To sell your fine wine, you must buy new bottles and bring your label to a printer. Obtain a small stall in one of the large roofed marketplaces in Barcelona, and price the wine at two and one-half times what you asked for it in Sitges. People of modest means shop in Barcelona as well as in the fishermen's village, but in Barcelona there are also prosperous businessmen and a wealthy aristocracy who buy the best and always have their eyes open for a new thing. You will sell your wine quickly.

"How much of a new pressing are you planning?"

Josep frowned. "A bit more than last year, but I'll sell most of my fermented juice for vinegar again. I need cash."

"You'll make much more from wine than from juice for vinegar."

". . . I don't have enough cash to get through the year, Monsieur."

"I'll advance the working money you need, in return for the exclusive right to two-thirds of your wine in barrels."

He looked at Josep. "I must tell you, Josep, that if you don't accept my offer, you will soon have many others. I've bumped into half a dozen French vintners looking to buy wine here. From now on they will be a common sight in Catalonia and elsewhere in Spain."

Josep's head was awhirl. "There are important decisions that must be made. Do you mind if I leave you for a short time and give it thought?"

"Of course not," Mendes said. "In the meantime, I'll stroll through the rest of your vineyard and enjoy myself." He smiled, and Josep thought Monsieur Mendes knew exactly how the interval would be spent.

The house smelled richly of garlic and herbs and simmering chicken.

Josep found Marimar in the kitchen, shelling beans, a smudge of flour on her nose. "The only chicken Angel was willing to sell was a tough old hen that had stopped laying eggs," she said. "But it will be fine. I'm braising it very slowly with prunes in a little wine and oil, and we'll have a spinach omelet with a sauce of tomatoes and peppers and garlic."

She sat with him and listened quietly to his description of Monsieur Mendes' offer, asking few questions but absorbing everything Josep told her.

"It's a chance to establish ourselves as makers of wine. We should take advantage of the situation. The phylloxera, the French wine shortage . . ." He broke off and looked at her.

He was apprehensive, because he knew she was fearful of change and found security in familiar patterns, even harmful ones.

"You want to do it, don't you?" she said finally.

"Oh, yes. I really want to do it."

"Then we must do it," Maria del Mar said, and she went back to shelling beans.

It was a very nice dinner. When their visitor complimented Marimar and spoke with special warmth of the small pastries she had served with their coffee, she laughed and told him drily that they came from the local grocery, whose proprietor was an accomplished baker.

When Francesc had said a drowsy goodnight and gone off to his pallet, their talk quickly returned to wine.

"Is your own vineyard in danger?" Josep asked.

Mendes nodded. "Phylloxera perhaps will reach us next year or the year after that."

"Is there nothing you can do?" Maria del Mar asked.

"There is. The plague came to Europe in grapevines imported from America, but there is an American grapevine whose roots the aphids don't eat. Perhaps the roots contain an element poisonous to the aphids, or maybe they simply taste very bad. When cuttings of our doomed vines are grafted onto these American roots, the aphids don't bother them.

"I've replaced 25 percent of my vines annually with grafted stock, for the past three years. It takes four years before one can get a crop. Perhaps," Mendes said, "you may be interested in converting your own vineyard."

"But Monsieur, why would we?" Maria del Mar said slowly. "The phylloxera is a French problem, no?"

"Ah, madame, soon it will be half Spanish!"

"Surely the aphid will not be able to cross the Pyrenees," Josep said.

"Most experts believe it is inevitable," Mendes said. "Aphids are not eagles, but on their own tiny wings they advance about 13 miles a year. If there are strong winds the insects can be blown far and wide. And they have help from man in their travels. Each year many people cross the border. Aphids can hide anywhere, beneath the collar of a coat, or in the mane of a horse. Perhaps-who knows—they may may already be somewhere in Spain."

"Then it appears that we have no choice," Josep said, troubled.

Mendes nodded in sympathy. "At any rate, it is something to be given careful thought," he said.

That night they put clean sheets on the bed in the Vall house, and Mendes slept there. The next morning he was up soon after Josep and Marimar, and he announced he would leave early for Barcelona and his train to France. While Maria del Mar prepared a breakfast tortilla, he and Josep walked through the vineyard together in the fresh morning air.

Josep told Mendes he would buy 225-liter barrels and stack them on both sides of the cellar, on wide shelves.

Mendes approved. "That will work for now, because you can ship the wine-filled barrels to me after a relatively short time. But wine prices will remain high for years, and the day is going to come when you will want every drop of your wine to be sold in your own bottles. When that happens you will need to put another cellar in your hill, at least the size of the one you have now."

Josep made a face. "All that digging."

Mendes stopped walking. "One thing you need to learn, perhaps the hardest and most important lesson. Sometimes you must trust other people to do what you want done. Once your vineyard reaches a certain size, you don't have the luxury of doing all the work by yourself," he said.

After breakfast, Josep saddled the livery horse, and the two men exchanged abrazos.

"Monsieur!" Marimar came hurrying from the masia with a sack containing a bottle of the good wine and a portion of tortilla to be eaten on the train. "I wish you a safe journey home, Monsieur."

Leon Mendes bowed. "Thank you. You and your husband have fashioned a wonderful bodega, Senyora," he said.

62

The Disagreement

*T*hree weeks later, Josep and Maria del Mar had the first serious quarrel of their married life.

Both of them had been working hard and had spent long hours discussing the problems of the bodega and their plans for the future

They had decided to begin replanting their vineyard after the next year's harvest. Each year for four years they would replace twenty-five percent of their vines with grafted stock, as Mendes had done in Languedoc. Josep liked the fact that this would give them this season and the following one in which to make wine from their entire production of grapes. After that, because the grafted plants would not bear a crop for four years, each year as they planted a new portion, their income would decrease by twenty-five percent. In the fourth year they would have no harvest at all, but with the new high prices for wine, they would have accumulated plenty of working capital, and they agreed to spend that cropless fourth year making improvements in the winery. That was the year in which they would have a second cellar dug, and not only the cellar—if they could afford it, they would also have a well dug somewhere on the Alvarez piece. With all the scrubbing and rinsing, to say nothing of irrigation when it was required, hauling water from the river was a constant waste of time and labor. A winery needed its own well.

What a new and unfamiliar pleasure it was to have money to do things that were necessary!

One evening Marimar returned from a walk in the village with a bit of gossip.

"Rosa and Donat are searching for a house."

"Oh?" Josep said. He was only half listening, wondering when the bottles he had ordered would be delivered "Why do they need a house?"

"Rosa wants to put tables in the living quarters above the grocery and make a proper cafe where they can serve real meals. She's a wonderful cook and baker. You saw how Monsieur Leon loved her pastries."

Josep nodded absently.

After all, he was telling himself, he would not need the bottles for many weeks. A more immediate need was for him to decide which sections of the vineyard to harvest first. To crush so many grapes, it was necessary to follow a clear harvesting plan. He would have to discuss it with Marimar.

Maria del Mar broke into his meditation.

"I would like to give them the Valls house."

"Who?"

"Rosa and Donat. I would like to give Rosa and Donat the Valls house."

Josep snorted. "Not likely."

She stared at him.

"Donat is your brother."

"And his wife would have taken my land. And my house. And my vines. And my bar of soap and my drinking cup. I will never forget that."

"Rosa was desperate. She had nothing, and she was trying to protect her husband's inheritance. Our situations are so different. I think," she said, "if you allow yourself to get to know her, you will like her. She's *interesting*. A hard-working woman with nerve and lots of different abilities."

"To hell with her."

"She's pregnant also," she said.

She waited and looked at him, but there was no reaction.

"Listen to me, Josep, we have no other relatives. I want my children to grow up among family. There are three houses on the bodega. We live in this one, and we need Quim's house for storage. But my old house is empty, and I want to give it to Rosa and Donat."

"It is no longer your house," he said roughly. "I own half of it, just as you own half of this house and half of Quim's house. And listen well: *You are not to give away things that I own.*"

He saw her expression change. Her face became pinched and guarded and somehow older, a look she had worn when he had first moved back to Santa Eulália. He had forgotten about that expression.

In a moment he heard her climbing the stone steps to the bed chamber.

Josep sat there, brooding.

He cared for her so deeply. He remembered the vow he had made to himself, his promise that in act or word he would never treat her cruelly, as she had been treated by others before him. He saw that he had the power to injure her, perhaps even more than those other bastards.

As he sat there feeling rotten and self-accusitory, he replayed her words in his mind and sat straighter in his chair.

Had she really said that Rosa was pregnant, *also*?

If so, had she misspoken? Or could it be that Rosa really was pregnant *also*!

He left the chair and bounded up the stairs to go to his wife.

A few days later, on a Thursday morning, a freight wagon pulled by two pairs of horses came. Josep directed the driver to Quim's house and helped the man carry forty-two slatwood cases of bottles inside and up the stairs. Stacked in two layers, they took up almost half of what had been Quim's small bedchamber. When the driver left, Josep opened one of the crates and took out a gleaming and virginal bottle, identical to all the others waiting for him to fill them with wine.

He heard voices as he left the storage house. Drawn by the sound, he walked to the Valls house and found Maria del Mar with his brother. "When you go to sleep and when you wake up," Marimar was saying, "in this masia you will hear the river sounds."

"Hola," Josep said, and Donat returned the greeting awkwardly.

"I was telling Rosa this morning," Marimar said, "that it would look so pretty if we could plant more wild roses close to this house. It would be nice to do that near our house as well, Josep. Do you think you've already moved too many roses from the river banks?"

"It's a long river," Josep said. "I might have to walk a while, but there are plenty of roses."

"I'll go with you to dig them," Donat said quickly.

"Rosa loves the flat pink roses," Maria del Mar said. "She can have all of those. I want the little white ones for our house."

Donat laughed. "We'll have to wait until they bloom in April to tell which is which," he said, but Josep shook his head.

"I can tell the difference. The pink ones make a higher bush. We can get them in the winter, when there is more free time."

Donat nodded. "Well, I'd best get back to Rosa and the store. I just wanted to take a look at the row of stones that has to be repaired at the back of the house."

"What row of stones?" Josep asked.

They moved to the rear of the house, and Josep saw and counted eight good-sized stones that lay scattered on the ground.

"I knew there was one loose stone in that wall," Maria del Mar said. "I've been meaning to mention it to you, but—what caused this?"

"I think it was the Guardia," Josep said. "They must have noticed the loose stone and removed it, then pried away the others to make certain that nothing had been hidden here. They really don't overlook the smallest thing."

"I'll repair it," Donat said, but Josep shook his head. "I'll do it this afternoon," he said. "I like stonemasonry."

Donat turned to go. "Thank you, Josep," he said.

For the first time, Josep took a good look at him.

He saw a portly, affable person. Donat's eyes were clear, his face was calm, and he seemed to have a sense of purpose as he prepared to go back to work he enjoyed.

His brother.

Something within Josep—something small, cold, and heavy, an icy sin he had carried unknowing in his very core—melted and vanished.

"For nothing, Donat," he said.

Coolness came to the village from far away, from the mountains, from the sea. Would the wind howl and destroy? Would it carry hail or tiny specks with wings? Autumn rain fell three times, but each time it was a mercy— gentle rain. Most days the sun still shone during the hours of light to warm away the chill brought by night, and the grapes continued to ripen.

He realized that when they replanted it would be an opportunity to make vines in large blocks of single varieties, because now he had to pay for the carelessness of his ancestors, going here, there, and everywhere in the jumbled rows to pick according to variety.

Josep wanted as much ripeness as possible in everything that was picked, but he didn't want grapes to rot while they waited on the vine, so he planned the picking order as if he were a general going into battle.

The oldest plants with the smallest grapes seemed to ripen last, perhaps because of their terroir. These were the grapes from which he had made his blended wine, and he had a special fondness for their wizened, very old vines and would not replace them until and unless he had evidence that they were doomed. For now, he gave them a few extra days of ripening.

So it was that early one morning he began the picking by taking the fruit of ordinary vines, vines that until this very harvest had put out grapes that became vinegar each year.

He had lots of help. Donat had let the village know that during the week of harvest the grocery would be open only from midday to four p.m., and he and Rosa had joined the pickers and would tread grapes at night. Briel Taulé was there as usual, and Marimar had hired Iguasi Febrer and Briel's cousin, Adriá Taulé, and they would pick and tread as well.

Late that afternoon Josep came down to the grape-filled trough and scrubbed his feet and legs.

Others would join him soon, and they would work in shifts, some picking and culling fruit while others were treading grapes. But for the moment he was alone, and he drank in the scene. The tank was filled with gleaming purple-black grapes. Nearby tables held tortilla and pastries from Rosa, under cloths, and cups and cántirs of water. In a crude fireplace of stone, wood waited to be ignited, and lanterns and torches were placed around the stone cistern to provide warmth and light against the dark chill when night arrived.

Francesc came, running unevenly, and watched as Josep put first one foot and then the other into the grapes.

"I want to do it," he called, but Josep knew the grapes were piled too deep and Francesc wouldn't be able to move.

"Next year you will be big enough," he said.

He had a sudden rush of regret that his father had not lived to know this boy and and his mother. That his father had not witnessed what had happened to the Alvarez vineyard.

That Marcel Alvarez would never taste his wine.

He knew that he stood on his father's shoulders, and on the shoulders of all those who had come before. For perhaps a thousand generations, as day workers in the fields of Galicia, and before that as serfs, his people had worked in the soil of Spain.

He had a sudden dizzying vision of his ancestors as a castell, each generation raising him higher on their shoulders until he could no longer hear the music of the drums and the grallas. A castell a thousand levels high.

"And Francesc is our anxaneta, our pinnacle," he said, and he scooped up the little boy and transferred him to his shoulders.

Francesc sat with his legs dangling on either side of Josep's head. He gripped Josep's hair in both hands and crowed.

"What do we do now, Padre?"

"Now?" Josep took the first steps. He thought of the hopes and the dreams and the hard work that went into the grapes, the constant struggle to bring them to wine. He breathed in their scent and could feel them popping beneath his weight, sensed the vital juice as it ran free and claimed him, the blood of the grapes separated from his own blood only by skin.

"Now we walk and sing, Francesc. We walk and we sing!" he said.

Acknowledgments

I didn't discover the glories of good wine until, already a middle-aged man, I began to travel to Spain, where I soon developed a deep appreciation of. the Spanish people, their culture, and their wines.

When I decided to write a novel about them, I chose to focus on the mid-nineteenth century because it was the period of the Carlist Wars and of the phylloxera plague that destroyed vineyards throughout France and Spain. I located my fictional vineyard in the Penedès region of Catalonia because living there would offer my protagonist easy access to both Barcelona and the wine country of Southern France.

Some elements of this novel are based on historical fact and some are invented by the author. The Carlist struggle in Spain was only too real, of course, as was the phylloxera disaster, but the village of Santa Eulália and the Pedregós River exist only in *The Winemaker*.

Members of royalty are taken from history. General Juan Prim lived most of his life as a soldier and was a politician and a famous statesman when he was slain. As with the assassination of President John F. Kennedy, there are many rumors about the plot and the people behind Prim's killing, and there is the likelihood that neither assassination will ever be truly solved. To learn about General Prim's murder, I went to the late Professor Pere

Anguera, author of the definitive Prim biography. I tried to utilize the assassination scene as Professor Anguera recreated it for me. The details—the substitution of one horse-drawn coach for another, the lighting of matches when the coach turned into a new street, the halting of the coach by two blocking coaches, and the mob from which gunmen fired at the president of the Spanish government council—are presented as closely as possible to the historic facts that were so generously shared with me by Pere Anguera. I am grateful for his information and for his subsequently vetting the pages of this book devoted to the shooting.

Because the real-life drama of the assassination was never brought to closure with the conviction and punishment of the killers, I felt free to add my own characters to the scene. So it is pure fiction, drawn wholly from my imagination, that young men from a village called Santa Eulália participated in the assassination mob.

For answering many questions, I thank Maria Josep Estanyol, professor of history at the University of Barcelona.

Accompanied by my wife Lorraine and my son, Michael Seay Gordon, the first Spanish bodega I visited in my research for *The Winemaker* was the Torres winery in Penedès, the region of the vineyard in the novel. It was an auspicious beginning: Albert Fornos, who spent his career as a winemaker there, gave us a splendid tour, and Miguel Torres Maczassek presided over a five-course dinner, at which a splendid wine was poured with each course.

Michael and I made several trips into the Priorat and Montsant wine regions. Almost invariably I have found that vineyards are located in beautiful places. Tucked into a small, lovely valley we found Mas Martinet Viticultors, the bodega of the Pérez family. Sara Pérez Ovejero and her husband, René Barbier, both have fathers who have won distinction as wine pioneers, and they are busily carrying on the family tradition, making successful and delicious wines. Sara Pérez has produced several volumes in which she mounted and described the leaves of the various grape varieties so that her children were able to begin their grape-growing education early. Munching on Spanish cheese and sipping her good wine, I was an appreciative student as I went through the books with her.

On several other occasions Michael and I drove a narrow and precarious road along the lip of a much larger valley, ultimately climbing a small but steep mountain to the village of Torroja del Priorat, where in 1984 Maria Ángeles Torra founded her family winery in a former monastery. It is managed by her sons, Albert and Jordi. Their grapevines are planted nearby, some on steep slopes, and several of their sought-after wines are made from grapes whose vines have persevered in the slate soil for more than a hundred years. I am extremely grateful to the brothers Albert and Jordi Rotllan Torra for reading the manuscript of this book.

In June of 2006 I was awarded a special literary prize by the city of Zaragoza, and while I was in that region, author and journalist Juan Bolea provided friendship and guidance and made it possible for me to visit two vineyards. I am grateful to Juan and to Santiago Begué Gil, president of the Wine Denomination of Cariñena, for his hospitality and wine lore.

On the Finca Aylés, a vast estate of 3,100 acres, where wine was first made in the 12th century, the winemaker Señorío de Aylés has planted 70 hectares of grapes, the end and beginning of each row of vines marked by rose bushes. I was thrilled by repeated sightings of eagles and to learn from owner Frederico Ramón that the lovely spot is designated by the European Union as a special zone for the protection of birds. I thank him for his hospitality.

In an enormous valley that reminded me of some of the great valleys of the American West, we visited The Bodega Victoria. I am grateful to José Manuel Segura Cortés, president of the Grupo Segura Serrano, for providing a lunch of regional foods and for giving me a tour of his winery.

Since writing this book, I have visited a number of other winemakers in various Spanish locations, and

I have a great appreciation of Spanish wines and the men and women who create them.

I am grateful to Alfonso Mateo-Sagasta, prize-winning historical novelist of Madrid, for information about village elections in the nineteenth century and for a description of the architecture and construction of the small village homes of the period.

I thank Delia Martínez Díaz for bringing me to the city of Terrassa, where I spent time in one of the most interesting museums of my experience. Housed in the sprawling brick buildings of an early textile mill, the Museu de la Ciència i de la Tècnica de Catalunya brings a visitor into direct touch with the technological revolution. One walks through exhibits that were the guts and machinery of the early mill, and I was able to see how the advent of steam power had created jobs such as the one filled by Donat. For infinite patience in answering my questions, I thank the museum director, Eusebi Casanelles i Rahola, conservationist Contxa Bayó i Soler, and the entire staff.

I thank Meritxell Planas Girona, a member of the Minyons de Terrassa, for answering my questions about castelling.

Ángel Pujol Escoda answered innumerable questions about hunting and nature with sweet patience, and his wife Magdalena Guasch i Poquet told me different ways to cook a rabbit.

In the wonderful central market of Sabadell, Maria Pérez Navarro took time from selling pork at her business, Cal Prat, to draw an outline for me and to make clear exactly where Josep and Jaumet would find the choicest cut of meat in a wild boar.

Dan Taccini, of Braintree, Massachusetts, a wonderful creator of handmade furniture, told me how to make a door from scratch.

For details regarding the Catholic confessional I turned to our friend Denise Jane Buckloh of Ashfield, Massachusetts, the former Sister Miriam of the Eucharist, OCD, and I thank her. I also thank Dr. Pheme

Perkins, professor of theology at Boston College, for answering my questions about Catholic burial, sin, and penance.

I am a writer extremely rich in family and friends.

Lorraine Gordon has lived with me for more than 60 years and has given me sustenance that is better than food.

My daughter Lise Gordon again was my editor, providing arguments, polishing, and superb editing skills that made this a better book.

My son Michael is now my literary agent. He is—and was throughout the many research sojourns for this book—the very best of companions on the road, at times merry, always responsible, with a keen and reasoning mind and a strong arm.

My daughter Jamie, my favorite photographer, is ever faithfully on call despite my lifelong discomfort in front of a camera. I am grateful for her great skill and loving patience. Jamie, Lorraine, Michael, Charlie Ritz, and Ed Plotkin also read the manuscript of this book.

My daughter-in-law, Maria Palma Castillón, never refused a research question, and I am grateful to her and to the Centre de Promoció de la Cultura Popular i Tradicional Catalana, in Barcelona, for answering questions she posed on my behalf, ranging from the tolling of church bells to the practice of hiring women to weep at funerals.

Roger Weiss has served as my webmaster and kept my computer working. I thank him for his knowledge and his willingness to answer my calls for help.

All of the many persons named above have helped me; but this book is mine, and if it contains flaws and mistakes, they are my own as well.

I am grateful to Blanca Rosa Roca for publishing *The Winemaker*. I value my association with her, which goes back more than a quarter of a century. Under her skilled guidance this novel, as *La Bodega*, already has been a great bestseller in Spain and Latin America. Now Barcelona Editions and Open Road Integrated Media bring it to English-language readers everywhere, and honor me by including *The Winemaker* among their first joint American and international offerings.

Noah Gordon
Dedham, Massachusetts
July 8, 2012

About the Author

Noah Gordon has had outstanding international success. *The Physician*, soon to be a motion picture, has been called a modern classic, and booksellers at the Madrid Book Fair voted it "one of the 10 best-loved books of all time." *Shaman* was awarded the James Fenimore Cooper Prize for historical fiction. *The Physician* and Gordon's most recent novel, *The Winemaker*, are newly available in print. The above-mentioned books and four of the author's other novels—*The Rabbi, The Death Committee, The Jerusalem Diamond*, and *Matters of Choice*—are also published in digital formats by Barcelona eBooks and Open Road Integrated Media. Gordon lives outside of Boston with his wife, Lorraine Gordon.

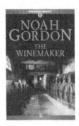   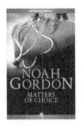